THE FIRST BOOK OF CATACLYSM

THE RAPTOR

G.A. Finocchiaro

THE RAPTOR Copyright © 2021 G.A. Finocchiaro

ISBN: 978-1-7373536-0-7

First Edition XXXXX 2021

writingbloc.com
www.gafino.com

Edited by Cari Dubiel
Cover Design by Rachel Perciphone
Interior Design by G.A. Finocchiaro
Author Photo by Ashley Griffin Photography

SCALES is a shared universe of stories written by G.A. Finocchiaro.

Chapters bearing SCALES symbols are connected to the larger story arc set within the SCALES universe. It is not required to have read these stories to enjoy The Raptor—however, having read the below will provide additional insight not provided within this book.

List of books within the SCALES series:

 The Knightmares

 Quibbles

 Grace Falls

 Bogey

For more information, please go to gafino.com and click on SCALES.

prologue

Someone. Somewhere. Somewhen…

"Confess!" said the voice. "Lest you be judged."

"Confess?" I questioned. "It's more complicated than that."

"Confess!" it demanded. "Or be judged."

"Confession implies guilt. I am guilty and I do not attest otherwise, but life, sometimes, is more complicated than guilty or not. It's not black and white. We're shades—light, dark, color. What we are and how we live is built around perception, emotion, motive. To offer up a choice of confessing guilt or being judged by my actions without explanation is unjust, and it flies in the face of all we were created to be," I replied.

When they did not respond, I knew they were confused. I mentioned life, but they did not live in the same way. They were never human.

"Let me tell you a story."

MALUS
Somewhere.
Then.

Ragnarok, they call it. The end of days. The gods of the Norsemen threatened their devoted with fear to command their loyalty. If you kept a man afraid and offered him salvation in return for nothing more than useless faith, you could command that man till the day he died. The remaining gods, one by one, have either fallen from their perch high above the animals that walked the earth or have resigned to follow the strongest. They have aligned themselves for the inevitable, the ever-approaching end.

Odin promised his faithful an eternity walking the halls of Valhalla, his kingdom in the next world. A kingdom of glory for those who would offer their mortal lives up to him on the battlefield.

Lies.

Puppets. Humans are puppets.

To what end they are needed depends upon the one in need.

Some humans were more special than others. For that very reason, Ragnarok came early.

Today was the end of days for Odin. The old god threatened it would be the end of all there ever was. His faithful believed him, blinded by their fear. Ragnarok would not be the end of all. The world was much larger and much more important than the Norse god and his kingdom.

Ragnarok was day one. What came next was my destiny.

A woman hit the floor at my feet and shattered my ruminations as I leaned against the cold brick wall, staring into the darkness. Such actions have caused me to lose my temper on other days. He knew he was pushing the limits.

Her hair was matted in an equal mixture of blood and sweat, though the blood was not her own. I could smell two distinct scents from her body. The stone floor and vaulted walls made her every annoying sob and movement echo. She anxiously twitched, making the torchlit shadows dance across the room.

"No praise for a task well done?" he asked. There was little light in the room, but he positioned himself so that I could see his prize. It was not the woman. His prize was tightly gripped within his right hand. It was an unspoken threat.

His lean, wiry muscles clenched as he shifted within a blood-spattered coat made of furs. His blue eyes were furious, and his blonde hair was wild and overgrown. He was not a formidable-looking man, but his prize, the large stone hammer, was.

"I expect a job well done. To give compliments for what is expected is to promote failure," I said, before I pushed away from the wall and leaned over to inspect the woman. She kept her head down, a shroud of hair surrounding her face. Her dress was made of skins and other primitive fabrics, like a woman out of time. For all her weeping, I was expecting to see more damage.

Loki was gentle with his sister.

I gave him a smirk and noticed his pained expression, twitching on the brink of explosive rage. His sneer was dissolving into a mask of anger.

"It was not without loss," he said, stifling emotions. "I lost my son."

"Which?" I asked.

"Jormungandr."

"Children are expendable. Make another," I told him.

His knuckles went white as he regripped the hammer.

I did not care for any of Loki's vile children. Jormungandr, the slithering serpent, could stretch the length of the world and bite its own tail. It was a powerful beast I was content to have lost. It was foreseen that the serpent's death would come to pass. The great and mighty Thor would fall after pacing nine steps from the dead carcass of Jormungandr. Dying from the venom that burned inside his godly veins from the fateful bite of the slain worm.

If it was foretold—unshakable destiny—then why remorse? Why feel pain over something that was not within one's ability to control? Why expend sorrow when nothing could have deterred the outcome? I learned long ago that control was all that mattered. Control was everything.

"Tell me your name," Loki demanded. It was not a question. I could feel the other eleven sets of eyes narrow their gazes upon me, watching through shadow. I knew all twelve of their true names, including the maniac, Loki, with his hateful eyes burning like spears of hellfire.

"No. My name remains mine," I said. After all, the contract was still binding.

This was not the first time Loki had challenged me. I could not blame the trickster for his frustrations. He spent immortal lifetimes as a follower, equal to his king, Odin, but never the one who sat upon the throne.

Now he takes my orders. Always a bridesmaid, I suppose.

He flinched. A flinch was all I needed.

Before Loki's wince matured into a charging rage, the stone brick floor beneath him cracked under pressure. A ghostly presence grasped onto him with spectral hands, rendering him motionless, as if encased in cement. He yelled and bashed at the dead hands with his new hammer, but for every hand he smashed to spiritual dust, two more took its place. Once he had fallen to one knee, bent by the pressure of the dead servants, his body relented.

"Your name will be revealed," said Loki through heavy gasps. "When it is, your power over us will be gone."

"Perhaps," I replied. I had waited far too long for this moment, and I would not wait any longer. Loki was a powerful ally—albeit a begrudging one—and had completed the most important task yet. If I was unsure of Loki's usefulness, I would have let the dead consume him. It would have been a poetic end for him to die at the hands of the dead, considering the vast number of humans slain or fatally tricked over the centuries by the trickster god.

I placed my hand beneath the woman's chin and kindly lifted her eyes from the floor to mine. She was older than I expected, but traces of beauty and grace were still there. Her eyes were swollen and raw from tears, but their gemlike clarity was the stuff of legend. She leaned back from her knees as I pulled her chin higher, exposing her neck to me. Even for my kind, exposing one's neck was a show of submission.

I backed away and allowed myself to summon spirits from the earth to shackle her wrists.

Then I spoke her earthly name, Frigg, but she continued to sob. I needed her attention, to fully gauge my need and to properly offer her gift, and I knew just how to get it.

"Yaliel," I said, and her trembling suddenly died away. Something as simple as speaking a true name—the one bestowed upon us by our maker and whispered into our ear at the time of our creation—gave us all the power we could ever desire over another creature. Immortals acquired many names the longer we lived, for the very purpose of burying our one true weakness in time. The magic of names, dominion, was as old as the gods. "Today your kingdom fell. A destiny you had Seen centuries ago. I am curious, do you know why I have sought your company?"

She looked at me in shame. Her entire kingdom and family were destroyed, all because of her special gift. A special gift I needed.

"Yes," she choked, as a look of recognition crossed her face. Frigg could only see the answers to questions she was asked. Such an unfortunate limitation to her precious talents. Had she this information prior to today, she may have changed her fate.

"Tell me," I asked politely. She turned away, bracing herself against my words with a pained look and trembling lips.

"The girl will be born one-thousand nine hundred eighty years after *the year of their Lord*. She will have hair as red as hellfire and eyes of emerald. Seek her on the new continent in the realm of the great empire no less than thirteen years from the time of her birth. It is only then, as her biology matures, that she may forfeit what you seek," Frigg explained, the answer flowing freely, as if it needed to be expelled from the prison of her lungs.

"Where is she?" I asked.

She sighed. "She, like many others who drift toward the sinistram, are drawn to the darkness and dark places," said Frigg, her eyes fluttering away from mine. "Where two cities meet—felicity and atrocity—upon a black mirror, one reflected above the other, where the Fates fall thrice. A city you have once visited upon your journeys—where the land decays like cancer beneath your feet. Power attracts power, like flies to honey. Vengeance brings you destiny, Pale Demon."

"Once she's found, how do I make the girl forfeit?" I asked. The problem with a Seer, particularly one as old and as wise as Frigg, was that they often spoke in riddles. They'd tell all you *want* to know but withhold the one thing you absolutely *need* to know. One must be thorough.

"To gain what you seek, she must first love you, truly. You must make her yearn for you with all her heart. Captivate her mind with all your charm. She must lust for you, her flesh to yours. And she must need you with every ounce of her soul so that there is no beginning or end to her without you. Once that is obtained, take her to the holy land that was lost and locked away. There you may acquire what you seek by performing the sacramental contract."

At that, I was satisfied. I took two purposeful steps forward and slashed her throat clean to the bone with my knife, preventing her from speaking before one of the other twelve in the room could ask my name or any other regrettable thing. She bled out quickly, her life force draining, but I ended her suffering with one final thrust deep into her chest and ripped out her still-beating heart.

It was only a matter of time before *they* became brave enough to ask Frigg my name—so I took her life and made her mine forever. Eleven sets of eyes retreated to the comfort of the shadows. I recalled the dead and released Loki, who left my presence in defeat, carrying the trophy hammer he had hoped would give him an advantage. He'd destroyed his brethren for nothing more than a chance to eliminate me. Sometimes, even a god could become a puppet.

I returned to my thoughts, leaning against the cold brick wall. For thousands of years, I'd survived in the dark black void, listlessly passing centuries, restlessly searching for a destiny that evaded me. Destiny was now mine. My path was laid out before me, giving my immortal life purpose in a world where purpose was limited. This was my time, and it all began with one extraordinary girl.

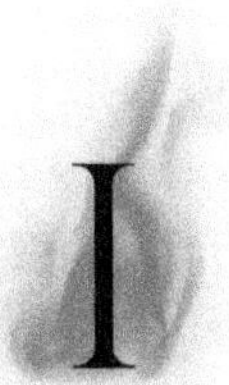

dreams in black

TONY
December 19, 2013
Now.

It began in black.

Lost.

Dark.

Without hope.

It was cold and wet. Not raining, but the air was thick and damp and hard to breathe. At first, I couldn't see a thing, and then, slowly, I could make out shapes—my eyes adjusting to the dark, as if fading from nothing into something.

I was in the woods. It had to be winter—the towering bare branches stretched into the stormy gray sky and a thick blanket of decaying leaves was as deep as a snow drift. I was standing at the bottom of a steep hill. There was a yawning crack in the earth, with a creek running through it—eroded rock that formed a natural boundary. The water flowed sluggishly, like it was on the verge of freezing.

I took a standing leap and landed on the other side in the thick, rotted-leaf-covered covered soil. The loose dirt crumbled away with every footfall, forcing me to climb the other side of the hill on all fours. Dense white vapor billowed from my mouth with every exhale, and the chilly temperatures penetrated my skin to the bone. I slipped and clung to a small sapling at the base of an old oak, the treacherous climb taking the best of me. The bark was wet and slimy, with frosty moss covering its north side, making it difficult to grip.

The closer I got to the top of the hill; the more dread infected me. My fingers went numb with anticipation and my heart pounded uncontrollably. I was a train without brakes, propelled toward the inevitable, unable to steer. The outcome was unavoidable, but I continued anyway, charging straight for the horror that awaited me.

I dragged myself to the top of the hill, scratching and clawing, and hatefully apprised my destination.

I knew where I was going. I had been there many times before.

There was a clearing at the top of the hill, filled with brier and tall weeds, and at the center were two old buildings with rusted metal, rotted wooden planks, and broken cinderblock walls. The buildings appeared like a dream, blurry at the edges and sliding in and out of focus. There was a rumbling, like thunder, with a rush of water falling and crashing into a rocky pool below.

A waterfall, with water as black as night.

As I trudged through the overgrown brush, I noticed the stillness of my surroundings. There wasn't a bird in the sky or a critter scurrying at my feet. All was dead and gray. The massive building ahead, one of two in the clearing, was broken and abandoned long ago, yet I knew my path laid within it. It drew me in magnetically—I had no other choice.

An old tree had fallen, and its decayed trunk laid across my path. I climbed over it, then up to the old barn door. The handle for the sliding door was as slippery as ice. One of the rollers was off its track and the door dangled haphazardly across the entrance. I slid it aside as the wind picked up, whipping and twisting violently. A warning.

When I stepped inside, I was struck all at once by the scent of stale air and rust. It was a warehouse, tall and wide, with rusty chain and broken old machinery from a bygone era. The warehouse was once a booming industry, with shelving, metal catwalks and offices, and vaulted ceilings with timber rafters as long as trees. Old paneless windows lined the walls, and the dusty floors were like a soft blanket under my feet. My eyes scanned the room, glossing over the finer details in favor of the important bits that needed my attention—like the stairs that led up to a door on the second level.

I imagined what it must have been like restored to its former glory when a flash of light stole my concentration. A storm surge brewed, lightning struck in the distance, and the warehouse trembled uneasily.

Everything about the experience made me want to turn back. The walls seethed as if they were alive, protesting my appearance, and the path ahead distorted like a funhouse. My skin crawled, my forehead dampened with cold sweat—my body trembling like I was suffering through a flu.

Why couldn't I just turn back? How could I continue when I knew what was coming?

And just when I felt like there was a way to change this course—to avoid what I was destined to see—I heard her voice.

The soft elegance of her call floated down to my waiting ears like a feather gliding on the air. She beckoned for me. *Hurry.*

But I couldn't understand her words. I strained to hear her, to decipher her message, but nothing cohesive formed out of the wordless call—except the frantic tone of her desperation.

She needed me.

My stomach soured and my pulse quickened. I was on the verge of a panic attack.

Why did I put myself through this over and over again?

I followed her whispers past dusty crates and over to the stairs, then followed them up to the second floor. The door swung open, and I passed through as another clap of thunder shook the building.

I followed her pleas into a great suffocating gloom—as voluminous as the thickest fog. It fed off my fear and stripped away my courage, then left me panicking for air, my hands on my knees and buckled over. I fought to slow my gasps, to pull myself together, the great silence threatening to swallow me forever—when I rose to my feet and found I was standing at the beginning of a long dark hallway. A long, terrible hallway I knew all too well, and my panic matched my rage.

It was an old unfinished hallway with wooden floors and walls. Lightning flashed through the windows, illuminating the dark hall briefly before returning it to the swallowing darkness.

The floor creaked with every forward step as I paced into the shade. The storm arrived with a great deafening crash—its intensity as sudden as a stroke—and my heart slammed against my ribs like a caged animal. A flash of lightning lit the room, followed quickly by a second and a third, allowing me to finally see my destination. The hair on the back of my neck prickled like pins when the red-faced demon came into view, a black doorknob dangling beside its hideous grin. Its malevolence stared me down, with sinister fangs and twisted horns, and snarled in cadence with the thunder.

A shiver ran down my spine, a death rattle that absorbed my strength and sent me tumbling into the near wall. I braced myself against it, struggling to suck wind into my lungs as the demon mocked my weakness with laughter.

I wanted to run. I wanted to turn away and leave this nightmare behind, but there was something inside me that wouldn't let go. It held me hostage and forced me to relive the horror. I was never free to change the outcome. I was shamed into this torture. I was my own prisoner, forced to see it through. A one-way trip, straight to the devastating end.

My entire body trembled. I pushed on, through spasms and buckling knees. The further I traveled down the hall the longer it extended, never ending, like a piece of elastic stretching into the distance. Every excruciating effort forward moved the laughing demon door further out of reach.

I should have given up, admitted defeat and succumbed to the hallway.

I couldn't change what had happened. I couldn't change the past as true as I couldn't change the outcome. I would have if I could. I would give anything. I would give anything to change what happened.

For her, I would have done anything.

I wished the nightmare would consume me, to take away the pain and the ensuing numbness. If only will was enough, I could have spun back time, pushed aside mountains and solved ancient riddles. I never wanted anything more than to start over. My self-hatred and frustration collided into something more powerful than the two alone—the collision shattered self-doubt and the flood waters rose into fury.

The levee inside me broke and cascaded through my body like the raging storm—its intensity increased along with my own.

"I'll never let go," I growled through gritted teeth, and I meant it—equally a curse and a blessing.

Tears burned my eyes while furious flashes of light burst through the windows along the unending hall. The steady glow lifted the shadows, and I could finally see her.

She peeked out from behind the red demon door, waiting for me. Her flowing crimson hair obscured everything but the emerald of her eyes flaring like beacons.

The sight of her lifted my paralyzing fear and replaced it. I knew what was coming. I accepted fate and allowed the anger to take over.

"Leave her alone!" I screamed, as a monstrous hand guided her back into the room and shut the door.

"No! Leave her alone!" I screamed again and broke into a sprint. With every stride the hallway stretched on, the door perpetually looming in the distance. I pushed harder, my blood igniting into liquid fire, burning away my remaining humanity and consuming me with fiery rage. I ignored the pain as the storm ferociously shook the very foundation of the building, striking the windows as I raced past.

My will be damned. I couldn't let it happen again.

Everything culminated in a furious display of anger—the storm, the hallway, and me, struggling for dominance. Like an unstoppable knife, I pierced the elastic barrier, finally outpacing the hallway's capacity, and crashed through the demon door. The jam splintered into a thousand pieces and scattered throughout the room, while I collapsed hard onto my knees against the floor, exertion threatening to drag me into unconsciousness. I doubled over, heaving, as the storm passed and left a stray roll of thunder in its wake.

The room was large and nearly empty. There was an old, blue and gold plaid couch, a knitted throw draped over the back with the initials M.S.U. crocheted into its pattern. There were two ripped and worn recliners at either end of the couch, as well as an old, scuffed coffee table sitting on a ratty area rug. A cheval mirror with peeling white trim sat in a corner with other junk—beer cans and bottles—littering the floor.

As the moments faded, small volleys of distant lightning lit the room with a soft phosphorescent glow. As empty and still as the room was, there was something stirring about. It was a presence that made everything feel alive, like it was buzzing with an unseen energy.

As I walked past the mirror toward the back of the room, something caught my eye in its reflection.

I was being watched.

Behind me, her shadowy veiled glance reflected in the cheval mirror. Two green eyes like shining stars snatched mine like a thief in the night. She was sitting on the couch, watching me.

"Tomorrow's not a promise," she said, her voice beautiful and crisp. Then the mirror cracked and shattered, falling to the floor in pieces.

When I turned, I found her lying on the couch, crimson hair covering her face, hands neatly folded on her chest. She was wearing an old, faded green sundress with yellow flowers—its frayed hem caked in mud and dirt.

I approached the sofa apprehensively, as if I didn't know what I would find—as if I didn't know how awful it was—as if I didn't know it would destroy me.

I held my breath and hoped for the impossible.

My hand gently dragged the hair from her face and caressed her cold cheek. What I found was no surprise, but that did not make it any less devastating.

She was lifeless. Her green eyes fixated on mine with pools of wet tears covering the small constellation of freckles on her cheeks—and the missing half of her skull, shattered and spilled, just above her left eye. Blood dripped from the walls, seeping into the floor from the great spatters that drenched them in crimson.

I had seen it a thousand times before.

"No," I sobbed. "Who would do this?"

I already knew the answer.

From the mirror came movement. The shattered glass had mysteriously reassembled, and I was staring at my own reflection.

"You," she answered, her voice like a whispered song. "I thought you were the moon."

Within the reflective glass I stared at an image of myself, unfamiliar to me. My eyes were wild and discolored, my face misshapen, like a devilish beast. Blood dripped from my mouth and chin, staining my skin and shirt, while my hands grappled with gore. The image should have been enough to drive anyone mad, but something inside me wouldn't allow it.

☾

"It was guilt," I said. "I feel so guilty every waking day of my miserable life." I sat upright and took a deep breath while I wiped the sweat from my brow before it began to run.

"Why do you feel so much guilt, Tony?" said the doc. I immediately thought the guy was just fucking with me. How could I not feel guilty? Didn't he have my files—my history—on some printouts stapled to that manila folder laying open on his desk? I took a deep unnecessary sigh and slid back onto the doc's couch while he waited for my answer.

The room was bright but dim, with overcast skies casting a desaturated filter over everything. Framed degrees and certificates lined the geometric patterned wallpaper behind a large wooden desk. The official nameplate read "H. Hammond, Psy.D." His perfectly arranged mahogany bookshelf was just a few steps behind the desk, loaded with red and blue hardcover books, like the whole collection of Encyclopedia Britannica—clearly, Doctor Hammond didn't Google. Together, it wasn't an uninviting room. It was cozy, especially the couch—was it memory foam?

Marshall always told me that I needed to stop using humor as a defense mechanism. He said it was his "thing," not mine. I suppose he's right—jokes were hard to come by these days, and I was scraping the bottom of the barrel. I pushed the people who cared for me so far away that I was hanging on by a solitary thread—and I was holding the scissors.

Seeing a shrink was an embarrassing final step for me. A final step backward that seemed to be the only direction available—albeit conditional. I suppose that's what happens when your mind fractures like a bowling ball meeting a windshield at sixty miles-per-hour. The state makes you check in from time to time.

My eyes darted around the room as I searched for a focal point. I didn't feel comfortable spilling my guts to a stranger, let alone looking them in the eyes while I did it. Not after my past. I felt like I had spent way too much time healing and talking and healing and talking, and not enough time living. I was feeling a PTSD flashback from recalling prior PTSD flashbacks.

"I think it's pretty obvious," I replied.

"Tony, why are you here?" the doctor asked me from behind his reading glasses. They sat extra low on the bridge of his nose, and I was waiting for them to come tumbling off. He had a yellow legal pad in his lap and was jotting down furious notes about my recurring dream like he was cramming for a midterm.

"Mandatory check-in. Part of the terms of my release. And because I made a promise to my buddy Marshall," I said, then added, "And to my nosy landlord—you know, some people should mind their own damn business, don't you think?"

"No, I mean, why are you here?" he said, then capped his pen and leaned forward in his leather recliner, making a few uncomfortable gassy noises I swore I wouldn't comment on or pun. "Today was your first visit with me, despite the referral being dated nearly two years ago. You come in, quickly introduce yourself, and begin to tell me about your dream, and ask for clarification about what it all means.

"Medicine of the mind doesn't typically work that way. Most patients come to me on a regular basis—some quite frequently, others maybe once or twice a year. We cannot expect to unpack your dreams before we unpack your life and what led you here today."

"So, you want my life story?" I said. The guy really didn't want to hear all that, did he? Everyone has baggage. I have luggage.

The doc looked like your average Dr. Freud impersonator, fitted with the stereotypical beard and glasses. "I've met plenty of patients who build walls around who they are to hide away the painful parts of their existence. It's a natural defense mechanism. A way to survive. Please don't take what I'm about to say next as an insult, but you are not a special case, Tony. There is nothing extraordinary about your current condition that I have not seen before. If you want to lead a healthier life, after all you've been through, I suggest we start at the beginning."

"Far be it for me to make your job any easier," I quipped, and Doctor Hammond smiled.

"No more walls, Tony." From the framed photos on his desk, Doctor Hammond had a lovely wife and three kids. I began to wonder how this man had ever met and married a woman—he was as humorless as a wet rag. "You need to be free of your demons."

"Okay," I said.

"Okay," he repeated.

"My name's Tony. Anthony Oscuro. I am 33 years old, and I live in the city of Philadelphia. I am generously five foot, ten inches tall with exceptionally dark hair and eyes—and a face for radio—*mayyybee* YouTube. I have a fair amount of scruff covering my face and chin, carefully fashioned—after all, I am not a heathen."

"That's not what I meant by start at the beginning," said the doc.

"I know. Sorry," I said, and sighed for the thirtieth time since entering his office. "This time of year has always been difficult for me. I've been so depressed for so long that I don't know where to begin."

"It is very clear that you're depressed, Tony." There was nothing more depressing than being told by a professional that you're depressed.

"Why don't you start at the beginning of the events that led you here? Why don't you tell me about *her*?"

I smiled, humorlessly. "Yeah."

"Or you could go back further, and tell me about your mother," he suggested.

"No," I said sternly. "One ghost is all I'm willing to discuss."

"Okay. Take me back to the beginning," the doc said. I looked at my watch and began to weigh my priorities, but he interrupted. "Don't worry about our session. After reading through your files, I made sure to set aside plenty of extra time for us to talk."

I promised Marshall I'd get help—I'd put this off for too long, and there was a chance the state might come calling if I didn't get reevaluated from time to time. Weighing priorities—help versus financial stability—was a difficult decision. I'd spent the last six years in a constant state of struggle, battling myself for a single moments' peace, and realized that the only path forward was through.

It was time I fixed myself instead of running away.

"Have you ever had that one moment in your life when you realized your destiny?" I said, starting with a free flow of consciousness that seemed to make the most sense. "That exact second your life went from meandering around in circles to a clear path forward? The split second before that very moment, your life was meaningless and forgettable, like an old pair of socks, but then something unforeseen happened and thrust your life into a whole new and amazing direction? As if the big bang went off inside you, spreading outward at the speed of light and making that very second the center of your universe? I remember that second. I remember every detail. It was the second I began to live. It was the day I met Jacinda O'Neill."

II

a lifeless nothing

TONY
December 19, 2013
Now.

I walked out of Doctor Hammond's office two hours later, past the receptionist's desk and a handful of patients in the waiting room and slid out into the hall without a word. Lucy, the receptionist, attempted to stop me by politely asking to schedule my next visit. I'd do it by phone, if I ever decided to come back.

I needed to be outside and into the cool air. I needed to numb.

Telling my story was like ripping out surgical staples. I bled out on Doctor Hammond's office floor, and nothing about the experience felt therapeutic. I thought therapy was supposed to heal?

Work had been calling my cell phone every fifteen minutes, but there was nothing about my current state of mind that would allow me to prance back into that office and slap on a fake smile for the remainder of the day. They would have to cope without me, even if that meant a pink slip.

I pulled out my headphones and began to bombard my eardrums with music streaming from my phone. That traveling library of music at my fingertips was the best invention of the century. It provided a secure personal space, keeping me safe despite being surrounded by strangers.

My music was life. There were ten bands that got the most plays on my phone, but Stabbing Westward was by far my favorite. Despite the memories associated with the band, they were a part of my soul. There was something about the dark industrial sound that filled me with enough strength to turn everything else off.

I put my head down, eyes to the floor, and paced around the next corner toward the exit. There was nothing to see walking these hallways. The office was as sterile as a hospital, with neutral wallpaper and mass-produced artwork for décor. I peered through the slender windows on the doors into the other office suites and saw packed waiting rooms with people's heads shoved into old copies of Time magazine. Their kids played with the sticky germ-infested toys that kept them occupied during their lengthy waits.

I couldn't help but conflate the hallway with my life—isolated and confined to my own path while the rest of the world moved on without me.

"Sir?"

I had been through a lot of uncomfortable situations in my life, but there were few worse than being caught with tears in your eyes. Especially when all you wanted was to be left alone.

When I looked up, I was caught. By looking, I had accidentally acknowledged I had heard him—but I played it off like I was looking toward the elevators and rubbed my eyes.

"Sir?" he asked again—was that a pocket watch in his hand? "You look distressed."

He was a shrink—he had to be. If it wasn't the balding head with the big white beard that gave him away, it was the nervous aspect with which he cleaned his old-timey glasses. And that suit? It looked like it was made of wool. My skin got itchy just from looking at it.

I sidestepped him as the elevator doors opened and felt relief the moment they shut and left me alone with my thoughts. Really, that's all

I wanted from life—to be left alone with my thoughts.

Once outside, the cold winter air hit me lovingly in the face. It soothed my frazzled nerves and dried my eyes. I let the cold wash over me and willed myself to forget.

Most people avoided the city when the weather was cold or rainy. Nothing emptied the streets faster than a blustery cold day with swirling winds that cut right through the fabric of your clothes. I understood the obvious setback rain and wind caused in an unprepared situation, but I always felt that there was something therapeutic, cathartic even, about walking in the cold.

If it was cold enough, the bitter weather could sweep away all the things on my mind that needed forgetting. Sort of like pinching your arm after stubbing a toe—it helped focus the mind on something else. The city itself added a distracting element that kept my mind in the present. There were always people running for taxis and commuter trains, and buses were known to clip people who weren't paying attention. The city always kept me on my toes, for better or worse. And best of all, Philadelphia was a great place for distraction—

—or burying the past.

The doctor's office was only fifteen blocks from my apartment. It was convenient, near city hall where the streets were clean, and the architecture was beautiful. There was so much to look at that didn't involve interacting with people. It kept my mind moving, because once it slowed down, that's when things got...*difficult.*

I moved to Philly two years ago from Mercy Point when Marshall offered me a job. Marshall was my best friend, and recognized my need for a fresh start—though, he and I remember that conversation differently—

"C'mon man! Philly is where it's at!" he'd said over the phone. "The girls here are something."

"Hot?" I asked, playing along.

"Are they hot?" he replied in a questioning tone. Witty banter was Marshall's constant state of being. "What is hot, really? Let's just say they're warmer than Alaska...in winter."

"Boy, how fast can I get there?" I said, like I had just been invited to a textiles convention.

"C'mon, T. Look, you need someplace to start over. It's closer to where you grew up. You have other friends here. It's a good situation." He paused, then added, "Mercy Point hasn't shown you any, you know? Mercy. Leave the bad memories behind. Come down here and play with me. We'll get Cheesesteaks and wooder-ice, throw some snowballs at Santa."

"Whoa whoa whoa, too far," I groaned. "The snowball incident was from 1968 and totally out of context!" I was an Eagles fan, yeah, come at me.

"Okay, move here and put the context straight. Fly Eagles, fly," he sang. "You start two weeks from Tuesday."

Then he hung up on me.

Marshall always got his way. Especially when I couldn't disagree with his argument. Mercy Point had not treated me kindly.

The city of Mercy Point was your typical fifth- or sixth-tier metropolitan area, on par with other great American cities without a major sports franchise, like Tulsa or Boulder. It was located in Pennsylvania between Philadelphia and Pittsburgh and had the distinct feel that was typical of the northeast. I went to college twenty miles north of Mercy Point—Milton State University, with an enrollment of 60,000 each year, was tucked away into the corner of a small suburban town named Grace Falls, known for the beauty of its three waterfalls.

That's where I met Marshall.

At their best, Mercy Point and Grace Falls were the settings for some of the greatest days of my life.

But that was then.

The city of Philadelphia was a lot of things, but one thing it was never? Boring. I passed all kinds of murals, street art and performances every day—and for a guy with a passion for art, it was always inspiring. Every now and then, however, I'd come across something new that would make me stop for a closer look. Beneath the overpass on Fifth Street was the newest piece by Philadelphia's own mysterious graffiti prophet, whose work had sprung up in every section of the city over the last few years.

This one was as ominous as it was majestic.

"THE 13 ARE COMING," it said in big, bold red letters that streaked down the side of the brick façade in runny drips.

"Think it's a warning?"

"Excuse me?" I asked, removing my headphones.

Did I have something written on my forehead? The rule was—head down, eyes at the ground ahead, and nobody would ever talk to me. Clearly, I had invited this man into a conversation I did not wish to have by the mere friendly nature of my scowl.

"The thirteen are coming," he said, gesturing toward the message. He was tall, with dark brown skin and a graying beard—his worn eyes were kind, but experienced, like he had seen some shit in his day. In twenty years, I expected my eyes to look the same—I had already witnessed a lifetime's worth of shit. "What do you think it means? The book of Genesis has always—"

"—sorry," I said, spinning away, "I'm late for a…sandwich." It was the first thing that popped into my head.

Contrary to recent events, I'm not a jerk. I don't hate people. I wanted to get home, to get behind the four walls of my sanctuary.

This was my life, and after all I had been through, I was content with quiet normalcy. I never once complained that I had been dealt a bad hand. I just wanted to be left alone.

Some days I even believed that.

Perhaps the antidepressants *were* actually working.

My apartment building was located on a dead-end street beside the Ben Franklin Bridge in Old City. Despite the surrounding bridge traffic, it remained a quiet little pocket within the busy burg. It presented lots of secluded comforts, including neighbors I rarely saw.

The streetlamp awoke as I entered the apartment building, while a nasty gust of wind picked up. It was perpetually gloomy inside, the lights in the hallway hadn't worked in years, and I relied on muscle memory to slide my key into the lock for apartment number 4. The lock clicked and the door swung open on its own, revealing a shadowy room with drawn shades, lit by a dim neon glow from the power button on the cable box.

I started my nightly routine by blindly tossing my keys onto the coffee table. They landed with a dull thump on a thick wad of bills as I tossed my messenger bag and coat onto a nearby chair. Then, in one fluid motion, I plopped onto the couch and pressed the red power button on the remote. I could care less about what was on; I just needed the noise—it helped muffle my mind like a blender to the brain pan.

"...this bizarre phenomenon cannot be explained. We asked Doctor Thomas, Physics Professor and electromagnetic expert at Milton State University, about the probability of lightning striking multiple times at the same spot. Doctor Thomas, welcome to the Evening News."

"Thanks, Judy. Glad to be here."

There was no such thing as the perfect escape, especially from one's past. Trying to ditch a former life was like trying to lose a limb. You could hack it off, but that would only cause additional pain—best to just turn away and pretend it's not even there. However, no amount of pretending could ever solve the problem—you're stuck with this whole other limb you don't want anymore.

Seeing Doctor Thomas was like finding that unwanted limb. I knew him—I took his class. I clawed at my thigh as the associated memories forced me to remember things I wanted to leave buried.

"Doctor Thomas, what can you tell our audience about what hap-

pened here today?"

"Sure. Well, there are a lot of factors when speaking to the probability of lightning strikes. The odds of a person being struck by lightning is greater than the odds of winning the SuperBall lotto."

"It was reported by eyewitnesses that The Gates of Hell, a statue by Auguste Rodin, was struck by lightning four times in a row this afternoon. Can you explain that, Doctor Thomas?"

"Heh, well, no, I can't. Hell froze over, I guess."

Doctor Thomas always did have a good sense of humor. He once told me I had potential. In the world of physics, that was equal to a wicked *"yo mama"* burn.

When my cell phone buzzed at six o'clock, I got up, grabbed a glass of water from the kitchen, and downed the whole thing with my pills.

I had been on various antidepressant cocktails for almost six years but recently began chasing them with sleep aids. My session with Doctor Hammond was like gouging a hole into a healing wound, and all I wanted to do was sleep. It was Friday, and there was no need to get up in the morning.

"…continuing on an already strange news day, was the botched implosion of the Divine Lorraine Hotel, on the corner of Broad and Fairmount Avenue. Our Lester Kelly has more."

"Good evening, Judy. The scheduled implosion of the famed Divine Lorraine Hotel came to an anti-climactic pause when crewmen attempted to trigger the blast and nothing happened. After several attempts, the bomb squad and members of the demolition crew bravely entered the building and found that most of the charges had miraculously disappeared. Authorities are now investigating…"

"That's scary…" I said to myself while raising a suspicious eyebrow. The idea of some loony running around the city with explosives made me anxious. Then I remembered why I never watched the news. It had been some kind of weird day out there, but then again, I didn't know much about ordinary to tell the difference.

What exactly was an ordinary day?

For a moment I pondered the world outside my box, thinking of how the average Philadelphian lived. Was it waking up to slave away at a 9 to 5, texting friends and lovers, hitting the gym, grabbing a salad to-go and sipping wine or scotch from the couch while watching TV until you retired at sixty-five? Seventy?

I made up my mind a long time ago that I would not live ordinarily. I was once on top of the world, knowing I was on the trajectory to great things, but that didn't quite go as anticipated. Maybe if I had noticed the signs? Maybe if I had done things differently?

All these thoughts.

"Tomorrow's not a promise," I said to myself.

The Doc, with good intentions, had dredged up things I had kept behind layers of pharmaceutical walls and carefully-laid mental bricks. But now the mortar had crumbled, and all those things locked away were peeking through the cracks.

Since rolling out of bed that morning, I felt wrong, but couldn't pinpoint the feeling. Something was amiss. Maybe it was the full moon? Maybe I had failed to respond to a chain letter? Was it Friday the 13th?

"In other news, there was a home invasion on the 800 block of Snyder Avenue."

The news then devolved into the usual—murder, pain, suffering. All the stuff that depressed healthier people—but I felt numb. I changed the channel to a popular syndicated sitcom and allowed myself to chuckle at the first punch line, then set my glass down onto the coffee table and walked into the bedroom.

My bedroom was always a bit untidy. Clothes never returned home to closets and drawers after being washed, maintaining a semi-permanent residence rolled up into wads on the floor or on top of the dresser. Dirty clothes always found their way into the hamper, but the clean ones were elusive—unless I had company, which was next to never.

I peeled my shirt off after every inch of skin broke out into a dewy layer of perspiration and tossed it into the hamper. Anxiety attacks were always an instant away. All it took to set off an attack was a single mental image from the worst day of my life. I'd confronted that image twice today and foolishly thought that maybe, this time, I might not cave.

"Keep it together. C'mon!" I scolded myself as I slipped on a fresh t-shirt.

The unearthed memories were difficult to re-bury. Every few seconds another resurfaced. My wall—that big strong wall I had built and become so proud of—was crumbling to dust.

I was hyperventilating.

It had been six long years without *her*. I often asked myself how I'd survived this long but never had any answers. My protective wall was down, and charging through it came every sad and happy memory of *her*.

It was excruciating. It was torture. I shook, like my demons were fighting to escape through every pore, and fought back sobs, suffocating in grief. Then I fell into bed and wept until the sleeping pills finally took me away.

An autoimmune disease is when the body fights itself. It recognizes a healthy part of you—tissue, organs, etc…—as a foreign invader and sends antibodies to fight it off, like an infection. My brain was similar to the disease—it tried to exploit every weakness and every doubt through dreams, attacking it from every possible angle.

I wish I could have controlled my dreams, to manipulate their outcomes to a more desirable ending. I haven't had a happy dream in years—at least not one I could remember.

The recurring nightmare I'd recounted to Doctor Hammond had been a steady part of my life since Northcreek. They all started in the woods at the bottom of a steep hill.

This dream was the same, until it became so very different.

The forest floor was damp and squishy beneath my feet. I was walking, following the path to the gully. I leapt across and was hiking up the steep incline when I heard the single engine overhead. It soared just above the treetops like a giant metal bird, then climbed high into the sky.

I was no longer standing in the woods.

I managed to avoid being strafed by friendly fire and flattened my dive before the engine stalled. My wingman broke formation and engaged the enemy. The combatant was a more proficient pilot than Simon had anticipated. It dove toward my plane, putting us both under the bullseye.

I wasn't ready for this. I wasn't ready for war.

We were a search and destroy team. Air support for a battalion of ground troops who stumbled into trouble along the Rhone river. We simply had to find them and drop bombs on enemy lines to soften their advance, allowing our countrymen to retreat.

Only, we ran into trouble.

France had been decimated by war, towns and cities flattened to dust. So much destruction and disregard for human life. I had watched too many brothers die in combat. Shot down or massacred by the unstoppable German war machine. Was there an end to this hell?

My engine restarted and I took evasive maneuvers. Diving ahead of the German plane—the sound of machine gun rounds zipping through the air past the cockpit—was both terrifying and jolting.

Luckily, Simon was a good pilot. He clipped the German's rudder with his machine gun.

The plane spun wildly. The Iron Cross painted onto the wings flipped over and over, then crashed into the trees below, leading a trail of smoke. One less fascist in the sky was one less threat to our men on the ground.

☾

December 20th, 2013

I woke up gasping for air.

I was holding my breath and clenching my jaw. Covered in sweat, and drowsy from the medication, my head pounded like a bass drum—like the worst hangover of my life.

After stumbling into the kitchen to the laughter of a late-night talk show playing on the living room TV, I grabbed a cold bottle of water from the fridge and downed the whole thing at once, then headed back to bed.

I felt feverish. My temperature so hot, I felt cold.

As I adjusted my pillows, I recalled my dream and chuckled at the thought.

A French fighter pilot? Sometimes my mind defined obscurity, and other times I questioned why I wasn't still at Northcreek. All in all, it was refreshing to be dreaming of something other than her, no matter how strange.

"What? Repeat. Over," I yelled into my radio.

I wasn't speaking English—was that *French*? At least it sounded French.

Simon yelled something over the radio that crackled under heavy static.

He sounded flustered. I twisted inside the tiny cockpit, attempting to peer out over the starboard wing into the empty air between Simon and me, facing south. I saw nothing in the darkening sky but a blooming thunderhead thick with storm clouds. One moment the sky was clear, and the next the remaining light was being swallowed up. I was checking back and forth between nose and starboard, levelling the stick so I didn't veer off course or go spiraling out of control, when I saw it. A black mass of *something* quickly moving toward the wing.

"What is that!?" shouted a voice.

A chill ran up my back.

There was someone in the plane with me. My tiny single engine plane didn't have a lot of space behind the pilot—perhaps enough for a single person. What I found was a large young man jammed into the space like he had been wedged in with a shoehorn.

"Who are you?" I yelled, catching a glimpse of his chubby face.

"Who am I? *Who am I?*" he shouted back, as if appalled by the question—then tapped his finger against the glass canopy. "What is that!"

It was too small to be another plane. After spotting it in my peripheral vision, my first instinct was to call it large bird. But it flapped strangely and glided on the air, much too large to be a bird. I tore my eyes free to straighten the nose—the shock caused me to push forward on the stick, and I was losing altitude.

I pulled back, flattening my dive, then looked back over my shoulder at the wing—

What I saw there made my skin tingle.

"Oh shit! Oh shit!" shouted the young man.

Someone gently touched down onto the starboard wing—and stood there, impossibly unaffected by the force, as if he were standing on the ground! A man in black with long blond hair was standing on my wing. Just standing there, effortlessly. His clothing and hair were whipping wildly in the wind as my plane pushed on at high speed.

I pulled up, gaining altitude to 6800 meters, and looked back. I expected him gone, but he was still there, untroubled by the angle and altitude.

"Shake him off! Shake him off!" shouted the young man.

"Who the fuck are you?" I shouted.

"Stop worrying about me and worry about that!"

The man on the wing was stalking toward the cockpit.

I dove and rolled, my stomach clenching, and when I flattened, I took a deep relieving breath. Nothing could have held on under such pressure and force—if not the friction, the gravity should have tossed him free.

But he was still there, like none of it applied to him. As if the physics of flight—thrust, lift, drag, gravity—were his to control.

I tried everything, before a loud slam preceded his bare fist breaking through the canopy's protective glass, and the rush of wind stole the air from my lungs. I withdrew my sidearm, ready to defend myself.

"Shit! Shoot him! Shoot him!" cried the young man.

This was crazy, it was only a dream! It was only a dream!

He ripped the canopy from the plane and the friction burned my face raw.

I fired my gun into the man's arm as he reached for my collar, but it was like shooting a ghost—he didn't bleed; he didn't even flinch. With a tug, he ripped me out of my seat, snapping my safety harness to pieces, then raised me over his head.

The young man kept screaming while the plane fell from the sky. My stomach lurched as the force from the freefall thrust my guts into my throat. I was suffocating while gravity twisted, pulled, and threw me, but it didn't break the man's vice-like grip. I couldn't steady my arm enough to fire the gun, yet the man stood there unbothered and smiled.

"We're gonna die! We're gonna die!" shouted the young man from the cockpit, but this man—this Kraut? Demon?—paid him no mind, as if he weren't even there.

I was dead. I knew I was dead. Either by this demon, the fall, or the crash—nothing about this predicament could lead to survival. I was going to die in moments, but I refused to die alone—I was taking him with me, one way or another.

"Confess," said the man over the deafening wind. "I know what you are. Confess to me now."

I tucked my fear away and summoned every vestige of concentration I had left, finally placing my gun between his bright blue eyes, then squeezed the trigger.

As my brain sent the command to fire, the man thrust his free hand deep into my chest and the instant pain forced the gun from my hand. He tore apart my ribs—sick popping sounds followed by deep thudding crunches, tugging at me from the inside. Then, with one last fatal pull, my body went limp.

Before darkness ushered me into the abyss of what came beyond, one word echoed through my mind, surfacing through the sporadic thoughts of a dead man.

Summanus.

THE RAPTOR

III

serendipity

TONY
December 19, 2013
Yesterday.

"Have you ever had that one moment in your life when you realized your destiny?" I asked, starting with a free flow of consciousness, selecting a beginning that made the most sense. "That exact second your life went from meandering around in circles to a clear path forward? The split second before that very moment, your life was meaningless and forgettable, like an old pair of socks, but then something unforeseen happened and thrust your life into a whole new and amazing direction? As if the big bang went off inside you, spreading outward at the speed of light and making that very second the center of your universe?

"I remember that second. I remember every detail. It was the second I began to live. It was the day I met Jacinda O'Neill."

"Dramatic," said Doctor Hammond, getting a small chuckle out of me. "Tell me, how'd you meet her?"

I looked away from the doc and stared at a particular section of the office wall, where the wallpaper pattern formed a pair of abstract eyes. They almost looked like hers. "Labor Day weekend. 1997. Before my senior year of high school. Grace Falls, Pennsylvania."

"Good start." Doc nodded.

"I think it was a Friday. I remember because Fridays had that certain glow, like magic was in the air." I took a deep breath, tore down my protective walls, and let it all come back to me. "You know, I talk a big game. I know you believe it's a defense mechanism, and you're one-hundred percent correct. I pretend like I don't remember and push the memories away the moment they surface. The fact is, I remember all of it as if it was yesterday."

August 29th, 1997

At just seventeen years old, I was already a completely helpless, irrevocably hopeless romantic. In fact, I was the epitome of the term. I knew what I was, but I didn't know who I was. There's a difference, and all of that was about to change because of a girl. A beautiful girl, on a magical night.

But I warn you, this isn't a love story.

I was good at sports, mostly baseball, but I wasn't the typical athlete. Don't get me wrong, I was good, but I was also the odd combination of art-geek meets jock that didn't quite mix with the mainstream. I didn't fit in with either group but was always striving to belong somewhere. I could discuss sports as easily as I could talk comics, art, movies, and the finer aspects of the Evil Dead franchise. When you don't fit in to a specific group, you don't fit in with any group. I felt invisible, and I wanted to be seen.

"T! Will you just enjoy yourself!?" screamed Amanda.

The problem was, I was much too shy to be seen.

"I am enjoying myself," I complained. I was lying.

I met Amanda in the eighth grade. She moved to my small suburban town in New Jersey from Grace Falls, PA, having lived there her whole life. We met in art class and ended up best friends. Without Amanda, I don't know where I would've been. She kept me afloat, and in a lot of ways, I did the same for her.

She and I were a lot alike.

Amanda had a darkness inside—her brother died when she was a kid. He jumped off a waterfall on a dare and never came back up. She left those demons behind when she moved away. So, when she invited me to tag along to visit her grandma in Grace Falls over Labor Day weekend—her first time back in several years—I couldn't say no. She would have done the same for me.

"You look terrified." She laughed. "This's the event of the year in Grace Falls."

"Not much to do up here, I guess," I joked and received an immediate shove from Amanda's free hand—the other one hoisted the largest waffle cone of ice cream I'd ever seen.

Grace Falls was the kind of small town that grew too big too fast and still believed it was a small town. It had malls and department stores right down the street from mom-and-pop shops, and a town square that was plucked straight out of the 1950s. It had its own yearly rituals, like the Labor Day Fair, which was the largest in the state. There was food, amusement rides, games, crafts, and enough things to see and do that it took more than one visit to observe it all.

For someone with introverted tendencies, it was overwhelming.

"Come on!" she groaned. Amanda was constantly trying to coerce me out of my shell to experience new things. "This was my favorite part of living here. Joey used to take me around to see everything." Most people winced when they thought of departed loved ones, but every time Amanda mentioned Joey there was a sparkle in her eye—like she knew he was still there, somewhere, watching over her. "I've got it. Follow me!" A suspicious grin crossed her face that made her look downright evil, and she set off at once with me tailing along.

Amanda was tall for a girl, with straight blonde hair that turned heads. She was pretty in that approachable way that everybody wanted to know her—but she made a point of having only a few very close friends.

She dragged me through crowded lines, past the delicious aroma of frying funnel cake to the far side of the fair. We ducked through tents and sidestepped children on sugary snack highs, finally arriving at a booth with a flashing sign that said *Speed Pitch*. For two dollars, you were given three baseballs to throw with a radar gun that would rank your speed. The fastest thrower per age group would receive a trophy and a cash prize at the end of the weekend.

I took my throws while Amanda argued with the booth operator about Rick Jansen—the recorded fastest thrower of my age group. "Don't tell me that jerk is still winning at everything?"

For a seventeen-year-old, I held my own. Rick threw almost fifteen miles per hour faster, but that didn't stop me from shoveling out six more bucks in an effort to climb a little higher. I got within five miles per hour and called it a day, satisfied I had left my mark on Grace Falls.

"See? Now you're having a good time. I can tell," gloated Amanda.

"I am. But only a little," I joked. "Hey, let's do the mirror maze."

"You're stalling," said the Doc.

"Just creating context," I said. "Amanda was my best friend. She was introducing me to Grace Falls. And, in a way, my destiny."

"Amanda sounds like a good friend who genuinely cares about you. Where is she now?" asked Doc.

"Yeah, she was, and she did. We had our ups and downs," I said, purposely avoiding his question.

As the sun slumped over the horizon, the crowds died away. The musical entertainment began by a wooden stage surrounded by hay bales and fire pits that formed a makeshift amphitheater.

Amanda found an old friend named Maynard. She called him Morris—his last name, as always—and we joined his friends watching the local talent. Morris and his group were misfits—Trent, Cyndi, Tori, and Kurt. They were punk, goth, and artsy, and I immediately felt like I might fit in. We critiqued every act in debates that often ended with Tori offering two thumbs down and a fart noise with her tongue. Most performances were country crooners I preferred to ignore, but there were some quality exceptions.

We promised Amanda's grandmother we'd be home before ten, but we lost track of time the moment we sat down with them.

I was glad we did.

The previous band, Marauder, front-manned by a guy in a black studded jean jacket, wrapped their set with a song called "The Ballad of Veronica Green." It was a dazzling display of energy and volume, and maybe that was why the next performer snuck up on us. We were still buzzing about whether or not Marauder was terrible, lousy, or al-most-maybe-good when a girl with an acoustic guitar crept onstage to a courteous applause. Her hair fell in waves of blazing red, and she wore torn jeans with a leather jacket and green Converse Chucks.

I was immediately smitten. "Who's she?"

Morris squinted through his glasses and nudged Amanda with an elbow. "Look who it is," he said.

"Who is she?" I asked again.

"My old neighbor," said Amanda. "O'Neill."

Amanda called everyone by their last names. She had a tough time calling me Oscuro, so she called me "T" instead—but that was after she tried "Ant" and "Tone" and "Scuro" and a variety of other awful op-tions, including "Anton," then later "Twan"—all of which never stuck, thankfully.

The stage was three feet off the ground, large enough to hold an entire six-piece band. The stage lights were hung from professional scaffolding and beamed hot and bright onto center stage. A stagehand quickly reset the microphone and placed a stool beside the mic stand as the crowd quieted.

When O'Neill was introduced, she was visibly nervous. The pol-ished acoustic guitar shivered in her hand. She slung her instrument over her shoulder and propped herself against the stool, looking into the crowd as if she was peering right through them. She smiled sheepishly, adjusted the microphone, then waited for the nerves to settle.

She looked tiny on that huge stage. The light crowned her crimson hair with a blazing red halo, and even from the distance, I spotted her green eyes.

"Hey, I'm Jacinda O'Neill," she said into the microphone once her trembling ceased. "How's everybody doing tonight?" There were a handful of cheers, followed by loud woos from Tori and Cyndi, which sounded antagonistic.

Jacinda looked absolutely beautiful under the lights, and she held her aged guitar as if it was her most prized possession. "This guitar was given to me by my Grammy when I was four. She was the best," she said, then paused to remember her Gram. "I'm going to play a couple songs. This is my first time, ever, playing for an audience. I'm a little nervous." Then she half- smiled and continued. "I want to play a few songs that inspire me, and hopefully, you too."

She brushed her hair behind her ear and checked the guitar one last time. "Okay, I think I'm ready," she said, taking a deep breath. "The first song is 'We Belong Together' by Ritchie Valens."

Then she began to play.

"She was awful."
"What?" asked Doc, raising an eyebrow.
"Dreadful. Categorically dreadful."
"Wait, what?" he asked, as he shook his head.
"I'm kidding," I laughed. "She was absolutely, undeniably amazing."
"You had me going."
"Yeah, the look on your face. Haha!"

It was like nothing I had ever experienced, watching this stranger— this amazing girl— play the guitar and charm me. She was graceful and brilliant. Bewitching. I couldn't blink.

But nothing—absolutely nothing—could have prepared me for her voice when she finally began to sing.

"You're mine, and we belong together. Yes, we belong together, for eternity," she sang. Her voice was strong, powerful, beautiful, enchanting, and pristine. My eyes watered, enraptured by her voice.

I had to know Jacinda. I had to know all about her. And lucky for me, my best friend knew her.

"Many people would argue, wisely, that you can't fall in love with someone unless you've seen them at their best and worst.

"I don't disagree with that.

"However, I fell in love with Jacinda O'Neill that moment. I was starstruck. I was without a doubt, in love with that girl. For all eternity," I said, and the Doc jotted a few notes onto his pad.

Next, she performed "Summertime Blues" by Eddie Cochran, then finished up her three-song set with "Wish You Were Here" by Pink Floyd. When she finished, she thanked everyone, said goodnight, and left the stage to smattering applause and a few heckles from the crowd.

"The crowd heckled her?"

"Yes," I replied.

"Why was that? You said she was good."

"Thus began the mystery," I said, like I was introducing a Scooby Doo episode. "I didn't know it at the time, but she had a contentious relationship with some of the local kids."

"What kind of contention?"

"You'll see."

"Amanda?" said Jacinda. "Hey!"

I would have been lying if I said I didn't see her coming. I had a tractor beam on that girl. I was aware of where she was at all times, even when I wasn't looking. In fact, my entire body became hyper-aware of everything—including how fashionably lame I was, and why I had chosen to wear those shitty shoes that night.

When Jacinda saw Amanda, she rushed over with her arms wide for a hug, as I did everything in my power to behave. She was so much cooler than me—I simultaneously wanted to hide beneath a hay bale or show off with a Bruce Campbell one-liner.

"O'Neill, hey," said Amanda, with a voice that sounded fake. She got up from her seat next to me and gave Jacinda a quick hug.

"It's been a long time," said Jacinda. "How's your mom and dad?"

"Good," replied Amanda, her genuine warmth beginning to burn through the artifice. "How's your family?"

"They're alright," said Jacinda. "Are you back? Or just visiting?"

I couldn't tear myself away from their small talk, hanging on every word as if I might learn something important—like her birth sign, blood type, and marital status. Eventually Morris leaned over and said, "You've got a little drool on your chin, Romeo," loud enough for everyone to hear.

"O'Neill, this is my best friend, T, from back home. He's an artist and an athlete like you."

"Oh, cool," Jacinda said, her eyes landing on me for the first time. All at once I felt powerful and weak, immune and sick—opposites that shook me like an unbalanced washing machine. "Hey T. What do you play?"

"Oh, I'm not that kind of artist—I'm no musician," I mumbled. "I draw."

"But he does play a mean skin flute," said Morris to his friends, and they giggled.

"No," she said, smiling, as Amanda looked mortified—like she could slap me and Morris both. "I mean, what sport do you play?"

"Oh," I said, then hopped to my feet to join them. I held out my hand and Jacinda shook it, and I swear I nearly lost my nerve at just her touch. There was a mini-debate turned epic argument inside my head as to how much pressure with which to grip her hand. I shook it firmly but gently at the same time, like I was holding a wiggling hamster. Our hands met for what seemed like forever, and I almost lost my thought until it came spilling out of me. "I play baseball."

"Nice to meet you, T who plays baseball," she said. "I paint and play soccer. I run some track too."

"What do you paint?" I asked. "And it's Tony."

"Anything. Everything," she said with a smile. "O'Keeffe is my favorite. Sometimes I try to paint like her."

"I know O'Keeffe," I said, then gestured to Amanda and added, "We learned about her in art class."

"I go to the art museum every time her exhibit comes through. You should go see it sometime." She paused and looked at me in a way no girl ever had. The look was profound, and I couldn't comprehend the entirety of it. "You have to see them with your own eyes."

"I am not a particularly attractive man," I explained.

"Your self-esteem could use a booster-shot, Tony," the Doc interjected before I could say anything else.

"Look, I'm being honest. I've never felt noticeable when I walk into a room. But Jaycie looked into my eyes and saw someone else. She saw the good that was there. Even the good I didn't see myself. I felt drawn to her, and I'd like to believe she felt the same. It was magnetic, like we were meant to meet."

"What happened?"

"Nothing."

"Nothing?"

"Amanda invited Jacinda to join us, but as time drifted on, Morris and his friends left. When Amanda ran off to say goodbye to them, she left Jacinda and me alone. As far as awkward moments go, and as much as my idiot-brain tried to ruin it, Jacinda looked right past it. I had a moment, a fleeting one, when we were talking about the planets and stars, and I had my chance to kiss her."

"Did you?"

"No."

"Why not?"

"Birds."

The moment seemed perfect. It was a beautiful night—warm and cozy by the fire in the early autumn air—and the moment was set. As the crowds thinned and the fire pit slowly burned out, Jacinda and I leaned back on the hay bales, looking up at the stars.

"There's a solar eclipse on Monday," she said, pointing to the crescent moon. "A partial one."

"Really? Is that rare?" I asked. I knew very little about astronomy or astrology. She could have said it happened daily and I would have believed her.

"A little," she said. "What's that?"

"Hmm?" I asked, before following her eyes down to my chest. "This?" I held up the chain around my neck, with an old brass skeleton key dangling from the end.

"Is that the key to your heart?" she asked jokingly.

"Yes," I said, playing along, and our eyes snagged like Velcro.

"Where'd you get it?" she asked.

"I found it when I was a kid," I said, and we drifted closer. The details of how I came into possession of that key didn't need to be told. Saying I found it was best to maintain the moment.

"Oh, and where are you from, exactly?"

"New Jersey," I said. "Small, one-stop-light town."

"I see," she said, now inches away.

"Did you grow up here?" I asked.

"Yeah," she said with a sigh.

"What's it like? Does your high school suck too?"

"Grace Falls has more ghosts than people," she said mysteriously. "Where are you going to college?"

"I don't know yet. What about you?"

"I don't know. Milton State has a good music program. Maybe I'll go there."

"Where's that?" I asked, gesturing with my hands.

"Locally. It's in Grace Falls." She was smiling, like she realized something cute about me. "Are you a lefty?" Then she clarified. "You use your left hand a lot when you talk."

I nodded. She was observant. She was paying attention to me, soaking up details. No girl had ever paid attention to me like that, and it was mutual. I wanted to know everything about her too. "You?"

She nodded.

I could feel her breath against my cheek, and her eyes were so big and pretty, I felt dizzy staring into them.

The moment was perfect. Too perfect.

As we leaned toward each other under the crescent moon, neither of us noticed the visitors perched on the wooden rail behind us. On cue, as my heart and brain finally conspired together to lean in and kiss her—

—a crow squawked, like someone had clipped its tailfeathers.

The squawking prompted the amassed others to join in. They were everywhere, flocking to the fair after hours to pick at all the leftover food on the ground.

The noise stole Jacinda's attention, and the moment vanished.

"Sorry," she said as she sat up. "I've gotta go."

"Yeah, okay," I said, inwardly cursing myself out like a New York taxi driver. "Will you be back here tomorrow? The fair's open all week-end, right?"

"It is, and maybe."

"Maybe? Just maybe?" I said playfully.

"I'll look for you." She smiled and nodded.

"Me too," I said, then quickly clarified, "for you. I'll look for you."

She laughed, as if she found me charming. "Tomorrow's not a promise, Tony. Gotta earn each one." Then she backed away from me and waved. "It was nice to meet you."

"Then Jacinda walked off and out of my life."

"She wasn't there the next day?"

"Nope. I forced Amanda to go back to the fair, and we stayed all day. There was no sign of Jacinda, not anywhere. It wasn't the first time I felt crushed, but this was different. This wasn't some silly infatuation with some girl—this felt real. Amanda and I got into a fight, but she wasn't actually angry with me—not yet, at least. The truth was, she was furious with Jacinda."

"Why's that?"

"My crush was just another reason for Amanda to hate her." Then I paused before adding, *"I warned you, doc, this isn't a love story."*

IV

persistence of memory

TONY
December 20, 2013
Now.

I woke up to the sound of laughter coming from my living room. It was a laugh track, like something that played after every awful joke on an old sitcom. I often fell asleep with the TV on and thought nothing of it. I yawned and rubbed my eyes, feeling at ease to start my weekend fresh with the sunlight creeping through the cracks in the drawn shades. I sat up and let the disorientation wear off before I attempted to stand. My head throbbed like I had been asleep all day, and I took a random glance at my alarm clock.

It was six in the evening.

"Fuck," I groaned. It wasn't the first time I had accidentally taken too many sleeping pills, but half the weekend was now gone.

As I rolled over, part of the bedsheets around my pillow looked scorched, and I wondered if I had forgotten to blow out a candle the night before—despite the fact I didn't remember lighting one. It also wasn't the first time I had gaps in my memory as a result of taking too many pills.

Another canned-laugh track followed yet another bad joke, only this one was accompanied by a giggle and the rustling of a plastic junk food bag.

I froze, registering the sound of a real live person in my living room. Who was in my apartment?

I reached down beneath my bed and slowly extracted my intruder and theft protection device—an aluminum baseball bat—as soundlessly as possible. The bat was old and scuffed but still hard enough to dent heads if someone came busting through my door. The bat was seeing its first action since I'd tried out for the city league team in Mercy Point. It still felt good in my hands, like my own personal Excalibur.

Being asleep for twenty-four hours produced side effects. Extreme grogginess and poor equilibrium were just the two I could identify despite the intruder alert raising my pulse. I stumbled out of my bedroom, bat raised, ready to swing for the fences.

"Get out of my house!" I yelled, attempting—and possibly achieving—to sound like a badass. The adrenaline was soaring until I realized who it was—on *my* couch, eating *my* tortilla chips with *my* salsa. I let the bat drop from my shoulder and used it as a crutch to keep from falling over.

"And good morning to you too, buddy! And good afternoon. And good evening!" said the stocky asshole, with great enthusiasm, from my couch. His shoes were off, and his feet were on my coffee table. Marshall was the only loyal friend I had left in the world, and this was him at his best—or worst—depending on the point of view. There were holes in his socks, from my perspective. "That was a fierce entrance. Can you do it again? I'd like to take a pic and post it for the 'gram."

Perhaps my mind was still groggy, but I was having a hell of a time figuring out how he got in and why he was sitting on my fucking couch.

"What's going on?" I asked. I was trying not to sound shocked or annoyed, but I wasn't sure I succeeded in either.

"Well, Jerry's mad at George because he let Kramer borrow Jerry's toothbrush, and we all know that can't be good. Also, Elaine's on a lunch date with a pansy English guy who eats toast with a fork," he said with a straight face.

I always felt Marshall missed his calling as a standup comedian or improv specialist. The guy was always funny, even when I wasn't in the mood.

"Hey buddy," he said, stuffing a loaded salsa chip into his mouth, "you sleep in those clothes? Bed-wrinkled is a great look for you."

The dizziness was passing, but not fast enough.

"Thanks. Why are you here?"

"Why am I here? On this earth? Metaphysically?" Marshall could twist anything around from any angle he desired, without hesitation. "Hope you don't mind, but I found a two-year-old bottle of beer in the back of your fridge-full-of-only-condiments." He picked up the bottle, took a swig, then studied it closely. "In fact, I think I gave you this beer two years ago, right about the time that relish on the door expired. You know, if you have purple relish, it's probably not edible."

Whenever we hung out, he made me wish life was different. Like it used to be.

"How'd you get in, Marshall?"

"No hello? No, *Hi Marshall? Thanks for getting me the sweet job I ditched for a whole half-day without telling anyone? Thanks for helping me actually pay the bills without needing an advanced physics degree to balance my checkbook on a monthly basis?*" he said, shrugging, then let out an exasperated sigh.

I felt the rising shame, and my own sigh carried the subtext of the phrase, "shit, I fucked up"—his guilt trip dug into my conscience. Marshall had gotten me the job, and I had already called out a half-dozen times for random reasons—mostly anxiety-related—and exceeded my accrued time off. It was difficult finding a job with my records. I used to be great with responsibility and obligations, but now I couldn't get out of my own way. I was like a slinky that fell down the steps instead of gracefully gliding its springy way—its only purpose was to be a spring, and it couldn't even meet that. That was me, a professional waste of cubicle space.

"Hello. Hi Marshall," I replied sarcastically. "Thanks for getting me a sweet job that pays the bills."

"That sucked, but I'll settle for an *I love you*," Marshall quipped.

"Well, that ain't happening," I said while tossing the bat onto the couch beside him. I continued over to the kitchen sink and splashed some water onto my face.

"Okay, okay. I'll settle for a proper Marshall-Tony adventure. Tonight," he proposed, and I gave him a negatory glare upon returning to the living room. "Ya know, hit up a few bars. Maybe a fancy club and see some hot young honeys shaking their tooshies around." He performed a small booty-shaking jig from the seat of his pants, although said seat never left my couch. Then he hopped to his feet and discarded his beer. "Damn, that beer is dreadful! No wonder you didn't drink it."

"I don't know," I said. "I don't feel like going out tonight."

Marshall's disappointed face was mostly a bulging lower lip coupled with baby eyes that I'm sure worked on someone at some time in his life. Just not on me.

"You're joking," grumbled Marshall.

"I've got shit to do." I stalked into the bedroom to avoid the conversation.

"Bullshit! It's Saturday night!" he retorted.

I walked over to my desk with its aging computer and rummaged through a stack of papers, pretending to look for something.

"Tony, man, we haven't been out together for any kind of actual fun since before the last time I was single. That was freaking six years ago! We're rapidly approaching our mid-thirties! Time's a-wastin'! You need to pick up the pieces and try and become whole again, man."

It wasn't the first time someone had told me that.

"That's not true," I said. "We went out on Halloween."

"That was a work event, T," he grumbled.

"I don't think—" I started to say.

"You don't think what?" he groaned, aggressively cutting me off. "That it's a good idea? Everything that happened, happened six years ago. It's time to move on." I kept my back to him on purpose—I didn't want him to see me struggling. "You've spent a lot of time cutting off from all your friends. I'm the only one stubborn enough not to give up on you. I know you went through hell. I don't know if you're actually stupid enough to be suicidal, but it's shit or get off the pot time. Just do something and get it over with!"

Marshall had been saving that up for a long time. He had a right to say it. I'd put him and everyone else I ever loved through a lot, and it was human nature to give up when you didn't see change in someone who desperately needed it. Though not everything he said was true. My family was gone, and most of my friends left because they were either too scared or ashamed of me. I didn't realize my actions were affecting Marshall, and he obviously didn't come here looking for a fight—even though he looked ready to punch some sense into my face.

Yet I had to admit, I was a frustrating friend these days.

I stopped pretending to sort through papers, which had accumulated for months, and hunched over my desk. Through the mess of random papers, mail, and bills, an old picture of *her* stared back at me.

The picture was taken more than ten years ago. There was a roller coaster in the background, brightly lit under a starry sky, a mini-golf club in her hand and a smile I could never forget—even if I wanted to. Her red hair was drifting in the breeze, and she wore a green barrette that highlighted her eyes.

She was so happy that night—the best of my life—and I remembered every detail. It was special for reasons I'd only ever shared once— yesterday with Doctor Hammond. It hurt just to think of it. Could I ever heal from a wound this deep?

I was careful never to leave pictures out in the open, and this one should have been buried in the drawer at the very bottom of the stack. I always kept them locked away and out of sight.

Marshall paused and eased back.

"I'm sorry, man. I can't imagine what it's like to lose the woman you love. Not like that," he said, shaking his head. "You've been through the wringer. It's no wonder you're seeing a shrink." He paused, planning his next words carefully. "She was the best."

I looked away from the photo and faced Marshall. I didn't realize I had tears in my eyes until they ran down my cheeks. "You know I'm seeing a shrink?"

"I followed you," he said. "You walked out, right past my office yesterday, and never said a word. I wanted to make sure you were okay." He glanced at my desk and saw her photo peeking out. "I want things to be like old times."

"I do too."

I looked down at her picture again, allowing myself a moment to admire her, then gently placed it into the top drawer and slid it shut.

Marshall and I settled in at the bar and started a tab. We both agreed the music was awful, but the beer was to our taste.

Cheap.

"Okay, seriously, how'd you get into my apartment." I took a swig from a fresh mug. "No shit this time."

"A true magician never reveals his tricks!" he shouted over the lame music. "Lucky for you, I am no magician." He took a hearty gulp and resurfaced with a foam 'stache he wiped away with the back of his hand. "You gave me a spare key when you moved in. Said you needed someone who could check up on you if you suddenly disappeared." At this, he provided the key, holding it up between his thumb and forefinger. It was brass-colored metal and struck a memory I quickly stifled with another gulp of beer.

"You sunnuva—"

"Ah! Ah! Ah!" he scolded, wagging a finger in my face. "My mother is no B-I-T-C-H! She's doggish, but I deal."

Marshall was looking stylish. Black and white wingtip shoes and a fancy blazer—it was a far cry from what he wore in college. He was the kind of guy who wore those awful vanity t-shirts that said something provocative like "My Jeans Were Washed in Windex—I Can See You In Them." I was proud of his new maturity. He did well for himself—successful, stable, and it was only a matter of time before he charmed some lucky gal into something special.

He deserved it.

I, on the other hand, still dressed beneath my maturity, but it felt nice to throw on some nicer clothes and reclaim some identity. Leather jacket, black boots, a shirt with actual buttons, and dark jeans made me feel like a new man. There was a part of me that felt happy to be out enjoying myself, even though another part felt guilty.

"Hey man, speaking of keys," said Marshall suddenly. "Where's that charm? That key you always used to wear around your neck?"

"I got rid of that years ago," I said with a forced smile and quickly changed the subject. "So, this is good right? Has it really been six years since we last did this?"

"Yeah, I think so! Last time we went out to a place like this—Jaycie was rocking the stage. You, me, and Anne were hanging in the back, waving our lighters through the air at the end of every song. It was New Year's, wasn't it?" He gave me a quick glance, seeing how I reacted to the memory before deciding to continue. "Actually, Anne called the other night."

"No way!" I was shocked. The way things ended between them was not on what anyone would call *good terms,* which made me feel guilty all over again. "Pensez-vous qu'il pourrait y avoir une romance dans le futur?" I teased.

"What?" asked Marshall. "Was that French?"

"Huh?"

"You just spoke in French, or something," he said. "When did you learn fucking French?"

"I didn't." My head felt like it was already swimming in alcohol. I looked at the glass as if it had some secret ingredient making me say weird things.

"Maybe I misheard you. What did you say?"

"Do you think there might be some romance in the future?" I asked again.

"Maybe," he said with optimism. "She just moved here from Pittsburgh. We'll see. I swear you didn't say that the first time." Then he gulped down the remainder of his glass and proclaimed, "I need another beer!"

I lasted another half-conversation before I decided to take a piss, not just to relieve myself, but to relieve the pressure building between my temples. Being out with Marshall was great, but the problem with old friends was the reminiscing of days gone by. Looking back made looking forward impossibly hard.

I told Marshall I had to "break the seal" and jumped from the barstool, headed for the back past a group of drunken college kids. The restrooms were down a hall opposite the kitchen near the back exit. It was a gloomy hallway filled with a red glow from the exit sign and the loud clanking of pots and pans emanating from the kitchen.

"I wouldn't go in there."

"What's that?" I didn't even see the guy at first, leaning against the wall, opposite the restroom door. My hand already rested on the handle.

"I wouldn't go in there, my man," said the guy. He wore military fatigues and looked serious—despite deadpanning an apparent fart-joke.

"Thanks for the warning," I said, then chuckled and opened the door, debating on whether or not to hold my breath. Did the military guy drop a *bomb* inside a public restroom?

"Sweet Caroline" played on the restroom speakers as I walked to the end of the urinal row, sampling the air—nothing fouler than the usual noxious stink of public restrooms. Some hipster guy zippered up and left without washing. I chose the final stall, hoping he wasn't a bartender or cook. There was a gurgling sound coming from the drain, making the unflushed piss-water bubble. Rather than rue the day with soiled pants, I quickly sidestepped to the previous stall and started my business there. I was nearly finished when the drain groaned, and the urinal flushed on its own in a violent tremble that made the pipes inside the wall whine.

Public city restrooms could look perfectly clean, but they always managed to find a way to disgust you. The nearest toilet stall had what appeared to be a mountain of feces piling up over the bowl, and I gagged a little as I passed. Heathens. Who the hell walks into a public restroom and unloads half their body weight, then bolts without a courtesy flush?

Most of the sinks worked, but some were stuffed with paper towels and refused to drain. As I selected the least offensive sink and began washing my hands, I felt a sharp pain behind my eyes. Dizziness overwhelmed me, and my reflection seemed to lag behind my motions, like we were out of sync. I thought about my beer, and I thought about how long it had been since I drank. Was the chemical cocktail I ingested daily, to help keep up that beautiful, protective mental wall, a bad mix with fermented hops, barley, and yeast?

According to the medication labels, undoubtedly so. That was, typically, the first item listed under the warning.

"Fuck," I said under my breath and pressed a wet palm against my eye.

"Fuck," said my reflection a second later.

It was almost amusing at first, if not totally terrible like a bad trip. I thought I could push through, splash some water onto my face, cool off, and suck it up—but then came the queasiness, like I was filling up with hot air. Was I having an anxiety attack? Was I getting sick? Neither would be surprising—it was flu-season, and I was out with my oldest friend talking about the good ole days I wanted to leave behind.

I closed my eyes, took a few deep, relaxing breaths, then opened—

—but my reflection was already watching me.

Jolting backward, it followed, still a moment behind, but something was amiss…

Suspiciously, I leaned forward to study the me in the mirror and how it moved. It was mimicking me, but not perfect, like a bad game of shadow.

"What the hell's going on here?" I said aloud.

"Hell has nothing to do with it," said my reflection.

A hand erupted from the mirror like it was breaking water and snatched my throat. I punched and clawed at it, trying to break free as it began to crush my windpipe.

"Confess, spark," the mirror-me threatened. I was caught by the neck like a mouse in a trap—dangling like windchimes in a hurricane. "Confess your secret."

I felt the world darken around the edges and blur. I was passing out.

The urgency of the moment took away the fear. I was desperate. Either I was going to get out of this, or I was going to die. There were no other options.

Propping a foot against the sink, I grabbed hold of the hand by the wrist and used my leverage to pull myself away. As I fell, I yanked my copy through the mirror. What surfaced from the other side was not my doppelganger, but a man with long blond hair, a beard, and a heavy brow that shaded his angry eyes.

He looked as mean as his grip suggested, and vaguely familiar.

He dropped me like a rotten pest and maneuvered to free himself of the mirror, stepping through the reflective façade—with one foot planted into the clogged sink—like surfacing through a pool of quicksilver. Then, hopping off the sink and onto the floor, he straddled me from my back as I gasped for air.

"Confess your secrets or be damned," he demanded, as the hair on my arms went rigid, like a static charge was filling the room.

"Damn dude, it's not even midnight," whined another hipster who came stumbling into the restroom. I was on the floor, gasping and sweating—but I was also alone. There was no sign of the blonde-haired man. "Seriously, bro, if you're gonna trip, do it from your own home."

"You look like you saw the mound of poo," said Marshall with a big grin.

"What?" I asked, as I steadied myself on the barstool next to his, massaging my throat. My head was still spinning from the lack of oxygen.

"That fucking enormous mound of shit in stall three," he said, laughing, "which I assure you, I had nothing to do with. But I'm impressed all the same."

I passed off my near-death experience as a medicated hallucination—the white-label warning not to mix alcohol with my prescribed dosage of dopamine inhibitors—or was it Northcreek all over again? My throat was fine moments later, as if I had imagined it all. Besides, there was nothing a shot of alcohol couldn't fix.

After all, nothing I experienced inside that restroom made any sense—and it wasn't the first time I'd experienced things that weren't real.

When the bar got lame, Marshall insisted we hop to the next. After two more hops, he decided we'd finally found the right bar, with the optimum lady-to-guy ratio, good music, and a drink special that made his wallet happy. He was trying too hard to make the night memorable, but nothing had the same magic as back then. We'd been young, with friends and two pretty ladies who adored us. I was happy to hear that Anne was back in the picture, but the woman who adored me was gone. It was a hard reality to ignore.

"Have you heard from the guys?" I asked.

"Heard from Brad a few months ago. He's still short," joked Marshall. "And an asshole for abandoning you. I tell him all the time."

"It's okay."

"I haven't heard from Sid. I know he moved down here almost ten years ago. Said he had important business."

"He was always a little mysterious," I said.

"A little? Loved the guy, but he definitely kept secrets—hey, hold on a sec," he said, hopping off the barstool. "Tonight is to moving forward!" His voice boomed as he held his beer up for a toast. "Whatever forward may be."

"Whatever forward may be," I repeated, and took my last sip for the night.

Marshall reached over and snagged our waitress with a sharp finger snap. "Hey, bring my man here a RedBull and another beer. He's deader than my grandma. She died in '85, so that's pretty dag-gone dead."

December 21, 2013
Midnight.

By midnight, things took a bad turn. A girl with red hair walked in and set up three stools down. I got hot and clammy, and Marshall immediately ushered us out and on to the next location before I had a complete meltdown.

"What's the deal with you and redheads?" he asked.

I didn't respond. I had a deal with one redhead—*singular*.

"Hey," said Marshall, slurring enough to show he wasn't sober. "Do you remember that time we scraped the cream out of Brad and Sid's Oreos and replaced it with Crisco?"

"And the second time we replaced it with minty toothpaste?" I replied.

Marshall immediately turned and puked all over the sidewalk.

We were walking from South Street toward Society Hill when that random memory nugget wandered into Marshall's mind. Even I chuckled at the thought. Payback was a bitch, but we didn't stop laughing—not even after Brad revealed he took a piss in the orange juice.

There were others walking along 4th Street, some just going out to the bars, but it was time for us to call it a night. Marsh could drink like a fish but could never hold his liquor, and I was in no mood for a mid-thirties hangover come morning.

"Maybe it's time I took you home," I said, but Marshall glared like I'd spat in his face.

"Are you joking?" he growled. "The night's just begun!"

"Yeah, for college kids and professional DJs named Scribbles," I joked, when I caught the smell of something—*different?* It was unlike normal smells, like warming metal, ozone, rotting fruit and marigolds, and provoked caution. My gag reflex wanted to trigger, but the goosebumps flaring and prickling across every inch of skin suppressed the retching.

I froze, like I was in the throes of another stupid, ill-timed panic attack.

"What's wrong?" asked Marshall.

"I don't know." I groaned when I spotted someone staring at us from across the street, standing beside an old tree and a wrought-iron fence. The long blonde hair. The beard. The caveman brow.

It was the man from the mirror.

"You see him, right?" I asked, pointing.

"The douchebag watching us?" said Marshall, full of liquid courage. "Sure do."

But there was something else—something warning me to run. Something that cursed and swore and screamed at me until my brain finally heard my livid subconscious.

The restroom mirror wasn't the only time I'd seen that man. The blonde hair and the long black coat was from a reverie—some hidden memory from somewhere else—and recognition struck as chills flew up and down my spine. It was the man from my dream. The man who flew through the sky, tore me from my plane and ripped out my—I mean, the French pilot's, heart.

And he was *still* staring at me.

"I think we need to go," I said.

"What?" shouted Marshall. "First time we hang out in years, and you're cutting early? This is an all-nighter, partner."

"I can't," I said, my stomach souring.

"Well, I'm not going home!" shouted Marshall.

"Then stay," I said, as the goosebumps sharpened. Something was wrong. My body was going berserk and I needed to leave. I backed away from Marshall, who eyed me suspiciously—and I understood I was acting weird. How could I explain it? Something effed up was happening, and if I stayed, I knew I'd end up in a padded cell by morning.

"Come on, Tone," he complained. "I'm sorry. Did I say something stupid? I'm drunk. I probably said something super-duper-stupid."

The man stepped off the curb, his long gait aimed at me. His expression never changed. His eyes trained on me, like he had a serious issue with my existence. I had seen that look before. It ended with blood, broken bones, and stitches.

"No, you didn't, but I gotta go," I said, my eyes dashing toward the oncoming stranger. "I'll call you." Then I took off.

"Damnit, Tony!" he yelled, followed by indecipherable curses.

I felt bad, but there was something about that creepy man that set off every internal warning system my body had at its disposal, including a few I never knew I had. At the first intersection, I made a right onto Lombard Street and managed to sneak a peek behind me. He was following, but from a safe distance. It was a busy street, so I decided to take the most public route home.

I don't know why I felt like going home would make me safe. I had scuffled with bigger, brawnier assholes than that guy. That dream? The restroom mirror? Those weren't real, were they? Just figments of my fucking psycho imagination, right?

As I debated the improbable—the man, the mirror, and my dream—something completely impossible happened. It was as if someone plucked a nightmare straight out of my head and into reality.

As a group of people exited a restaurant, crossing my path and forcing me to swim through them as my stalker closed in, a woman with red hair stepped out ahead of me. She glanced back playfully, her movements attracting my attention like they were stolen from a memory.

"Help me," she whispered, flashing her emerald eyes. Her face was hidden beneath shadow and crimson locks.

She strolled ahead as I pushed through the crowd and eventually turned into an alley—looking back and smiling as she went.

"Help me, Tony," she said—sweet, desperate, entrancing whispers.

Was it the alcohol? Was I hallucinating? Again? Was it real?

When I approached the alley, I stood in its dark mouth and stared into the black abyss. My mind had foolishly abandoned the threat to investigate this new mystery, like I was no longer in control. I couldn't see anything beyond the darkness, but I could smell her perfume—strawberry and lavender—enchanting me, as a shock of memories flooded through my mental walls and swept me away.

A lamp flickered on several yards into the gloom, and she stood beneath it, shrouded by crimson hair. I knew it wasn't real. I knew it couldn't be real, but my heart wanted it more than my mind knew to turn away. I moved into the alley with slow methodical steps, like the ground might give way beneath my feet—like this was all some trick or trap. When I stepped into the spotlight, just three short paces away from her, the light blinked out, and I was stranded in a sea of darkness.

There was laughter—a woman's high-pitched cackle—and I awoke from my trance with a startle. "My boy, never believe anything you see in the witching hour," she said. A cold grimy hand snatched my wrist in the dark, and then I felt a burning sensation that seared into every limb. "Master, he is yours."

"Let go of me!" I growled and tugged at her grip, pulling and scratching at her bony old hand, but I was lost in the dark and shackled to some woman whose scent and sound made my skin crawl.

"You've been marked, boy," she said as the burning cooled. "Run if you must. They will find you," she sang, then let go.

The man was standing in the mouth of the alley, watching us. His eyes visibly smoldered through the darkness, like a hellhound tracking its prey.

I heard the caw of crows and the flapping of feathered wings, then suddenly the alley lights snapped on and the woman—the redheaded imposter—the witch—was gone.

I ran.

I ran from the man deeper into the alley. The stench was easy to ignore when the fear of death, or worse, was driving you. I jumped over broken pallets and climbed over piles of garbage, then ducked around a bend and hid behind a dumpster. When I looked back, there was no sign of him. There was no sign of anyone.

I felt hot. The alcohol haze burned out of my blood. I panted for air while my pulse pounded in my own ears, deafening the call from above.

The crows. They were cawing again and circling overhead, eliciting an old memory or two, like déjà vu. I leaned from my hiding place to get a clearer view when the man stepped out of the shadow and into the moonlight. He charged at me, his teeth clenched like a snarling animal, and launched into the air like a rocket.

Instincts are strange. Ever have a really large dog charge at you with a ball in its mouth? All it wanted was to play—for you to throw that ball—but your knees buckled with the urge to flee—like it triggered some dormant code in your brain. Somewhere in your DNA were hard-coded instructions that large beasts charging toward you were a cause for danger, and your brain engaged the fight or flight response.

When that man launched himself into the air, my instincts took over. I leapt and rolled away—an acrobatic feat I had never once attempted prior to that moment—and watched the man soar overhead. What happened next defied logic. It defied the laws of physics, gravity, and all that I knew was real. The man landed on the wall next to the dumpster. The force of his landing cracked the mortar and brick, shaking dust free from the very top of the building. Then he stood up from the wall, perpendicular to me—he was some kind of Spider-Man or reality nightmare. He then looked up at me and smiled like a viper, sharp teeth and fury hidden behind a veneer of calm deviousness. He didn't fall. He didn't even appear to struggle at the trick.

It was, without a doubt, the scariest thing I had ever seen. I was overloaded with fear. The kind of fear that pins a person down and cripples them, like a deer that can't move away from headlights.

"I know a secret. I know what you are," said the man. His voice was as deep and sharp as a canyon—ferocious and distinct.

"What do you want?" I asked.

"Paradise," he seethed.

A flame then ignited in the corner alley from where we came. Then another. Both danced on the air parallel to one another, growing larger and hotter every moment. Their light slowly revealed a silhouette—another man—and he was walking toward us—strobing like a flickering VHS tape—like the world had gone "funny"—like something wrong had just happened—with both of his fucking hands on fire.

innocence lost

TONY

"I warned you, doc, this isn't a love story."
"Why did Amanda hate Jacinda?" he asked.
I took a deep breath and smiled.

September 1997
Then.

The entire ride home to our small New Jersey town from Grace Falls was done in near silence. Amanda and I had fought before—this fight was far from the worst of them—but she was struggling to articulate her frustration. I wasn't in the mood to discuss something that bothered her when I hadn't done anything wrong, and I didn't feel the need to apologize.

We didn't speak again until the first day of school three days later. Our paths crossed at 7:45 AM that Wednesday morning, in front of the high school we both shared complete and total disdain for. I behaved like nothing had happened, and she did the same. I wasn't interested in finding out why she was upset, and I decided it wasn't worth being angry at her when everything seemed fine.

"Why did you dislike high school, Tony?" asked Doc.

"Didn't you?" I replied. "I don't understand people who had great experiences in high school."

"Why?" he asked with his head cocked to the side, as if I was being set up for the 'gotcha' moment.

"Because," I said, then paused as I gathered my words. "It was artificial. It was superficial. It was prejudicial." Then I smirked at my rhyme. "People were separated into groups and subcategories and told that's where they were, and that's where they'd always be. I was sorted before I was even old enough to know what was happening. Before I was old enough to know who I was."

Growing up without a mother made me an easy target. Every "your mom" joke took on new meaning when flung in my direction, and kids can be cruel. School was difficult for me. My dad and I were lower middle class, a single-parent family. Not too low on the totem-pole to be desperate, but not high enough to be comfortable. It's not something I'm ashamed of, but I felt like it stunted my identity. While all the other kids were learning what they liked, and what represented them, I was wearing hand-me-downs and off-brands.

Things like that weren't important to me at the time—they still aren't—but it made me an outlier with my peers. It made me a cast-off.

I didn't know who I was, and I wouldn't for some time, which made me the perfect target.

Our town had a problem with bullying—when good-ole-boys have boys, they teach them how to be like them. The apples fell right to the foot of the tree and sprouted their own roots. My earliest memory of being bullied came in the second grade, when Billy Woodward pushed me into a puddle during recess.

I never fought back when I was a kid. I let these things happen. Looking back, I realize I was to blame for not sticking up for myself, but would it have changed anything? Would it have made things worse? Life's not a movie. When you stand up to the bullies in the real world, you don't hash out your differences then magically become best friends. They don't back off realizing the error of their ways because you suddenly hit back. When a bully gets a taste of their own medicine, they only learn to come down harder.

A week after Billy Woodward pushed me into that puddle, I tripped him face-first into some mud on the playground. We were playing soccer during gym class and I missed the ball. I wasn't intentionally going for his ankle as much as I wasn't intentionally going for the ball either. From that day on, every opportunity he had to make my life hell, he took.

I had dealt with Billy Woodward for years when Amanda moved to town.

"How'd you two meet?" asked Doc.

"We were in the same art class," I said. "But how we became friends? That's a good story." I had a grin on my face just thinking about it.

Our eighth grade school trip to Washington D.C. was early in the school year—October, a few weeks before Halloween. We boarded a pair of cruise-liner buses and cruised down interstate 95 for the two-hour drive to the nation's capital. I was separated from my friends who had boarded the other bus and was drifting in and out of sleep. Watching the scenery fly by my window, I felt something oozing in my hair, then heard laughter. Billy had maneuvered behind my seat and spat onto my head.

Amanda was there. She saw the whole thing and told the chaperones, who made Billy ride up front with them. From that moment on, Amanda joined the ranks of Billy's victims.

Billy was a popular kid. He came from a rich family, and for whatever reason, the other kids thought he was funny. The only difference between him and me that made any sense was income—he was a C student who had anger issues and bad teeth. I was an A/B student who wore hand-me-downs, plus I was an artist and an athlete. Tell me, why was I the bullied and he the bully?

I spent a lot of time hating myself because of that kid…

We had already toured the theater where Lincoln was shot, and one of the Smithsonians—the air and space museum—when we stopped for lunch. There was a cafeteria in the lower level of the museum, populated by business professionals and staff who saw an infestation of rowdy kids as a daily annoyance. I grabbed my lunch and sat down at a table on the far side of the food court—I wanted to eat and be out of there as quickly as possible. I was separated from my friends and surrounded by strangers—I felt exposed, vulnerable, and I wanted to go home.

I was eating by myself, head down, when Amanda sat next to me. She took a bite of her dry hamburger and said, "Needs ketchup. I don't like ketchup. It tastes like fake tomato and processed sugar, but this meat disc is as hard as a hockey puck…" She removed the meat from the bun, then banged it a few times against her food tray as if she was performing a vital experiment. "…or a murder weapon."

I pushed the red ketchup squeeze bottle toward her, and she smiled.

"Thanks, Oscuro," she said, then wrinkled up her face. "Whoa, that won't do. Oscuro does not roll off the tongue."

"Sorry," I said, as if I needed to apologize.

"What's your middle name?" she asked.

"Ambrogino," I replied, which made her jaw drop open like a drawbridge.

"This really won't do," she groaned. "I can't call you by your first name. I just won't."

"You don't have to call me anything," I said. Years of bullying had left me socially defeated, especially around women. I had not a single friend who was a girl, and I was prepared for the punchline—for Amanda to lead me into a false sense of security, then rip my still-beating heart out, like something from *Temple of Doom*.

"If we're going to be friends, I'm pretty sure I need to call you something," she said.

"I'd be lying if I said I didn't have a crush on her. She was the first girl who had ever shown me any kind of attention. She was pretty, blonde, and had an overflow of personality. She made me feel special—and I hadn't felt special since I was a little kid..."

The doc looked at me, expectantly. But I shrugged it off and kept going.

While Amanda was trying to figure out what she was going to call me, exhausting herself with different options that ranged from "Antonio" to "Double A," there was trouble brewing right behind us. Like a heat-seeking missile, it would have found us anywhere we went.

"Hey guys, I found the loser table," said Billy, echoed by a handful of laughs. I didn't need to turn around to know he was flanked by his girlfriend, Lisa, and the Trevors—two guys with the same name who had been best friends since they were in kindergarten. There were others, but I didn't know them, and I didn't feel like looking up to notice.

Amanda courageously turned to them and said, "Good, I guess you know where you'll be sitting."

"The mouth on you," said Trevor #1.

"C'mon," groaned Lisa. "Let's eat. I want to see the history museum."

"You're such a drag, Lisa," whined Billy.

"Such a drag," said Trevor #2, while Trevor #1 laughed.

"Yeah, go eat, asshole," said Amanda under her breath.

"What was that?" demanded Billy. He was still carrying his food tray but came walking up to our table like he was about to dump it on our heads. Neither of us moved, but when he took a ketchup-soaked fry from his tray and tossed it into Amanda's hair, I sprang from my seat like a jack-in-the-box. I don't know why I did it. I had stopped caring about being bullied, but there was something about seeing her being bullied that made me angry.

"Oh, look it!" laughed Billy, and the Trevors and crew started chuckling. "Look who's defending his new girlfriend?"

"Leave her alone," I said, unfirmly. I wasn't scared, but I was wrangling in too many emotions and sounded like a chicken—literally. My voice was cracking like a chicken cluck.

"Or what?" said Billy. Then he smiled evilly and said, "Are you gonna tell your mommy on me? Oh! That's right, you don't have a mommy, do you?"

"Shut up," said Amanda. She was standing just behind me, and I felt her guide my hand behind my back. She pressed something plastic into my palm, then whispered, "When I say go, squeeze."

Billy raised his tray like he was about to dump it, and said, "Hey you two, you have something on your shirt."

"Go," said Amanda.

Each table in the cafeteria was supplied with two large condiment squeeze bottles—one red ketchup bottle and one yellow mustard bottle. When Amanda said "go," we each came up spraying, with my watery yellow mustard splatters and her red stream of ketchupy goo. Billy caught big wads of each in both eyes, his shirt stained in crisscrossing patterns, and the Trevors were doused. Even Lisa got hit in the crossfire. But the best part? There was so much ketchup and mustard on the floor that Billy slipped and fell, then slopped his whole tray on top of himself—open chocolate milk carton and all.

Amanda and I stood there, watching the chaos. From the look on her face, she'd never expected it to work half as well as it had.

"Don't cross the streams," I said quietly, quoting one of my favorite movies.

Amanda smiled and replied, "Try to imagine all life as we know it stopping instantaneously and every molecule in your body exploding at the speed of light."

We smiled at each other, both of us in that moment realizing we were Ghostbusters fans.

"I'm going to kill you shitheads," said Billy as he slipped attempting to climb onto his knees.

"Gotta catch us first," said Amanda as she grabbed me by the shirt and ran, dragging me along for the first few strides. We ran up the stairs and into the museum, with Billy screaming at the top of his lungs, and hid in a space-pod exhibit so nobody could find us. We ducked beneath the front seats and the dash.

"I can't believe you did that," I said, after the danger had passed.

"Me?" she questioned. "We did that. You and I together, T." Then she smiled brightly, like the lightbulb had finally flicked on. "T, that's your nickname. Simple. Elegant. I like it."

The rest was history.

Amanda and I needed each other to survive. She was the only person I told my deepest darkest thoughts to, and I provided her the same service. I had other friends, but she was my closest, my rock. We had the kind of bond that transcended everything, including fights.

That's why I ignored what happened in Grace Falls. Neither of us spoke of it. We ignored what happened and moved on, letting it fester under the surface.

Looking back, maybe I was obsessed. I spoke of Jacinda every chance I had, asking Amanda for more information, and wondering aloud if Jacinda and I liked the same things—as if she were an absent third in our conversations.

"She said, 'Grace Falls has more ghosts than people.' What do you think she meant by that?" I asked Amanda while she was trying to enjoy a soggy PB&J from her brown bag lunch. You would have thought I rubbed her nose in dog shit.

"Of course O'Neill would say that," she grumbled.

"What do you mean?" I asked.

"Damnit, T! Can we just stop talking about O'Neill?" she growled, raising her voice and calling the attention of half the cafeteria.

I wish I could report that I stopped straightaway and never brought it up again, but that's a lie. That night with Jacinda was the closest I had ever gotten to a girl, and I didn't know how to handle it any other way other than to share the experience with my best friend.

I was there for every Amanda heartbreak. I was there every time she took a chance on a guy, and I was the one who helped pick up the pieces when he inevitably ruined it by being a jerk. We'd binge horror movies and spend the entire day swapping from DVD to VHS, from Carpenter to King adaptations, from B Movie Slashers to Alien Terrors, and everything in between. We'd recite dialogue, eat pizza and ice cream, and laugh until she didn't feel the need to cry.

"So, understand, when I say I was confused about Amanda's frustrations over Jacinda, I wasn't being naïve," I said, and the doc jotted something down onto his legal pad.
"What happened next?" he asked.

October 31, 1997

It wasn't until Halloween that things finally overflowed. Amanda never had eyes for me, but she was secretly in love with Paul Lucas. Paul was a semi-silent weirdo with borderline sociopathic tendencies—drawing, painting, sculpting death and murder in every class. Yet if you conversed with Paul, he was almost a regular dude, despite being dressed head-to-toe in off-the-rack Hot Topic fashion and a dog collar. Paul had a way of luring Amanda in, then breaking her heart in a vicious cycle that repeated itself every year since she'd moved from Grace Falls. Why she kept running back to him was beyond my comprehension. Even when I attempted to understand, she skirted my probing questions like she was a politician pivoting to unrelated talking points.

On Halloween night, Amanda and I dressed up and went to John Monk's annual party. Thad Spector and Chris Withers were there, along with thirty others who showed up to enjoy that year's spectacle.

Thad was a tall guy, with shoulder-length blonde hair and a goatee. He knew more about books, movies, and the internet than anyone else I associated with.

Chris was tall, with well-combed brown hair and glasses—a nerd of the highest caliber—a former Boy Scout with a super-IQ.

And John? He was a heavy-set guy in all the AP classes, with a baby face and a filthy mouth—but he was a heck of a lot of fun.

John always managed to entertain by cleverly scaring his guests with something unique and twisted to be discovered at some point in the night. Each year was different. Last year's exploding cake was a big hit with everyone but his parents—he'd actually put firecrackers in the cake. It was that kind of commitment to his craft that made John brilliant.

The party started at 7PM, and by 7:30 we were already enjoying a conversation around the finer points of *Star Trek* plot lines and *Crimson Justice* comics when Paul Lucas showed up.

I was dressed as Roddy Piper from They Live, while Thad and Chris both arrived as Tom Baker's Doctor from Who—a fun coincidence that was met with laughter, high-fives, and plenty of spoofing hijinks. John was wilting within his Fox Mulder FBI-grade suit and tie, while his sister Meghann joined us dressed as Carmen Sandiego.

Amanda, however, stunned us all when she arrived in a silver mini-dress with knee-high white boots, her blonde hair in pigtails. She claimed she was dressed as Baby Spice, and I immediately felt suspicious. It was unlike her to do something so…mainstream? Risqué?

Amanda wasn't the kind of girl who slipped into something provocative for Halloween. She liked gore and crazy wigs and monsters—not that she couldn't clean up. She often wore dresses and makeup to school, but nothing like this.

I was so busy trying to figure out what she was up to that we hardly spoke. She could tell I was suspicious and drifted from me, presumably not wanting to be analyzed by her best friend.

When she left our group to accompany Paul to the kitchen, my suspicions were reinforced. Amanda was pulling out all the stops to capture Paul's attention.

He was dressed as The Crow for the third straight year—a topic that was not overlooked.

"That costume could use a washing," said Thad. "Or at least a couple squirts of Febreze sometime in the last three-hundred-sixty-four days."

"Yeah, smells a tad ripe," added Chris after catching a whiff.

"Holy hell," added Meghann. "Smells like pit stains and desperation."

"Something is seriously wrong with Manda's nose," I said, then focused on John. "Why'd you even invite that guy?"

"Ambiance," said John as he popped the cap on a fresh beer. "He really spooks up the joint."

Amanda spent the next hour talking to Paul as he chugged green punch and devoured a couple chocolate cupcakes with gummy-worms slithering out of them.

"How'd that make you feel?" asked Doc.
"Jealous," I responded. "I won't deny it."

We managed just fine without Amanda, but the party felt wrong without her. Eventually she followed Paul into the room, where they shared a seat on an ottoman and listened in.

"Sublime is way better than Nirvana," argued some guy dressed as James Bond.

"Shut your dirty mouth," shouted Thad, and we all laughed.

"He also likes Smash Mouth," I said. "I think that invalidates anything he says."

"The worst!" shouted Chris, laughing and shaking his head.

"Christ, who invited that guy?" Meghann scolded after finishing her second beer.

"I did," said John, "and now I'm revoking it. Get out!"

While we were laughing, Paul stood up and threw a mask over his head, grabbed Amanda by the hair, and put a knife to her throat.

A whole friendship—four years of loyalty, laughter, and tears, came down to that one moment.

There was a second when the only things in the room that moved were heads and eyes. It took everyone varying degrees of time to recognize the situation and assess the threat.

Seeing Amanda threatened like that, I reacted instantly. Without another thought, I sprang from my seat on the sofa, took two full steps, and slugged Paul in the jaw before he could hurt her.

Paul dropped like a sack of laundry as the knife bounced off the ground twice and jiggled at Chris's feet.

"Fuck, dude!" yelled John.

"Hey, it's rubber," said Chris absentmindedly, pointing at the knife.

"What are you doing?" screamed Amanda, pushing me aside to check on Paul.

"What's going on?" I asked as the room gridlocked with confusion.

"It was a gag, bro," said John. "Oh man, is he okay?" John lumbered his big frame over to Paul, who was still wearing his creepy mask, and nudged his shoulder as Paul began to stir.

"What gag?" I asked.

"That was the gag," said John. "This year's scare."

I'd never seen Amanda so furious. She could hardly look at me without her eyes tearing up like she wanted to strangle me. I heard someone say, "What an asshole." Chris and Thad read the room and quickly escorted me into the kitchen and away from the angry crowd.

"You saw your friend in need and you reacted. I think most people would recognize that as a good quality, despite the obvious mix-up," said Doc.

"Yeah, you'd think," I said. "I felt awful. I didn't like the guy, but I didn't mean him any ill will. When he came to, I was told he was ready to grab a real knife and come after me."

"What happened with Amanda?"

I was sitting outside on the curb with Thad and Chris watching trick-or-treaters who dared to be out past curfew when Amanda finally exited the house. She paced back and forth from the porch before she came down to the curb and asked for Thad and Chris to give us room to talk. She sat down next to me, her pigtails flapping around as she tried to summon the right words.

"Sorry, I didn't know," I blurted out, deciding to cut her off at the pass.

"You seem to be suffering from ignorance a lot lately," she said.

"What's that supposed to mean?"

"You're my best friend, T, and yet you've been on and on about O'Neill for two whole months now."

"What does that have to do with this?" I asked. I knew I may have overstepped asking Amanda questions about her former friend—but why would that matter?

"O'Neill and I go way back," she said, "and there was a time when she was my best friend. We were neighbors—me, Morris, and O'Neill.

Morris never liked her much, but we all played together, because of me. When we were in the seventh grade, O'Neill became trouble."

"What do you mean, trouble?" I asked. It was such an ominous word, trouble.

"She—," Amanda began, then paused, as if she thought better of what she was going to say. "She'll break your heart, T. Besides, you'll never see her again."

"Why won't I see her again?"

"Why are you so obsessed with her?"

"I'm not obsessed," I explained. The whole conversation was quickly circling the drain. "I finally met someone who gets me."

"Sometimes, you can be such an oblivious asshole," she said with tears.

"Damnit, Amanda, what the hell is going on?"

I wanted her to tell me what was on her mind, to explain everything in easy, digestible pieces. What I learned was that people don't communicate that way, at least not in the moments you need that kind of clarity. Emotions were sometimes more complicated for some people to sort through than they were for others. Amanda wanted me to reach her conclusion on my own, but I was incapable of that. I didn't even know what the problem was, let alone how to read her mind.

"Maybe we should stop hanging out so much," she said.

"What?" I asked, a choking sensation gripping my throat. "Why? So you can spend time with stinky Paul?"

"Are you jealous?" she spat.

"What? No!"

Then she smiled. It was the kind of smile that ends conversations. It was the kind of smile one gives when they've decided to let go.

"See ya around, T."

"And that was it?" asked Doc.

"For the most part, yes. We saw each other in art class. We even hung out a few times with Thad and Chris and the others, but never just the two of us."

"No further explanation?"

"Not at the time, no. I tried once or twice, but gave up when she started dating Paul."

"How did this experience make you feel?"

"Helpless. Confused. Irredeemable."

"Irredeemable? Why?"

"I had great friends like Thad, Chris, and John, but there was only one Amanda in my life. She provided something I never had."

"Which was?"

"Female companionship. When I lost her, I felt like I'd never be good enough, for anyone. Not Amanda, and definitely not Jacinda, the girl who never showed up."

The doc then jotted down several notes.

VI
malus

MALUS
December 1st, 1996
Then.

I heard them bickering back and forth in voices inaudible to the human ear. They fought for information. They whispered, exchanged scandalous clues, and dug through their ancient memories for scraps. What they searched for had either withered through the sands of time or became lost in the bowels of their own memories.

Information was bound to be forgotten when you lived forever.

They asked for my name, but they knew me only as Malus.

I gave myself that name. Perhaps pretentious, but when choosing a name, perception was most important. What was I if not malicious?

I was leader of the feared, The Thirteen, a king of the damned, conqueror of Hades, destroyer of Chernobog, and master of Chronos. I won the Helm of Darkness and tricked the Stygian Three. I walked the river Styx from shore to shore and ascended Mount Sinai. I executed the greatest king, assassinated the mightiest god, and mastered the dark arts.

Who was I by any other name?

A name was precious.

Beyond meaning and definition, to know one's true name was to have power over them. Our true names were ours alone to know and own, and they had to be protected at all costs.

Some of us took many names, burying their truths through the ages. Some of us walked this planet while it was still molten ash. Their ancient names were now gone, lost to this world.

Still, just because a name was lost does not mean it could not be found. Quite the contrary...

I was content to be Malus. I wielded power that made my rivals wither like dried weeds in drought. I was a ghost, a beast amongst beasts. I was the greatest of Thirteen. The Pale Wanderer. The Pale Demon.

Soon, when all my plotting came to fruition, I would be more than that.

Soon, I would be anything I desired.

Every step I took was measured and planned toward my ultimate goal. There was no rest for the wicked.

Frigg, goddess of foresight and knowledge, a Seer, was kept within a small windowless cell. She was shackled, restrained, and filthy. She was dead—her heart torn from her chest—but when I bound her to my ring, she was mine. Undead and unable to answer to anyone else.

Loki secretly questioned her, but my true name was still a mystery. His words could not elicit a single answer from Frigg. Only my questions could bring answers from her lips. Such was the power of my ring.

She lingered within her cell, passing in and out of a dreamless sleep, until the day she was no longer useful to me. And on that day, she knew I would release her to the Unbecoming, where her husband, Odin, awaited.

For many years Frigg endlessly suffered alone. Until today.

"Have you succeeded? Have you found the girl?" she asked. Her voice was hoarse. She spoke through the ragged throat I'd torn out to silence her.

"I have."

"Ask your question," she rasped.

I thought for a moment, gathering my tangent thoughts into one cohesive question, to receive the most accurate answer. "I found the girl. I now seek entry into the holy land that was lost and locked away—Eden—so that I may remove her burden. How may I gain what I seek?"

Spontaneously, words began to fill her mouth.

"To gain what you seek, you must start on the first day of a single calendar year in which the previous contained no less than two solar eclipses, two lunar eclipses, and with the rare transit of Venus across the sun. You must wait until the vernal equinox to retrieve the first key of Eden, the Key of Capricorn. Next you must endure until the summer solstice for the second key of Eden, the Key of Libra. Then you must idle until the autumnal equinox for the third key of Eden, the Key of Cancer. Alas, you must languish until the winter solstice for the fourth and final key of Eden, the Key of Aries. To possess the keys, you must have patience, passing through the Zodiac as the stars cycle the heavens. Then, and only then, after the full year has passed, on its dying day before rebirth, the four keys must be taken to their hidden gates at the four corners of the Earth. Eden will be revealed to the world of man when all four locks are freed, where the roots of the world grow deep."

"The World Tree," I said. "How may I find the keys?"

"You may find what you seek between the lines along the celestial sphere, marking both the northern and southern limits where the sun cannot advance beyond. Seek the Key of Capricorn along the path the sun travels upon the vernal equinox, to the floating continent where the sun rises first. The first key will lead you to the second. The second to the third. The third to the fourth. Each key was provided a guardian who will die to protect it. A Fallen given new duty by the Host." She exhaled and slumped against the wall of her cell. "I have given you answers. Please let me pass," she begged.

"Does anyone oppose me?" I asked.

"Yes, Pale Wanderer. There are many who oppose you." I was given the name Pale Wanderer because of my platinum white hair. But that, although memorable, wasn't the same as my genetic gift—though some called it a deformity. My left eye gray, and my right brown—heterochromia iridium. Some said I walk in two worlds, and maybe they were right—just not in the way they intended.

"Please, let me pass…" Frigg continued.

"Those who oppose me, should I fear them? Are there any legitimate threats against my plans?"

She thought for a moment, then said, "There is not one alone who may oppose you with a legitimate threat." Then she begged once again. "Please, let me pass…"

"You have performed adequately," I said.

"If I have served you well, then please, let me go to rest amongst my brethren."

"You know where you'll go once I release you. Why do you hurry toward that fate?"

"It is better to cease than to live in captivity."

"That it is," I said and left Frigg to rot alive.

December 21, 2013.
Ecuador, South America
Now.

The air was heavy and humid. Even breathing felt like a chore. The jungle was thick, and the sun beat down on the trees above, leaving scattered rays of light dotting the ground around me. I heard the snakes hiss, welcoming their brother, and the furrier creatures scattered. If there was one modern invention I appreciated more than another, it was the creation of sunglasses. I hated the light. I slipped a pair over my eyes and marched directly west with the sun at my back. It was morning, a groggy hot morning that was only getting hotter.

Tourists flocked to the ancient temples of South America, snapping photographs and running up the great staircases and laughing, oblivious to the truth of those ancient civilizations. If only they knew what horrors lingered in the ground beneath their feet.

The temple I sought was not on any map, nor was it crawling with tourists. It was hidden from the world, deep within the Ecuadorian jungles along the equator. It was said that the last of the giants lived there—their last refuge, far from humankind.

I saw them once, upon the battlefield a long, long time ago.

I stood on an incline facing a mound of dirt as a tropical rain began to fall. There were no obvious signs of a hidden structure, but the ghosts there told a different story.

Loud thuds slammed against the mound of earth before me. Each thud grew louder until the dirt gave way and collapsed. Just beyond the dusty entrance were two skeletal guards, ready and willing to do my bidding. I commanded them to take their spears and follow me into the darkness.

The tunnels wound deep into the earth toward the temple. There were skeletal remains that did not belong—some were thieves who ventured too deep and others merely victims dragged to their deaths. None could recount what attacked and killed them, only that they died in the throes of the greatest fear they had ever known. Something lived down there in the dark, below the temple, and it was not natural.

I removed my sunglasses as I entered rooms that had not seen a single particle of light in centuries. The stale ancient air was cold and smelled of wet soil and rot. Roots from the vegetation above had broken through the ceiling and walls, and at times they created narrow passes, wide enough for only one.

We crossed another corridor and into an open room with a giant calendar carved into the walls. It had remained untouched by the world of man, hidden away from their prying eyes. It was taller than the ancient lizard beasts and as wide as a farmer's field. At its center was a large concentric circle, with a smiling deity surrounded by energy and light.

The calendar was a piece of art as much as it was an astrological marvel. It was perfect and precise, marking every day from the beginning to the end, and far beyond. Certain entries were marked, perhaps signifying important events, and I was amazed to find four dates marked in blood. Four dates that coincided with the solstices and equinoxes of this year, 2013. Nothing in this world was coincidence. Everything was connected, one event to the other, the Fates weaving upon their mighty loom.

The keys pulsed violently, urging me into the blackest pitch at the far end of the room. A wall of stone barred my path, and with a touch I could sense it was as thick as I was tall. I ran my hand along its face and found it surprisingly smooth and without a single fault or crack. It was much too dense to penetrate with the dead, and my anger flared with frustration. I had come too far to turn back. I had only one day to retrieve the final key or wait for the next cycle—when two solar and lunar eclipses occurred in the same year that Venus made its transit across the sun.

"Give up," she said, but she could never understand what I had sacrificed to be there. The centuries. The plotting. The loss.

The three keys around my neck were trophies. I needed only one more.

Anger was a great motivator, and as I ran my hand across every inch of the wall's surface, I found a single slit in the rock as thin as paper. It was there for a reason.

It made sense that the key's master would have assurances built to protect it. The Great Maker did not intend for the keys to be taken by the Fallen. Most Fallen did not have the ability to conjure the kind of power that I could.

I summoned the flames inside, let them burn angry and hot, until I had what I needed just beneath my skin. I channeled fire, pushing it into my arm, down my wrist and into my hand, letting it flare into a hilt and swarm into a flaming blade. A burning sword, just like the one Michael used to banish The Morning Star, a power only afforded to the most powerful of Angels. The flames hissed and cracked, burning bright enough to banish shadows inside the dark hall.

I thrust the sword into the narrow slit and let the hellfires burn. A perfect crack appeared, glowing and traveling at equal speed from the fault to the floor and ceiling. The rock split into two equal pieces. Halves split into perfect halves, carving a single square stone block—my entrance into the adjoined room.

The chamber beyond was a marvel of ancient architecture and artisan design. There were jewels embedded into statues, reliefs carved of gold—enough riches to make the greedy weep. Pictographs recounted the histories of the people who called this temple home.

They were giants. Great extinct beasts lost to time.

Pairs of stone pillars broke the room into three equal parts, each of them carved with ghastly faces from floor to ceiling. This was a place of terror. There were no ghosts here, for anything that died within this room was consumed by the creature that called it home. The creature was not malevolent. It was a protector, a guardian given eternal duty.

I strode down the very center of the room, unafraid, with my skeletal guards on either flank. My sword's fire began to lift the shroud at the end of the chamber. There, at the edge of the room, it slept where the shadows were at their thickest. It was made of black stone and perfectly posed, like a statue. It had the head of a hippopotamus, with two large, sharp horns protruding from its snout. Its mouth was agape with a single, stark white tooth jutting from its lower jaw. Its body was massive, like that of an ape, with large, clawed hands and thick hooved feet. It was like a toxodon, but three, if not four times the size.

The Mayan people called him Votan. His name was scrawled from floor to ceiling, equally in praise and warning. The black, toothless god, they called him. A Devourer of souls. He was a Destroyer once—an angel made to destroy cities and assassinate great evils—his scent told me that.

The game within a game was learning their true name. The shock of hearing their secret was often followed by an offer—their service to my cause—a plea for mercy. Knowledge of names was power. In Votan's case, my knowledge would be his destruction.

"Leave," whispered a voice. "Please leave, or he'll devour you." A young girl, no older than six, apparated in front of me. From her modern clothing and the bow in her hair, I suspected she had wandered off from her parents and fell into a dark place she should never have been near. An innocent lost forever.

"He knows what you are," she said. She appeared as a phantom, but she was no ordinary ghost. Her soul burned brightly inside Votan's belly, forever his slave. Still, the dead were the dead, and I was master of all dead things. "He knows why you've come, and he is giving you one chance to leave."

Was he attempting to frighten a necromancer with a ghost? With all my combined power, there was only a handful of beings who could destroy me, even with my true name. Votan was never one of them. I summoned my power and the ring on my finger vibrated. With a simple thought, I reached out and took control of the specter.

"He says," the little girl began to say, when she stopped and blinked thrice, accepting my control. Then she turned to face her former master. "Heed your threats, Votan. Give the stranger the key, and he will spare your life."

There was no response. Just silence as Votan's magic dissolved, and the little girl along with it. The stillness seemed to last for minutes, and I began to wonder if the ancient god had fallen asleep like an old man on duty.

The floor began to tremble. Mortar dust fell from the ancient canopy, clouding the air, when the statue moved. It was a slight movement, like preparation. Then the rumbling subsided, and the room went perfectly still once again.

When it appeared that nothing would come of the standoff between us, Votan leapt forward with a ferocious howl. He was as large as an elephant, but quick as a leopard lurching after its prey.

The very moment Votan moved, I grabbed for each and every soul burning inside his great stomach. In one quick pull, I ripped them all free.

He fell instantly, two steps from his roost. The souls of the dead seeped from his burst gullet and spilled onto the ground in a slimy pool of ectoplasmic gore. Votan was too wounded to move and twitched from the floor. His side was split wide open with the glow of the devoured souls oozing from the wound.

I stepped forward to take his eyes and claim the key. Death was just another journey for us. Eyes were portals of the spirit—without them, we were sent back to our own realm—to the place we belonged. For Votan, it would send him straight to the burning pits.

I placed a hand on his mighty brow, spread wide one of Votan's eyes, drew up my sword and aimed—when a new vibration on the air caught my attention.

There was movement behind me.

That small distraction was all it took for him to attack. Votan slashed at my chest with his clawed paws, slicing open a wound that immediately began stitching itself back together, while his gaping wound did the same. I ordered my skeletal guards to investigate the movement, and they left my side in an instant as Votan rose up before me. He was twice my height and with the wound in his belly nearly healed, I was in for a battle.

His great toothless mouth snapped as I dodged and ducked away. The single gleaming white tooth whistled as it missed cleaving my face by a fraction of an inch.

I slashed my sword across his shoulder, which did nothing but enrage him further. He lashed out as quick as a tiger, shredding my shirt. As I rolled away, I could hear a scuffle brewing behind me. A figure in black attacked my skeletal guards, and the power emanating from him made me question my decision to come alone. If I had brought the entirety of the deka-tria, my Thirteen, this battle would have already ended.

Votan roared and chopped down on me like an axe. I blocked it with my sword, but his mighty paw overpowered my stance and slapped me across the room. The impact crushed one of my guards when I slammed into his fragile remains and rolled all the way to the wall. Bones across my body broke and reset, but the distance provided time to alter my attack.

The most powerful of us could bend the rules of the physical world, like gravity, thermodynamics, magnetism, and relativity. I shifted gravity and found myself falling towards the ceiling as another swipe of razor-sharp claws tore into my shoulder. From the ceiling, upside down facing Votan, I could look him in the eye. As he snapped at me with his toothless bite, I came upon a fortuitous realization. Votan was a toothless god—not a *nearly* toothless god.

His shiny white tooth was the Key of Aries, and it was hidden in plain sight.

"The tooth?" I asked, and he replied with an angry roar. The next time he snapped his jaws at me, I was ready. I dodged and slashed his muzzle, severing most of his jaw.

Votan furiously wailed and thrashed, and I pounced before he could recover.

"Now you may rest forever, Mahvriel," I said, speaking his true name. I ended his misery with a stab through the heart, and the earth quaked when his life ended. He died knowing his secret was exposed. A dishonor for a Fallen.

It took all my strength to wedge the key free from the jawbone, and it came loose as the bone cracked and split. It was made of ivory and shaped like a tooth, with intricate root-like spokes that could be entered into a lock. It hummed along with the other three and pulsed with energy. They held secrets beyond my understanding. The legend of the Holy Keys was true—they carried with them untold power.

As I admired the spoils of victory, the sounds of battle went silent.

My last guard was defeated, and my nerves sharpened. The man in black had bested the warrior and was waiting for me somewhere in the room.

What was he after? The key?

Or me?

A ball of fire exploded against the wall with a hiss, showering me in sparks and glowing embers.

"Parlor tricks!" I yelled, laughing.

His arms were alight with hellfire, and his hair was long and black. I did not recognize him, except—

—the scar!

It had been a long time since I saw that mark. A scar in the shape of a crescent moon wrapped around his left eye. The mark of Gabriel. Tattooed or branded, the scar told me everything I needed to know about his loyalties. When an angel falls, the halo snaps, the wings are clipped, and the mark upon their face scars over. He had fallen shamefully, like the rest of us. Over time it might heal, but only when the Fallen had given up all hope of going home.

Who was he?

He stank of enchantment and black magic, but very little Grace. He was a powerful *spark*, not a true Fallen nor a god. He held a tiny fraction of real power. The mystical surrounded him like an aura. He had done *things*—dark things. The evil on him grayed out the good. He was a tormented soul—I could sense it.

"You look like you've seen a ghost, Pale Demon," he said. There were places where people still cowered in fear of that moniker.

"I've seen ghosts. I command ghosts. You are no ghost, not yet," I said and dashed at him, slashing for his head with my flaming sword. He dodged and flayed the flesh from my forearm with hellfire.

"How did you get here?" I demanded.

"Revenge. You took something precious from me. I did some pretty horrible things to find you," he said, gasping for air. The adrenaline pumping through his beating heart gave him power, fueling his body like gunpowder on a roaring fire. "I may never get back all you took, but I refuse to let you live."

Pitiful. When you have walked the Earth as long as I, you learn a few things about equilibrium and the Cosmic Scales. Revenge, although a powerful driving force, one that I slaved to for centuries, can never heal the broken. Even if the spark could defeat me, his half-life was built on recklessness, and revenge would swallow him. He'd end up in the pit sooner or later.

He came at me in a flashing storm of hellfire. I slashed for his legs as he leapt over me and raked my back with fiery claws, ripping my skin apart like warm butter. I slashed and cut him across the chest, but as my wounds healed, his did not. He staggered backward, and I pushed again and again, forcing him back onto his heels. The spark was running out of room but managed to sense the wall behind him and sprang upon it, walking up its side with ease.

Sparks were like demi-gods—weak angelic beings with small portions of Grace that gifted them luck and sometimes great physical gifts—but altering gravity should not have been one of them. He was like a magician without the proper dexterity, performing miracles with sloppy sleight-of-hand.

When he spun to race away, I plucked him from the wall by the throat and held him above my head. The pain extinguished his hellfire and left him defenseless.

"What good is revenge when you are incapable of achieving it?" I asked, my hot breath sticking to his face. I could see the abomination in his eyes, the atrocities committed rivaled only by my own. We were the same. Two creatures who would do anything to get what we wanted and had crawled through the bottomless filth and wretches of this world to achieve it.

"I won't give up!" he growled.

"Why?" I slammed him into the wall. The rock at his back crumbled from the force as I threatened to crush his body through it.

"Because," he said through clenched teeth, "she would never give up on me."

A surge of heat poured from his body, and his bones began to glow like molten lava.

The amount of power he possessed was impressively raw. His spark was dim, the empyrean spirit inside him was minuscule, and yet he fought back. He was more than a spark, yet so much less than a Fallen, but I was not impressed by such small, insignificant things.

I threw the spark to the ground and rammed my burning blade into his chest, straight through his black heart—

—only I missed.

He was fast. Kicked free of my grasp and rolled away. I kept after him, offering no recovery.

I was being careless. My hubris was getting in the way. No more games.

With a simple command, I collected all the dead within the room, every freed spirit ever consumed by Votan, and pooled them into a spool of psychic terror and ectoplasmic suffering. Then I lobbed them at the spark and watched him get torn to shreds.

The spool lifted him off the ground, tore at his mind and flesh, and slammed him into the ground. He skidded across stone, smearing his blood along the floor like a squashed bug.

I was standing over him, watching his pathetic body suffer, when he sprang at me with a makeshift knife, stabbing for my eye. I caught his hand by the wrist, twisted it painfully, and studied the knife. It was fashioned from a familiar tooth.

"How are the Stygian Three these days?" I asked. My prior encounter had left them in a less-than-desirable state.

"Dead," he said, as he spun and jammed the knife even closer to my eye.

It was those words that struck me. This spark had killed the Stygian Witches? I was dealing with something I had never encountered. His hunger for revenge was a force of nature.

I drove my clawed hand into the wound at his chest and dug for his heart, mortally wrenching it loose. The spark ripped himself away and fell to the floor, his dying heart stuttering behind his broken ribs. He was critically wounded and shifting around with pathetic tears in his eyes.

"I failed her," he cried. Only the spark knew who she was and just how long and dark his path had been. He carried scents from other realms, places between spaces and beyond.

"Come now, failure implies a chance of success," I said. He was formidable for a spark, but in the end, he was nothing. "Let me end your misery."

"This is the end of me," he sobbed, then removed a piece of thread from around his neck. "But it's only the beginning." He tied the thread into a strange knot, one that I had never seen. "I'll pass on my Light."

"What is that?" I asked, stepping closer. He scurried away, putting as much space between us as possible. What trickery was this? What threat was held within that tiny thread?

"I lost everything. All I had was a vague whisper that came to me in a dream. *Thirteen Evils hunt Four Keys to open Eden.*"

The blood in my veins ran cold. The treachery within my own ranks ran much deeper than I thought.

"I searched for you through the darkness and into places beyond mankind. That's where I found this. My fate," he said, gesturing to the thread. "Stolen from the Fates themselves. You have no idea what I had to do to get this." He sobbed. "You'll see me again."

"And I will kill you," I threatened, as he pulled the knot tight and vanished.

VII
white knight

TONY
Then.

"How did this experience make you feel?"

"Helpless. Confused. Irredeemable."

"Irredeemable? Why?"

"I had great friends like Thad, Chris, and John, but there was only one Amanda in my life. She provided something I never had."

"Which was?"

"Female companionship. When I lost her, I felt like I'd never be good enough, for anyone. Not Amanda, and definitely not Jacinda, the girl who never showed up."

The doc then jotted down several notes.

February 16, 1998

The Monday after Valentine's Day proved to be an interesting one. There were few days in the life of a teenager that were more stressful than Valentine's Day. The school provided an anonymous service where you could send someone a Valentine lollipop and a brief message for two bucks—a fundraiser for the cheerleaders. For an extra dollar, you could send along a balloon as well. They were called Candygrams, and they were the worst.

Every year, there was always a mixture of anxiety when it came to that fateful afternoon when the Candygrams were delivered—would I be lucky enough to get one? Or would I be unlucky enough to not get one? And what if I got one, and it was from someone I didn't want to get one from?

Teenagers had enough stress when they weren't making up their own imaginary nightmare situations. However, I already knew what was going to happen—I hadn't received a Valentine since elementary school, when everyone gave out those cheap pre-made cards they sold at the grocery store. My dad always had me make my own from construction paper rather than spend the twenty bucks like everyone else—and the kids always knew who gave them the crappy hand-made card, not the one licensed by *Barbie* or *G.I. Joe* with a message like "Loving is Half the Battle—Go Joe!"

However, just because I didn't get one didn't mean I never sent one. I'd sent Kelly Cavendish an anonymous Candygram every year since the eighth grade and even made sure to send the optional balloon as well. Kelly, however, was dating Billy Woodward our senior year, and rather than tempt fate, I was going to forego sending one altogether—

When the cheerleaders pushed their squeaky cart into my seventh period history class and announced who should come up to the front and claim their Candygram, they called out Amanda's name. Her nose was buried in her book and the summons caught her unaware. It took a nudge from the girl behind her before she realized they had called her name. We sat on opposite sides of the classroom, and I watched her get up from her desk and walk over to the cart where Lisa Henwick, Billy Woodward's ex-girlfriend, begrudgingly handed her a Candygram—Lisa was still sour over the condiment bath from four years before.

The problem was, they didn't give Amanda her balloon—I know, because I paid for it. I nearly protested and squirmed in my chair when

Lisa announced Amanda's name a second time, to a chorus of gasps.

"Why did they gasp?" asked doc.
"Because only the prettiest, most popular girls got more than one Candygram," I explained. "Amanda was one of the prettiest girls in school, but she didn't want to be popular. She was content watching Evil Dead, wearing band tees and Chucks, and reading comics. The girl was anti-popular—a bookworm and a smartass. Amanda Hemmels getting two Candygrams was like Jamie Lee Curtis getting an Academy Award for Halloween."

When Amanda grabbed her second Candygram, it came with my balloon and message. I'd spent the better part of three days writing her a message that said how sorry I was and how much I missed her. When she read it, she shot me a glance from across the room, and I turned away. I didn't want to get caught watching her read my message.

The entire day passed without her acknowledging me or my Candygram—but she was forced to carry that balloon with her everywhere she went for the remainder of the day, and that included art class with Paul Lucas, her boyfriend.

You wouldn't have known they were fighting, let alone in a relationship. The two of them hardly spoke to one another in school, but I had witnessed them together in public more than enough times to know they had an equally strange relationship outside. A relationship that involved Paul's obsession with whiskey.

"Are you suggesting that at seventeen, Paul was an alcoholic?" asked Doc.
"The kid brought a flask to school," I explained. "Yeah, I'm suggesting he was an alcoholic."

On the following Monday, Amanda didn't show up to school, but Paul was there, and he appeared more moody than usual. Feeling brave, I managed to ask him if Amanda was out sick. Paul stared me down like

I had stolen a sip from his flask without asking, before saying, "Yeah, you could say that."

His answer was so ambiguous that I didn't even have to pressure Thad to give her a ring on my behalf after school. We were at Thad's house, Chris on the couch playing old-school *Legend of Zelda*, when Amanda's mom picked up.

"Hi, Mrs. Hemmels, is Amanda there?" he asked, holding the phone away from his ear so I could hear too.

"Who's calling?" she asked.

"Thaddeus," he replied. "I noticed she wasn't in school and I wanted to see if she was okay. Plus, I have her homework assignments."

"Hi Thaddeus," said Amanda's mom with a sigh that carried enough context to inform us something was wrong. "Amanda had an accident this weekend. She fell down the stairs at her boyfriend's house."

"Is she okay?" he asked, and I could feel the blood draining from my face as Chris swatted away crab-creatures jumping around the television screen.

"She has a broken arm," said Mrs. Hemmels, "but she'll be back in school tomorrow."

"Okay," said Thaddeus. "Let her know we hope she feels better."

Then Thad said his goodbye and hung up.

"What did they say?" asked Chris, his eyes glued to the game.

"She had an accident," I said.

"Is she okay?" asked Chris, seemingly unperturbed.

"She fell down the stairs," said Thad.

"Oh man," said Chris, "yeah, the stairs at her house are pretty steep. I fell the last time I was there." This wasn't new information. Chris was slightly less coordinated than the average Joe, but we all knew Amanda's house was old, a fixer-upper with loose floorboards and stray nails.

"No," said Thad, "over at Paul's."

"That's interesting," said Chris as he paused the game. That phrase never left Chris's mouth unless he had something interesting to attach to it.

"Why's that?" I asked as I plopped onto the couch beside him.

"Paul lives in a one-story rancher," said Chris. "His house doesn't have stairs. Not even a basement."

There was no worse combination than jealousy and hearsay. The two could combine to form the worst possible scenarios, and the imagination was only limited by suspicion. At that time, there was nothing stopping my mind from leaping to the worst possible scenario.

Twenty minutes later, John Monks picked us up from Thad's house after we called his beeper and left him a 9-1-1. We all had driver's licenses, but no wheels unless we were borrowing from the 'rents.

"What's the emergency?" he shouted out of the passenger-side window after pulling up out front. He was red-faced and disheveled, having climbed through a death-trap of seatbelts to manually roll down the window. He had an old multi-colored Ford Bronco with patches of rust on the frame. We called it the "Calico Kid" because of the various panels of color stripped from other Broncos by the previous owner. As far as first cars go, John didn't need fancy or sleek, just reliable enough to get him from point-A to point-B, and it always started up on the second try.

"We need a ride," said Thad. "Obviously."

"A ride?" groaned John. "To the hospital? The dentist? Chiropractor?"

"Just a ride," I said, specifically leaving out the destination.

"Why the 9-1-1?" he screeched and rolled his eyes.

"Would you have come if we hadn't?" I asked.

"Fuck," whined John. "No…"

Chris laughed and hopped into the back, then said, "I told them not to do it."

"It was Chris's idea," said Thad.

"Yup, it was," laughed Chris.

"You guys are assholes," groaned John as we loaded in. "Where to?"

"Paul Lucas's house," I said.

"You confronted Paul?" asked Doc.

"We did," I replied.

"On what grounds?" he asked.

"On the grounds that he hurt Amanda," I explained.

"Are you sure that's what transpired?" he asked. "What if she really had fallen down stairs? What if it was a complicated situation that was easier to explain that way?"

I shook my head. "He admitted to it. Sorta."

We arrived at Paul's house on the other side of town. He lived down a long country road that led into the boondocks of the boonies. Our small country town was in the middle of nowhere, a speck on the map that nobody had ever heard of. We were so far out into nowhere that there were no longer road signs, and the streets went from paved to gravel.

Paul lived in a small blue rancher in the middle of the woods. If his house was a log cabin, I would have feared finding a book of the dead in its cellar. John parked along the side of the narrow road—there was so much mud in Paul's driveway that he feared the Calico Kid would get stuck and need a tow.

"Quaint," said John. "When was the last time you were here, Chris?"

"Ninth grade," he replied.

"Paul was in our Boy Scout troop," said Thad.

"There's a lake in the back, and we took the canoes out looking for tadpoles and frogs," said Chris. He appeared lost in thought as he recalled that day three years prior. "Paul's a strange fellow. Peculiar. But his father is far stranger."

"What do you mean?" I asked.

"Ever see *Tremors*?" said Thad.

"Yeah," I replied.

"Remember Burt Gummer?" he said. "Paul's dad is a hillbilly with an arsenal that'd give Burt Gummer a chubby."

"Did you just say *chubby*?" said John.

"He did," I replied, and John guffawed. "What are we waiting for?"

"Maybe we should rethink this," said John. "Nobody wants to get murdered tonight."

"If I find out he broke Amanda's arm," I said as I hopped out of the Calico Kid, "there will definitely be a murder."

"Cripes," said John, as Thad and Chris exchanged a look.

I had only walked ten feet when Thad hopped out of the truck and said, "Maybe we should let this be. Amanda's not dumb. If Paul really did hurt her, she'll break up with him."

"Does that mean he should get away with it?" I asked.

"No," said Thad, taken back by my question. "But maybe we shouldn't be the ones to exact revenge, either."

I stood there, looking at my friends in the darkness. A yard lamp on top of an old telephone pole was the only light anywhere for miles. I could just make out John and Chris's faces, tinted red from the truck dashboard. They were imploring me with looks to reconsider.

"You don't hurt a woman," I said. "There are certain things you just don't do." Then I looked at them all and said something sentimental—something I meant, but never could articulate at any other moment. "Friends are the only thing worth fighting for."

Thad followed me as I turned and strode toward the house, probably to be a peacemaker if needed. I stepped in the thick mud and nearly lost a shoe, and I heard him groan that I was "leaving evidence."

The truck door slammed twice in the distance—John and Chris finally following as I approached the front door. The house was on stilts—the entire yard was a bog, and it was clear there was no basement, no stairs.

"The Bog of Eternal Stench," groaned Thad—and he wasn't wrong. The whole place reeked of methane gas. John went to light a cigarette, and Chris politely put his hand over the lighter, preventing him from striking the flint. Whether or not it would have ignited the gas was science I couldn't explain, but it was certainly safer that way.

"Smells like farts," said John.

When I knocked on the door, Paul answered. He didn't look surprised. He didn't look welcoming. He didn't look like anything at all. His face was impassable as he opened the screen door and stepped out of the house.

"What do you want?" he finally said, looking at Thad.

"Did you hurt her?" I asked.

"Who?" asked Paul. I was suddenly very aware of how tall he was, as if he had grown three inches since the Halloween party.

"Amanda," said Chris. He only said it because he couldn't stand the silence when the answer was so obvious.

"Why would I hurt Amanda?" he asked.

"You tell us," I demanded.

"I can't tell you that," he said. "But maybe you can tell me why you're so jealous of us?" He was finally looking at me. The guy never looked me directly in the eyes, at least not since I slugged him.

"Jealous of who?" I asked. "You and Amanda?"

He nodded. "You sent her a valentine," he said.

"You sent her a valentine?" asked Thad.

"A Candygram," I replied.

"That's a valentine," said John.

"With candy," said Chris, clarifying.

"Why?" asked Thad.

If we were there to intimidate Paul, we were doing a foul job of it. Chris and John were as unthreatening as they come—and Thad? His body language was uncomfortable, and he seemed to be mediating like a school counselor.

"Because I wanted to apologize," I said.

"You could do that with words," said Paul. "You didn't have to show me up by buying my girl a valentine like that." Paul then cracked a bit, showing emotion. "You did it on purpose, Tony. You were trying to show me up, and you succeeded. If you considered Amanda a friend, maybe you shouldn't have waited four months before you tried to apologize. And maybe you should have said it to her face, instead of trying to make me look bad."

I felt awful. He was right. And I could tell he knew he had me on the ropes without a single punch thrown.

"Paul," said Thad as he began to back away, "see you in class tomorrow."

"Sorry, Paul," said John.

"See you in class," said Chris with an awkward wave that was caught somewhere between shame and indirectly suggesting we were all still friends.

I was reeling, too distraught to realize the four of us were retreating to John's truck. I was too caught up in my own bullshit and deciphering what was going on between Amanda and me that I had lost track of the part I played.

"Wait," I said, when something struck me—something he had said that didn't sit right. I turned back and Paul was already reaching for the screen door. He turned back to face me with an annoyed posture that reminded me of the way Billy Woodward would petulantly react to the teachers whenever he was caught misbehaving.

"What?" groaned Paul.

"You said I showed you up," I said. "I got her a Candygram with a balloon. That's not exactly a bouquet of flowers and a handwritten poem."

He shrugged and shook his head. "What are you suggesting?"

"What did you get her, Paul?" I asked.

Thad and John groaned, and Chris kept walking, not realizing the rest of us had stopped.

"What does it matter?" said Paul. "What does it fucking matter?"

"You didn't get her anything," I accused. "That other Candygram was from someone else. You got showed up by two different guys."

The look on Paul's face was incredulous. He looked like he wanted to hit me, like he had the night of the Halloween party.

"Scandalous," said John in a high-pitched voice, his mouth unmoving like a ventriloquist.

"You know, Paul," I said, taking two steps toward him. "You've had Amanda chasing after you for three years now. The least you could do is put forth a little effort."

"Fuck off," he said.

"Two guys that aren't even dating her thought more of Amanda than her own boyfriend, who sat on his thumbs instead of spending three bucks on a silly Candygram."

"Sitting on his thumbs? I bet he liked that," said John in the same high-pitched voice.

"Two bucks," said Chris.

"What?" I asked. At some point Chris realized we weren't walking along with him and had doubled back.

"Two bucks for a Candygram," he clarified. "Three for an added balloon."

"Correct," I said. "You couldn't be bothered to spend two bucks on her. So, what happened? Did she confront you about it? Did you hit her?"

"Okay," said Thad, stepping in. "You proved your point, he's a bad boyfriend, but this is going too far—"

"Women should know their place," said Paul.

Thad dropped his hands to his side, looked me in the eyes and said, "Did he really just say that?"

"I think you guys should leave," said Paul, as he retrieved something from his belt. I didn't react straightaway because it didn't feel real, but the gun in Paul's hand was every bit reality. He took two steps toward me and raised it to my head. "Think you're a tough guy? How tough do you think you are, Tony?"

I could smell the alcohol. It was sweating from his skin.

Nobody moved. Nobody said a word.

Very little went through my mind. I thought about my dad, and I thought about what was going to happen if Paul pulled the trigger. And I thought about Amanda, and how she would react after learning Paul had murdered me. I felt like a bug who had wandered too close to the pretty blue light before the zapper shocked me dead.

The stare-down that followed was so intense that none of us heard or noticed the car pull up or the sound of the door slam. In fact, it was so far away in the back of my mind that I didn't even know I was hearing my own name until she was standing right in front of me.

"What the fuck, Paul! Tony?" screamed Amanda. "Put that away!"

"I wasn't gonna do nothing," whined Paul as he finally lowered the gun. "Safety was on the whole time."

"Are you serious?" growled Amanda. She slapped him. She slapped him so hard it left a handprint on his face, and Paul looked startled. "Never do that again. Never ever do that again." Then she turned to me and said, "What are you doing here, Tony?" I didn't recognize my name when she spoke it because she actually used my full name rather than calling me T. She was angry. Her eyes were flared, and her arm was in a sling.

When I didn't answer, John said, "Hi Amanda," in the same ventriloquist voice.

Paul moved next to Amanda, presenting them as a united front. When he placed his hand on her hip, she shrugged it off and said, "Go inside." When he started to argue, she shot him a furious glare.

"I don't think you should be out here with them," he said.

"You know, Paul," said Amanda, revving up like a fuel-injected engine. "It's bad enough you didn't do anything for me on Valentine's Day, and trust me, I hate that holiday as much as the next person—but you could have at least made an effort to do something, not just sit around on your couch watching South Park and drinking. But when I fell, you didn't even help me up. You let me drive myself to the hospital, and after thinking about it for a full weekend, I can't be with someone like you."

"That sucks," said Chris. He wasn't saying it to be a smartass. He said it because he really felt that it sucked—hence why Amanda gave him a thin-lipped smile, as if to agree with him.

I thought everything was over—the whole confrontation, and that Amanda dumping Paul was the start of us being friends again. I was wrong about Paul hitting her, but I wasn't wrong about him being a shitty, psycho, apathetic boyfriend—and a piece of shit. But when Amanda turned to me, anger still in her eyes, I knew she wasn't done.

"T, I love you, I will always love you, but you don't know boundaries! I don't know if I can be friends with someone who knows everything about me but can't seem to figure me out. I don't need a white knight—but you need to be one, and damnit, T, I can't have that."

"What does that mean?" I asked.

"It means giving you space doesn't work."

"Space?"

"I thought we were on the same page, but then you go and do this," she said. "I know you mean well. I know you only ever follow your heart, and that's such a good quality—but not for me. Not when we're such a mess of co-dependency."

Then she turned to the other guys and said, "You all have been like brothers to me. I needed that. I needed that after losing Joey a long time ago. But replacing him is impossible." Then she turned directly to me, as if what she said next was specific for my audience. "I don't need another brother. We need to figure ourselves out. Separately."

"What happened next?" asked Doc.

"She took a deep breath, then walked away," I explained. "Nobody followed her. Paul drunkenly stumbled away as if it was no big deal, then went inside and turned off the outdoor light, leaving us in the dark. But I was doubled over. I was sobbing so hard you'd think I had been punched in the gut."

"It was interesting what she said to you."

"What part?" I asked.

"About being a white knight." He had just finished jotting down copious notes. Enough to fill a whole page in his doctor-scratch shorthand.

For the next three months, I survived without Amanda. I avoided her whenever I could but was friendly and cordial when I needed to be. I spent plenty of time with Chris, Thad, and John. We had some good times, but it always felt like a piece of the puzzle was missing—like the fab-five was missing its heart and soul.

Baseball season came and went. Despite our school team's losing record and my mediocre grades, I was accepted to four different universities—one in Texas, one in Connecticut, and another in Philly. But I received a full scholarship to play ball at a university I had forgotten all about. I'd applied for a scholarship on a whim, and when I received the acceptance letter and the full ride to Milton State University in Grace Falls, PA, I was stunned. I could have followed my friends to college in Philadelphia, but for a single-parent family, a full ride was hard to pass up.

When the time came to make my decision, I signed the paperwork and packed my bags for northern PA. Saying goodbye to friends wasn't easy, but that was life. I was taking a bold new leap into the future and putting the past behind me.

August 1998

"What're you going to do with yourself?" I asked my dad as he helped me load up the truck. It was a rusty, beat-up pickup, but we had gotten the most out of it.

"Work. Food. Sleep. The usual," he replied with a smile.

"If you need me, you know I'm only a six-hour bus ride away."

"Only a six-hour bus ride?" He laughed. "That's like saying you've only eaten two-thirds of the food in the house for the last eighteen years."

"Seriously though, you'll be alright?"

"Of course. Let me know your game schedule, and I'll be there in the stands."

By noon the next day I was settled into my room—a two-bedroomed, four-bed, concrete cell that I had all to myself. I was scheduled to have three roommates, but they wouldn't arrive for two more weeks. Student athletes reported early for training and orientation. Having the whole room to myself was the most grown up I had ever felt. Without any supervision, I enjoyed three full days of pizza, tacos, and delivery from the local favorite China King. Amid my freedom, I was able to do some self-reflection.

It was then I realized how much I missed Amanda. I wanted to talk to someone, to share my life, and she wasn't there.

"To this day, I miss her. I think about her all the time, about what she might say to me now, after all I've gone through. Would we even be friends? Would we have common ground again? But, truthfully, I don't know if I will ever be healed enough to allow someone that close to me."

"Why? Why do you believe you are so far gone?"

"What makes you believe I'm not?"

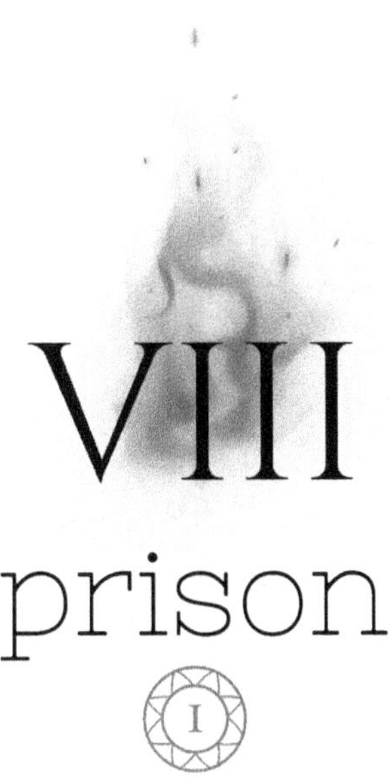

VIII

prison

TONY
December 21, 2013
Now.

The man's hands were burning. The fire crackled and hissed, like his skin was kindling. He strode forward, large strides, and in a moment, he was upon us—me and the blonde-haired man, who was still standing on the wall like he was freakin' Lionel Ritchie, *dancin' on the ceiling.*

"More flesh for the feast," said Lionel, welcoming the third.

"Who are you people?" I shouted. I wanted to run, but to where? Could I outrun a man who could walk on walls? And another who burned like the Human Torch?

Then, as if it all wasn't strange enough, something weird happened. Maybe the fear clenched my bladder full of too-much-beer so hard that it broke a blood vessel in my brain, or maybe I was having a stroke—whatever it was, something inside my mind opened up, and two words fell out like a bonus bag of chips falling into a vending machine basin.

Summanus. Then, "Oriel," I said aloud, my mouth on autopilot.

If I had wanted to slip away, I should have just kept my mouth shut. That word—his *name?*—was like a bomb exploding between us. He looked shocked, angry and defiant, and launched himself at me without hesitation.

I was impacted—twice—once by Summanus driving me across the alley toward the far wall—then again by the burning stranger, knocking me free and sending us all sprawling in the dirt and mud of the grimy alley floor. As the other two stared each other down, growling like mad dogs, I made a run for it.

I hadn't run like that in years, and the rust on my body was evident—an athlete no longer. I felt like I was moving within a vat of molasses, laboring through every stride. That's when I heard the cackle, and the world went dark. The woman was back, and her laugh echoed within my head. Every direction was cloudy, like I was swimming in a lake at night—able to see only three feet ahead in any direction.

"Lost boy, don't run too far," she cackled, then skittered out of the darkness toward me. She was as old as dirt and twice as ugly, with a hooked nose and straw-like white hair. Her eyes were covered with cataracts and her skin was leathered and wrinkled.

She spat in my face—a mucousy wad of saliva that burned like acid.

I screamed in pain as my face melted, trying to wipe the acid from my eyes before I went blind, when someone said, "It's all in your head."

Then the witch burst into flames.

Almost immediately the moonlight returned, and the spit stopped burning. There was fire all around me, growing and spreading from every surface. The heat was intense, swallowing all the oxygen and starving my lungs.

I ran.

This time I escaped the alley and ran two city blocks, dodging people along the sidewalk, before boarding a city bus. The doors were closing as I jammed myself inside, flipped the TrailPass from my pocket, and the driver waved me on.

When I sat down, I was shaking. I stared out of the bus window, trying to calm myself through a variety of methods—none of which were working—when the bus passed a samurai standing on the corner. He glared at me—his hair was traditionally bound, and he wore a bluish gray kimono with a sword tucked into the belt.

"What in the actual fuck is going on?" I asked myself as I began to hyperventilate.

My nerves were shot, and I was beginning to feel muscles I hadn't used in years. It was almost 1 a.m., and the bus was nearly empty. A drunk couple got off at the next stop, leaving me alone with the driver and my thoughts. I wasn't far from home. Walking would have taken less than a half hour, but I wanted to be off the streets as quick as possible and away from the chaos—away from my hallucinations.

I saw impossible things and tried to analyze them. What had happened? What had I witnessed? I felt like I was cracking—like I needed new medication—like it was Northcreek all over again—when the bus lurched into the air.

I was thrown from my seat as the lights and engine cut off. It sounded like a wrecking ball had bashed into a wall of plastic. The whole side of the bus was crushed as something ripped right through the fiberglass and metal, nearly slicing it in two.

When everything came to a full stop, I crawled out from where I had landed beneath the seat and walked to the gaping hole in the bus. The driver unbuckled himself and stood on the other side of the gap, staring into the hole with me. We could see the street, chunks of metal, electrical wiring, and motor oil sprayed over the asphalt.

"What the fuck was that?" he asked.

I shrugged, but I had a good idea. Pick your poison—the wall-walker or the flamer. Was it impossible to think one of them could have destroyed a city bus?

I left immediately through the gaping hole and ran, stumbling the wrong way for a full block before I turned left down 5th Street, toward home. I don't know why, but for some reason I thought I'd be safe locked within those four walls—like it was my palace of isolation—a fortress of solitude. I had walked that stretch of dark, lonely sidewalk many times, and never once was I ever struck by crippling fear or knee-buckling terror like the overwhelming despair that infected me as I raced past the brick wall to the Christ Church Burial Ground.

Benjamin Franklin was buried there. It was an old cemetery, with worn headstones older than the country itself. There were tours, and it was seen as a local ghost attraction—leave a penny behind and the spirit of Franklin would wisely toss it back at you, fulfilling his Poor Richard's prophet-eering.

The problem was, what I saw stepping out of the cemetery ahead of me was no penny, nor the ghost of good 'ole Ben—it was a dark silhouette against the halogen streetlight from the corner across the street. It was tall—taller than any man, with two pointed ears that stretched up to the stars, and it was slowly being consumed by a funerary fog that crept from the cemetery and into the street.

I took three long strides before I stopped, as if my brain was registering and reacting to stimuli faster than the rest of my body. Every joint from my ankles to my hips was swollen, and every muscle was aching. I was a geriatric thirty-three-year-old, and whatever it was that stood in my way was going to kill me. Even its posture proclaimed death, as if it was the living embodiment of quietus—a final silencer from somewhere beyond.

I was stuck—the proverbial rock between multiple hard places—the creature in front of me, the wall across the street, and the cemetery vomiting its eerie fog. I had never met anyone good at making split decisions—some impulses in the moment were better than others, and when I saw the wrought-iron gate on the far side of the cemetery, it looked as good an option as any.

I sprinted into the cemetery and aimed for the gate, cutting through the sacred ground and leaping over headstones until the fog had grown so thick, I couldn't see two feet in front of me—when the inevitable occurred.

The solid marble headstone practically leapt up out of the fog and tripped me, sending me sprawling forward into the cold dark mist. My head smacked into something hard and bounced off, and I went skidding across the ground.

My head rang like a bell tolling in the far distance. Was I down for a minute? Five? I tried to move, but everything was slow and muddy, like I was swimming. While I was down, the fog had thickened, and I stood up to the suffocating cold of the mist—ice drifted within, snowing and covering every surface with a thin layer of white and gray.

I wanted to run, but there was nowhere to go. I couldn't find direction. I couldn't even find my hands in front of my own face. Shifting through the cemetery, I maneuvered like a blind man, when everything became quiet. The city, at its quietest, was still a low buzz of streetlamps, tires against asphalt, and the faintest thump of bass from a sound system blazing down the expressway. At that moment, when things went quiet, there was no sound at all—

—until something moved.

It was close, like a scratching against the ground, but disappeared as quickly as it began. Every thought scampering through my whirring skull was praying that whatever made that sound was innocent or equally lost within the mist.

For several steps, I hadn't hit anything, not a stumble over uneven ground nor a brush against headstone, and I was beginning to move more confidently through the dark. Then the scratching sound started again—this time, from two different directions.

It was surreal.

The whole night was a bad dream.

"You're losing your shit," I said to myself. "Get it together. Get it together. Get. It. Together!" I rubbed my eyes and pulled at my hair, but nothing changed the circumstance. Even at my lowest, I had never experienced anything like this. How could it be real? A man was walking on the fucking wall! He grabbed me from within a fucking mirror! Another's hands were on fucking fire! It was too much. It was all too much.

Then someone placed a hand on my shoulder.

"Sir?" it garbled.

I had lost my shit. I was seeing things and was wandering around the cemetery like a total doofus lunatic, and some good Samaritan was going to help me snap out of this—

"I'm okay," I said, spinning around.

In moments of great confusion, the human body typically does two things:

1. **Flinch** – When we see something unexpectedly close, we flinch. It doesn't matter what it is—a person, a projectile, a fucking firefly—the human body's first reaction is to keep whatever it is from getting into our two most precious outer organs—our eyes.

2. **Freeze** – There is something about absolute terror that makes our legs and feet grow roots, stabilizing us in the one place we wish not to be.

I both flinched and froze as the grimy face of decay snapped its rotted teeth, going for my neck. My flinch deflected the teeth, which sank into my coat collar instead.

"Sirrrrr," it gargled. "Mayyyy IIIIIIII helllllpppp youuuuu?"

My fist connected with the side of its head and crushed the weakened skull with a sickening thunk. And in a blink, they were all around me—gargling and yawning disenchanted messages from their departed lives—hands of the dead, grabbing and groping for a handful of shirt or jacket. Something even clawed at my leg when two lights sprang up in the distance—like candles, and I was being pulled down into an empty grave. Pulled down into the dark hole as the dead swarmed and pulled me under.

When I hit bottom, I was spat out like a half-chewed wad of gum and landed on something hard and flat, like cold concrete. My head pounded—my pulse zipped behind my eyes like speed metal bass drums and clanging cymbals. I was free. The dead were gone, and I was flapping around on the ground like a beached fish looking for water.

It was dark, and every movement I made caused a circus of echoes. Nothing was grappling for me. Everything was suddenly calm, except for my thrashing about. I took a moment to breathe, and after wiping the dirt and grime from my eyes I was able to see shades of black—and as my eyes slowly adjusted, I was struck with a horrifying discovery.

I was in a cell. Four by eight feet, with old rusty bars caging me and a narrow cut in the ceiling where moonlight crept in. A series of clouds swept past in the sky above, casting the cell into total darkness until they drifted on. In the corner was an old rusty bedframe, the rot below was the remnants of the once-soft bed cushion, and the walls were crumbling, exposing the old brick.

My heart rate hadn't slowed, and it wasn't going to. Every move I made echoed back to me as if it was coming from beyond the metal bars, or from the next cell beyond the brick walls. I had no understanding of how I got there, why, or how I was going to get out, and I was petrified—because I knew exactly where I was.

I had somehow been transported more than twenty blocks in a single second and locked within the middle of an historic, haunted, prison.

The Eastern State Penitentiary was known for torture, murder, suicides and more when it closed down in 1971. It was said to be one of the most haunted places in the country.

Last year, Marshall had sponsored a work trip after hours to visit the haunted attraction the Penitentiary hosted every Halloween. The attraction never actually went inside the real haunted parts, and I was generally unamused by the theatrics of it all.

But Marsh was excited.

"Got you out of that apartment, finally!" he shouted, then handed me a flask he had hidden in his jacket.

"Yeah, seems like the place to be," I said, noting the long lines wrapped around the block as I took a sip and handed it back, discreetly. The penitentiary looked like some kind of fortress, with ivy crawling up the pale stone walls.

"Lots of honeys running around," he said, elbowing me like we were a couple of boomers. Marsh was trying so hard to get me *back in the saddle* that he probably didn't realize how it made me feel. It was like calling attention to something new inevitably reminded me of what was lost. "What do you think about Corrine?"

"From Sales? She's cool," I said. "Thinking of asking her out?"

"Oh no, not for me," he said. "For you, Captain Spock."

"Spock?" I said, thinking it was some kind of compliment.

"Yeah, he's an emotionless husk," said Marshall. "C'mon, man. Live a little. Those drugs they got you on have you watching life go by."

"And you think Corrine is the key to my living?" I asked.

"She's a start," he said with a grin. "C'mon, she's a fun gal, and maybe you hit it off. Maybe she even invites you over to her place…" He let his words linger on a high note, as if he needed the tone to land his insinuation.

"You know that feeling when you need a shower," I started to say, but averted all eye contact, "like you just feel disgusting all over. As if a single whiff might make you gag?"

"Oh, you're talking about Sundays," he deadpanned.

"Imagine it's not your skin," I said, pushing past his joke, "but your insides. Your vital organs and guts, they all feel dirty. Grimy. Rotten. That's how I feel all the time." His face changed, and I think I might have really scared him. Then I gestured at Corrine and the others in our group. As they enjoyed themselves, I found myself slinking away until Marshall swooped in to help me socialize. "And no amount of time, effort, *or Corrine*, will ever wash it clean."

"Alright," he nodded after a long pause. "But this isn't over. You hear me, T? This is not over." Then he smiled and dug his hands into the tense muscles in my shoulders. "However, tonight, we venture into the scariest haunted attraction this side of the Mississippi!"

"So, everything west of the Mississippi is scarier?" I questioned.

"Have you ever been to Mississippi?" he asked. "That's some scary shit."

We spent the next hour walking through dark corridors and listening to men and women scream like little kids and laugh.

Now that I was locked inside against my will, I was screaming too. I was screaming at the top of my lungs. I yanked on the metal bars that barely rattled in their locked fittings. "Let me out! Let me out!"

As my voice echoed back to me over the course of several seconds—one scream fading as another was just beginning, like a cascade of sound—I recognized the pattern of something else beneath my echoing voice—a mad chuckle that didn't echo. Someone or something was enjoying my breakdown.

The echoless laugh was taunting me, and for a moment I pondered why it didn't echo, and despite my belief that I was actually hearing it, the only other possibility seemed the most likely—it was all in my head.

There's a point, right at the edge of a nervous breakdown, when it feels like you're breaking through an invisible bubble. I began to check the boxes off one by one:

- Depression? Check – but that was an easy one.
- Insomnia? Check – if not for the cocktail of pills I took, I'd not be sleeping at all.
- Extreme Mood Swings? Check – Marsh would agree.
- Panic Attacks? Present.
- Paranoia? Double Check.
- Hallucinations? Absolutely.
- Anxiety? Trembling? Shaking? You betcha.
- Flashbacks of a Traumatic Event? …hope not. I was wearing good pants.

I was trying to keep it together, pacing my cell and focused on breathing, but my clammy hands wouldn't dry, and my stomach was tied in so many knots I was sure my good pants had nothing to worry about. I heard it again, the chuckling, like a maniac ghost was watching every shake and shiver, every mumble to myself to "keep it together."

When the giggling died away, I stood perfectly still in the middle of the room and wrapped my arms around myself, my hands stuffed under my arms. I closed my eyes and tried to clear my head, but my mind was like a relaxed muscle spasming. One moment it was blank, and the next conjured memories—her laugh, her eyes, her voice saying, "I thought you were the moon." Shaking, sweating, I was a mess, and as the pain inside me grew, so did the dark thoughts—there were more than enough sharp and rusty objects in the room to end it.

Could I actually survive till morning? Could I survive locked up in this insane place till someone came by and found me?

I couldn't.

I was already losing my grip. I was hearing things, was even starting to see things—shadows flitting through the darkness, and I felt surrounded, like the dead were dragging me back down into the black hole—

Whispers.

I could hear whispers. They started like small whisps, but eventually grew into sounds that were almost words. I did not imagine it—they echoed. Quietly, I placed one foot in front of the other, gently moving from where I stood to the cell bars, then angled myself to peer right down the hall, then left…

…someone was there.

It was as dark as I could ever remember inside that prison. Not even running through the woods with my dad—running into that clearing in the dead of night, not knowing where we were going…

The long blonde hair—I could see him. The man from the alley with two names. Summanus and Oriel. He was there, and he was whispering, almost bickering with…*nothing?* He was talking to himself as the shadow with the pointed ears drifted behind him. The shadow wasn't talking, but there was a second voice—a crazy voice, the one that was laughing, and it didn't echo as it replied to the man who could walk on walls.

"How?" asked Summanus. "The spark is mortal. He'll die if we twist too hard." His whisper echoed off the stone walls.

"I do not care how," said the disembodied voice. It was hard to hear without the echo bringing the words closer to my ears. "Just get the name."

The darkness parted like a tear ripping its way through black paper: jagged, hot, and swiftly splitting before it impaled into the floor with a metallic clack as loud as thunder—passing through Summanus in a shower of blood and hot sparks.

A spear—a burning spear was holding his lifeless body in the air, as a pool of blood spread across the floor like a river draining from the gaping hole where his heart once beat.

There was a loud bark, like an attack dog, followed by the sound of scuffling in the distance. But I was too entranced by the burning spear and the gore to fathom it. For several seconds I watched in horror—too terrified to blink, and too overwhelmed to move. Shaking, I witnessed as a trail of bloody footprints strolled away from the body, then disappeared mid-stride as it passed my cell—but not before the echoless words left me a parting gesture.

"Be seeing you, Tony Oscuro," said the voice.

The light from the spear was dwindling, or maybe it was the light in my eyes. Everything was beginning to feel far away, like I was peering into a far-off tunnel and out the other side—but all that changed the moment I saw *them*.

From the other direction, away from the scuffling and the riotous barks, a barred door swung open and slammed against the wall with a big crash. There were four of them, all dressed in black, with strange masks, pacing through the hall like the Horsemen of the Apocalypse.

Wearing a black blazer and a mask with some kind of glow-in-the-dark paint depicting a jagged smiley face, the man in front carried a sword.

To his flanks were two men—one in a similar mask depicting a horned circle lugged an old dusty book. The other wore black military surplus, with big claws jutting from fingerless gloves—he had four jagged vertical streaks on his mask.

In the back was the lone woman, wearing a leather jacket over a glowing skeleton body suit, her mask painted with a skull.

"There!" shouted the man in front, pointing at my cell.

"What is that?"

They were mystified by whatever was transpiring further up the hall. They were scared. Debating whether or not they wanted to step any closer.

"Anubis," whispered one of them.

"Oh?" replied the one with the claws in a deep voice.

"Luna, give us time."

"You got it, boss," replied the woman in the leather jacket. She took both hands and waved them like she was splashing water in a pool. *"I desire liquid fire."*

Liquid fire splashed in the hall, like lava, and lit everything with an orange glow. The barks from beyond my view roared and the entire structure shook with an intense impact. Dust fell from the crumbling cement and the stench of brimstone and burning hair flooded the room.

"Get that door open, Alchemist," said the leader with the sword.

"You got it, Borrower," shouted the guy with the book as he charged over to my cell.

"Who are you?" I asked. I had seen a lot of insane shit, and this wasn't any easier to swallow. If I was hallucinating, I was way beyond the scope of sanity.

"Nightmares," said the leader—did they call him *Borrower*?

"What do you want?" I asked, as the roaring continued. "What do you want from me?"

"Get Tony out of there," said Borrower, and Luna stepped over to help. "Now!"

"Why won't it open?" said Luna, while Alchemist sprinkled some kind of powder onto the cell bars and yanked.

"I don't know," said Alchemist as he removed a blowtorch from his belt.

The next thing I knew, we were flying away from the bars in opposite directions. They were flung across the hall, and I was being dragged through the cell, then up the side of the wall. Something had me by the neck, but when I tried to fight back, I couldn't breathe. The more I struggled against its grip, the closer it came to snapping my neck.

"Shit!" Luna yelled. "It's cursed!"

"What's got him?" asked Alchemist.

"A phantom," said Borrower, while the guy with the jagged streaks on his mask growled like an animal, and I got a flash of reflective eyes.

"How many are there?" asked Luna, realigning the glowing skull mask.

"Everywhere," he answered. "Ghosts everywhere." It was like he could see them.

"They're going to kill him," cried Luna, and the dark cell was growing darker while my heart rate slowed. It was the end. I felt the cold begin to overwhelm me.

"No," said Borrower, stepping up to the cell. He pulled a medallion out from beneath his blazer—a strange triangular trinket that sparkled like a disco ball.

"You can't," sobbed Luna, shaking her head.

"This is more important than any of us," said Borrower. "Get that door open! And Claws, nothing gets through till we get him out."

"Right on, brother," said Claws, the man with the glowing eyes.

With that, I passed out—and the next moment, as the darkness surrounded me in a cold, numb embrace, I was falling. It felt like I was falling forever into the dark void of nothing—when a flash, like lightning, lit up the sky—but it wasn't the sky at all. It was a cavern, deep, and in the distance was a pyramid—upside down—its point stabbing into the earth. The sight of it struck a deep fear in me that I startled myself awake with a great big gasp.

It felt like hours had passed, and the sounds of battle were like warbled pops and booms. In reality, I woke up moments later, as the door to my cell swung open and Alchemist and Luna were running toward me.

The Borrower was screaming, and jagged cuts were slashing through his clothes.

It felt like a dream. It felt like a nightmare. It was all moving so fast, and I was just too slow and too ignorant to understand what was happening.

"Can you move?" asked Alchemist.

Luna took her hands and did something that looked like she was turning up the volume on an imaginary dial, then said, "Cocoa bean, espresso caffeine!"

It sounded dumb—it sounded ridiculous—but I was on my feet before the full effect hit my head. It felt like I was turned up to the max setting—energy and awareness in tip-top form, and my sinuses cleared like I had eaten a mouthful of curry.

When we moved into the hall beyond the cell door, I got a clear look at Summanus, still impaled on the flaming spear—his dead eyes wide open, expressing pain and shock. The sight of his body formed a shower of cold sweat along my brow as I scooted away, and I realized just how afraid I was.

The truth was, however, I wasn't afraid of death—I was afraid of losing my mind—and the dark thing crawling on the wall toward us was made of terrors that could have cracked open the sanest nut. It was a man with the head of a jackal, and far behind him at the other end of the hall was the man with flaming fists, stalking toward us.

Borrower was still screaming, the phantoms were tearing him apart from the inside, but he managed to pull himself together and grabbed my jacket as I shuffled past. "Friends," he said, "are the only thing worth fighting for."

I felt like I knew the phrase. Like I had said that once, or maybe someone had said it to me. A thought popped into my head, but it was too impossible to believe.

Claws and the creature crawling on the walls squared off.

"Alchemist," sobbed Luna, "time to shatter."

She was crying beneath her mask, and Alchemist closed his book with a snap and placed a hand on her shoulder. "Friends protect friends. There's a better future coming. I know it."

"Get him out of here!" yelled Claws, just as the thing grabbed him by the arm and snapped it off. Claws let out a massive howl, but the pointy-eared creature—Anubis?—kept on coming.

"Claws!" screamed Luna, and Borrower crawled to his knees and lifted his sword, presenting the next line of defense. In a blink, Anubis twisted Claws' head clean off and flattened Borrower against the brick wall in a smear.

Alchemist backed away as he retrieved something from his belt while Luna put me behind her and placed a kind hand onto my chest.

Luna then said, "Shoo, fly. Save us all," just as Alchemist plunged the head of an old Roman spear into his own chest.

I was pushed, hard, flying through the air and through three cell doors before I hit the dirt in the courtyard beyond the jail, but still within the penitentiary walls. A green spark flashed from where I came, and an eruption of green flames came billowing out after me.

With a second to spare, I rolled onto my feet and ran.

I ran through the darkness. I ran until I found a door and fled.

I escaped the tall penitentiary walls in the space between a chained gate, wedging myself through, and ran until I got tired, and then I kept running. I ran all the way home and I didn't stop to look over my shoulder.

IX

grace falls

TONY

"Why? Why do you believe you are so far gone?" asked Doc.

"What makes you believe I'm not?"

"Tony," he said, "I have had hundreds, thousands of patients in my career. Trust me when I say I've seen much worse than you."

Then he set his pen down, sighed, and gave me the kind of friendly smile that made me think he was underestimating my trauma. After all, everything I had detailed so far was silly kid's stuff—but he'd asked me for my story, and that was what I was giving him, from the top.

"I've had patients that howled at the moon," he said, "who believed they were werewolves. I have had patients that murdered people and did other horrible things. Unspeakable things. But you are, from what I could tell, a good man who has experienced some bad things.

"Trauma manifests differently within people," he continued. "We cannot compare trauma because the human experience is viewed through various lenses and perspectives. I cannot tell you how to feel, but I don't believe you are broken."

"Maybe I'm not broken," I said. "But I'm not whole either."

August 1998
Then.

The town of Grace Falls was different than I had remembered. The year before, the town had felt alive with possibilities—like my future was there, waiting for me. Now, it felt—mundane? Less vibrant? It may have only been in my head, but I couldn't shake the feeling that I wasn't where I was supposed to be.

I left campus to explore the town the very first chance I had and walked every inch of the town square. It was a cute place with privately-owned stores circling a public park with a water fountain and cobblestone sidewalks—including an arcade attached to the bowling alley, aptly named Pin Falls. There was also the Bolt & Shield Comics Shoppe—a place Amanda used to frequent when she lived there—a Malt Shop where you could get any number of custom ice cream flavors, depending on the season—and there was no season in Grace Falls quite like the end of summer.

It was late August, and the town was preparing for the Labor Day Fair. Signs were hung and tickets were being sold, and one couldn't walk very far without someone talking about it. When grabbing a bite at the diner, I noticed their paper placemats were giant advertisements for the town's biggest yearly event, with every coming attraction listed—including the Speed Pitch Booth, sponsored by the Darby Sporting Goods store.

While I was exploring, I took a tour bus out to the falls on the outskirts of town—three beautiful waterfalls that had their own history, not all of it good. A simple microfiche database search at the school library returned quite a few eye-opening headlines…

…including one from 1984 about Amanda's brother, Joey. Reading the newspaper report was a sterile version of the story Amanda told me. How her brother was dared by a bunch of kids from school to crawl out onto a ledge of the largest waterfall—a section referred to as "Goner's

Cross." All to impress a girl. He slipped and fell and never resurfaced after hitting the water and rock a hundred-plus feet below.

Amanda swore she saw her brother years later in the woods behind her house. She told me that once when she was feeling extra vulnerable. I'm not sure she believed it herself.

I wondered if that was what Jacinda meant when she said *Grace Falls has more ghosts than people.*

My exploration of Grace Falls, however, wasn't just about getting to know my new home. If asked, I may have suggested that was the intention, but the deeper truth was that I was searching.

I was searching for Jacinda O'Neill.

Everywhere I went, I was always on the lookout for a flash of crimson hair, but I never once caught a glimpse of her. I investigated every redhead I came across—embarrassingly, that included a mother of two at the grocery store—as if I was Columbo chasing down every lead.

The redhead of my dreams was nowhere to be found. Maybe she had gone away to college? Maybe I was being stupid, but for those entire two weeks I felt as if I might bump into her at any second. As if my love story would start at any moment—

—what kind of stupid, moronic idiot goes to college to find love?

This guy. This guy right here.

Despite my disappointment, I had baseball to keep me focused. There were more ups than downs, but overall, college baseball was much different than the high school program I came from. I knew there would be differences, but at times they were drastic.

At times they were downright chaotic.

August 24th, 1998

At the beginning of my second week, I left extra early for the locker room, while the sun was just rising. I'd wanted to discuss some knee soreness I was experiencing with the trainer, but I stumbled into something totally different. I always had a knack for putting myself in awkward situations, but this time I faceplanted into a powder keg.

The bathroom stalls presented a lot of privacy if someone wanted to clear their mind. It wasn't odd to find a teammate just chilling in an open stall, taking a few moments to themselves. Training was intense at times, especially the way the coaches pushed and pushed. That morning I heard some awkward shuffling from inside a closed stall. I could care less what business others had within that small cubicle of privacy, but when I walked by, on the way to the trainer's office, the door swung open, and I saw something…*unexpected.*

One of my teammates—a guy as big as a freight train—was getting a clear liquid injected into the meaty part of his lower back by another teammate. I didn't need subtitles, I knew exactly what I saw, but before I could move along, they spotted me.

"Hey," said the big guy. He threw a towel around his waist and jogged over to me. "You didn't see anything, right, bro?" The other guy looked frightened, like I was going to rat them out.

It was hard to look at the guy and not feel angry. He was cheating, and we were all in competition for the few spots they had for freshmen on the team. I had occasionally dealt with guys like him in the past, but this time, I underestimated the situation.

"Sure," I said, walking away. Before I managed a few steps, I was violently spun around and pushed into a cinderblock wall.

"Listen, you little shit," he said, with fistfuls of my t-shirt jammed into my neck. He was twisting so hard the stitching popped.

I was above average height and athletic—to hear someone call me a little shit, despite its relative accuracy, was jarring. The guy was a blue-eyed, iron-jawed piece of granite, with a gravelly voice that furiously rattled when he threatened me. It was hard to believe he was only eighteen.

"Get your hands off me," I said, but he didn't comply.

"You didn't see anything, you hear me?"

"Dude, whatever," I said as he shoved me aside then stared me down.

"What's going on in here?" asked the trainer, charging out of his office.

"Nothing," said the guy. "Just looking out for my friend here."

Without wasting another moment, I stepped away and into the trainer's office, letting him follow me in. "Everything okay, Oscuro?" he asked.

"Yeah," I said. "Everything's fine." As the trainer began probing my knee, I asked, "What's that guy's name? The big one?"

I knew the answer before he could respond. It was like I had heard the name before…somewhere.

"Rick Jansen," he said. "Our top recruit. He's a legacy. His family helped build the town, including this university."

"What did you do about the confrontation?" asked Doc.

"Nothing." I shrugged.

"Why not?"

"What would that have accomplished?" I said. "That I'm a rat? I just got rid of a bully from high school. The last thing I wanted was another—especially someone who was twice my size. The guy was a linebacker. You could count every vein and artery in his neck and arms. He was a meathead, and there's one thing you don't do with a meathead."

"What's that?"

"Piss them off."

At practice later that day, I tried to make things right. This was college, not high school. Cooler heads would prevail. I'd go over to Rick, shake his hand, explain how we had gotten off on the wrong foot, and move past it. We were going to be teammates, and if there was one thing I understood, it was having your teammate's back.

"Hey man," I said, catching up to Rick after practice. As freshmen, we had to lug the equipment from the batting cages into storage behind the field after practice. I was carrying a dozen baseball bats, while Rick carried a single catcher's mask. Clearly, he didn't feel obligated to do his part.

"Hey, bro," said Rick, sarcastically, in return.

I was struggling to keep up with an awkward twenty pounds of bats in my arms. It was like wrangling an armful of loose groceries. I said, "Little help here?" and expected a kind gesture—even if it was minor.

Instead, he stuck the catcher's mask on the end of one of the bats and said, "There ya go."

At first, I rationalized it—the guy was being defensive. I'd caught him cheating, and he wasn't about to be cool with a guy who could destroy his college career. I dropped half the bats and said, "Rick, look man, I'm sorry."

Rick stopped walking. In fact, he not only stopped walking, he took a deep breath and turned back on me angrily and shoved his forefinger into my chest, then said, "Sorry for what? What are you sorry for, Oscuro?"

I was confused. I thought it was pretty obvious what I was apologizing for, even though I knew I didn't need to apologize—he was the one cheating, not me. I was merely being deprecating, trying to bury the hatchet. When I shrugged and said, "For seeing you shooting up in the bathroom stall?" I swore he would have buried that hatchet right between my eyes if he had one.

"What the fuck is wrong with you?" He grabbed me by the sweatshirt, again around the collar, then yanked me aside and away from anyone who might see us. I dropped the remaining aluminum bats as I was being flung, and they made the kind of racket Rick appeared to be attempting to avoid. "Are you some kind of faggot?"

"What?" I squawked. "No…" It was a weird question, and one that was none of his business, even if he was honestly asking. That specific accusation seemed to be a top five entry in the book of Bully's Greatest Hits—homophobia was a symptom of their disease.

"Then why were you paying attention to what I was doing in a bathroom stall?" Before I could answer, he continued. "I don't think you understand the pecking order around here. I'm only going to school here because I lost my scholarship."

"Why'd you lose your scholarship?" I asked, and he gripped my shirt so tight I started to choke.

"None of your fucking business," he said. "If you want to survive around here, I suggest you quit the team or get out of my way." Then he threw me to the ground next to a tree and grabbed one of the aluminum bats I had dropped. He swung it around playfully, like he was about to do a song and dance routine with a cane or umbrella, before he bashed it into a tree just above my head. The crack of the impact made my ears ring.

"I'm not going to lose another scholarship," he said with a wicked smile, then left me there on the ground, rubbing my neck.

"Neither am I," I said to myself.

August 26, 1998

The Wednesday before Labor Day was move-in day for all remaining students. The chaos started at 7:30 AM when a random guy in a hoodie, flip-flops, and mesh shorts stumbled past my door, dropping a lamp onto the floor—and it never let up.

It was a roar of white noise for no less than ten hours, as families cried their goodbyes and idiots tried skateboarding in the halls while others were still moving their stuff. I heard a bunk bed collapse two doors down and a girl fighting with her boyfriend over the payphone. I wasn't one to enjoy the quiet, opting for music or TV in the background as I completed mundane tasks like cleaning—but by noon I was praying the noise away to whatever god could hear me over all the commotion.

It was almost 3 PM when I heard a knock on the door and found a tiny Asian guy standing there with a plastic garbage bag over his shoulder.

I wasn't sure what was happening.

"Are you gonna let me in?" he snapped. When I stepped aside, he bounded into the room and stopped at the center. "What a shithole."

"Are you my roommate?" I asked.

"Who do you think I am? The garbage guy?"

I noted the black plastic bag slung over his shoulder. "Are you the garbage guy?"

"Was that racist?"

"Was it racist?" I asked, confused.

"Nah, I guess not." He laughed. "Brad."

Brad tossed his bag at the wall and shook my hand.

"Tony."

"Which bedroom's yours?" he asked.

"We have to split two bedrooms. I've already claimed half of that one," I explained, pointing at the far side of the room toward the open door. You could see a pile of clean, unfolded clothes on the top bunk.

"Fuck, we have to share?" Brad snatched his bag and flung himself into the empty bedroom. As soon as he disappeared, there was a second knock at the door.

When I answered it, the guy on the other side stared at me like he had just seen a ghost. He was black man with a Wu-Tang t-shirt and a goatee that surrounded a kind, chubby face.

I said, "Hi," but the guy continued his blank stare. I recalled several roommate horror stories I'd heard from older teammates.

Eventually he said, "boo," and rushed into the room. "What's up homie! Oh! Wait, I mean, roomie!"

"Nothing much," I said, overwhelmed by the strangeness of both personalities.

"Marshall," he said, dropping his things to provide a firm handshake. "Good grip there, buddy, you must work out." Then he winked and grabbed his bags.

"Tony," I said. "Hey, we have to split bedrooms. Two and two."

"You've settled in to that one," he said after peering into my room. "So, I'm going to set up shop over here." He took two steps toward the other bedroom when Brad stepped out. "What the fuck is that!?"

"Huh?" said Brad.

"Oh," said Marshall, "I thought he was an action figure. Or Legos or something."

"Fuck you, asshole," said Brad.

"He swears too!" said Marshall, who spun and walked the other way. "Well Tony, looks like I'm bunking with you. The little guy scares me."

"Brad and Marshall. They sound like quite the characters."

"Yeah," I replied. "Our fourth roommate never showed up. It was just the three of us the first year. Brad and Marshall made my transition into college life easier. Brad was a moody guy with a big heart, and Marshall was a loyal jokester who became my best friend—and believe me, I needed them."

September 12, 1998

I wasn't sure what I'd expected, but the reality of college wasn't it.

I woke up early to hit the gym, a mandatory obligation for all student athletes, then showered, dressed, and ran to my first class. After class it was reading, studying, and homework until my next class, with a quick bite in between, followed by more reading, another class, a snack, and then back home for additional reading.

By the first weekend, I slept till noon just trying to recover from the pace.

I woke up to Brad playing video games in the next room and Marshall cooking lunch. There was nothing more jarring than gunfire and explosions when sleeping, and I managed to incorporate them into my dreams—a restless dream, struggling to find the redhead of my fantasies in a creepy forest patrolled by dark soldiers.

"Hey roomie!" said Marsh. "Want a cheesy griddled square?"

"What?" I grumbled. I had different phases of awake—there was barely awake, sort of awake, and alert—and I was still transitioning between asleep and barely awake.

"A grilled cheese," he clarified. "If you're gonna be my roommate, T, you're gonna have to keep up the pace. Life goes fast. I go faster." Then he shoveled one of the sandwiches he was cooking with a hot plate onto the spatula and looked at me. "Coming in hot!"

Marshall launched it, but I didn't move. I didn't even flinch. The sandwich landed on the sofa with a soft plop.

"What was that?" I asked.

"A flying hot grilled cheese," said Marshall, still blinking at me. "I thought you played ball."

"I do, but not this second," I groaned.

"Whoa!" said Brad from the couch. He was still shooting things on the TV. "Who left this grilled cheese here?"

"T, you look like old dog shit," said Marshall. "We're only one week into the semester. How are you going to survive the next three months?"

"It's hot!" shouted Brad.

"It's called a *grilled* cheese, ain't it?" shouted Marshall.

"Bro, what kind of cheese is this?" he asked with a full mouth.

"Cheddar and brie," said Marshall proudly. The man took his cuisine serious. Especially comfort food. He'd made pancakes earlier in the week with peanut butter, bananas, and strawberries. He could cook a full meal with just a hot plate and a toaster.

"What the fuck is brie?" asked Brad.

"Cheese!" both Marshall and I shouted together.

"Oh, dang," he grumbled. "Didn't have to be rude about it."

Marshall turned back to the hot plate and began spreading butter on two new slices of bread, preparing them for the skillet as I grabbed something with caffeine from the mini-fridge—a two-liter bottle of soda with one gulp remaining. It had been full the night before—a thrilling reality of living with roommates.

"What do you fellas say to some roommate bonding?" asked Marshall.

"Like what?" I asked mid-yawn.

"Can't say," said Marshall. "I've only been here a week."

A big explosion sounded from the TV, and Brad put his hands in the air to celebrate—one with the controller, the other with a half-eaten grilled cheese.

"The town square isn't bad," I said. "There's also a mall on Gossamer Drive."

"A mall?" shouted Marshall. "Listen, roomie, I'm from Philly and no self-respecting bootstrapper from the hood is going to spend his first weekend away at college in a townie-infested mall."

"Yeah, but we're only eighteen?" I said, and Marshall gave me a patronizing look.

"I hate fucking townies," said Brad. "And malls."

"That's surprising," said Marshall.

"Why?" asked Brad, taking the bait.

"Because you get all your clothes from the Sears children's department."

"Fuck you," said Brad as he stuffed the remainder of his sandwich in his mouth and turned his attention back to the game. Then he started laughing and said, "It's actually true."

"Okay," I said to Marsh. "If not there, then where?"

That night, with the help of Brad's connections, I did something I never thought I'd do—I took a fake ID and used it to get into a bar. I looked every bit below twenty-one—Brad looked like he was fourteen and his height didn't help—but Marshall did all the talking.

"Hey, my man," he said as we approached the bouncer—some guy with a mean face and a meaner belly that sneered suspiciously as we approached the door. "My roommates turned twenty-one over the summer, and we are looking for a good time."

Brad whispered to me, "That sounded like a lie."

"Is it actually a lie if he says it loud enough?" I joked, but I was nervous and ready to run if things went sideways. A layer of perspiration miraculously appeared on my brow the moment the bouncer grabbed my ID and began to compare.

"You're wearing the same shirt," he said.

"Am I?" I asked, then shrugged like I had never heard something so preposterous.

Marshall's eyes widened like he had seen a ghost.

Brad facepalmed, then played it off like he had an itch.

"Alright," said the bouncer, handing the ID back to me. And somehow, some way, by Marshall's undeniable will, we got in.

"What did I tell you guys?" he said as we entered the crowded room.

"That brie is fancy cheese?" said Brad.

"That I did, Bradley," said Marshall, "That I did. But also, that we would not be denied this night. No, friends, we would not be denied."

The first time I walked into a bar was overwhelming. I found myself questioning etiquette. Do we go to the bar? Do we grab a table? Or do we wander around like livestock? But most importantly, I didn't know what to do with my hands—should I put them in my pockets? Fold them? Nothing felt natural and I was drowning in my own self-doubt.

Marshall sidled up to the bar between two different groups and wedged enough space for Brad and I to each fit a shoulder in.

"What a night, fellas!" said Marshall. "This is the place to be."

He wasn't wrong. The bar was filled with people our age and slightly older. The bartender was gorgeous, with a smile that kept the tips coming—and there were more women in one place than I had ever seen in my life. All we had to do was tell the cab driver to take us to the best bar in town, and this was where we ended up—somewhere near the mall, which almost sent Marshall into fits.

"If we end up at a TGIFridays, I officially went to the wrong school," he proclaimed as we drove by.

But it seemed like a cool place, with TVs tuned to football highlights and a loft with dim lighting and party booths. I recognized a few guys from the baseball team and settled in.

"In hindsight, it was a dump—and Down The Hatch was a much better bar in the town square—but, we'll get to that later…"

"I feel like you're stalling, Tony," said Doc.

"Do you want me to tell my story, or not?" Then I added, "If I don't tell it the right way, you won't understand."

"Okay." He nodded. "Continue."

We were there for a few hours, getting to know each other. I learned that Brad was adopted and from upstate New York. That he was the oldest of three and wanted to open up his own business. Marsh was from Philly—a bad neighborhood, and we shared the common heartbreak of being a Philly sports fan. Like me, he had a rough childhood, and we bonded over that. I think that was the start of our friendship. He wanted to be a chef, or a writer, maybe a lawyer or cop, perhaps even an engineer—really, he had no idea, but he was the first person in his neighborhood to go to college, and he was determined to be a somebody.

By the third hour we were chatting up a couple of girls next to us—upperclassmen at Milton who didn't believe we went to school with them. When I turned back to the bartender for another drink, I caught a flash of red from across the bar.

At first it only momentarily snagged my attention, like I'd caught the flight path of a housefly, then lost sight of it a second later—but then it reappeared through the crowd and became more prevalent—the long crimson locks swayed as she walked, like an avalanche of red in a dreary, colorless room. I slipped away from Marshall and Brad and began moving through the crowd to intercept her as she headed toward the door.

"Bro, where you going?" asked Brad.

"T?" questioned Marshall. "Where's he off to?"

"I don't fucking know," groaned Brad. "I just asked the same thing!"

The crowd had thickened since we arrived. It was now standing room only, sometimes three deep in line to the bar. It was like trying to walk through Disney World in peak season, and I was attempting to maneuver upstream. Weaving through people was an art form, shifting and saying "Excuse me" just loud enough for them to hear, but not so loud as to sound like an ass—an art form I failed to master as I chased down an opportunity that evaporated over every second wasted.

She was moving fast—like a phantom, sifting fluidly through the crowd like water through a colander. She was surrounded by three other girls, two brunettes and a blonde, and as they passed through the front door and by the bouncer, I had just stumbled my way out of the crowd.

The night was chilly—the Great Lakes air brought the nippiness of winter almost a whole season too soon. There was a line to enter the bar and crowds of smokers taking long drafts while chatting with friends. It was nearly as busy outside as it was inside, and I almost lost the redhead as she maneuvered away and met up with another group.

I don't consider myself lucky. It was rare that I ever got a fortuitous bounce or had something valuable fall into my lap. In fact, I'd say that meeting Jacinda was the luckiest thing that had ever happened to me. But, just then, when the redhead and her friends walked off laughing, a small wad of money fell out of her purse, causing her to stop to grab it before it blew away.

I thought I had won the lottery.

"O'Neill?" I said as I closed in. "Jacinda?"

The girl looked up at me just as a gust of wind blew her red hair into her face. My head was soaring. The anticipation was exhilarating, and when she stood up and swiped the hair away and said, "Who?" my heart sent a distress call—a mayday, just before it crashed into the side of a snowy mountain peak of despair.

"Oh," I said. "I-I-I'm sorry."

It wasn't her. Her face wasn't even close to Jacinda's beyond the red hair, and even that was suspect—it was a dye job. The girl had brown eyes and wore enough makeup to paint an entire O'Keeffe. I had no idea how I had made the mistake.

I wanted it to be her. I wanted it so bad that I only then realized how fast my heart was pounding and how disappointed I felt.

"Do you have a problem?" said a guy who stepped in between us.

"It's okay, Steven," said the girl. "He thought I was someone else."

"Back off," said Steven, and I placed my hands into the air as if to prove I was innocent.

"Starting trouble everywhere you go, Oscuro," said Rick. He was waiting in line with a few members of the baseball team, watching me embarrass myself. "Who were you looking for?"

"Nobody," I said as I backed away, while the girl and Steven marched off. A few of my teammates chuckled, but not Rick. He was staring at me like I had just confronted him all over again.

"What are you doing outside?" asked Marshall, catching up. I didn't know he was going to come after me. It was the kind of solidarity I would come to know quite well.

"Yeah," said Rick. "Listen to your mother."

"Excuse me?" said Marshall.

"Excuse you," replied Rick, stepping forward as if to invite a fight. I was taller than Marsh, and even I looked tiny standing up to Rick. Then Rick leaned in and said something inaudible that sounded a lot like a racial slur into Marshall's ear.

"Do you have disability," asked Marshall, "or are you just that stupid?"

The situation was going to explode. Marshall and I combined were equal to one Rick, and he had four friends who were watching and itching to prove how manly they were.

I put my hand on Marshall's shoulder and said, "Rick's my teammate. He's just joking around. Let's use some discretion and not do anything unwise."

"Yeah, listen to Oscuro," said Rick. "He knows all about *discretion*."

Marshall nodded and backed down. He saw the odds, and like me, he wasn't a fighter.

"See you at practice, guys," I said, and Rick smiled as we turned and walked away.

"Who's that lunkhead?" asked Brad, finally catching up with a beer bottle still in hand. "He looks like he's one dose away from 'roid rage."

I nearly laughed.

"Rick Jansen," I said. "You know you can't drink that out here."

"Oh!" squealed Brad, who looked left, then right, before deciding to chug the last few gulps. Once done, he handed it to some guy in line. "Hide this for me, bro."

"What happened?" asked Marshall. "We were having a good time, then I see your spooked-ass running out the door."

"Yeah, sorry," I said. "I thought I saw someone I knew."

"You've only been here three weeks. Who do you know besides us?" he asked. "And that dick named Dick with the microscopic dick back there."

"A girl," I said.

Both Marshall and Brad stopped in their tracks and looked at each other with big, cheesy grins. I spent the next hour telling them the whole miserable story—about Jacinda, the prude crows, and Amanda. When I finished, Marshall asked the bartender for a round of shots before he looked me dead in the eyes and asked, "Did you move all the way out here for some girl you met only once, a year ago?"

"Looking back on it now," asked Doc, "did you? Did you decide to go to Milton State based on legitimate reasons? Or was it because you were hoping Jacinda might be there?"

"Looking back," I said, "despite the scholarship, I really had hoped Jacinda might be there."

"Do you regret that decision?"

the echo

TONY
December 21, 2013
Now.

I fumbled with my keys until I realized the front door of my apartment building was unbolted. At times, other tenants would accidentally leave it unlocked, but after all I had been through that night, I was paranoid. It felt like death might creep in.

With the front door locked tight behind me, I hustled over to my apartment door and prayed it wasn't wide open. It was locked, just as I had left it, and my anxieties calmed into an even simmer.

Once inside, I flipped on the apartment lights and took quick inventory of my surroundings. An empty salsa bowl and beer bottles Marshall left behind were still on my coffee table. My baseball bat leaned against the far wall, and my work bag was on the chair, as expected. If someone was going to break into my place, the last thing they would have done was tidy up.

Most of the time, I preferred the dark, but tonight the lights gave me comfort. My apartment had fifteen-foot ceilings and a large bay window with the shades always drawn. The streetlamp outside filtered through the gaps and gave my apartment a soft glow at night. It was a charming apartment furnished with shitty fittings. I couldn't afford real adult furniture and had scavenged for most of my belongings, including a milk crate bookcase and a third-hand entertainment center.

Was I really thirty-three?

Tragedy stunts progress. I still felt like a kid, while the people I once held close to me were moving on into new life phases. Nice apartments with nice furniture, engaged, careers in full swing—maybe even pets or prospects of buying a house. But not me. I was stuck back at the beginning like I had landed on a Chute instead of a Ladder.

I plopped down onto the couch and closed my eyes. What I witnessed earlier that night were the kinds of reality-shattering events that had led to my last breakdown—only much worse. There were a million things I could have done, a million things I could have thought about, but I chose the easiest path. I thought of *her*.

I thought of Jaycie's smile and the memories locked away. It was a masochistic move from a desperate man needing an escape.

I was a total glutton for punishment.

I remembered how she used to play with her hair when she was lost in deep thought, and the way she would hold onto her laughs when she found something inappropriately funny. I thought of the constellation of freckles on her cheeks, and the way she would crinkle her eyebrows when she thought I was being weird. I recalled in perfect detail the way she shrieked with joy and jumped into my arms in celebration when she bowled a strike.

She could be so lucky sometimes…

My emotions got the better of me. I felt like I was going to pop and spatter the walls in decorative Jackson Pollock splats. It was my fault. I let too much through my mental dam.

It was too much.

Living like this was just too much. It was impossible to live when the past was so painful and the future so bleak. And now I was hallucinating—potentially—which made it even worse. My mind was crumbling all over again. This was what I got for spilling my guts to Doctor Hammond.

I was having a psychotic break. I was sure of it.

Pulling out my phone, I tried to find another distraction. I launched some stupid game and got frustrated moments into the load screen. I thought about signing up for a social media account. I could spend time uploading pictures and searching for old acquaintances, but who would actually connect with me?

Amanda?

Years ago, after everything that transpired, Thad sent me Amanda's number and told me to call her sometime. I tried once and got her voicemail. I still had the number, saved somewhere deep inside my mobile account, and with a few swipes on my phone, her name popped up.

I started to craft a text message, then quickly abandoned it after realizing the complete stupidity of what I wrote.

"Hey, it's T. Remember me?" What was I going to write after that? *"I'm having a psychotic break and thought I'd say hi? What's up? How's life? Mine sucks."*

Instead of sending that monstrosity, I did something rash—I hit the "call" button instead.

I heard it connect and ring before I realized I was holding my breath. It rang three times before I hit the "End" button in a panic—just as it may have picked up. But that didn't matter—it was the worst idea in the history of me—and I tossed my phone aside.

My nerves were shot to hell and my hands were shaking. It was time to take my meds. When you've been taking them for as long as I have, you can feel the effects tapering off. I walked into the kitchen, grabbed a dirty glass, and filled it with water. I closed my eyes and swallowed the pills and opened them to a dark apartment. The electricity had shut off with an audible snap.

Every muscle clenched, and the hair on my arms and neck stood straight up.

Creeping back into the living room, my hands groped at the wall until I found the old foam rubber-wrapped handle of my bat. I was ready to bash some brains or go down swinging.

It wasn't just the apartment lights—the streetlamps were out too. The room was as dark as the alley, with only the sparse light of the crescent moon drifting through the window.

Despite knowing every inch of my apartment and spending most of my time inside with little light, imagining what lingered inside the darkness with me was as terrifying as watching *Hellraiser* for the first time in Amanda's living room. She made fun of me throughout the movie as I grappled with a pillow for comfort.

Each step further into the center of the room left me with a less precise understanding of my whereabouts. I thought I was near the entertainment center, but my foot caught on the edge of the rug, and I went stumbling into the wall.

Nice. I'm a freakin' gazelle.

"I remember you being more graceful," said a man's voice. The words were spoken sarcastically and came from the opposite corner of the room. The shadows there were extra thick, obscuring the intruder's features.

"Who the hell are you?" I demanded.

"After all you've witnessed tonight, you come across a stranger in your apartment and all you can muster up is a weak-ass *who the hell are you?*" he said. "You might want to work on being a tad more intimidating."

That did it. Now I was angry. Whatever was going on—if it was paranoid delusions or a home-invasion robbery—I was annoyed and about to take out my frustration on this jackass if he didn't leave immediately.

"Fuck off." I felt as if I could have chopped down a tree with a butter knife. Taking four aggressive steps forward, I lifted the bat to take a giant, raging swing—when the bat disappeared from my hands and my momentum carried me forward without a weapon. "What the hell?"

"Really now?" said the voice. He was no longer in the shadowy corner ahead, but was somewhere—above me? "At the moment, you're way out of your league."

I looked up, following the voice, and saw the shadowy figure standing on my ceiling. His long black hair hung the wrong way—not at the floor like it should have been. Sir Isaac Newton was rolling around in his cramped, rotted grave. The stranger was holding my baseball bat. He placed it on the ceiling and leaned against it. Then he put his face into his palm and took a deep thoughtful sigh, like he had just experienced the longest, hardest day of his life. "I'm all tied up in knots. I tied too many, and now there's too many holes."

My knees buckled and gave way, and I fell onto my ass looking up at him. The reaper, this demon, was stuck to my ceiling, toying with me before ending my life.

"What are you?" I asked. My voice wavered and I sounded childish and afraid.

"Don't fear me. Plenty of time for that. You'll fear soon enough, and in ways you've never imagined," he said, but it wasn't a threat. He sounded tired, and his voice was shockingly familiar. The more I heard him speak, the more familiar he sounded.

"Cool trick. Are you going to keep showing off? Or are you going to kill me? Honestly, I'd rather you just finished it," I demanded.

Oh, so courageous! Invite him down from the ceiling to slaughter you. So much for self-preservation. My psychotic break was becoming a chasm. I was fighting against my own basic nature to survive.

"I forgot how eager you were to die," he said, then shook his head and added, "Too many knots." With his face still planted into the palm of his left hand, he groaned. "Avoiding death—that's instinct—but when you've nothing left to live for, you wait for death to catch up." He paused. "No, I'm not here to kill you. I saved you." Then, in one fluid motion, he dropped to the floor and landed on his feet, gracefully, without much of an impact. The bat dropped a half second later and he caught it without looking up—like a choreographed stage show. "Too many knots. I'm just an echo. Thus, the end of me, and the beginning of you."

My eyes were adjusting, and there was blood below him on the floor, leaking from a great big wound in his chest. I got nauseous just looking at it. I could see bone through the gaping hole, and the erratically beating muscle of his heart. He should have been dead, but there he was—the ceiling-walking undead.

"You saved me? In the alley?"

He answered by lighting both hands on fire. They crackled and popped like kindling, and the room momentarily bloomed with light. Then he extinguished the flames and wobbled slightly on his feet. His long black hair shrouded his face, but there was something wrong with it. Something disfiguring I couldn't make out.

"And on the bus. And in the Penitentiary. Don't forget about those," he said, like he was bragging.

"Sure." Credit where credit was due, right?

"Would've found you sooner, but they moved you around, like they were trying to hide their stash," he said, flailing his hand around in the air above his head. "Fucking portals."

"Who were the others? The people in the masks that got me out of that cell?"

"Old friends," he replied, then sadly added, "Dead friends."

There was a long pause as he sat down on my coffee table. I could hear the creak and whine of his bones and joints.

"The blonde man who attacked you was Summanus," he said, "but I think you already knew that, T." He chuckled and coughed, clearing a wad of phlegm from his throat. "I killed Summanus with a flaming spear. If he had killed you, it'd all be over, and that would be one big pile of fucked-up shit we'd all be swimming in right now. The other was Anubis, but he got away before the blast. They are just two of The Thirteen."

"Stop," I demanded. What the fuck was he talking about? The Thirteen? Like the graffiti message? "Who are you? How do you know me?"

"Of course I know you," he said, like I was being daft. Then he leaned forward and brushed the hair from his face. "I am you. I'm your echo."

At first, the reveal landed like a dry sponge—nothing sunk in. It was like an elaborate joke, only the punch line was lost in translation. He looked familiar, but something was off. Try looking at your own face on an entirely different person and see if it looks familiar. In a mirror, the reflection moves like you; there are no surprises or unpredictable movements. This was much different, much harder to comprehend. It was the same reason I spotted the differences in the mirror-me imposter back in the bar restroom.

His face was worn with cuts and bruises, and perhaps a little older, but not by much. The features were definitely similar, if not equal—he had the same incongruent lip that was slightly thicker on the right side, and a small divot between his eyebrows. Everything matched except for two major differences—his hair was shoulder length, compared to my own tightly cropped mess —and there was a large and very obvious crescent-shaped scar on the left side of his face. It started at the top left eyebrow and curled around his eye, finishing at the cheekbone. It looked old and cracked and simultaneously fresh. I had a similar wound once when I was younger, but it wasn't so perfect and neatly shaped— this scar had purpose, like a brand.

He watched me closely, waiting for a sign that I had acknowledged and accepted his revelation. It was impossible, but I had witnessed quite a bit of impossible today. The question was, could I trust him? Could I take him at face value?

Did I really just make that joke?

I was definitely losing my mind.

"This world," he said thoughtfully, "was not made for you. For me. It was made for people. You and I, we aren't people. We belong to an infamous group. We are Fallen—the guilty. Whatever our crime, it was bad. The balance of power hangs on the head of a pin, and that is our fault. It was our crime that started all of this, and it was set upon our shoulders to right the wrong, without help. Those are the rules. They can't help us."

"They? Who are they? What crime?" I shouted. I was still sitting on the floor, too petrified to move and too confused to sit back and ig- nore everything I didn't understand. What were we? What crime had I committed? I was trying to keep up with his vague explanation, but it was insanity. I had no point of reference or context, and what the hell was a Fallen?

In a sudden burst he was on top of me with hands on either side of my face, forcing my eyes to look into his. He moved faster than I could blink.

"This is going to hurt," he said, and he wasn't fucking kidding. His hands glowed red hot, and my bones felt like they were melting. I wanted to scream, but the heat poured into my lungs and stomach, searing through my veins—it felt like I was getting a jump from a super-juiced car battery. "Stop putting that impure shit into your body. The chemicals. The pills. You don't need them. They dull your mind and prevent you from being who you were meant to be. Purity is important."

In the throes of my pain, I saw an image of Jaycie. She was walking ahead of me, wearing a green peacoat, kicking through piles of orange and brown autumn leaves covering the sidewalk. I could smell their earthy fragrance, and I could hear her laughter as she teased me to catch up.

My mental wall, built with years of therapy and mortared with antidepressants, was completely down. It was gone. And the flood of emotions—the flood of real feeling—came rushing in for the first time in six long years.

When the pain subsided, he was sitting back on the coffee table, watching me.

"I'm sorry," he said, as I shivered. I wasn't cold or scared—the shivers came from years of being asleep. I was finally awake. "Listen closely."

I was staring at the wall, adjusting to the sensory overload—the sounds, the scents, the color, the emotions. He snapped his fingers and yelled. "Tony!" My eyes lurched at him and refocused. "I have done many things I am not proud of to get here. I traveled to realms that men should never step foot in, learned things that prepared me for the road ahead. My road is now ending.

"I never learned what crime we committed, but that's not important right now. What you need to know are the basics," he said, and I nodded my head as the shakes diminished. "Angels, Demons, Heaven, Hell— it's all real, just not the way it's taught in Sunday school. You and I, we're an angel—kind of," he said, then groaned and grabbed his chest. "So much to say, so little time.

"There are two ways to kill our kind. Destroying both eyes will send them back to where they belong. Think of it as a video game respawn straight to jail. Burn them with hell or angel fire—or destroy the heart—

that destroys the empyrean spirit and they cease to exist—no afterlife, just gone. True names even the playing field if spoken aloud. They are your best defense and offense. Names will come to you, and you won't know why, but be glad they do. I never fully understood the magic of names, but maybe you will.

"Paradoxes. They're dangerous, Tony. You know what they are—no Back to the Future shit. No Terminator 2 loopholes. What happens, happened. What was, is what will be. Causality! See some strange shit, like ball-lightning, freezing mist, fucking frogs raining from the fucking sky? That's a paradox. You saw the flicker, right? When you first saw me?"

I remembered it straight away—when he first appeared in the alley, two flaming hands, reality bent and wavered like old movie film going off track. "The paradox is catching up to me. I'm just a remnant, after all." He said it thoughtfully, like he had just learned something new. "Never mind that—Fallen can feel them, like ripples in a pond. Cause too many and the world, the whole fucking world, breaks apart like a plate smashing on the floor—they'll come and snatch you right up, Tony. Don't cross your own timeline, if you can help it.

"And the Thirteen. The motherfucking Thirteen are coming for you. They are vicious. Remember Doctor Celestine's Theology and Mythology classes in college? You'll need to remember. They were once angels, living as gods on earth. Now they're after you, and that's my fault."

"Why?" I asked, as he clutched his chest. He was dying and putting forth all his efforts into staying long enough to say what needed to be said.

"Because I poked the wasp's nest," he said with a smirk. "Do you have a Sharpie?"

"What?" I asked, then pointed to a cup next to him on the coffee table. He grabbed one of the permanent markers and took my left hand, drawing something quickly on the inside of my wrist.

"They'll be coming after you sooner or later. Because you have it. You have it, don't you?" he asked, then nearly buckled over in pain. I didn't get the chance to reply that I had no fucking clue what he was talking about when he continued. "When I'm gone, you'll have to fix this. You see, time is linear, like a long piece of string spreading out to infinity." He removed a strand of thread from around his neck and dangled in front of me. There were several knots in various places along its length. "You and I, we are one piece of string that runs parallel to Earth time. We don't exist here. We do not belong here. We exist outside of time, in the Empyrean Realm—Heaven, if you want to call it that. I found a way to break free of Earth time, in case I failed my mission, if I made the wrong choices, I could fix it—" Then he grimaced, stood up, and pounded his fist into his forehead, like one does when they forget something stupid. "Except we only get one do-over, and I just used it to come here, to you. Tonight is your awakening. You must do whatever you can to stop the insanity. Find a way. It won't be easy. You'll need help. Earth has rules about time. As long as you still breathe, there is hope.

"There will be a time—and it will be different for you than it was for me—" he said. His voice was manic, excited one moment, sadly preaching the next. "That you will have to make a choice. It will be a very difficult choice. I made the wrong one—I tried to end it before I was ready—but you, if you make the right choice, you will only be faced with another choice, and another, until you either succeed or fail. Tony, you may just find a way."

"What do I do? How do I know what choice to make?" I asked, choking on my words. I couldn't seize the actuality of it all. Was he talking about time travel? What was a paradox? And what—how—who—why was a thirteen after me!? It seemed far-fetched and so much bigger than me. My logic fought for every inch, screaming like hell to wake up.

"I can't tell you that. It was different for me. Things are already different. Things have changed." He coughed four hard hacks into his hand, and a spatter of blood appeared on his chin. He quickly wiped it away and continued. "Their leader, he will do everything in his power to destroy you. He will come after the people you love. He will try and crush you."

Then he stood from his seat on the coffee table, and I did the same from the floor. He stepped over to the bay window, then opened the curtains to look outside. "Death is coming for me," he said. "It'll take you too if I don't finish this." He held the thread in his hands and admired it. "I stole my own Thread of Fate. Do you know how fucking insane that is? What I had to do to get it?" I shook my head as bloody tears fell from his eyes. "One more thing to do. If I die before I tell you this, it's all over." Then he placed a hand on my shoulder. "Remember this. Try and memorize it, if you can." He ignited his hand and held it just below the thread, then looked at me sadly. "In a realm beyond ours, they speak of our world like fairy tales, just as we speak of theirs. I discovered one there about us—

"Thirteen Evils hunt Four Keys to open Eden.

Between two hearts, One maid torn.

The Light and the Dark, duality born.

If Her Love be true for the Righteous or Wicked,

Be with heart, with mind, with body, and soul,

Dominion shall be granted over all that is known.

So it was seen, so shall be done.

The Raptor against Thirteen,

The Spirit must become One."

Then he backed away from me and lit the thread with his hand. "Let her be your inspiration, Tony. Never let her go. Tomorrow's not a promise." His body ignited along with the thread, and as he dissolved into the flame, I heard his last words within my own head. "Too many knots. Sorry, T. This is going to hurt. A lot."

XI

mutiny

MALUS
December 21st, 2013.
Hours Ago.

The path through the caves was a journey deep into the earth. It was an intricate labyrinth, past monoliths depicting old gods and through chambers filled with unexplained technology from a society that rose and fell before the first man stood on two legs. It was an enormous underground mausoleum, and the dead were plentiful. I could feel their unending torment fueling me with their ghastly power, building me up like a chemical high. It was one of many strategic choices to dwell here, with an army only a necromancer could utilize.

Chernobog once ruled this underground city. An evil entity so powerful and ancient that it appeared in many cultures across many lands. The black god, they called it.

Yet even Chernobog was not the first terrible master of this dark place.

The time of those primordial gods had long since passed when angels fell. The Fallen became gods—demanding worship, loyalty, devotion, and most of all, love. We all craved the one pure thing we were denied. Some of us found fulfillment in new, dark, twisted ways amongst mankind.

Yet to say *amongst* mankind was like saying lions lived *amongst* rabbits. Our urges, our needs, were too much. We would feast on them, meddle with their lives, fuck their women, and slaughter every last one of them for nothing more than the twisted satisfaction of the challenge.

No, we could never live amongst them. We lived in ancient places, old and abandoned to time and memory. Shrines built to us, symbolizing our power, our greatness.

We were great once. We would be great once again.

I stalked through the next hall and approached the large stone archway—the entrance to the Sacrificial Chamber. The archway was a magnificent specimen of art, celebrating the grotesque powers of the lost civilization's gods.

Inside the chamber were two rows of monoliths with a stone altar at the end, and an open space where the masses gathered to witness ritual sacrifice. Evil seethed within the room at the countless atrocities committed within. Skulls and hideous beasts adorned the rocky wall face, gently illuminated in the flickering torchlight.

This place was my home—and there was a traitor in my house.

"Nemesis!" I shouted. I was rancorous. I wanted destruction.

The warrior goddess appeared at my side, stepping out of the Veil to do my bidding. She was clad from head to toe with trophy weapons won in battle. Her face was streaked in war paint, and her dark hair was braided. One could hardly tell there was a goddess of magnificent beauty beneath the warrior. "Bring me the Seer, now!"

Nemesis rarely spoke, and in my rage, I would have torn my most loyal servant apart if she had questioned me.

The Sacrificial Chamber came alive as the eyes of gods opened. They slept in shadow, passing time in the Dream Lands until needed. Immortals, like humans, preferred their time in fantasy over reality. The difference was, immortals had experienced all Earthly pleasures—love, hate, lust, war—and reality became empty. Boredom fueled our slumber until we could bear witness to excitation.

There were whispers amongst them.

Loki appeared, lounging on the altar, eating an apple and playfully tossing his hammer. He looked smug, like he was enjoying my frustration. The black storm shadow of Summanus glided away from Loki, like a child concealing his association with a troublemaker. Summanus's eyes gleamed like silver as he shifted into a shadowy crevice. He was not interested in my anger.

We were Thirteen in all—though some remained absent.

Loki, the trickster god, with his dead brother's hammer.

Summanus, the god of nocturnal thunder. An infernal assassin.

Thanantos, the god of death and plague.

The Morrigan, the phantom queen. Goddess of war, destiny, and fate. Her black feathered cloak like a shroud of blight.

Mammon, god of greed and covetousness. Perpetually thumbing his golden coin.

Hekate, goddess of magic, Queen of the Unseelie—hiding her face beneath a white owl mask.

Nemesis, goddess of retribution, with her enchanted and cursed weaponry—a collection of the fiercest Divine Devices.

Bacchus, god of wine and bloodlust—sipping blood from a golden chalice.

Dagon, the fish-god. Demon of the deep.

Astoreth, goddess of fertility, sexuality, and war. Naked and feared—her curves like glass edges. Supple flesh as hard as diamond.

Moloch, our newest member, the bull-headed god. A beast so large and ferocious, he dwarfed us all.

And Anubis, god of death, the jackal-headed god—master of alchemy and the arcane.

There had been others. Some were lost. Some had their contracts revoked. Together, we had no equal. Even a holy choir of angels could not withstand our might—when we were focused on a common goal...

Unaligned, however, we could tear ourselves apart.

Their mutinous whispers were about me, questioning my capability. They were concerned about the girl—the dead spirits in the room told me so. Did they truly believe I did not have spies everywhere?

Of all the Thirteen, Loki trusted me least. His hair was wild, blonde and unkempt—A reflection of his inner turmoil. He was after all, a Trickster. Nothing he said or did could ever be taken at face value. There were always ulterior motives where Loki was concerned. He twirled his trophy through the air like a child's toy—a large stone hammer with runic carvings, stained with the blood of its victims. It was Mjöllnir, Thor's Hammer, which Loki took from the Thunder God's lifeless body after he and his children destroyed Valhalla and set Asgard ablaze.

If I must be sincere, without Loki's contributions and the loss of his child, Jormungandr, we would have never found our prize.

As grateful as I was for Loki's sacrifice, I grew tired of his persistent undermining attempts at my position. Still, I had nothing to fear. There were contracts, and nobody of *this* world knew my true name to break them.

"Still plotting, Trickster?" I asked.

"That depends. How long have you been listening?" asked Loki with a smile.

"You have a new trinket," said Mammon, eying the trophy from the mouth of Votan. It dangled from a leather cord and stood out like a star in the night sky against my black shirt. "Tell us, Master, what is that you wear around your neck?" Leave it to the god of greed to take note of invaluable items. He leapt from the shadows, snarling like a coyote from beneath his ratty red hood. His taloned fingers played anxiously with his lucky gold coin, like a prestidigitator practicing his craft.

"Nothing that concerns you," I said when Nemesis returned with the prisoner, but she was not alone.

Dagon and Astoreth accompanied her—the latter of which had her diamond-sharp claws across Nemesis's face, ready to destroy her ancient gray eyes.

The fish-god's black cloak concealed his tentacles, like a cephalopod, wrapped around each of Frigg's limbs—the last around her throat. The excruciating pressure applied torqued her body unpleasantly.

"What is this?" I spat.

Mutiny.

By the time my mind decided on the proper response, I was impaled from behind by two great horns. They burst through my stomach and lifted me into the air. The beast, Moloch, had gored me, as Bacchus and Mammon shackled my wrists with their great strength, angling them to break and dislocate bones.

The pain was immense, but I laughed at the level of coordination it took these traitors to perform such a miserable insurrection. Loki sat idly by, swinging his hammer and watching, as Thanantos stalked into the torchlight. There were many things in the room that were built upon nightmares—Thanantos was the worst of them.

"In your absence, we have decided on new leadership," he said, his voice as deep as the pit itself. He spoke like a demon—cold, dark, and forever tortured. Thanantos's body had begun to decompose long ago, caught in a perpetual state of rot. His flesh was shaded in violet and putrefaction, held to the bone with straps of old black leather, staples and stitches. He removed his sickle—the Adamantine Sickle—the blade had killed Medusa and disemboweled a god—and smiled at the disturbed thought of using it. His smile ripped the stitches that kept his mouth from falling away from the jaw. "Where are the contracts?" he demanded.

"On me," I laughed. "Tattooed to my skin."

A furious wince crossed the death god's face. By inking their contracts onto my flesh, I guaranteed two things—1) They had to kill me to break the contract, and 2) in order to kill me, they had to break the contract—thus creating a paradoxical pact.

"Ask the Seer to tell us your true name, so that we may break our contracts," growled Thanantos.

Or they could speak my true name.

I said, "Go to hell," then laughed maniacally at the absurdity of my words. My laughter was cut short, turning to screams when my guts spilled to the floor in a steaming pile of organs and bile.

Thanantos licked his sickle clean and waited for my screams to end. The divinity of the blade kept my body from healing.

Pain was purifying. It could remove all fickle thoughts and leave a mind clear and precise. Sometimes pain was the only thing I still felt.

"Where is the girl?" he asked.

"What you seek from her cannot be obtained by feasting on her flesh," I choked as blood erupted from my throat. "Power that pure must be given freely."

"We shall take what we want," he said. "Ask the Seer for your true name."

When I killed Frigg, I created a contract between us—different than those between myself and the other Fallen within this chamber. She belonged to me and could not answer questions from anyone else. She was bound to me and my ring.

Bacchus and Mammon twisted my arms, threatening to rip them from their sockets, as Mammon clawed my hand for the ring. They were paying too much attention to me and not enough to the wild card in the room.

The hammer struck Moloch so hard, it nearly caved his skull inside out. The mighty bull god dropped a steadying hand to the floor, and I took care of the rest.

The air went ice cold as an invisible force of the dead scratched and clawed at Moloch before he could retaliate, slashing deep gashing welts all over his skin. His great bull head roared as he stammered on his hooves until finally falling to one knee.

Bacchus and Mammon followed, forced to bend the knee by the dead. The dead kept them pinned, unable to move or flinch.

I retrieved my guts from the floor and willed my body to heal as Thanantos swung his sickle for my chest. His blade never struck. The rotting arm of the death god stuck into thin air, inches from my heart. It wasn't the dead that stayed his hand, it was the contract.

"Does anyone else challenge me?" I screamed, as rage began to heat the air around me. I recalled my inner hellfire, letting it furiously burn just below the surface, and held it there as a deterrent. The air reeked of brimstone as my temperature rose.

Dagon released Frigg and fell to his knees of his own accord, followed by Astoreth. Nemesis spun, seeking retribution, but my dead restrained her as well.

I needed them. I needed them all.

One by one, they fell to their knees.

Loki stepped to my side. "Any one of you shits lift a fucking finger, and I'll crush your fucking face."

"Frigg," I called to the undead goddess. "You lied to me."

Her misery dissolved in an instant, replaced by a glimmer of hope. She'd lied to me on purpose. She wanted my wrath to release her from this world.

"My Lord, I cannot lie to you," she said.

"A spark attacked me in the temple of the Lost City of Giants. I slayed the mighty god Votan and took the Key of Aries," I proclaimed, holding my prize above my head. Mammon snarled, still unable to move—the god of greed should have grabbed the key while he had the chance. The white ivory key, along with the other three, had great power; they all could sense it.

"You went alone?" asked Loki. He wore a maniacal smile to mask his own displeasure. "You keep that filthy whore locked up, away from us, and then you go after the final key on your own?"

I could sense the piqued interest of the others, filling the room with anticipation. I was their leader, I was the one with the vision, the one who found the *loophole!* I gave them their part. I selected them. I gave their pathetic existence new meaning.

Maybe that was why I went alone—to prove that I could do it on my own—but I was wrong. The spark proved that.

"You have a contract," I said. "I do what I please."

I told them what they needed to know. They knew the girl was *special*. They knew about the keys and Eden. Was that not enough?

I was more powerful than any one of them, but all twelve combined? Contract, names, or not—I could not defeat them all at once.

"You said there were none who may oppose me," I stated, my eyes boring angry holes into Frigg.

"No," she said weakly. "I said there is not one *alone* who may oppose you."

She had tricked me with words. I should have paid more attention. "Who is the spark that attacked me?" I growled.

"He is Anthony Oscuro. Born to father, Martin Oscuro, and mother, Carol Oscuro. Anthony alone is nothing but a Fractured spirit of vast unimportance. The Raptor. He is one of many, born from dust to dust. As he is, there is no threat to you."

"No threat, indeed," I growled.

Then she continued with a conniving smile. "He currently dwells in the city of Philadelphia, but your paths have crossed many times. You are—"

I ended Frigg's half-life with a snap of my fingers. She was about to say something…unwise? Unfortunate? Her body collapsed and she ceased to be, at one with the Unbecoming. She was clever. She forced my hand.

"What the fuck was she on about?" asked Loki.

I paced the room and released the insurrectionists from the dead. "The Raptor? From dust to dust?" I questioned aloud. Frigg had spoken in riddles. "The spark was not a serious threat, but there is always more than one spark. A shattered spirit is rare—but there are always many pieces. This one in particular had knowledge and abilities that made him dangerous. We cannot underestimate any god, Omen, demon, angel, fallen, demi-god, or spark who seeks to oppose our plan." I gave Frigg's words another thought, then added, "Born from the dust of the beginning, till the dust of the very end. We must wipe them out of existence."

"Summanus," I called, "summon the Baba Yaga. Mark Anthony Oscuro's spark and destroy him." Then I turned to the rest and said, "Fill your mouths with the blood of the spark. Destroy them all from beginning to end. Go. Kill them all. Every *mark*. Every last one of them. Be back by sunrise."

Frigg called him The Raptor. Sparks were Fallen that fractured to pieces as they fell from grace—fractured by force as they fled the attacking Host. A single spark was part of a larger, powerful spirit, forced to live as human, incomplete.

I needed to know more.

The Thirteen fled into the next room, where the ancient tribe dumped the bodies after their ritual sacrifices, letting them drain and rot. I stood in the doorway and peered at the half-eaten carcass chained to the wall. They were the remains of the Titan, Chronos. He was still alive, and likely conscious of his existence in some manner of speaking, but the chains that bound him were no ordinary chain. Zeus bested his enemy and enslaved him in the Chains of Prometheus. Then with the Svefnthorn, a magical runic glyph, he put the ancient Titan into a half-sleep—both awake and asleep at once—in the hope of learning the Titan's power over the pathways of time.

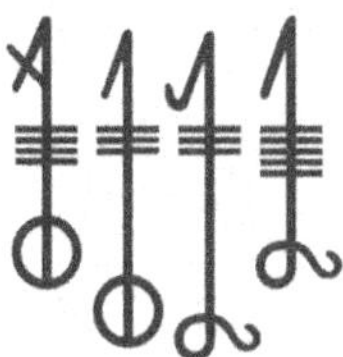

Where Zeus failed, I succeeded. Hidden within the Titan's flesh and blood was the answer to mastering time. With a single bite, one could travel anywhere in time and space, but there were limitations. One bite equaled one jump to wherever and whenever they chose.

They each chewed their allotted flesh and vanished.

"Trust between demons is folly," I said without turning. Loki was behind me, groping his hammer. "We are fated together if we are to succeed." Then I swallowed my own pride and said, "Thank you."

The grin on Loki's face widened, exposing more teeth than was possible for a single mouth to hold. "I love chaos, thrive upon it, but a Trickster always knows when there's need for order. I do whatever I do for me. When the time comes, I will take what is mine."

"So be it," I said, as Loki stepped forward, took two bites, and vanished.

The screaming started soon after they left. Her shrieks echoed through the house like a wailing banshee, relayed to my attention by the dead. By the time I arrived at her room, she had entered into hysterics. She banged on the door, the walls, and the boarded windows, frantically searching for a way out.

"Help me! Please! Somebody!" she screamed.

I calmly waited outside her door until she drained herself into an exhausted heap of nerves and tears, then prepared to enter her room.

She was special, and I dared not go in without a plan. There was too much at stake, so little room for error.

"Wait here," I said to Nemesis. "Do not let her out."

Nemesis was the only one I trusted. She guarded the girl when I was away, preventing the other Thirteen from making a serious mistake.

I opened the door by breaking a series of charms and unlocked an ancient Celtic knot that held the door closed. When I stepped into her room, she skittered into a corner behind the bed.

"Let me go!" she cried. Her blonde hair was a frayed mess of curls, and her blue eyes were soaked in tears. I could hear her pulse from across the room and taste the panic wafting off her skin. Her green dress with yellow embroidered flowers was dirty and torn, and she shivered at my every movement.

"No," I said. She sank against the wall, then broke into hopeless tears.

The house was once owned by an eccentric who had disappeared, leaving it conveniently abandoned. Like the rest of the old four-story estate, her room was structurally weak and decayed. The floor was uneven, the walls were crumbling, and mold grew behind the plaster.

Her room had a single bed in the corner with a dirty mattress. There was a table beside it, which had warped from the dampness of the room, and a glassless, cheval mirror frame propped against the wall. There were two boarded windows, allowing only modest shafts of light into the room, and nothing else.

"Where am I?" she cried, as she brushed the blonde hair from her face.

"My sweet, Lilly," I said, "don't you remember?" My Lilandra. My special Lilly. She was my prize. Or rather, she would relinquish my prize to me. "This is our house, and you are my fiancée."

She shook her head, confused.

The human brain was malleable. Memories were relative constructs. The difference between dream and reality was as thin and flimsy as wet paper if one had the means to manipulate them.

But that was the trick. Her mind was fractured and disconnected—a disassociated personality swimming through a sea of faceted memories. Her impressive will repulsed all attempts at breaking down the walls of her reality—so instead, I placed a new reality on top of the old, suppressing her mind.

Heart, mind, body, and soul. All four had to be mine before the clock struck midnight on the last and final day of the year—ten short days away.

The means to manipulate and control those four human pillars of love and devotion were through reality-altering spells called glamours. With them, I could control her experiences, and through the combination of my unique *gifts*, I could make her love me.

But even my pride had to bend. There were others more capable—others I could offer a contract if need be.

Inside my glamour, the walls were freshly painted, and the sun shone into the room on the chirps of songbirds. Lush green plants grew under warming rays of light, and the mirror happily reflected Lilly's imaginary world. It was "paradise" within four walls. A day inside her room could be weeks inside her mind, or, if I so designated, merely a second. If I so chose, we could dine in Paris or view the sights of Venice without ever leaving the confinement of her locked room.

Within the glamour, she saw only what I wanted her to see. She felt only what I allowed her to feel. I was in complete control, confining her mind and body to the stimuli I projected in order to mold and bend her will, to make her surrender. But every few days, her resilient will broke free—and it was beginning to happen more frequently.

"Please! What do you want from me?" she asked. She was terrified of me.

Inside the glamour, she also saw me differently. I was her true love.

"I want you, mind, heart, body, and soul," I said. Her reaction to my words was expected. She spat curses and hurled threats and took me for a lunatic rather than her warden. I had no interest in earning her affections—the glamour provided that for me.

When her hysterics evolved to anger—I could smell the fear turn to rage—I quickly put her down with a simple charm. "Sleep." The word had no sooner left my lips when she fell to the floor, unconscious. From there I could rebuild the glamour over time, like a castle, brick by brick.

"You know what they say, my love," I said. *"The race is not to the swift, nor the battle to the strong.* Rest now. We have just ten days till we are married. There is still plenty of time to make you love me."

My Lilandra was the most important human in all existence. An extraordinary girl. She was an anomaly, a paradox. A *loophole*. And so, to keep her safe and protected, I cohabited with her. In a house on a hill, old, rotted, and conveniently surrounded by the dead.

G.A. FINOCCHIARO

THE BRIBING OF MAMMON

983 A.D.

There was once a cave in a barren land, far from civilization. Within it was an amassed treasure that could not be rivaled by king or country. That cave was filled with more gold and jewels than any other collection of wealth in the entire world. All of it—every coin, necklace, ring, and crown—stolen, won, bought, or traded, but only when it was convenient. Most of the treasure was soaked in blood, both literal and figurative.

Mammon sat upon his mound of treasure, content to flip his favorite coin. He let it tumble over his foul fingers and performed sleight of hand tricks like an accomplished prestidigitator, passing eternity with his love—wealth.

When Malus found the cave, he entered Mammon's sanctuary with careful precision. There were traps for man, angel, and god alike, ready to be sprung if one so dared to steal even a single coin. Each step was carefully taken, every lump in the sand carefully scrutinized for magic or machinery meant to maim or murder.

After avoiding no less than six traps, Malus crossed the threshold into the cavern filled with gold. The sparkling metal reflected the sparse light and set the whole room glittering. Nearly every surface shone, reflecting his own visage back to him like thousands of eyes tracking his every move. It was then by chance that he spotted a shadowy figure behind him, reflected in just one glittering jewel.

Malus waited until the shadow was nearly upon him. He spun and raised his blade but found nothing there. The jewel's reflection maintained the shadow's presence, now just two steps away.

It was a trick, and Malus had tricks of his own. He let himself sink into the Veil, the world that overlapped reality, and slipped behind the shadowy demon.

Mammon stopped his advance and smiled viciously. "Looter! Come to steal my gold?" he accused while routinely flipping his favorite coin.

"On the contrary, I have come to add to your wealth," said Malus, reappearing behind the god of greed.

"Strangers do not come here to donate treasure. I am no fool, stranger," hissed Mammon.

"I have not come here for wealth or treasure but to offer an opportunity. For you, I offer every bit of gold and silver, every gem and jewel-encrusted artifact, every crown and king's ransom that your greedy heart desires. All I ask in return is your hand in a complicated task," explained Malus.

"How can I be sure you can fulfill such an offer? As you can see, my temple is filled from floor to ceiling with treasure. One can never have too much wealth, but to imagine my current wealth increased by infinite proportion arouses me, Pale Demon, and yet I am suspicious."

"For one that has so much wealth, greedy Mammon, is not the thrill of accumulating more than even you could imagine a risk worth taking?" asked Malus.

A few moments passed as the greedy god weighed his cynicism against his avarice. "How shall we proceed?" asked Mammon.

XII

the moon and the stars

TONY
Then.

"Do you regret that decision? Do you regret going to Milton State, in part, for a girl based on a single night's interaction?"

The doc's question was valid. Something I had asked myself a thousand times before. "Yes. I regretted it. Especially after what happened next."

1999-2000

The first few months flew by faster than I could stop and think. I blinked and was back home for Thanksgiving, and then rushing through the last few weeks of the semester with finals. Before too long, the frosty winter was thawing into spring, and all the training throughout the fall and winter were starting to coalesce into everyday practices.

There was one and only one thing I was looking forward to—playing my first game as a Milton State Red Devil.

"My dad arrived the day before our first game and took me and my roommates to dinner. There, I had to tell him I wasn't playing—in fact, I wasn't even going to be on the active roster. All that training, all that hard work for nothing."

"How did your father respond?"

"He decided to come to the game anyway and root for us. Then he said he wanted me to keep pushing. Work hard. Practice hard. He said the coaches would notice."

I felt like I had disappointed everyone who had supported my decision to play baseball three hundred thirty miles away from home. I watched as guys like Rick Jansen earned starting roles, and I was angry keeping his cheating a secret.

It was a tough time for me. I dropped out of classes that made me happy, like art and design, and took easy classes for easy grades so I could dedicate myself to the baseball diamond. I was too busy to make friends, and Marshall and Brad rarely saw me, as I was hitting the gym and taking extra practice.

The more dedicated I became to the team, the more isolated I felt. Whispers in the locker room fueled my growing paranoia, and it always felt like Rick Jansen was in the middle of it. I felt like an outsider, and the harder I tried to become a part of the team, the more I felt like I was falling behind.

Then tragedy struck.

I was tracking down a line drive deep into the outfield, and as it sliced overhead, I leapt. I don't know how high I jumped, but I heard cheers a split second before the groans. My mitt snagged the ball, and as I fell back to earth, someone else occupied the spot where I was landing.

Some say they heard it, but I didn't hear the pop so much as I felt it rattle my body—like breaking off a drumstick with a wet thunk.

"Hey Dad," I said from the hospital payphone. "Listen, I—uh—I blew out my knee."

"I bet that was a hard conversation to have with someone you didn't

want to let down."

"Yeah. You know, all I ever wanted was for him to be proud of me. To see me succeed so he knew I'd be okay in life. That I was a winner," I explained.

"Do you think that's what he thought of you? That you weren't a winner?"

"I think when he died, it wasn't with the greatest confidence in his only son."

January 21, 2000

I spent that entire summer rehabilitating at home. Thad, Chris, and John swung by to visit a few times. Their college experiences were so much better than mine. I felt like I was missing out. I felt like the world was spinning and I was standing still.

One day, toward the end of summer, I saw Amanda at the grocery store. I hobbled down a snack aisle and exited the store before she saw me pretending to compare bags of Cool Ranch and Nacho Doritos. I was avoiding any kind of awkward confrontation. I didn't want her to see me in a knee brace and depressed.

When school started up in the fall, I re-enrolled in the art classes I'd dropped the previous year, and things started to improve. My knee was healing, the brace was off, and I attended my first college party.

Marshall and Brad were extra friendly with girls from another dorm who were hosting a floor party. They hyped it up as a party I'd never forget, and they weren't wrong.

We arrived sometime after ten, and it was already wild—a girl puked in the hallway as we entered the floor, chucking up chunky vodka-soaked bits that Brad thought was the funniest thing he ever saw.

"Yup, it's a party," he said, and clapped his hands like he couldn't wait to get on his own path to puke-town. "Man, kids these days can't hold their liquor."

"What's the room number again?" I asked as we sidestepped a balance-impaired couple making out, flopping from one side of the hall to the other.

"Uh, four, something-something," replied Brad with a shrug, and I realized they were lying to me the whole time.

"What the hell, man?" I groaned. "I thought you guys were friends with these girls?"

"Friends?" questioned Marshall. "More like good acquaintances."

"Acquaintances? How'd we get invited?" I grumbled.

"My excellent eavesdropping skills," explained Brad.

"Oh my god, you're basically creepers!" I said incredulously.

"Am not?" shrugged Marshall, half-agreeing to disagree that he wasn't agreeing to anything I just said.

We swam through crowds of drunken coeds for almost an hour, searching for two random girls none of us knew. I felt like a minnow in a sea of people. It was hot, dark, and the music was too loud to interact with anyone. Everything strobed and pulsed, and in a blink, I lost Brad and Marshall—both off chasing their white whales.

I learned one very important thing about college floor parties that you don't learn by watching TV or movies—they are hot as balls—as hot as big, hairy, humid, juicy, balls.

I felt sick. I was overdressed and the movement made me nauseous. Rather than sweating it out in a corner, I made a break for fresh air. I forced my way to through the crowd to the nearest exit and hastily into the stairwell, barging through the doors and sucking down huge gasps of cool air. My insides felt hot, like I was going to melt from the inside out.

"You have impeccable timing, Oscuro," said a gravelly voice. "How's that knee?"

Rick Jansen was standing down a flight of stairs on the landing below, surrounded by friends and teammates. They were looking up at me, wide-eyed, like I had caught them in the act of scandalous activity.

"Healing," I said after establishing a few deep breaths.

Rick's gaze lingered on me suspiciously before he turned away and leaned into a shady guy wearing a Steelers cap. He discreetly removed something from Rick's hand, then patted him on the shoulder and left down the stairs. Then Rick and our mutual teammates climbed the stairs toward me like a pack of wolves, narrowed eyes gauging my level of trustworthiness.

"Good to hear," said Rick, as the others surrounded me passive-aggressively, like they were attempting to intimidate me. One of them, our ace pitcher, got so close to me that I thought he was going to hit me—or kiss me—I couldn't decide which. I had been in this spot before, but this time, I didn't have Amanda slipping condiment bottles into my hands like pepper spray.

Someone pushed me from behind, and I slammed into someone else—who then took offense and shoved me back the other way. Fists were clenched, then suddenly—

"Fellas," said Rick. "Cool it."

They listened, though they weren't happy about it.

"Bro?" questioned Ace.

"Get lost," said Rick. It took a long drawn-out moment, but they eventually dispersed through the doors into the party, leaving Rick and me alone on the stairwell landing.

"Sorry about that," said Rick. "The guys, they just don't trust rats."

"I'm not a rat," I said.

"Good," said Rick, patting me on the shoulder, then gripping it extra tight. "I'm glad to hear you say that. I mean, I'd be willing to help you out. You know, an awful injury, you just getting back on your feet, literally. You might need something to help get your edge back."

"I appreciate that," I lied, "but it's not for me."

"Suit yourself," said Rick, and he sounded disappointed. "Hey, it's a party, right? Want a hit? Free for a friend."

In the palm of Rick's hand was a small plastic baggie the size of a nickel holding something that looked like sugar or flour, but I knew it wasn't either of those things.

"No thanks," I replied.

"Are you sure?" Rick asked. "You look like you need it."

"Nah, I'm good."

I realized then, that Rick needed me to take it, because then he would have control over me. He'd have dirt on me. Without it, I had control over him, whether imaginary or not. The only way to trust me was to put us on equal ground. What he never understood was that I wielded the power I had over him merely in the interest of being left alone.

"Suit yourself," replied Rick. "So, listen, I'm sure you know not to speak of this. Our interactions are beginning to make me wonder about you."

"Wonder about what?" I asked. His tone was friendly, but the implication was threatening.

"Teammates need to trust each other. So far so good, you haven't said a thing, but I want to ensure you remain a good teammate."

I was never a good liar. I had the kind of expressive face that left nothing to subtext. When I looked at Rick, I looked at him as someone I couldn't trust, really didn't like, and actually loathed, even though I nodded my head and said, "Sure."

"Good. Good man, Oscuro," he said as he patted my shoulder again, then took my hand into some kind of buddy-shake I was unwilling to participate in. He gripped my hand so tight he popped veins in his neck. "Keep rehabbing that knee. We need you out there next year. Gotta earn that scholarship."

With that, Rick Jansen and I were firmly off on the wrong foot for the second year in a row. And to make matters worse, that was also the night I met Julie.

"Who's Julie?" asked Doc.

"A freshman. I bumped into her outside the men's room. The queue for the ladies' restroom had gotten so long she decided to "switch sides," as she put it. It really doesn't matter who she was. She was the first in a long string of awful women."

"Elaborate."

"Okay, so the way I met Julie should have been a sign. To her, I was nothing more than a flavor of the week. We dated hot and heavy for a few weeks and then it was over as fast as it started. No discussion, no notice. I went to her dorm room and found her there with two guys."

"Oh."

"I can't say the rest were any better. I felt like an experiment. Like these women were just toying with me."

"A lot of people view college as an opportunity for education, but also

for the opportunity to see what they like and don't like," he explained.

"The problem was, Doc, their experimentation came at my expense," I said with a sigh. "And my wallet."

"So, you had some bad experiences, and—"

"Hah, no," I laughed and shook my head. "It was a lot of bad experiences. One after another. I was stood up, dumped on New Year's Eve, slapped, laughed at, ridiculed, used, embarrassed, and my favorite— robbed, all within a span of four months."

"Sounds like you had a lot of opportunities."

"Maybe. I think I was just chasing a dream."

"A dream?" he asked.

"Yeah. I wanted to find someone who saw me the way I wanted to be seen. Someone I connected with. Someone who understood me."

"That kind of chemistry takes time to develop," said Doc. He had a point, but he wasn't there back then.

"You're right. It does, but if you're seeing early red flags, isn't it smarter to move on?"

"I suppose."

"I was miserable, Doc. I always felt like I was missing the point— like I was missing my purpose."

"From our short time together," he said, "I can accurately deduce that you are at your best when you feel like you are in service. When you play baseball, you are conforming to the team. One part of the whole. When you are loved and in love, you are in service to the partnership. When you have a close friend, like the friendship you had with Amanda, you feel devotion and purpose. This is not unique to your life experience. Many people struggle through similar situations."

"How do I fix it?"

"You're not broken," said Doc.

"I am broken. I'm very broken," I said, and couldn't stop myself from crying right there on his couch. "Who's going to hold my hand when I die?"

The Doc gave me space to sort myself, though I knew he was perplexed and wanted me to elaborate. We were getting ahead of ourselves.

After composing my emotions, I said, "Then one night, I thought

I saw her."

"Who?"

"Jacinda O'Neill."

April 13th, 2000

"Hey man, it's not all bad," said Brad. "At least you got laid." He was chilling on our couch watching *That 70's Show* and eating a huge bag of Doritos. I had been visibly depressed for months, and my mood was finally starting to sour my roommates as well.

"You'd get laid too if your farts didn't smell like nacho cheese," groaned Marshall from an old rocking chair we lifted during last year's trash day. Brad unleashed a wicked fart and laughed as Marshall and I ran for cover into the hallway. "One day, I'm going to murder that kid. In his sleep."

"We could do it right now and nobody would know," I suggested, half joking. "He'd fit into a suitcase. We wouldn't even have to cut him up."

"Tempting. Instead," said Marshall, "why don't we go down to the quad for some food, maybe hit up a movie? I hear there's a new vampire flick playing. I know how you like those suckers. Come on, it'll cheer you up."

"Nah," I said after considering his offer. "I'm gonna go for a walk."

Marshall didn't try and stop me. He knew I needed to sort things out on my own. Living in tight quarters for nine to ten months a year was hard, especially when all you wanted to do was get some peace and quiet.

It was a brisk April evening. The sun was down, and campus was quiet. I had no destination in mind, so I walked and kept walking.

I walked so far, I ended up in downtown Grace Falls, and sat on a bench by the fountain in the town square. The fountain was donated by a Philadelphia artist, who created it after touring the town's waterfalls. It was a three-tiered fountain, with the moon chasing the sun around a globe held on the shoulders of Atlas. Water sprang from the globe in three spots—symbolizing the three waterfalls of Grace Falls—and into the pool below where satyrs and nymphs playfully shot water into the air. The tentacled arms of the Kraken reached up from the lower pool to spill the second tier into the third. There was a plaque bolted into the concrete that read, "We all shine on, like the moon and the stars and the sun." A John Lennon song.

I stared at the fountain for a long time, deciphering all the symbolism—like a cross between art history, and my mythology and theology classes with Dr. Celestine. Then finally, I rested my head and gazed up at the stars.

There was a crescent moon in the sky, and I heard the words "Nice to meet you, T who plays baseball," dancing in my head.

As I sat there thinking about that night, two-and-a-half years earlier at the Labor Day fair—the thought of the "girl who got away" filled me with such frustration that I nearly thought about leaving. Why did I wait so long to try and kiss her? Why did I even come to Grace Falls? Why was I such a loser?

Reliving regrets made me feel worse. It was getting late, and I had to start walking home.

Just beyond the town square was a corner bar—the kind that catered to locals and university students alike—called Down the Hatch. I couldn't get in, I was only twenty at the time, but the applause from inside was enough to grab my attention, just not enough to keep it. As I passed the bar to the opposite corner, then jumped the curb beneath an old tree, a loud noise from above stopped me.

CAWWWWWW!

A crow was throwing a fit, cawing and squawking as I walked by. It was that simple pause, when I looked up at my feathered friend, that changed everything for me. The sound of an acoustic guitar and a voice, like a memory, hung on the air.

I paced back toward the bar and attempted a peek at the performance through the cloudy windows, when her beautiful voice hit the chorus. She was singing "Instant Karma (We All Shine On)," the same Lennon song embossed into the fountain plaque.

My pulse quickened, but my eyes needed to see for themselves. I had to know. I rushed to the door and was immediately rejected by the bouncer, despite my fake ID throwing him for a loop. I tried begging, then bribery, and settled on simply asking who was performing, but the bouncer refused on all accounts.

Dejected, I waited outside and listened for the next twenty minutes, until she wrapped her set with a "good night" and a "thanks for coming out," without so much as a name drop. It was another fifteen minutes before the side door opened, where the dishwasher was taking a smoke, and a girl with blazing red hair stepped out into the cold night air with a guitar case in hand.

"Hey, good set," said the dishwasher.

My body paced toward her on cruise control. The side of the building was dimly lit, but if I could just see her face—even a glimpse would have been enough for me—to know it was her.

"Thanks!" she said, approaching a red cabriolet parked along the side street.

As I opened my mouth to call out her name, the words catching in my throat, a figure stepped out of the shadows and stopped me with a stern hand to my chest.

"Hey man," said a guy with sandy blonde hair. He had a small scar above his right eye and an unlit cigarette hanging from his lips in the kind of way that spelled trouble. "Got a light?"

"No, sorry," I said, then shrugged him aside.

I silently cursed my bad luck. Did I need another obstacle to prevent this one simple thing? But by the time I had evaded the guy who went out of his way to ask me, and not the smoking dishwasher for a light, the girl had already gotten away—her taillights glowing as she drove off.

I kicked at a crushed beer can and cursed at myself for letting the opportunity pass.

When I turned back, ready to growl at the stranger for stopping me, I was alone. The dishwasher and guy with the scar were gone, leaving me with my angry thoughts.

It took over an hour to walk home, and by the time I got there I expected both roommates asleep, either in bed or on the couch. However, when I opened the door, I found Marshall and Brad entertaining a third.

"Where the hell have you been?" yelled Marshall, leaping to his feet.

"Yeah, you were gone so long, they sent your replacement," joked Brad.

"What?" I asked, as the third guy, with sandy blonde hair and a scar over his right eye, got up from the couch.

"Hey man," he said, holding his hand out for a shake. "I'm your new roommate, Sid."

XIII

reunion

TONY
Then.

"Your new roommate, Sid, was he the same guy from the alley?" asked Doc.

"It was dark, but yes, I think so. There were moments when I felt the world was conspiring against me. That was one of those moments."

"Apophenia," said Doc, and I almost thought he sneezed.

"What's that?"

"When one mistakenly perceives connections between unrelated things. Even if Sid was the guy in the alley, that doesn't mean he was purposely attempting to keep you away from finding out the identity of the woman. Did you ever ask him?"

"No," I said.

"Why not?"

"It felt unimportant. Sid was a cool guy and fit in perfectly with the rest of us. He was a real positive influence to have around, and I didn't want to know—I didn't want to hate the guy, so I let it go."

"Why were you getting a new roommate so late in the year?"

"Apparently Sid and his former roommate didn't get along. Rather than force them to spend the next few weeks in an untenable situation, they decided to put him in an available space."

"I see. So, what happened next?"

"Fate."

October 13th, 2000

By the time junior year started, I was feeling much better. My knee was healed, and I was ready to participate in practice. Adding Sid into the household had brought with it an added dimension we didn't expect. The guy grew up in Grace Falls and knew all the best spots in town. He got us into bars, and we had dormitory Nintendo tournaments playing old games for cash prizes. The guy knew how to keep us distracted and having fun, despite the loads of homework and growing obligations of baseball practice.

It was mid-October in Grace Falls. The mountain weather was getting cooler, and the trees were turning orange and dropping their leaves. It was warm enough that people still enjoyed leaving their homes, but cold enough to wear a jacket and jeans.

I couldn't speak for my roommates, but that was my favorite time of year. It always felt like anything could happen, even the most unexpected things. Maybe that was why I took a chance giving Amanda a call. Thad passed her number to me over the summer and suggested I give it a ring sometime—except she never picked up, and I left the lamest voicemail ever in the early history of cellphones.

"Bro, why are you being such a Debbie Downer?" asked Brad from the couch. We were watching a rerun of a Saturday afternoon low-budget TV show that was akin to *Baywatch* in space.

"No reason," I grumbled. I was sitting in our beat-up recliner with the Kool-Aid stains—or at least we hoped to high-heaven it was Kool-Aid—with my feet kicked up. I was fidgeting, wagging my foot back and forth and distracting Bradley's soft-core-space-porn.

"I don't know, man," said Sid from a beanbag chair on the other side of the couch, "he's looking kinda mopey." Sid was a work-a-holic. I never saw the guy sleep. He was always doing research or taking walks around campus.

"Hey bro!" screamed Brad at the top of his lungs. When no answer came, he screamed it again. "Hey bro!"

"What do you want, my little taquito?" said Marshall, poking his head into the living room from our shared bedroom.

"Fuck, I'm Korean, bro! I'm not some fucking Mexican dish!"

"Have you ever had a taquito?" said Marshall to anyone in the room.

"They're small, fried, and tasty," I replied.

"Exactly!" laughed Marshall. "Brad, my little taquito, what are you yelling about?"

"You guys are such assholes," he grumbled. "Why is Tony being such a mopey bitch?"

"Have you asked him?" said Marshall.

"Yeah," said Brad.

"Nicely?" refined Marshall.

"Of course fucking not!" growled Brad.

Marshall eyed Brad up cautiously. "Such a spicy taquito."

Brad cursed, but I'd learned to tune him out. The guy gobbled up all the sensitivity out of the four basic curse words. Now, if it wasn't an amalgam of three or more, it hardly registered as foul language.

"Hey," Marshall said to me, "let's get some air."

Sid tagged along for a walk around campus. It was early evening, and the sun was just starting to set. The lamps along the campus sidewalks were slowly waking up, and student life was winding down for the day. We had only walked a short distance from our dorm when Marshall asked, "So what's got you down, buttercup?"

I laughed, then said, "It's nothing." But before we paced another ten feet I admitted, "I gave Amanda a call this morning."

"No shit," said Marshall, shaking his head. "How'd that go?" He knew the story. We'd spent many a night up late discussing our pasts.

"It didn't," I replied. "She didn't answer. I ended up leaving a *voice-mail*." When I said the word "voicemail" I made sure to say it in such a way that explained the levels of uber-awfulness saved for the worst pit-witches of hell imbued in that message. "Somehow I mumbled my way through an apology, and I think I accidentally called myself a *dingus*, like five times."

"That's terrible, man," said Marshall. "Sorry to hear that."

"I actually like the word *dingus*," said Sid.

"How does that actually happen?" asked Marshall. "I mean, you have other words. I know. I've heard you use them plenty of times."

"I choked," I admitted. "One moment I was saying hi, the next I was saying sorry and trying to deprecate myself without saying something too damaging—I instinctually started saying dickhead, but I pulled back at the last minute to go G-rated and the D stuck."

"I think the problem is, you don't get your D stuck enough," zinged Sid.

"Wow," said Marshall, shaking his head and stifling a laugh. "Up high." The two high-fived at my expense.

"I lobbed that one right up there," I groaned.

"Sorry, T," said Sid as he put his arm over my shoulder. "We tease because we care."

We walked in silence for a little while, when I heard someone shout, "Oscuro!" from across the quad. Rick Jansen had a way of making it appear like we were friends, when really, he just took every opportunity to show he knew who I was, and that he was watching me. He waved like he was making a statement, and all his cronies laughed at my expense.

Marshall said, "Want me to kill him? I'll jam a few dozen hot dogs down his throat and make him gag on his own homophobia."

"That guy's a total douche," added Sid.

"Do you know him?" I asked Sid.

"A little," he said, but didn't elaborate.

"Where are we going, Marsh?" I asked. He appeared to be steering us at random.

"Have faith, ye of little faith," he replied.

"That's not how the saying goes," I said.

"Ah, but it should!"

"Anybody ever tell you that your jokes are pretty fucking lame?" asked Sid.

"Never," replied Marshall.

"Not true. I said that just yesterday," I added as we crossed the quad.

"C'mon! You don't count!" shouted Marshall. "Everybody knows your jokes are lamer than mine. You've disqualified yourself."

We bantered back and forth for the next several minutes while Marshall led us into the unknown. Marsh wasn't the kind of guy to just do things at random. He was a meticulous planner—his school notes had appendices and his calendar was filled out six months in advance. It wasn't like him to meander, which should have been our first clue.

After a third u-turn, Sid and I were about to mutiny when Marshall finally said, "Aha, there it is!"

"Reitman Hall? The performing arts building?" I asked. "Why are we going there?"

"My friends," boomed Marshall preparing a dramatic speech, which prompted Sid to righteously groan. "There comes a time in all men's lives when the saccharine call of a lady fair beckons a fella to step up his game, and sally forth into the night with his best brothers at his side in order to win her delicate hand for the sake of—"

"Fuck off," Sid and I grumbled at the same time.

"I'm serious, boys!" exclaimed Marshall.

"Who is she?" I asked while rolling my eyes.

Marshall had no trouble meeting women. He seemed to meet them all the time, which was the complete and total opposite of the rest of us. However, he was behaving oddly and was wearing his special cologne—that should have been our second clue.

"Her name is Anne, and there is no maiden more fair than she!" he said, like a royal proclamation. "For real, my homies, she's awesome."

I gave Sid a glance, but he was staring off at a nearby tree with a gathering of birds on a bare branch, like he was purposely trying to ignore the conversation.

"What is it?" I asked him.

"Nothing," said Sid, then looked at me. "Noisy fucking crows."

"Okay, fine," I said to Marshall. "Let's go see this Anne."

"Diggity," said Marshall with a wild smile. That word was his favorite. Marsh was the kind of guy who had to be different. Instead of saying *cool* he would say *diggity*.

The performing arts building was filled with small auditoriums, stages, props, musical instruments, and studios. We walked through a labyrinth of fake trees and passed a rack of hats and bright colored wigs before we reached twenty feet beyond the door. There were students everywhere, rehearsing a theater performance for their upcoming production of *Faust*.

"Where's Anne supposed to be?" asked Sid. "It's a big building. We're not just going to walk through the whole thing and hope to run into her, are we?"

"No, not at all," said Marshall, hiding his guilt.

I looked at Sid and shrugged, "Wouldn't be the first time." It had been over a year, and I still hadn't let Brad and Marsh off the hook for the floor party.

We pushed on into the building and passed a group of violinists. "We must be close," said Marshall.

"Why's that?" asked Sid.

"Those were violins," he replied.

"She plays the violin?" I asked.

"No. The cello."

"So why do you think we're close?"

"I don't know. Similar instruments and all," he responded with a frustrated shrug.

Sid and I fed Marshall a glare worthy of a thousand angry suns and allowed him to walk off ahead of us.

When I started after him, Sid grabbed me by the shoulder to hold me back. "Man, this is not what I wanted to do with my Friday evening," he said, as Marshall wandered around the next corner.

"Yeah," I said. "But he'd do it for us."

"You're right," admitted Sid, albeit apprehensively. He looked like he was weighing a moral judgment but couldn't find the proper way to articulate it. "I have a bad feeling about this."

"Why?"

"Tony," said Sid, looking as cold and stern as ever, "the sooner you come to the conclusion that there are no happy endings, the better off you'll be."

"Wow, Mr. Crappy Pants, who crapped in your pants today?" Every now and then we called Sid that because he could be so dour and dramatic.

"Ugh, never mind."

"C'mon man, we're wingmen. We have to make sure Marsh lands safely." Then I jogged out ahead to catch up with Romeo, but he wasn't there. Not around the corner. Not at the end of the next hall either.

Marshall had vanished.

We ducked into a room or two, but there was no sign of where he'd gone. The man wasn't exceptionally fast, and the mystery thickened. "Which way did he go?" I asked.

"Maybe he found her?" Sid suggested with a shrug. "He's spry for a chubby black guy, ain't he?"

"That's what *all the girlies say*." I finished the quote from an Offspring song. "When Marsh wants something, he goes after it."

"Then why the moral support?" asked Sid.

"Marsh may seem like he's this unstoppable force, but he never had a family. Did you know he was a foster kid?"

"No, I didn't," he replied, as we ducked into a few classrooms to check for any chubby, spry Romeos.

"Yeah, his mom was murdered by some cult-loony when he was six."

"Shit," Sid said under his breath. He said it like he should have known, then looked at me with an inquisitive expression and said, "Wait, didn't you—"

"This way," I said, cutting him off after finding a stairwell to the second floor.

When we entered the second floor, we were surrounded by another mob of students. We waded through and found the next stretch of hallway was quieter, but nobody had seen Marshall, despite the bang-up job the two of us had done at mimicking him as we asked around.

One student told us the stringed instruments department was down the hall to the right, and we set off like Frodo and Sam in search of our bud. We were trading ideas on what we were going to do to Marshall once we found him—I suggested freezing his underwear, Sid suggested putting vinegar in his cologne—when something remarkable caught my attention.

"Have you ever had that feeling like you were stepping into a moment?" I asked Doc.

"Elaborate."

"I had the overwhelming feeling that I was suddenly on the right path. That in the next few steps, I'd find destiny. Like this whole charade to help Marshall find Anne was somehow helping me find my own future."

A gentle trickle of muffled musical tones came from the hall ahead. There was something about it that swarmed my attention—so much so that I didn't even hear Sid's ranting.

The music got louder the further we moved down the hall and seemed to be coming from beyond a set of metal double doors to a small auditorium. A second entrance was twenty feet beyond the first, where the doors swung open and a student carrying a microphone charged through, allowing the music to flow gracefully into the hall.

I heard an acoustic guitar followed by a sweet voice that cut off the second the pneumatic doors released and slammed shut with a loud bang, muffling the music once again.

"Come on," said Sid, tugging at my jacket, "I think Marsh went the other way."

"Hold on," I said, as I walked ahead with Sid apprehensively following. "He's probably just around the next corner."

I felt strange, like I had just arrived home after being terribly homesick. There was something about it, something that made me tingle all over. It was like a wave of relief after being startled awake from a horrible nightmare.

When we passed the first set of metal doors, I took a casual glance through the narrow window, but only caught a glimpse as I kept pace. We continued a few steps to the second set of doors, allowing another quick peek before my body screamed at me to stop.

My heart pounded, causing my throat to throb and my head to hammer. I was emotional, and I couldn't explain why, only that there was some strange, impossible hunch that kept insisting I take a closer look. I stepped back, as if trying to sneak up on something while Sid plowed ahead without realizing I had drifted off.

My mind rationalized that I didn't just see what I thought I saw. It was fantasy. It was fiction. It was just a figment of my imagination, and yet I continued to play along, too curious not to turn back—because, *what if?*

I snuck over to the door, tiptoeing like a cartoon creeper, as if taking another look were against the rules. When I got to the window, I took a long gaze inside, gathering up as much of the scene as I could. It was a dark amphitheater with a lit stage and several rows of plastic blue seats. A handful of students in the corner were putting the finishing touches on a set piece in the shape of a giant cloud. That cloud was one of five other clouds that surrounded the performer on stage like an angel singing in a ray of heavenly light. I only allowed my eyes to look at her last. I was afraid of what I might see—

—and sure enough, I saw *her*.

She had the reddest hair I'd ever seen—a hot fiery blaze of color and warmth. Her locks were long curly waves of crimson, flowing and framing her perfect complexion. I could see her emerald green eyes shine and sparkle in the light every time she looked up from the old polished acoustic guitar she held in her hands. The same acoustic guitar her grandmother had given her when she was just a little girl. She strummed gracefully and sang sweet and powerful into the microphone in front of her. Her voice was stunningly beautiful, with soul and passion, making my heart thrash wildly in my chest and eliciting a name that had gotten lost in my mind over the last few years.

She had become a myth. A legend from a time long ago. I had never forgotten her, so much as I had placed her aside for a rainy day.

Jacinda O'Neill.

It was her, without a shadow of doubt, it was Jacinda. She looked like a dream rather than the faded memory I'd tried so hard to remember until giving up hope of ever seeing her again. She was older, and more beautiful than I remembered, like age had brought forth the woman she was destined to be. Even the way she dressed and angled her head while singing, swaying smoothly to the rhythm of the music, it was all the same. My emotions exploded my chest into sporadic heart thumping that caused an acute case of hyperventilation. My head felt dizzy and my mouth felt dry. My knees felt weak, and suddenly every sense was heightened to emergency levels. Most importantly, a part of me I thought was dead came surging back to life, and for the first time in a very long time, I felt hope.

"Dude, are you coming?" asked Sid. He looked frazzled and sweaty. Frustrated.

I was too busy staring at the girl who got away to acknowledge his question.

"I'll catch up," I finally said, waving at him to go on without me. He cursed to himself and said something indecipherable, then scooted on in search of Marshall.

Jacinda's eyes were glued to her guitar as she played, paying no mind to the commotion around her. The stage crew finished their work and dispersed. Some of them disappeared backstage, while a small group moved up the aisle toward the doors I was peeking through. I backed away as they opened and scampered on without giving me a second look. As the doors hung open, slowly closing with the hissing pneumatic press, I stuck my head inside the room. I hung on every strum and chord, fascinated by her.

I could have watched her for hours.

Then, without warning, the hissing noise cut off.

BAM!

When the door slammed into my head, I saw stars. The world spun, and I nearly lost consciousness. The bang was so loud, I thought the whole building had heard it. But it was the whining sound that came from my mouth when the doors slammed against my head—a cross between a rabid squirrel and a peacock in labor—that left me truly humiliated. I ripped my head free and fell backward onto my ass in the hallway.

"Idiot," I scolded myself as I rubbed my head and grimaced. Did she hear me? Did she see my stupidity? I prayed that just this once my awkwardness would go unnoticed when my worst fears were realized.

"Hello? Are you okay?" she said over the loudspeaker.

Huge trampling waves of dread and embarrassment killed the pain instantly.

I could have run away. I could have frozen. I could have done a million things, but none of them matched the split-second genius I patched together in that moment.

"Are you okay, man?" I said as I walked through the doors on the opposite side of the auditorium—pretending to have witnessed some other idiot's idiocy. "You should put some ice on that."

I strode in like I was sauntering into a bar, cool and confident. Jacinda put a shielding hand above her eyes, to see through the spotlight and into the shadowy seats below the stage. "What an idiot, right?" I used my thumb to gesture back toward the hallway.

"Yeah, I guess," she said with a suspicious half-shrug.

"Smooth," said the doc.
"Thank you."

There was a certain level of comfort I took while she was on stage and unable to see me in the shadows. She didn't seem to recognize who I was, and I hadn't planned my approach this far through. What was I supposed to do? What was I supposed to say? *Hi Jacinda, remember me? Labor Day Fair? 1997?* That was lame. Lame lame lame lame lame!

The seconds ticked by and we both stood there without saying a word. I was frozen solid, trying to come up with something, anything at all that wouldn't sound stupid.

As I waged an internal argument over what to say next, she stepped away from the mic and hopped offstage before I could react. I was dumbstruck and had turned back toward the door when she called out.

"Wait!"

I stopped and said, "Yeah, uh, what's up?"

"Turn around," she demanded. She said it in the most curious and suspicious way, like she knew something was up. She was only a few feet away and moving closer by the second.

"Me?" I asked with my back to her—like she could have been asking anyone else in the empty auditorium.

"Turn around, Tony," she demanded.

I deflated. I was caught. About to burn in a slow horrible death. Like I was trespassing or caught waltzing through the girl's locker room.

I turned to face her with a guilty look on my face along with what was supposed to be a cute, confident smile—but I'm sure it probably appeared more like constipation.

"Oh my God, it is you!" she yelled with a big beaming smile.

"Hey," I said with a geeky wave. Then she hugged me. She literally leapt into my arms. It wasn't one of those polite lean-in hugs—it was a real hug. She smelled wonderful, like strawberries and lavender, and I think I may have had an out-of-body experience.

"What are you doing here?" she asked after stepping back. Her smile was big and bright and absolutely amazing.

"Wait, what am I doing here?" I said defiantly. "What are you doing here? I've been here three years, and I've never once seen you around campus. I think I would have taken notice."

She smiled sheepishly. "I just transferred here. This is my first semester."

"Music major?"

"Yeah. Music production. What was your first clue?"

"Right," I replied, nodding.

"I'm also minoring in literature," she added after catching me staring. I couldn't help but take her in—her eyes, the cute constellation of freckles, her lips—

"I can't believe you actually remember me," I said, speaking aloud what should have remained inner monologue.

"You're Amanda's friend from New Jersey. I could never forget you. How is she?"

"Amanda?" I asked, and she nodded. "I don't know. We haven't spoken in years."

"Oh," she said, then quickly changed the subject. "So, did you like it? My song?" She had another suspicious look on her face, smiling like an evil genius playing an evil little game. She was trapping me.

"I didn't hear anything. Why? Were you playing?" I asked innocently. I wasn't a very good liar, but I was too embarrassed to admit what had happened—that I got my big stupid head caught in a big fucking door.

"Tony, I know it was you. The side of your face is bright red, and your ear is scratched," she said, giving me a prideful I-got-you kind of smile.

"Yeah," I said with a laugh. "Sorry. I saw you from the window, and I—"

"Uh huh, mmm hmmm," she said, mocking me. I smiled, but my blood pressure was up, and I was probably sweating in all the bad places one does not aspire to perspire. "So, how are you?" she asked, quickly bailing me out of my own mess.

"Good, I guess. You?"

"Getting there. I think things are looking up," she said with a twinkle in her eye. My heart wanted it to mean something, a connection, but we hadn't seen each other in years. "So, what are you doing here? You're not a music or performing arts major, are you, T who plays baseball?"

"No," I said playfully, "still semi-undecided. Graphic Design major, I think—but I have a scholarship to play ball. My roommate came down here to talk to a girl who plays the cello."

"Oh?" she said with piqued interest.

"Yeah, Marshall. The way he's acting, he might be in love with her. I think her name's Anne, or something?"

"Marshall, huh? You don't say," she said, something hidden in her voice.

"T, what's up buddy?" said Marshall, strolling through the doors behind us, followed by Sid and a slender girl with dark curly hair—Anne, presumably. "Who's the lovely lady with which you are so gallantly conversing?"

"Hey, this is Jacinda. We met a few years back through a common friend," I said, introducing them—and both Marshall and Sid tried not to appear surprised. They both knew the story, how I met this redheaded goddess named Jacinda when I was seventeen and never let it go. Marsh hid it well, but Sid looked outright flustered. "This is Marshall, and that's Sid."

"What up?" said Sid, as Marshall nodded.

"Hi guys. Call me Jaycie," she replied.

"Sid's from Grace Falls too," I explained.

"Yeah, never met," said Sid, and Jacinda shrugged to admit the same.

"Hey, Jace," said the girl with the dark curly hair.

"Hey. Tony, this is my roommate, Anne," said Jacinda. Both girls had the most conspiratorial smiles I had ever seen—like we had just been caught in an inside joke.

"Hey, uh, hi, Anne," I said, giving her a wave. I quickly shot an inconspicuous look at Marshall, and we telepathically exchanged dreadful thoughts.

I could almost hear him scolding me as he raised an eyebrow. *Did you know about this? Oh, I'm gonna kill you!*

"We're having a party tomorrow night," said Jacinda. "Think we should invite them, Anne?"

"Yeah, I guess we can give them a trial run," she said, playing along.

"Party, huh?" I asked.

Jaycie smiled, and I swear she almost blushed.

XIV

forged

TONY
December 21, 2013
Now.

Agony.

I was being reforged. Tempered with fire and pain.

There was more pain than there was body to receive it. The suffering was constant, like riding a never-ending wave. I was tossed like a ship on a stormy sea. Molten like metal in a smelter's furnace. There was no beginning, no end, there was only searing agony.

I was surrounded by flames, but they did not consume. It was like I was being prepared—fundamentally changed. Crafted into something new.

They all screamed at once, thousands of lives ending and banging away inside my head. There were so many emotions. Too many thoughts and feelings. So much loss and suffering. I felt as though I was slipping away into the darkness, lost in the multitude of individuals fighting for control—fighting for a voice.

Their last moments came to me as a dream and ended as nightmare.

August 5, 1966
Vietnam

"Hey 'Toya!" said Sergeant Murphy. It was informal. Given the circumstances, I supposed a little informality was just fine.

"Yes, Sergeant?" I replied, attempting to sound unafraid. There were few things in this world I was scared of—only bears, alligators, and big fucking leeches. Problem was, I wasn't sure what we were dealing with here, and none of it felt natural.

I could almost hear my mother's voice telling me to say my prayers, but I never saw a man get out of a jam by folding his hands and falling to his knees.

Faith was useless to me. Maria, she was the one with the faith. She made sure Gabriela and Junior said their prayers and took their vitamins. Good mothering—

Sergeant Murphy dropped into the mouth of the foxhole beside me, as silent as a man carrying a B-40 and an M-16 could rumble through the jungle, then situated himself on the embankment on the side, opposite my position. It was dark as hell, hot as shit, and home was calling my name in two weeks.

"Call me Murph."

"I feel uncomfortable with that, Sergeant," I said as I aimed my M-16 into the hole. This wasn't a typical spider hole. The Vietnamese soldiers were a special kind of crafty. Sometimes they'd dig whole systems of tunnels that left us scratching our heads.

We were members of Tiger Force, a long-range reconnaissance patrol unit of the 1st Brigade—and this wasn't the first tunnel we'd found. Last time we went into the *black echo*, half of us didn't come out. The Army paid an extra $10 a month to crawl through the black. All sorts of creepy crawlies lived down there, and I wasn't talking about Charlie.

Have you ever been really good at your job, but hated it? That was me. I enlisted for a better life for Maria and my kids. I wanted to marry that girl, but I couldn't keep my nose out of trouble. If you want to scare a man into going honest, send him to war in a jungle far from home. I'd give anything to be back home with them in Sedona.

"Montoya," he said—it was the first time he had ever used my full name. He had a look in his eye like he was about to suggest something crazy. Sergeant Murphy was known for doing brash things that often went boom. I should know, since I carried out most of those orders. I was a demolition expert—I could disarm a mine in two shakes of a pecker—blow enemy bunkers like I was born for it. "You think it's that *thing*? The jungle demon?"

Sergeant Murphy was referring to some fucking acid-trip story some of the men had been gossiping about like fucking schoolgirls. The whole 1st Battalion 9th Marines were slaughtered on a Search and De-stroy last week. Only a chaplain, Petty Officer 3rd Class John Mona-co survived, along with some kid who kept screaming about "ong ba bi"—a jungle demon. Now my CO had that silly shit in his head, and I was starting to believe it.

Two weeks, man! Two weeks and I was out of this hell hole. Honor-ably discharged. Service to my country paid in full. And I was out here in the middle of this shit?

"I think you need some rest, sir," I suggested as I refocused on the hole and tried not to let such nonsense play tricks on my head. It was a man. Maybe a tiger? Did they have fucking tigers in Vietnam? I had a flashlight stuffed into my belt but didn't want to put a target on my head by shining it around in the dark. "Where's Littleman? Mayweather?"

"Dead," said Murph.

A chill ran up my spine. "Both? How?"

We were camped for the night, with lookouts posted. We were the best of the best. Nothing got the drop on us. Ever. Until twenty minutes ago.

Hunk—this kid from the Bronx with more brawn than brains, but fucken hell he could line up a target—was snatched right out of his boots. His gun went off, and that was when the whole mess started.

Four of us tracked the fucker into the jungle: myself, Sarge, Little-man, and Mayweather. Then we fanned out once we lost sight of him along a ravine. In the jungle at night, there were two shades of dark—

black and black-black—and I saw something black disappear into the black-black black hole after Sarge opened fire.

Now it was just me and Sarge, and the odds seemed to be worsening by the minute.

"I don't know. I don't know what I saw," said Sarge in a panic.

He was cracking. Even the coolest cat could lose their marbles out here. But this was different. This felt very different.

"What does that mean, my man?" I asked, trying not to lose my own cool. If there was one thing that got my wig flipped, it was people who couldn't keep their shit together.

"I saw something. I-I-I just don't know—"

I wasn't supposed to be the level-headed one. I wasn't supposed to be the leader. If I was going to get out of here, I was going to have to pull us out, one way or another.

The hole was dug into the side of a hill and surrounded by plants as thick as the hair on my uncle Jorge's chest—that is to say, goddamn thick—and so dark that he could be sitting right there, listening to us, and we'd never know.

Tick. Tick. Tick. Tick.

There was a ticking sound, like someone had dropped a basket full of matches on the ground, and it was coming from inside the hole.

"My man, what's that sound?" I asked.

"You have a light?" asked Sarge.

What kind of demolition specialist would I be if I didn't have a light? Using a flashlight out here at this time of night was like sending up a flare—so I fished the lighter from my pocket and struck the flint. When the flame lit, I immediately wished I hadn't. All forms of crawly critters were streaming out of the hole—snakes, rats, scorpions, spiders as big as a fucken toaster, and thousand-leggers bigger than the fucken snakes. My boots weren't thick enough to squash bugs that size. It was a parade—they were fleeing something, and I started to get a real bad feeling about—

Sarge had already loaded up the B-40—it was Littleman's—and was about to do something that even I thought was stupid.

"You know, Sarge," I said carefully, "I'm not one to question my superiors, but as far as superiors go, you're behaving entirely un-superior."

Sarge leaned away from the embankment into the mouth of the hole and took aim. He was squeezing the trigger when a flash of pale white skin breached the shadow. Two clawed hands, like a predatory bird, snatched him around the belt, then pulled. He collided with the rim of the hole and broke in half—bent backward at the waist as he was yanked viciously into the narrow opening. His B-40 went off simultaneously, firing wildly into the embankment and exploding on impact just five feet away.

There was fire and blood—and I struggled to remain conscious as a silhouette stood over me amongst the flames.

"Maria," I cried when the pain erupted in my chest and hip. I wasn't going home. I knew with absolute certainty that I was going to die. I thought of my daughter and the way she smiled at me from her crib. I thought of my son and his unrelenting sweet spirit. And I thought of Maria—I could never give her what she wanted—what she deserved.

Something grabbed me by the throat, as a thought drifted through my mind and surfaced from beneath my grief. "Morrigan," I whispered, as the eyes of my killer flashed beneath her feathered hood. Crows circled overhead, while her teeth and claws burrowed into my chest—

April 4, 1892
London, England

"Henry," said Martha, "would you please come to bed?"

She was in her sleeping gown, standing by the stairwell with the concerned look she often reserved for her students. It was no secret that my work had consumed my every waking thought—even nocturnal thoughts in some cases—but it was necessary. I was on the verge of a breakthrough!

"I will, Martha," I comforted her. "Just a few minutes longer."

"My love," she said as she paced over to me at my desk. The oil lamp was running low. Had I really used almost half the font? "You cannot be at your best if you do not get the proper rest."

I sighed. My wife was always correct when she rhymed. She was indeed the better half—sacrificing for us, for our children—and there were days when the guilt was so great that I could not breathe.

"I may have found the key to unlocking the mysteries of dementia praecox," I said, with enough passion that I might have awoken the boys if they had not married, had boys of their own, and lived in houses of their own. It seemed like only yesterday… "My patients hear voices. They see things. They experience reality differently. I think these phenomena could all be interrelated."

"Henry, I understand your passion for your work," she said with a soft smile. "Come to bed soon, my love." She gave me a kiss on my balding head before she left.

I readjusted my bifocals and loosened my tie. If only my wife knew why I was so passionate about my work. I'd never once shared with her about the voices and the dreams. I was as much a patient of my work as those I studied.

Minutes, or maybe hours, had passed when I heard a creak along the wooden floor.

"Martha," I said, "I promise, I will come to bed this instant."

"Eternal slumber, you shall have," said a voice unlike any I had ever heard. The stench was unbearable, and the fright that rose within me was like a mighty tremble.

I was dead before I could speak the word that entered my hippocampus, as if I were recalling a long-lost memory. "Mammon."

October 10, 1632
Kaga Province, Japan

"Remember, even a fool has one talent," I said, before bowing to my students. They bowed in return, respectful as always for their teacher.

"Master Doshin," asked Atsuki after I dismissed them to their daily chores.

"Yes, Atsuki?"

"My father would like to speak with you," he said.

Atsuki's father was one of the village elders I was sworn to protect. If

I was summoned, it was my duty to go. Such a summons was not uncommon. The elders often needed escorts as they travelled the roads from our village. My men and I provided protection from the bandits that prowled the forests. They were frightened of the samurai and often remained hidden when my men and I rode our horses, our katanas at our sides.

Before the sun had climbed over the highest peak, we had been saddled with horses and provisions, leaving at once with a small caravan of goods. Atsuki's father, Hiroki, needed an escort to transport valuable harvests of rice and grains to the market in the next town.

We travelled the road south from the mountains, beyond the rocky foothills and into the thick forest of pine and bamboo, where the panda and the macaque were as bountiful as the crane and duck. The road was worn and flat, which allowed Hiroki's wagon easy passage.

The skies darkened with the eastern wind, and the drifting cold brought an uneasy chill amongst the horses as they clapped their hooves in protest—or perhaps they could sense something more? As the caravan moved on, deeper into the wilderness and the forest path narrowed, something appeared at the center of the road amongst the thinning mist. The form appeared as large as our wagon and remained as still as rock.

"What is it?" asked Hiroki.

I did not answer. I was as perplexed as anyone. We had traveled these roads the prior week without issue, and there were no rocks then, nor foothills the object could have fallen from. I dismounted my horse and commanded my men to do the same as they grew incensed by the growing stench—each man with a ready hand resting on their katana. The situation felt wrong—it felt like a trap.

I walked from my position next to Hiroki's wagon and through the ranks of my men until I was standing at the very front, pacing toward the obstruction.

At first, I thought it was a trick of the eye within the mist. The rocky obstruction seethed as if breathing—like shoulders rising and falling in slow, heavy gasps.

And then the beast opened its eyes and lifted its mighty head.

It appeared more than twice the size of any man, with horns like the mountain ram, but vastly larger and more pointed. Its deep, raging breaths puffed great plumes of vapor from its mighty nostrils, and I immediately understood this beast did not answer to our gods. It did not feel as if it belonged to our land—it was like it had wandered there on accident.

I could not determine what it was, and it quickly galloped off into the forest like an animal. I turned back toward the caravan and gave the signal for the men to remount their horses. It was in that moment when a sense of dread filled me like water into a shallow bucket and the white feathers of an egret grabbed my attention from the corner of my eye. It flew into the air, agitated, and called out in anger. Then a sapling fell, torn from the ground, and dust sprang up in the misty distance.

Before I could shout my warning, the great beast charged into the side of the caravan, flipping the wagon and goring horse and man—ripping them to shreds—then disappeared once again into the forest.

The remaining horses fled in fear, and my men drew their katanas while others inspected the trampled victims for survivors. We could see it coming—the beast charging through the forest, turning wide and rushing toward us—whole trees were broken in half as it roared and leapt free from the thick underbrush. It threw the wagon into the air, tore a horse in half and swung its mighty horns, destroying everything that stood in its path.

We were no match for the beast. A few men ran to save their own lives, those that stayed were slaughtered, and I was the last, defending a broken Hiroki who lay trapped beneath his wagon. My sword was drawn when the beast walked out of the forest like a man upon two legs, facing me.

I had no time to question our bad fortune—what the beast was, or where it came from and why, but something else troubled me. It was like I had envisioned this moment in a dream.

The monster charged me with bloody rage in its evil eyes, thundering like rocks sliding down a mountain. My katana flashed, but it was far too meager a weapon against a creature so fierce, and as its mighty horns tore through my body, I spoke the only word that came to me in my dying moments.

"Moloch."

January 30, 2096
New Delphia, Pennsylvania

My name's Jamaal, and I have a problem. Twenty-two-year-olds are supposed to have romantic problems, or trouble finding jobs in an economy that automated ninety percent of its labor force, with sixty-six percent unemployment and a compulsory sundown curfew. My problem, though, was nothing of the sort.

I had a genius IQ, an eidetic memory, and a sparkling personality with epic levels of snark and charm—however, I hadn't left my apartment in four fucking months. Do you know what agoraphobia means? It basically means I'm afraid of everything and anything that makes me uncomfortable. For a three-hundred-thirty-pound black man with an acute case of social anxiety living in a metropolitan city of more than forty million people—there was a slim-to-none chance that I might have the courage to make it out of my apartment anytime in the next decade.

Pizza delivery arrived fifteen minutes ago. I wired the money via the delivery app by throwing coins into a register on my phone—get five direct shots and earn a ten-percent discount on the next order—then waited for the bot to leave. For some reason my whacky brain told me I hadn't waited long enough for the delivery-bot to vacate the hall. So I couldn't grab my pie—despite the mouthwatering smell and the roiling growl in my always-hungry stomach.

At twenty minutes, I finally gave in and grabbed the pizza before it got cold.

For a guy who can't leave his apartment, you might be wondering how I made the eighty bucks to buy a measly pizza? It's not like they come cheap these days.

How can I put this into humble terms?

"I am the greatest OverCraft champion that ever lived, sucka-suck-as!" I yelled into the built-in microphone of my X-Vision Gen5 headset. In 2096, one could become a multi-millionaire without ever having to leave their couch. I flipped the X-Vision onto my forehead so I could grab another slice—sausage, mango, and ricotta—and demolished it before getting back in game. My rig was top of the line, full haptic response with a built-in port for direct interfacing with the brain's cortex.

"Hey JamAll," said Curtnee4U over the in-game audio. I loved it when she used my handle—tee hee. "Need a partner to raid some interstellar bug pits? I'm looking to grab some loot before I sign off for the night."

"Oh baby, you talkin' dirty now," I flirted.

I liked Curtnee4U. We met once at a virtual café after our Spark Auto-Match swiped right. It was going so well that we disabled our avatars. Reality's a bitch. I thought she was gorgeous—her response was a little less stellar. However, we remained friends—could I have expected anything more than that?

"Let's go! Before it gets too late."

"It's only 11PM! We've got all night to tear this jawn up."

"Jamaal, some of us have real jobs at sun-up."

"Oh, right. Society. Civilization. I've always found that word misleading."

"What word?"

"Civilization. What's so civil about it?"

 She sighed. "You might enjoy reality if you lived it a little more."

"Doubtful," I responded as I chewed on my last mouthful and slid the X-Vision back over my face. But when my eyes focused on the digital interface, there was something there that didn't belong. I checked to see if I had loaded the wrong game. The OverCraft logo was on screen with interstellar marines slaughtering giant alien bugs—however, standing amongst them was some fucked-up weirdo, like something out of a horror game. I never got into the Whisper Hills franchise—those horror games creeped me out and gave me anxiety. The gangrenous monster was staring at me from on top a mound of dead buglings. "Are you experiencing any bugs, Curtnee?"

"Um, yeah! Loads of them. I just mowed down a whole mob of ugly buglings."

"No, I mean a programming bug," I said as I checked the system logs and found nothing but smooth code.

"How would I know? I'm not the one who's a genius," she said.

"I'm sure you'd know," I said as the freak walked toward me and removed a pair of sickles from the skin of his shoulders. His body looked like it was decaying right off the bone—held together by tightened straps of leather. "Hold on, Curt. Let me run a quick diagnostic."

"Ugh, c'mon!" she whined. "Hurry back."

When I removed my X-Vision to run a diagnostic on the headset, the lunatic with the sickles was there in the room with me. Never mind the impossibility of it all, or the fact that it somehow got through my high-tech security system—sunlight didn't even get into my apartment unless I gave it permission—I was frozen. My mind shut down as I felt my condition seize every biological system in my body. I was scared shitless, and I couldn't even defecate to prove it.

"I shall feast upon your flesh and soul, spark," it said. "It will be exquisite."

"Thanantos," I said out loud. The words traveled from mind to mouth—the only function my body was capable of as he gutted me alive.

I could hear Curtnee crying through my X-Vision headset as I screamed in agony.

June 15, 1851
Russellville, Ohio

"Great sermon today, Chappy," said Mrs. Taylor.

"Thank you, Constance," I said. "I am energized by my flock every Sunday." Mrs. Taylor was the last of this morning's congregation to leave the church. I stood on the front stairs waving goodbye as they walked into the sunny afternoon. Once they had all gone, I strolled back into my church and began my own daily prayers.

My father built this church, thirty years ago, when I was still a young man. Ohio was a "free state," but that didn't mean this building and its congregation were accepted. Before the year was over, after the last shingle had been hammered, my father was found hanging from a tree on the other side of town.

I was lost in prayer when the church doors opened and closed. I quickly finished my silent thought and turned back to welcome my guest. I was surprised to find nobody there—perhaps they decided not to come in after all? I went to the doors to welcome in the shy soul in need of guidance and found the front lawn as vacant as the church.

"Strange," I said to myself and shut the doors. The sunny skies had darkened, like a storm was rolling in.

"Is it strange?" said a voice.

She was standing with her back to the window. The light behind her left a shaded silhouette, but I could tell by the halo of light that backlit her body that she was naked.

"Ma'am," I said kindly. "This is a house of God. Could I offer you some clothing?" I began walking toward the closet in the back where I kept clothing and blankets for those in need. "Are you in need of help?"

"I come for flesh, and you offer help?" she laughed. "Are all holy men so short- sighted?"

"My dear, I'm not sure I understand."

Within a single blink she crossed the room, then inspected me curiously by forcefully moving my head from side-to-side. She was beautiful, tan, with long, flowing dark hair and pale gray eyes. I was too shy, too respectful, and too frightened to offer myself a weak look down at her body. Men like me hung for much less.

"Your people came here in chains, yet you pray to your oppressors' God? Not your own?"

"We are all His people," I responded as she ran her icy cold finger down my cheek. It was rock hard and sharp, despite being as supple and rounded as the rest of her body. I felt it cut shallowly through my skin, like a paper's edge.

"No," she said. "I am *his* people. You are *his* toys." She smiled. "Come now, holy man, does your passion not burn when I'm near? Do you not lust for your queen?"

"Astoreth," I said. The name came to me as if someone had whispered it into my ear. Hearing that spoken aloud made her grimace, like I had hurled rotten insults at her.

"You know of me," she said. "But you do not know me."

As another name, a secret name, whispered into my ear, she buried her teeth into my neck and tore me apart like an animal. There were no screams, just the snarling animal masked by the maiden.

NOW.

Like broken glass, my sharp edges were heated and prepared for reassembly. As if on cue, shards of a larger whole were collected from across space and time—lives destroyed but not gone. Instead, they were collected and harnessed, becoming something whole. What it was meant to be—becoming what it once was.

...it came out of nowhere...

...it was evil...

I was a good man...

I was a gypsy...

...I saw it there, within the shadows...

Loki...

...what was that?

I was a King...

I was a carpenter...

...I looked into the eyes of a devil...

Hekate...

...it was there, in the sky...

...how can a man be so fast?

I was a master thespian...

I was a poet...

...it looked at me with hate...

Dagon...

...it grabbed me. I couldn't fight it!

I was just a man...

...I loved her more than I loved myself...

...I would never see him again...

I was a knight, in service to a corrupt King...

Morrigan...

It may have been several minutes, or several hours—days even, I couldn't tell. Time dragged on like an eternity with all of them jammed inside one mind. I felt them all, unique and different, each soul its own life. Hundreds of names and faces—languages and cultures—loves, ambitions, and accomplishments, returned and collected. I was swimming in the thoughts of others. Treading water in an ocean of personalities. Right when I thought I was about to succumb, when the pain and the torment from the raging fire and the overwhelming screams amongst the voices pushed me under, a simple human reminder from Tony Oscuro's era pulled him—me—back to the surface.

My phone was ringing.

It was more like a trill than a ring. Like a computer facsimile of what an old phone ring used to sound like—back when there were rotary dials and analog voices.

I woke up on the floor, naked, and in the middle of a scorch mark. My cell phone was on the sofa, buzzing and ringing until it suddenly cut off. I'd removed it from my pocket last night when I got home and made an ill-conceived phone call, before my *visitor* arrived. Good thing— looks like every item I wore had become ash on the floor around me.

When I finally crawled to the couch and grabbed my phone, there were thirteen text messages. All thirteen were from Marshall, not including several missed calls and four voicemails. Without listening to his messages, I called him back and waited as the phone rang twice before an irritated voice answered.

"What. The. Fuck," he yelled.

"Yeah. Trust me, I'm feeling the same right now," I said.

"No. No! You're not going to disappear this time, damnit! You do this every time—" he said, but I immediately cut him off.

"I'm coming over," I said.

"What?"

I could tell my demand took him off guard.

"I need to tell you something," I said as I got up and paced into the bathroom. When I flipped on the light, the air in my lungs shot out as if I had been punched in the gut. "Oh shit!"

"What? What is it?" asked Marshall.

How the hell was I going to explain this?

"Nothing. I'll be over in a few," I said.

"Okay," was all I allowed him to say before I hung up on him. I was too stunned to talk any further.

Several things presented themselves to me at once in my reflection. For starters, the weight gain I had suffered through since turning thirty was gone—replaced by a flat stomach and biceps I hadn't seen since I was in college. However, the big shocker my fingers were probing was the crescent shaped scar that ran from the left side of my forehead, around my eye, to my cheekbone. It looked like someone had cut my skin with a knife down to my skull, then cauterized it with a hot iron. It was bumpy and ugly, but it didn't hurt—it was, however, hot to the touch. My visitor—the other me—my echo—had one just like it.

There was movement in the mirror—a shadow shifting against the wall behind me in the bedroom. I instinctually moved aside and slunk into a position that allowed me to move from the bathroom to my bedroom. As I stepped through the doorway, I was enveloped by a black nothing. Imagine a room with no walls—just open space that expanded into infinity.

Was I under attack?

I didn't feel threatened. I felt at peace—if not at home. Choosing a direction, I began walking and paced out into the nothingness. After a short while I came upon a man dressed in an old-fashioned wool suit and wireframe spectacles of a bygone era. He was staring at his pocket watch and eyeing me up suspiciously.

"Good morning, sir," he said. He had an accent—British maybe?

He looked familiar—especially the pocket watch.

"Good morning," I replied, checking my naked wrist for the time by instinct.

"I have been waiting for you," he said to me sternly, as if I had made him late for an appointment.

"You have?" I replied, checking my surroundings. It wasn't like I was sitting in the man's office for an important business meeting. "Who are you?" The words left my mouth with less patience than I intended.

"My name's Henry, and I am a piece of you," he said as he removed his glasses and began to clean the lenses on a piece of cloth he pulled from his suit jacket pocket.

"A what?" I replied.

"The only piece, apparently, who seems to have any amount of information privy to this," he said, paused, then added, "situation." He spoke like a well-educated and cultured man. Like an Oxford graduate with the implied arrogance.

"Are you a shrink?" I asked. He reeked of psychological evaluation—like he and Doctor Hammond would be friends. They'd go to the pub and drink a neat scotch while discussing philosophy over a plate of tater tots.

"Hmm? A what?" he replied, baffled by my slang.

"A head shrinker. A psychologist."

"I am—or rather I was," he corrected himself. "What I am—what we are—is something much more."

"I don't understand," I admitted.

"Tony, we need to discuss—" he said, but I was already past him.

"Can't talk," I said, looking back as I paced away. Whatever this place was, I was sure it had a deeper meaning. I was balancing on a psychotic break, and I just happened across a psychologist? When I turned back, I ran straight into a serious-looking Japanese man with a sword drawn to my throat.

"Listen," he demanded. If I moved, even to breathe, the blade would cut me open. He looked like the guy I saw on the bus last night—the samurai who glared at me from the corner.

That's when I realized I was surrounded. They were there in a blink. All of them. Strange men, even a few women, dressed like the extended cast of the Village People—Time Travelers Edition. There were teachers, farmers, pirates, and knights. There were Vikings, cowboys, politicians, and wainwrights. Every nationality and ethnicity were accounted for, even those that had their borders moved and nations renamed or assimilated.

There were thousands.

"This isn't real," I said, cracking.

"You may be right," said Henry. "What is real may be a relative term at this juncture. Are we here?" He gestured to the others. "We are figments of your subconscious manifesting themselves in order to make peace with what you—or rather, we—have become."

"I don't understand," I said. Some of the faces looked familiar to me, as if from a fading dream.

"Hey, my man," said a guy wearing army fatigues and a helmet. He was carrying a big-ass gun, with a sly grin that made me want to like him. "I'm Jose, but everyone just calls me Montoya." He was the army guy who warned me not to go into the bar restroom—was he actually ever there? Or just a figment of my imagination.

"Tony," I said, shaking his hand, which felt real enough.

"Yeah, I know," he said. "We all know you, my man."

"You do?"

"Young man," said an older black man with silver hair and beard. "I think you may want to listen to the gentleman." He was nodding to Henry, who appeared to be impatiently waiting for me to return my attention.

"Do you understand what you are?" asked Henry.

"I wish I knew," I said, unsure what was being asked of me. It sounded absurd to say what my echo, my doppelganger, explained to me last night.

"I think you know, son," said the older man. It was the guy from beneath the overpass. The one who wanted to discuss the book of Genesis.

"I mean, let's be real," said an obese kid with a big mouth. I immediately decided I liked him. "Being an angel is some extreme bullshit, ya know? Saying that shit out loud sounds arrogant as fuck."

"That's true," said Montoya with a nod. "I'm an angel." Then he looked at the kid and said, "How did that sound?"

"Yeah, kinda douchey," he replied.

Montoya then leaned over and said, "Hi, I'm Montoya," and shook the kid's hand.

"Jamaal," he replied—and I vaguely imagined him crammed into the single-engine cockpit.

"Do you agree?" Montoya asked me.

"Total d-bag. And yeah, I guess we're angels?" I replied with a question.

"Partly right. We are not angels. We are an angel. Singular, not plural," said Henry.

"What do you mean?" I asked.

"You, me, and all the rest of us are part of a singular being. One divine being which, for some reason or another, fell from grace. During its descent to this world, its spirit was shattered into thousands of pieces and scattered throughout time. As individual pieces, we were too weak to maintain our forms, so we were given bodies, lives, mothers and fathers. We were given human life, and we would remain human, until a time when we were forced from our bodies and reassembled as one."

"Forced from our bodies? You mean death?" I asked. "But I'm not dead."

"We all arrived here at various times. Many of us as bewildered as the rest, but a few are self-conscious about our predicament. Then we waited for you to arrive. I knew it would only be a matter of time."

"Waiting for me? Why?" I asked.

"Because, sir, you are the largest piece. We are mere fragments of a whole celestial being, and when our lives ended, we cascaded through time and collected into the largest available portion."

"I'm the largest piece?" I asked rhetorically. "What does that mean, exactly?"

"I do not know for sure, but I believe that means you are in charge. Without one voice, we would become nothing but an amalgam of personalities and conflicting thoughts. We are all one, and we must become one," he explained.

"The spirit must become one," I said, recalling something my echo told me.

"Come again?" asked Henry.

"I was told that the spirit must become one. It was part of a saying, or something. It talked about four keys and Thirteen evils. I think this was all meant to happen. That we all had to come together, in order to do what we're supposed to do."

"Perhaps. It does indeed make good sense that the pieces must be collected," he replied.

"One of them killed you, right?" I asked somberly. It wasn't until I stopped to understand what happened to realize how it happened.

"Correct. I was murdered by a rather hideous beast named Mammon. I do not know how I came upon his name, but it was there when he attacked me from the shadows."

"Yeah," said Montoya. "Me too! Mine was some crazy bitch named Morrigan."

"Oh snap!" yelled Jamaal.

"Exactly! Snapped my bones like I was nothing but twigs," he continued. "What about you, my man?"

"Thanantos. Ugly fuck," said Jamaal.

"And you?" I asked the older man.

"Call me Chappy," he said, stroking his beard. "Astoreth. She was called Astoreth, but I sensed more information was available, I just could not get to it in time."

"I am Doshin," said the Japanese man. "Moloch. The name surfaced like a long-lost memory."

"Yeah! Me too!" said Montoya. "I bet we all have a similar story."

There were nods amongst the crowd, but not all were as excited as Montoya. Many appeared graven, even mortified about their situation. A sense of deep loss permeated throughout the crowd.

"They all had lives taken from them," said Henry. "Shattered by these creatures. We all have a common enemy and purpose."

"I'm sorry," I apologized, then I turned to the crowd and said louder, "I'm sorry." I even spotted a French World War II pilot, who nodded at me knowingly.

"Thank you for your sympathies," said Henry. "As I was saying, you are the largest fragment, and therefore you are in control. We are all small pieces of a larger whole, but we each cannot be part of a single consciousness. At least not yet, not until we are fully restored. It is your body, therefore we have agreed it is you who shall be the primary entity."

"What does that mean?" I asked, as the crowd hung on each and every word. Their attention was completely undivided, like they were looking to me to be some kind of entertainment, or preacher.

"It means that we shall become a part of you. We will lend our talents and skills. Whatever we were, you now have at your disposal," Henry explained, speaking on their behalf. "We all know our future is with you—or us, as it may be. As you said…" He reached out and grabbed my hand. "…The spirit must become one."

Henry then dissolved into me. After he was gone, each member of the massive crowd moved forward one by one and extended their hands. Like Henry, they dissolved into nothing, absorbed into me until I was alone in the black.

When they were gone, I turned and began my journey back. The black nothing faded and left me once again in my bedroom.

I needed help. I needed to talk to someone. What if I really was losing my mind? What if this was Northcreek all over again?

I ran for the front door and stepped out into the hallway before realizing I was naked. It took ten minutes to find the proper clothes—jeans, black thermal, Doc Martens, and my brown leather jacket. I pocketed an old zippo and a pocket-knife, texted Marshall that I was on my way, then left at once.

unrequited

TONY

"Did you go to Jacinda's party?" asked Doc.
"We did," I said. "And we weren't the only ones who showed up."

October 14, 2000
Then.

Marshall started getting ready three hours before the party. He showered twice and ran an electric razor for at least an hour. Sid, Brad, and I hurled insults at him from the other side of the bathroom door as he sang "My Girl" to himself to drown out the distractions.

We left an hour late, but only because Brad saw what Marshall and I were wearing and decided he needed to freshen up as well, calling us his "competition."

Jaycie and Anne lived in an apartment building off campus across Main Street. It was mostly filled with students, tired of dormitory life, who could afford it. It was a nice building that put ours to shame, with pest control, working lights, and solid plaster—and that was just what we could compare with our eyes on the way up to their second-floor apartment. Everything was spotless and neat, and the hallway floors were shiny—not sticky.

After a small debate on who should knock, Brad decided he was man enough, and called the rest of us female genitalia before making three hard raps on the door. When nobody came to answer, he tried again—knocking continuously until Anne finally opened.

"What up, gorgeous," he said. "My name's Brad, but you can call me B-Rad." He then took her hand and brought it to his mouth, kissed it, and genuflected like she was royalty.

"Don't mind him," said Sid as Anne stepped aside to welcome us in. She was still at a loss for words when I passed.

"We have to let him off the leash sometimes," I added.

"If he starts humping legs, we'll tie him to a fire hydrant," said Marshall. Anne gave him a hug, and the two of them scooted away, leaving the rest of us to fend for ourselves amid a total sausage-fest.

"Sausage fest?" asked Doc. "I'm unfamiliar with the term."

I shot the doc a raised eyebrow and said, "Tons of dudes." He nodded with a smirk and allowed me to continue. "They had Jaycie surrounded. I almost decided to go home."

"So, where's this chick of yours," said Brad, huffing into his palms to sniff his own breath, "so I can swoop in and steal her right out of your loser hands?"

"Is he always this obnoxious at parties?" asked Sid.

I hardly heard them.

I spotted Jaycie right away, surrounded by a group of guys who looked like various incarnations of 90s era Brad Pitt—from *Legends of the Fall* through *Fight Club*. At that moment, it wasn't about confidence, it was about realism. She was surrounded by guys who were supremely better looking than me—and why not? Wasn't she gorgeous? Wasn't she charismatic and fun? Wasn't she my dream girl for a reason?

My hopes were crushed.

As I was in the process of putting my tail between my legs and wandering off to some corner to mope, she spotted me, smiled, then waved excitedly. In slow motion she started moving toward me like she was skipping, as if I were the only guy in the world.

"You're making this up," said Doc, wearing a humorous grin.

"Of course I am," I said. "It was like the clouds had parted and a happy little sun burst out from behind them. Like my thumping heart was the Kool-Aid Man making an entrance through a brick wall. I felt as light as a feather, and I heard the faint tune of 'Walking on Sunshine' in my head before I realized it was actually playing on a boombox by the window." Then I took a deep breath and fought back a sob that had been steadily rising in my throat for the last twenty minutes. "She moved toward me like none of those other guys mattered. She even side-stepped B-Rad as he swooped in, popped collar and all."

"Hey!" she said to me—her radiant smile gave me jitters. "You made it. I was starting to think you were gonna flake."

"Flake? Me? No! Never. It's fashionable to be late," I said with a joking smile, then shot Brad a quick glare to let him know his fancy golf shirt wasn't worth the lost time. "You look amazing."

I surprised myself with my sudden burst of confidence, but Jaycie managed to bring out the best in me—even if I was pretending like I hadn't gotten my head caught in a pneumatic door.

At first, I thought I had only imagined speaking those words, but then she reacted, and I realized, gladly, that I had actually said them.

After all those years of striving to mature into a more complete, more aware person, I had finally done something that wasn't just masking a shy, bullied, little boy—I wasn't that kid anymore. I was growing up. I was twenty and refused to make the same mistakes I made when I was fourteen.

However, that didn't mean the outcome would be any different.

"Thanks, you too." She blushed, and her smile quickly faded. She seemed suddenly nervous around me, like we had swapped places.

"Thank you," I laughed. I wasn't used to compliments and immediately set off on a mental journey to decipher if she really meant it. The closest thing I had gotten over the last year was a quick "that's cute" from a girl who collected Troll dolls. I still had nightmares of those hideous things staring at me while I was sleeping.

"You still wear that key?" she said, noticing it dangling from my neck. It had slipped out from under my t-shirt when I bent to tie my shoes on the way over.

"Yeah, I never take it off," I admitted, hoping to leave the subject behind.

"Why?" she asked curiously as she reached out to touch it.

I was stuck between honesty and a lie. I never wanted to lie to her, even if it meant saying something awkward. It was far too late into the conversation to lose my courage and back out. I wanted her to know my intentions. I didn't want to be friends.

"I told you that I found it, but actually, I wear it because it was my mom's," I said. "And it also reminds me of you—the night we met."

I had not admitted that to anyone. Not to Amanda, Thad, Chris, John, Brad, Marshall, or Sid, nor any friend or love interest who came into my life. I had denied it, to myself and to others—and if someone asked about it, I replied, "it's the key to my heart."

But after meeting her that night at the fair years ago, it symbolically became her key. As the years passed and I began to forget about Jaycie, I would look down at the key and get an image—a feeling—of who she was—or who I thought she was. A pleasant reminder of how love should feel, of what she represented to me. It was a huge relief to admit it out loud, and a whole other experience to know I had finally admitted it to Jaycie herself.

"Oh," she said.

That was the entirety of her response.

She looked shocked. I imagined her walking away, storming off and never speaking to me again. I scolded myself for ruining things so quickly. I came on too hard. It was too much.

She still appeared shocked when she reached out and grabbed my hand.

"Come with me," she said. "I want to you to meet someone."

She took me into the gathering of Pitts on the far side of the room, where she stopped and said, "Rick, I want you to meet someone."

"No," said Doc, shocked.
"Yeah."

"Yeah, babe, Oscuro and I are old buds," said Rick as he wrapped his arm around her waist and pulled her in.

"How do you two know each other?" I asked. I was dead inside, going through the motions to appear relaxed. My body pretended to be okay, but my eyes spoke differently.

"We went to high school together," said Rick.

"Just our junior year," she clarified. "But we've known each other since we were kids. Our dads were good friends."

"Yeah, Jaycie had the biggest crush on me back then," he said with a snide smile. I could have been imagining it, but it appeared like he was rubbing it in. "We bumped into each other her first week home. The rest is history." Then he glared at me, like a warning.

"History," I said, nodding. "Yeah, cool."

"We good, Oscuro? You look like you've seen a ghost," he said with a grin. He could tell what was happening. He read it all the way, including the downward spiral behind my eyes.

"Oh yeah, we're fine. I have a paper due tomorrow, so I should probably get back to it," I explained, overacting just how *FINE* I really was. I was as *FINE* as a paraplegic on ice skates.

"Tomorrow's Sunday," said Rick, and Jaycie winced—even she knew I was trying to get away while I still had some pride. "You have a class on Sunday?"

"No, I—I promised myself I'd have it done tomorrow. I have tons of stuff to do. Laundry. And you know, stuff? Time budgeting, you know?" I explained it all in a nervous ramble. "Catch you guys later." Then I ducked away before I said something stupid…

…something *else* stupid.

"See ya at practice, Tone!" shouted Rick.

I managed to drift to the door before Marshall stopped me and asked,

"What's wrong?"

I looked at him, then to Anne—they were having a great time, and I didn't want to ruin it.

I patted Marshall on the shoulder and said, "Enjoy yourself, bud. You deserve it."

Then I left.

"I almost didn't survive the walk home."

"What do you mean?" asked Doc.

"I wanted to throw myself over a bridge. Or jump from Goner's Cross. People died leaping off that ledge, and I didn't want to be alive. I was devastated, and I don't remember how I made it home."

The next morning, I woke up in an empty room after suffering through a night of endless nightmares. Marshall hadn't come home, and Brad was passed out on the floor next to the sofa. Sid was sleeping off a hangover with the door closed.

I was making my way to the kitchen for breakfast when a key slid into the door lock.

There are few things you expect to see the miserable morning after you frustratedly bawl yourself to sleep—and before you've fully rubbed the rust from your eyes or soothed a dry throat with a glass of water.

List of things I expect to see in the early morning:
- Brad sleepwalking naked through the room.
- Marshall returning from an early morning Bagels-2-Go run to apologize for the all-night fart-a-thon.
- Sid arguing with maintenance because someone unbalanced the washer and left it running through a full cycle at 4AM.

A beautiful redhead was not on the list, for good reason.

And she was accompanied by my best friend and his new girlfriend.

"My grammy used to bring me here when I was a kid," said Jaycie as we sat on a park bench beneath an old hemlock tree in downtown

Grace Falls, near the cemetery. It had only taken me five minutes to get ready as the others waited—but that was after the fifteen minutes it took to convince me to go for a drive with them. Eventually I decided to go, against my better judgment, after Jaycie pleaded and promised to make it up to me.

I didn't respond and sat as far away from her on the bench as possible. Marshall and Anne were on the swings, keeping their distance.

"I'm sorry," she said eventually.

"What for?" I asked.

I had no idea what she was apologizing for, other than her bad taste in men.

"I didn't know."

"I thought you invited me for a reason," I said.

"I did," she explained. "We weren't going to invite Marshall and not invite his roommates, that's completely rude." She was trying to joke and lighten the mood. When I didn't laugh, she continued. "I invited you because I wanted you there. As strange as it sounds, I'm new in my own hometown. I don't have many friends here. I thought it was an opportunity to get to know more people."

Then she added, "And I'm dating the captain of the baseball team. I thought maybe I could introduce you, or something. Maybe help you score some points?" She saw me sigh and my face contort, then dropped her head into her hands. "I didn't mean to lead you on."

It was hard to be angry at someone so contrite—especially someone I had built up to be more than human. Despite her awful taste, she seemed to be exactly that—human.

"After the party, Marshall told me everything," she said. "He's a great friend. He's a good man and I think he's a good match for Anne."

I wondered how much Marshall had explained, and if he brought up the uneasy ground between myself and Rick Jansen.

"Yeah," I sighed. Marshall and Anne were ridiculously cute together, which made me feel guilty for being so annoyed with it. "What did he tell you?"

"He said your friendship with Amanda ended because of me. He said you held me up on a pedestal for years, based on a single night, and that when women didn't meet up to those expectations, you moved on."

"Not entirely accurate," I said with a hint of petulance, despite the relative accuracy.

"I didn't ask for you to put me on a pedestal, Tony," she said. "I hardly know you."

Her words hit me like a cartoon-bubbled *"POW!"* from the old Batman TV show. She was right, even though I hated her saying it.

It was true. We hardly knew each other. She could have been a complete asshole who deserved to be with Rick for all I knew—despite my intuition otherwise.

"I'm sorry," I said.

"Why are you sorry?" she replied. "I'm flattered you see me that way. But it's not real. It's not based on reality." Anne laughed as Marshall tripped and fell attempting to jump from his swing, then laid there too embarrassed to move as she laughed even harder. "I've been through a lot of pain in my life, Tony. I ran away from home when I was seventeen, and I just returned eight months ago. I feel like I'm finally rebuilding. You seem like a great guy, and I'd really like to surround myself with good people."

I was dreading what she was about to say. It was inevitable. The kiss of death.

"Can we be friends?" she asked.

I imagined Rick sitting on a giant scale, being weighed against "good people," and felt the need to say something—but left it unspoken.

Instead, I said, "Okay, I'd like that," despite it being the furthest thing from what I wanted. But there was one undeniable truth about Jacinda O'Neill and me—I wanted her in my life, one way or another.

For the next several months, my relationship with Jaycie was purely platonic on the outside, while I screamed internally every day about how awesome she was. It started slowly at first, meeting up twice a week to study or grab a quick lunch, and later we began hanging out multiple times a week.

We had a good thing going.

The problem was I was falling in love with her. Real love with the real her. Something based on real interaction and feelings, and every day I asked Marshall to scold me for putting myself through that torture.

"You dummy! You idiot!" yelled Marshall. Then he politely touched my shoulder and asked, "How was that?" as I was sitting at my desk, rubbing my temples to help ease the heartache.

"Perfect," I grunted. "Keep it coming."

This was a typical evening's Jaycie-inspired berating.

"You candy-ass, spumoni eating, cheesesteak wit' whiz guzzling, calling red-sauce fucking gravy slurping, Italian hillbilly, masochistic piece of Sicilian shhh—

"Dude?" I groaned. He had gone a little too far.

"That was awesome," said Brad, chomping on popcorn from the doorway. "Can I try?"

"No!" we both shouted, and Marshall slammed the door shut.

It was an effective way of keeping my hopes grounded.

"What is love to you, Tony?" asked Doc.

"What do you mean?" I asked, feeling like this was an odd time to asking me something so nebulous.

"A moment ago, you told me that you didn't really know Jacinda enough to be placing her on a pedestal," he explained. "Now you're telling me you were in love with her." I nodded. "Explain to me what changed. What did you see in Jacinda that you didn't see before?"

I took a deep breath to think about his question and realized I could talk about Jaycie for days on end.

"Jaycie was a starry sky, and I was just a kid with a telescope, staring up at the heavens. She was an atomic force. She had a beautiful, curious, opinionated mind. She could banter with the best and had a way of making people smile when they felt at their worst. I'd humiliate myself for her smiles. She made me better just by smiling with me.

"There was no limit to Jaycie. She was endless.

"The way I loved her wasn't for me. It was unrequited. It was unsolicited. I loved her for her, because it was truth. She deserved authenticity, and I could not honor that by stifling what was in my soul—what was so obvious to me."

"Which was?"

"That Jaycie was the best thing that ever happened to me. And I was so hopelessly in love with her that I never saw the warning signs of what it might do to me when she realized our non-relationship had gone too far."

It was silent within the room.

Finally, I said, "Was that adequate?"

"Yes," he said. "Yes, it was."

THE EXTRICATION OF NEMESIS

128 A.D.

Deep within the Thracian mountains was a narrow path. That path led, treacherously, to the top of the highest mountain, whose peak could be seen by many kings across many lands. The path was not meant for man, but for a creature whose natural talents gave them access to places that could not otherwise be visited. There, upon a small landing at the very top, was the rumored perch of Nemesis, goddess of retributive justice.

Once upon a cold spring night, Nemesis, daughter of Night, was summoned to the mountain under a banner of peace. An apple-branch was left at the foot of a statue that had been erected in her honor and likeness, within the city of Rhamnus, in southern Greece. It was a message that Tyche, goddess of fortune, had identified an assailant in need of punishment, for which Nemesis would be judge, jury, and executioner.

Only, Tyche had not sent that message.

Arriving at the mountaintop, Nemesis awaited Tyche carrying the assailant's name. Justice would be swift, finished before the sun climbed over the horizon. She waited until the moon was at its highest, when a message was delivered, albeit not the message she was expecting.

The mighty goddess was a skilled fighter, a true harbinger of death should her sword's blade be leveled. But she was ambushed by Aphrodite and Artemis—a quarrel over lovers and broken hearts. The battle was fierce, but the vengeful goddesses prevailed. Beaten, it was said that Nemesis stayed upon the mountain in shame, for two inferior warriors had bested her, and there was no greater shame than that.

When Malus arrived at the top of the highest peak, he could sense her presence but could not find her. The entire mountain top was not vast, nor did it have many places with which to hide. There was a large boulder and an assortment of rocks, even a small tree that grew from the craggy soil, but there was no goddess, not there, not anywhere.

"What do you seek, stranger?" called a voice, weak and small.

"I seek the goddess of retribution. I seek Nemesis," spoke Malus.

"What do you need of her?" asked the voice.

"I offer the goddess an opportunity. A chance to avenge all wrongs," offered Malus.

"The goddess is weak. What use is she to you?" asked the voice.

"I have heard stories. Legends. Nemesis was rumored to be the most powerful creature in all existence upon this plane. She has untold power that might be useful to me."

"Her power is unreliable. One moment it flows like a raging river after a storm. The next like a drip, ice melting under a winter's sun."

"If Nemesis signs my contract, I offer a cure to her ailment," said Malus. "May she have inexhaustible power to exact her own retribution—for vengeance on those who did this to you."

"What must she do? What impossible task must you ask of her?"

"That depends, my dear," said Malus, as he approached the great boulder and lowered himself onto his knees. "How long would you like to remain a poor ant, holding that great boulder upon your back?"

XVI

recompense

TONY
December 21, 2013
Now.

The outside world was chaos.

In *The Wizard of Oz*, remember how Dorothy goes from the black and white mundane world of Kansas, then steps into the bright technicolor realm of OZ after being caught in a trans-dimensional twister? Dorothy's awakening in that strange land had nothing on the sensory overload I experienced as soon as I stepped into the outside world.

Beyond my front door, the world exploded with new stimuli. My senses had been given wider breadth—a depth that explored new ways in which to feel.

Every direction exploded into sound, color, taste, and sight. I could hear walls, smell car horns, taste atomic properties, and see probabilities. Every piece of matter was emitting something into the world that was picked up by my new senses.

The city was no longer the white noise background I could ignore to survive like a living zombie, zoning in and out from one day to the next. It was now a dazzling array of overpowering information. Smell and taste were nearly indistinguishable and elevated to equals of sight and sound. I could hear the crawling of ants, smell the rats scurrying below the city pavement, and taste the pollution in the air. It was dizzying.

Up was down and down was left, which left me not right at all.

I felt—wrong—yet correct.

"Steady, my man," said a voice.

"Who said that?" I asked.

"It's me, my man. Montoya," he said, standing beside the blue mailbox on the corner.

"How?" I grimaced. The sensory overload was starting to hurt. The sun was too bright, the noise too loud, and everything smelled and tasted awful.

"Sir," said Henry, placing a comforting hand on my shoulder. "We are constructs of your imagination. We are here to assist you, should you need us."

"Deep breaths, son," said Chappy.

"Focus," said Doshin, stepping up to stare into my eyes like he was giving me the Miyagi.

"Master Doshin is a samurai, for real," said Jamaal.

The five of them from that place—that realm inside my mind—were there with me, but were they really? I could see them. Heck, I could feel Henry's hand on my shoulder, but when a woman dressed in scrubs turned the corner and passed straight through Jamaal, I was left feeling crazier than ever.

"Focus," repeated Doshin. "You are in control." Just thinking the word "focus" brought my overload down to a manageable level. It was all still there, but accessible as needed. "Good."

"Tony," said Chappy. The way he said my name made me feel like I was about to receive a lecture—I was not a religious man, and there was something about the way priests and preachers spoke that always left me irritated, like an itch I couldn't scratch. "Do you believe talking to your friend is going to help you solve anything? I believe it could bring unnecessary danger to the people you love."

"Marshall's always been there for me," I said as I walked toward the corner. "I don't know what I'm doing, and I don't know where else to go."

"I understand, but—" warned Chappy, but I had already leapt into the street, crossing before the light changed. Chappy then looked to Henry and said, "What good are we if he doesn't heed our advice?"

Henry nodded. "He will come around."

I heard them. After all, they were only in my head.

Marshall lived in the Fairmount section of the city. On a normal day, walking, it could take me close to an hour from my apartment. I jogged there in under ten minutes without so much as a drop of sweat. I was in top form—strong, agile, and as fast as ever, and yet only scratching the surface of my new ability. The trip could have been done more efficiently if I wasn't struggling against the sensory overload.

Marshall lived in an old row home subdivided into apartments—his was on the second floor, with an outdoor metal staircase that led to a private entrance. When I knocked on his door, I could hear the voices inside as if I was in the room with them, but even with that foreknowledge, it didn't stop the shock of seeing her.

Literally…

"Tony!" said Anne excitedly.

Seeing Anne set off a chain reaction—a thought, followed by another, and suddenly I was thinking about the last time I saw Anne, at the hospital in Mercy Point.

"Hey," I said.

I wanted to be happy. I wanted to hug her, but all I could do was feel the rush of panic—and the rush wasn't holding back.

"Hey buddy," said Marshall. "Look who came by for a booty call last night!"

Anne laughed, but I felt wrong—like I was sweating on the inside. A pressure built inside my head as if someone had stuck an air pump in my ear to inflate a flat basketball. I started to speak—maybe it was a "Hi" or a "Hey"—but instead of words, there was a sudden shock that busted all of Marshall's lightbulbs in a shower of sparks and glass.

Then I fainted on his doorstep.

I awoke two minutes later on Marshall's couch, and my body ached all over. Anne and Marshall were in the next room having a playful argument, and I actually smiled for them. They were meant for each other. Some people just have that chemistry.

"What do you want me to do?" said Marshall. "Throw the guy back in the loony bin?"

"No, I'm not saying that," said Anne. "He's clearly struggling. You said so yourself. The guy needs help."

"He needs friends too," argued Marshall. "He needs us."

"I'm not saying he doesn't," she said, lowering her voice after she spotted my stirring. How did I know? I could hear the inflection in her voice matched by movement, and a faint but subtle change in her pulse. "I'm just saying that he needs more than just you and me."

"You and me?" Marshall questioned. "You and me as in—we?"

Anne laughed and I could hear them kissing.

"I would say get a room," I joked, "but it seems you've already got one." Sitting up on the couch was like trying to move after the first few days of baseball training. Every muscle was sore and joints audibly popped and whined. "It's like déjà vu all over again."

"Hey, that's what you get for taking the top bunk," said Marshall, perfectly remembering the time I accidentally caught them mid "flow" as I got up for a glass of water.

They entered the living room and glared at me as I lounged on the couch. I felt like I was about to be scolded by parents.

"What's up with your face?" asked Marshall. "And how'd you lose twenty pounds in a single night?"

"Tony, are you on drugs?" Anne asked.

"Funny you should say that," I said, looking at them both. "Today's the first time in years I'm not on anything."

Anne grimaced. She wasn't following my logic—as if anyone could follow me into the places my mind was weaving. I was losing it, for sure, but in an entirely different direction.

"What's going on, T?" asked Marshall. "Are you in trouble?"

"Ha ha!" I laughed too hard. Then, a wave of emotion nearly brought me to tears. I was on a manic rollercoaster, rising and falling on waves of thoughts and feelings. Then I sat up in such a rush that Marshall took a step back.

"Are you okay?" asked Anne like a worried mother.

"I'm not insane," I said. "Something happened last night."

"Yeah, and you paid for it with your face," said Marsh.

"Ha!" I laughed. He was right. The scar on my face wasn't pretty.

I was about to explain—to attempt to explain—when I caught a whiff of something drifting with the darkening skies developing outside Marshall's windows. "Do you smell that?" I asked them cautiously. The smell was getting stronger, like vomit and brimstone with a hint of something sweet that made me very uncomfortable. It wasn't the smell that made me uncomfortable, but rather what my instincts told me it meant. I leapt from the couch and paced over to the window, looking out in paranoid angles like something out of a spy movie.

"I don't smell anything, T," said Marshall. "Sit down and talk."

I could tell I was making them nervous. Hell, I was making myself nervous. What the hell was that smell?

"We'll talk, but we need to find out where that smell's coming from first."

"Tony! What the fuck is going on!" yelled Marshall, smacking the back of his couch. Anne winced at his outburst, but the look on her face spoke volumes. She was just as annoyed as he was. "You have this big fucken scar across your face that wasn't there yesterday! What the fuck have you gotten yourself into!?"

"Marshall, I don't know where to begin," I said, ignoring the foul stench for a moment. He was on the verge of losing more than just his cool. He was about to pop.

"Try!" he demanded.

"It's difficult to explain, I—"

"Try!" he yelled, cutting me off.

"I'm not exactly human," I explained, my voice as serious as stone. I mean, I was operating under that assumption after last night, right?

"If you're asking me, sir," said Henry, "that is indeed correct."

"Yup," I replied to myself. "I'm not human. The shrink in my head told me so."

"Oh yeah? If you're not human, then what are you? And, okay, what *is* that fucken smell?" he said, looking over at Anne. It was so rank in the room that I was beginning to think they had lost their olfactory ability. It had grown from just a whiff into something overpowering.

"It smells like something's rotting," said Anne, as she shot Marsh an accusatory glance. "Something probably went bad in your fridge."

"I don't think so," he said, as Anne stepped into the kitchen. Marsh had an open floorplan, and I could see her the whole time as she stepped over to the fridge. When she opened it, there was a brief moment when the scent intensified. Maybe it was just rotted food.

Then a clawed hand seized Anne by the throat and pulled her into the fridge, and the door slammed shut behind her.

"You know, it might be Tuesday Surprise. I cooked something on Tuesday and—hey, where'd she go?"

I leapt over to the fridge before Marshall finished his sentence, flinging open the door and closing it before he could see inside.

He didn't want to see what I just saw.

"Where'd Anne go?"

"I don't know," I lied.

"Tony, where did Anne go?" he asked, and when I began to shake my head he screamed, "Tony, where the fuck did Anne go?"

I stepped away against my better judgment, letting Marshall inspect the refrigerator for himself. There was very little my mind could process after seeing what was inside. My emotions were feast and famine—one moment I couldn't control them, and the next I witnessed something horrible and couldn't even muster up a pained expression.

Marshall wasn't what you'd call a "believer." He was a staunch unbeliever, atheist, and all-around "the truth *isn't* out there" kind of guy.

Everything had a rational explanation for Marshall, and up until the early hours of this morning, I was the same way.

Grabbing the handle, Marshall whipped the fridge door open and stared into the stainless-steel box like he was searching for something to eat. The condiments on the shelves were still wobbling when he said, "There's nothing in here."

"What?" I asked. My hands were shaking as I peered over his shoulder into the fridge.

"What did you see, Tony?" he asked, but before I could answer he called out, "Anne? Anne? Where did you go?"

There was movement in the room, like a draft, only there was no one else in the apartment with us. I would have *heard* them. I would have *smelled* them. I was still acclimating to this new body, soaking up all the info there was to gain from the room we were standing in.

"She's dead," I said, and Marshall ignored me. Tears ran from my eyes as my grief finally caught up. Everything felt so out of control. "We need to go."

"Anne?" he called out again.

"Marshall!" I yelled and jumped in front of him. "You have a three-room apartment. One bedroom, one bathroom, and one room for everything else. Where could Anne have gone?"

"You tell me? Why'd you make me think she was in the fridge?" he asked.

"You're not going to find her," I said, my voice cracking. "She's gone, man." My body began to shake. Doom was all around us.

"She's not gone!" yelled Marshall.

"Did you hear the front door open?" I argued. "Where else could she be?"

Marshall jumped back to the fridge, placed his hand onto the handle and screamed, "Look! She's not in the fridge!"

He swung the door open and swept away by a wave of blood and bone, striking him so hard he fell backward and slid into the oven. I grabbed him by the collar and dragged him free of the bloody geyser as he spat and coughed up blood.

"Marsh," I said, grabbing his face so he could see the seriousness in my eyes. "We need to get out of here."

He was in shock; I would have noticed from across the room by the way his eyes were dilated. Grabbing him by the shoulders, I lifted him to his feet like he was nothing more than a toddler and began ushering him from the room. "What just happened?" he asked, but I couldn't answer. I heard a sound, like floorboards creaking and stopped.

I caught the sight of a shadow moving in a reflection. My head snapped to a framed photo sitting on one of Marshall's end tables. It was a picture of us with our old roommates, Brad and Sid. There was a dark shadow in the reflection between Brad and me, moving like it was approaching from somewhere far away. I looked around and saw nothing in the room with us. The walls were painted white, and despite the overcast skies, there were no shadows in the room.

"What's wrong?" Marshall asked as he noticed my eyes darting around his apartment.

"There's something here with us," I said. I could feel it. I could *taste* it.

"What's going on, Tony? Where's Anne?" he asked. Marshall was out of it. He was spiraling, and I knew I had to pull us through. I couldn't crack. I repeated that to myself over and over like a mantra.

"We have to move, now," I said, feeling pulse quicken through his skin. I even heard it thump and accelerate.

I followed his eyes to the TV. We were perfectly reflected in the glass tube, but behind us, standing over Marshall's shoulder was a dark, ominous shape. It did not move, but stood there, waiting.

"How is this possible?" asked Marshall. He kept looking over his shoulder then back to the TV. Even though there was something in the reflection, it was not actually there. He even reached out to the area where the black contour stood, casting his hand back and forth. His hand disappeared within the shadow in the reflection with each pass.

"Stop," I suggested, and Marshall listened instantly.

"What is it?" he asked. He was scared, and so was I.

"I don't know. Just stay away from it. Stay in the light," I said.

"That shouldn't be hard, except all my lightbulbs are broken," he said. "Did you do that? Did you make the lights go out?"

"Wish I knew," I said.

We maneuvered around the shadow by watching it closely in all the reflected surfaces of the room. Marshall took a long, exaggerated way around to be extra sure and stopped in front of me with a half-smile. We were only ten feet from the front door.

"Okay," said Marsh, "where are we going? Should we get Anne?" he asked, then winced, like something had shifted in his bowels.

Before I could answer, there was a spray of blood.

Through Marshall's stomach came a clawed hand ripping its way out. There was absolutely nothing I could do to save him. Marshall shook violently, clinging to the last seconds of his life as the thing ripped its way out from inside him into our world. Marshall's eyes locked onto mine, and we said our goodbyes telepathically, like we used to communicate years ago.

I wanted to grieve for him, but the thing that came forth made every alarm inside my gut go off—every sense told me it was danger—and there was no time for grief.

The skies dimmed as the creature stepped into this world. I could feel it sucking the heat and the energy out of the room, empowering it as it moved from one form of existence to another. Marshall's carcass fell to the floor, split in two, when the beast stood up at full height in front of me. It was no shorter than seven feet tall in long blood-red robes and old leather sandals. Its body was half man and half beast, with long grimy hair protruding from under its cloak. It watched me carefully and removed its hood, unveiling his awfulness to me. He had the face of a coyote mixed with man, morphed together in some twisted nightmarish way that seemed hastily unplanned. He had long yellow fangs and wild eyes with a snout and a set of wide pointed ears.

Mammon.

He was Mammon. He killed Henry, and the psychologist inside my head shivered at the sight of the beast.

Mammon's long arms spread out wide, funneling me into a corner. I don't remember backing away, but with every sliding step the creature took, I retreated an equal distance until I was backed into the wall.

Marshall's body twitched on the floor, his blood soaking into the carpet, and Anne was just a spatter across the kitchen tile. I felt loss. I felt crippling emptiness. Then I felt pain.

Mammon thrust a clawed hand into my left shoulder and lifted me against the wall, my feet dangling off the ground. I could feel his hand wrapped around the bone like a convenient handle to toss me around. He sniffed the air and enjoyed it.

"Yes, fear me," he said. His voice was like a whining dog. My fear and my grief were feeding him. He was enjoying it, and it made me angry.

I could feel something in my chest—a passion, filling up like gas in a tank. The flames. They had been gone for so long—and I remembered feeling them for the first time—that night at the Labor Day Fair in college. I'd stifled the flames for years behind chemical walls, and I could feel them igniting now, growing higher and hotter. I finally understood what they were for. The power had been there all along. I urged them on, building up a mass several times the largest size I had ever felt.

As Mammon breathed humid puffs of putrid stink on my face, I smiled at him. I let my grief infect me, and I used the pain to push the flames even higher.

Mammon sniffed the air with his canine snout and there was no more fear for him to feed. If a coyote could look stunned, that was what I saw in his eyes. "Tasty spark, time to die," he said, and his muzzled mouth opened and unhinged like a snake, forming a wild snapping alligator maw with barbed teeth that twisted like thorns.

But I did not fear him.

I hated him.

I hated what he did to my friends and I pushed off against the wall and ripped my shoulder free from his grasp, snapping the bones in his hand. He roared, not in pain, but surprise as the bones immediately grafted back together.

"I know who you are," I said, "Mammon." The room shook and the windows clouded over, cutting out all the light. Darkness grew around us as the beast pressed its will upon my own. "Wait, that's not your name." There was more to this beast, another name still drifting to the surface.

Mammon swiped at me, bashing me against the wall, and kept the pressure on my head as it tried to crush me. "What is your name, spark?" it asked.

"Tony," I squeaked between gasps for air.

"No," it growled, pressing harder, and I felt my skull bend between his hand and a steel beam behind the sheetrock. "Your true name!"

"Anthony?" I replied like a smart ass.

He raked his free claw down my chest, taking huge chunks of flesh with it, and came for more when I caught his arm at the wrist. I fought against his strength, willed myself to hold him back as he leveraged himself over me and began to press down with everything he had—when the name finally floated free.

"Echmet," I said.

Mammon's strength was cut in half and the light returned to the skies outside the window. He was still a terrifying beast and fought like a wounded animal, but suddenly his magic was gone. Knowing his name was like knowing the sun was nothing but a fiery star in space, not a deity that rose every morning and died every evening. Mammon was still a dangerous, terrifying killing machine, but he was suddenly less likely to kill me by infecting me with fear.

With strength beyond my capability, I pushed away from the wall and stood on both feet, grappling with Mammon's claws. His maw snapped at my face, and I ducked away and rolled toward the couch. But as I got to my feet Mammon launched onto me, pinning me to the ground.

"I shall rip that name from your lips," sneered Mammon, and I felt my muscles pop and give way.

I was going to die. I could feel my time slipping, like the last grains of sand were falling through the aperture on the hourglass of my life, when I felt the spark—no, not a spark—a roaring lake of fire waiting, pleading, begging, to be dispensed.

"No," I whipered. This could not be the end. No. My Echo told me to stay alive. No. No. I had to do it for her. No. No. No. No. I had to live for Jaycie. No. No. NO! NO! NO! NO! "NOOOOOOOOO!"

The beast unhinged his jaw, widening his bite to snap my head clean off.

"Fuck you!" I roared, raging over the loss of the only friends I had left.

In a flash, my skin ignited. Mammon tried to pull away, tried to avoid the flames, but I grabbed, held tight, and unleashed everything.

The entire apartment exploded.

XVII
broken

TONY
Then.

"Which was?"

"That Jaycie was the best thing that ever happened to me. And I was so hopelessly in love with her that I never saw the warning signs of what it might do to me when she realized our non-relationship had gone too far."

It was silent within the room.

Finally, I said, "Was that adequate?"

"Yes," he said. "Yes, it was."

"I never saw Rick and Jaycie together," I said. "She kept us separate and rarely mentioned his name, further perpetuating the growing hope I held onto." Then I took my fist and lightly pounded it onto my thigh. To tell this right, I had to remember things that were going to hurt. "My hopes got too high. I was Icarus, waiting to fall."

November 17, 2000

Our relationship, whatever it was, was the most precious thing I ever had in my life.

But there were moments, like seismic shifts, when the gaps between where I was and where I wanted to be were shrinking. Moments when I could sense I was collecting real estate in her heart—building equity and trust in her mind—a real connection that went deeper than friendship.

"You're enjoying this way too much," I grumbled amidst waves of Jaycie-giggles.

"You have to wear it," she said as she stifled the laughter. "You fouled. You pay the price. Them's the rules, kid."

We were at the local movie theater catching a matinee of *High Fidelity*, starring John Cusack, and we arrived forty-five minutes early with nowhere else to go. We shared a fondness for Cusack, one of the many things we had in common—we'd realized we were linked by more than just Amanda.

We grabbed sodas and a popcorn to share, and I was hungry, like always. I ate the entire bucket of popcorn with fifteen minutes to go before the movie started—a faux pas worthy of capital punishment.

"So, you're saying," I clarified, "that because I ate all the popcorn before the movie, I offended the local magistrate?"

She nodded and pointed to herself, helping me identify the plaintiff. "Yes," she giggled mischievously.

Before I could argue the point any further, she grabbed the bucket and dumped it over my head, then left it there like a fancy hat. Her face flushed, and tears streamed down her cheeks from the laughter.

"I think you made this up," I said. My voice hollowly echoed from inside the bucket.

I looked ridiculous, and it made Jaycie laugh that much harder.

It was beautiful.

"I would never!" she theatrically professed.

"You would!" I replied. "And you have."

"You are the bucket-head," she said, like a mantra. "Now that you are nice and fed, you wear the bucket on your head. It's tradition."

"Far be it for me to go against tradition," I said. Leaving the bucket on, I stood up and scooted to the aisle.

"Wait, where are you going?" she asked.

"To get more popcorn," I replied. As I finished speaking, an elderly couple walked into the theater and stopped dead in their tracks after seeing me.

"Roger, let's go sit on the other side," said the woman.

Jacinda made a high-pitched squeal as she tried to stifle the guffaws coming from her.

Eventually I returned with a new bucket of popcorn, and I made sure not to touch a single kernel, on principle. Later, halfway through the movie, I removed the bucket from my head.

"Jacinda," I whispered while she was taking a sip of soda. "My hair smells like butter."

From her mouth erupted a gushing spray. Never had such a fine spray of soda flown from someone's mouth. It spread across the next six rows and could be felt trickling down in a fine mist for a whole ten seconds afterward. I thought I was going to have to find her oxygen.

I never let her forget that day, and the word "butter" became one of many inside jokes.

But there were other moments too. Moments of inspiration rather than laughter.

December 15, 2000

Jaycie was determined to get me to stop listening to 80s rock, "not because it sucks, but because you need a more refined palate," if I was to continue hanging out with her. Up until that point in my life, I had no musical identity. The songs I listened to were odds and ends I picked up, but I never had the chance to explore the many possibilities that existed beyond my immediate scope. "No friend of mine is going to go through life thinking music is AC/DC to Kip Winger with nothing in between."

Where I grew up, it was country and hip-hop and nothing else. The school dances were either hoe-downs or bass and booty jams—which was partially why I never attended. If a song wasn't being played on the radio, I probably didn't know it existed.

"C'mon!" said Jaycie, as she dragged me into The Music Shoppe at the Grace Falls Mall. It was a popular place, filled with people who looked way too serious about their music. "Somebody once gave me a musical education and it changed my life. And now I'm going to do the same for you. I'm gonna rock your world, T."

"I'm already in college. Why do I need another education?" I grumbled, purposely dragging my heels. She was so adamant about teaching me music that it was becoming her obsession. She would have me listen to little bits and pieces of things she liked, to try and form musical parameters, but now she was taking my instruction to a whole new level.

"Because I'm a musician," she said, like I should know better than to ask such silly questions. "And no self-respecting musician can allow you to go through life with such awful flavor."

"Flavor?" I questioned as we paced into the store. "Like butter?"

Jaycie laughed, sweet big belly laughs. Every time she was reminded of my bucket-head, she couldn't keep herself straight.

"Like buttuh," she replied with a giggle.

The store was a filled with at least twenty rows of CD racks, with band posters and top-ten billboards as judged by the store's employees. In the back corner was a listening station with enough room for two, like a doublewide phone booth.

"Hey, don't I know you?" asked one of the clerks. It was a tall chubby guy with a black polo embroidered with the store's logo.

"I don't think so," said Jaycie suspiciously. *Do you know me?*

"Guess not," he shrugged. "A little girl freaked out here once. You look like her."

"Nope, sorry," she said with a shrug. "Not me."

Before the guy could reply, Jaycie shoved me into the listening booth and closed the door, sealing us inside. "That was weird."

"You have a truly remarkable way with people."

"Shush! We are in my holy place. Put these on." She handed me a set of earphones, then slipped her own over her head. "Ready?" She was excited, like this was the greatest thing to happen in the history of ever.

The station had hundreds of popular albums from the last several years, and Jaycie worked the interface like she was Arthur Fonzarelli.

When I nodded, she hit play and watched me with extreme scrutiny.

The first song that played was some kind of hip-hop I never heard before—not that I had much experience. I shook my head and she shook hers, agreeing. "Yeah, that's not you," she said, then added, "not me either."

"Then why'd you put it on?" I asked.

"I needed to make sure," she laughed. "Should we even try country?"

"Ugh, no," I said, and she smiled brightly. "I always knew you were cool."

"Thanks," I replied.

Next, she cued up a song by a scantily clad popstar I'd caught Brad ogling one night when he was up late watching TV by himself.

"Nah," I replied immediately.

"Agreed."

"Are you only going to play stuff you know I'm not going to like?" I asked.

"Hush, I'm trying to get a baseline," she said.

Then she played something that made sense. Something that hit all the right notes.

"What is this?" I asked.

"'Rain When I Die' by Alice in Chains." She smiled big. "You like?"

"Yeah," I said, way too loud.

"Thank heavens, you have good taste," she said, then grumbled, "Unlike some people in my life." She may not have mentioned his name, but it was clear who she meant.

After a few minutes, she hit stop and cued up the next song—"Still Remains" by Stone Temple Pilots. We had only really known each other for three months, and she could already read me, like my thoughts were printed on my skin in big bold font.

"Yeah," she nodded with a great big smile and did a little happy dance.

After that, she played "Lithium" by Nirvana. I stopped her ten seconds in and said, "Do you think I lived under a rock in the 90s? Of course, I like Nirvana."

"Excuse me." She laughed. "Okay, time for a deeper cut."

Silverchair's "Miss You Love" was a soulful experience with Jaycie singing along to the lyrics—some of the people in the store were listening in and smiling—and all at once I felt proud to be associated with the coolest, most talented woman ever, and yet saddened that I was crammed into a tight enclosed space with said girl, who was taken by the biggest lunk of wasted space I had ever met.

"I think we hit your sweet spot," she said, noting my approval.

But when she played a song called "What Do I Have To Do?" by Stabbing Westward, things shifted uncomfortably. She caught me looking her in the eye during the chorus and pulled away. It was my favorite song of the bunch, not just because of the industrial style, but because the lyrics hit so close to home that I felt them all the way down into the guts of my soul.

Awkward moments between us were to be expected. When the reality of our situation popped up like an unwanted houseguest, Jaycie always took it in stride, like she understood how tough it was on me.

"I think we've found your sound," she said. "Let's grab some ice cream."

She was doing her best not to let on that she noticed my forlorn stare and tried to pull us out of the nosedive. "Okay," I said. "On one condition."

She looked up at me like she thought I was about to say something regrettable. There was real concern—maybe fear?—in her eyes.

"What's that?" she asked.

"No *Butter* Pecan," I said, and she began laughing all over again.

Everything with Jaycie meant something. Every moment and every minute of time spent felt like it had a purpose. She created a monster that day—I passionately sought out new music everywhere I could and ended up the biggest Stabbing Westward fan that ever existed.

December 18, 2000

In my twenty years, I had never once bought someone, other than my dad, a Christmas present. Amanda's family was Jewish, and I was never close enough with my other friends to do so. I spent a whole week fretting over whether I should or should not get something for Jaycie, analyzing and overanalyzing every thought.

If I got her something, would that be overstepping?

If I didn't get her something, would I be wasting an opportunity?

Would she accept the gift? Would she be offended?

I tortured myself for days until Anne dropped by one evening and Marshall put an end to my suffering.

"Annie, baby," he called to her before she even removed her coat and mittens. She looked slightly frightened—all big eyes and bafflement. "There is a code between roommates. An unwritten code that says that we cannot ever get involved in their trifling affairs."

"This is true, I suppose," she replied, her suspicious eyes still as wide as canyons when Marsh strolled up and took her dramatically by the hands.

"I ask, dearest Annie," he said, theatrically weeping into the sleeve of his sweater. "Please, for the love of all that is merciful in this world."

"Amen!" shouted Sid, seemingly ignoring us from the sofa.

"Spit it out already!" shouted Brad from the beanbag chair.

I was in the bedroom, my face buried into my pillow as I continued down the path to a nervous breakdown over my lofty decision.

"Can you please inform my roommate if the redhead of his desires got him a Christmas present so he can decide whether or not it's copacetic for him to return the favor?"

"Hi Tony!" Anne shouted into the bedroom.

"Hey," I said and waved back, still face-down and muffled by my pillow.

"Yes, Jaycie got you a present for Christmas," she said.

I was hugging Anne five seconds later for her timely information drop, then immediately set out to find the perfect gift.

There was a Punk Rock Flea Market the next day, and Sid and I went to check it out. There, I found the perfect gift.

They spoke to me the moment I saw them: purple vinyl earrings that were die-cut out of old Prince records in the shape of stars. When she opened them the next day, she was blown away.

"Oh, fuck!" she yelled into the bitter wind. "These are cool as hell, T."

Anne and Jaycie had dropped Marshall and me off at the bus station for our six-hour trek to Philly, where my dad would pick me up for the holidays. The station was just a small booth with an outdoor seating area angled in such a way that the cold whipped through like a wind tunnel. Jaycie was bundled up, wearing a white knit cap with a pom-pom that wiggled every time she moved her head.

"Did Jaycie O just curse?" I said, looking left, then right.

"Hey, my mouth gets dirty all the time," she blurted out, then realized what she said and started laughing.

"Gutter or potty, you pick the dirty," I said. Jaycie appreciated wit, and that line was bursting with it, but she wasn't laughing. She was looking at me strangely, like she was holding back something important. "What?"

"I got you something too," she said, handing me a small box with a ribbon.

"You didn't have to," I said.

"Shut up," she groaned and rolled her eyes at me. "Just open it."

Inside the box was *Wither Blister Burn & Peel*, the Stabbing Westward album we had listened to days before, as well as two tickets to their show in Philly later that spring.

"Are you serious?" I asked.

"Yeah," she said. "Take whoever you like."

I wanted to immediately respond that there was nobody else I would ever consider taking other than her, but when I looked up at her to say those words, she already knew. I could read it on her. I knew her so well, so quickly, that I could read her as easily as she could read me—we didn't just read and speak it, we actually were each other's language.

"Thank you," I said. My words carried paragraphs of subtext. "So." I immediately scrambled to de-awkward-ify the situation. "Have any plans for the holiday?"

"Not much," she said. "Rick's house on Christmas Eve. We're supposed to go to Pittsburgh for New Year's."

"T!" shouted Marshall, rescuing me from the sting of reality. "The bus is boarding!"

Marsh and Anne were wrapped in a lover's embrace, and I couldn't help but wish that would one day that would be Jaycie and me.

When Jaycie gave me a hug and said, "Have a safe trip," I didn't want to let her go.

"See you in a few weeks?"

"I'm not going anywhere," she said and backed away. "I live here." Then she gave me a friendly wink. "Your music education continues when you get back!"

"You got it, professor," I said, just before I boarded the bus home.

Jacinda O'Neill wasn't who I thought she was.

She was better.

She was endless.

Through her eyes, I began to see myself differently.

February 2, 2001

"I want to show you something," she said one day when I followed Marshall over to her place to see Anne. I was creating artwork for an upcoming event flyer I wanted Jaycie to approve—her first gig on campus was at the end of the semester. We were discussing Dr. Celestine's mythology class when Jaycie grabbed me by the arm and led me to her bedroom.

Marshall joked from the living room, "Children, behave!" as Jaycie shut the door behind us. I wasn't sure what to expect, but my anticipation was squashed once I saw her inner sanctum.

"Sit down," she suggested with a smile, gesturing toward the bed. Her room was larger than mine, with a flowery bedspread and a few framed photos sitting on her nightstand. One of them was undoubtedly of her grandmother, and I imagined she'd look similar in sixty years. There was a poster of a Georgia O'Keeffe painting on the wall, and a small desk in the corner by the window with an opened textbook on its surface. She had two small bookcases—one of them held books, and where there wasn't enough room, she had stacked them on top. The other bookcase was filled with handwritten notebooks. At least fifty of them.

"Here it is," she said, pulling one of her many notebooks from its shelf. She walked over and hopped onto the bed next to me, curling her legs under herself. Then she handed me the book and watched with a shy smile. I could tell she was nervous, maybe just as nervous as I was.

"I've been journaling since I was thirteen. Some pages are just doodles, but most are my thoughts and song lyrics—sometimes from songs

I enjoyed, but usually lyrics of my own. This one is special," she said, tapping it with her index finger. "Go on, open it."

"Are you okay?" I asked. She was looking ill, shivering.

"I'm just really nervous," she said.

"Why? It's just me," I replied.

I was the one who should have been nervous. I was sitting on Jacinda O'Neill's bed—it was both at once a high-crime and misdemeanor against Rick Jansen, as well as uncomfortably seductive to be there with someone I was attracted to like an electrostatically charged ion—thanks, Doctor Thomas. I was her friend, and I planned on honoring that oath, forever if I had to.

"Just open it. You'll see," she said.

The notebook was filled with sketches, doodles, journal entries, and blocks of lyrics scrawled in perfect script, with small captions of places and dates, starting in August of 1997. One page was marked August 29th.

"Read it," she said. "Out loud."

"I played my first live gig last night," I read. "It wasn't the performance of a lifetime, but everyone needs to start somewhere." As I read it, I remembered the lukewarm reception and the way Maynard Morris and his friends responded to her. Jaycie was always so positive, and her outlook made me smile. "I played 'We Belong Together' and 'Summertime Blues,' two of Grammy's favorites, along with 'Wish You Were Here.' I remember hearing Pink Floyd on my father's car radio shortly after Grammy passed away, and it seemed like the perfect choice for a third song. I knew she was looking over me, because I ran into an old friend, Amanda, and made a new one named Tony. I know that not everyone comes into your life for long periods of time, sometimes we only get a moment, but I wish I had someone like Tony in mine. I hate to say it, but I'm jealous of Amanda, for having someone like that in hers. He made me laugh. He was sweet and made every self-doubt fade away. He's a prince, and I hope to meet him again someday."

"I wanted you to read that," she said.

I had been depressed since the holidays for a variety of reasons. Spending time with Dad was great, but he was depressed—that, in turn, left me feeling the same. I thought going back to school after the break would help, but I only felt worse.

My situation with Jacinda was at once the best and worst thing in my life. Over the holidays, I'd realized that her friendship was precious, but it was also the thing that was making me sick.

When I walked into her bedroom, I immediately saw the picture of her and her Grammy, but I selectively ignored the other two—both of Jaycie and Rick together in varying stages of a loving embrace.

"Why?" I asked.

"Because you're an amazing guy, and you need to believe it—no, you need to know it—like I do." She paused as she searched for the right angle to approach from. "I know you're struggling right now."

"No, I mean, why didn't you show up the next day? Amanda and I went back to the fair, and I looked for you."

"What do you mean?" she said, like she was confused.

"I asked if you'd come back the next day, and you said, 'I'll look for you,'" I explained.

Jacinda's eyebrows crinkled, she shook her head and said, "I don't remember that at all. I'm sorry."

"It's okay," I said. Again, it felt like the universe was conspiring. Sure, it felt good to know she thought so highly of me, yet she was still so far away from the levels of my own admiration. Was it my fault that I fell in love? Can one choose to love a person, or does it just organically happen, whether you choose it or not?

I absentmindedly flipped through her notebook and landed on a page with frantic writing and scribbles, illustrated by the silhouette of a man with white hair. The page was only opened for a split second when Jaycie's hand came down on top, snapping it closed. Then she quickly took it from me, like a toddler's mom swiping away something dangerous.

"Sorry," she said with a flustered giggle. "I'm not comfortable sharing all my secrets."

There was an awkward silence as she put the notebook back onto the shelf, a silence I aimed to fill as soon as something, anything, entered my thoughts.

"Hey, can you teach me?" I asked. When she looked up, she saw me pointing to her guitar. It was sitting on a stand beside her desk.

"Can I teach you?" she repeated with a laugh. "Of course, I *could* teach you, but then you'd learn all my secrets and would never come out to any of my shows."

"That's entirely untrue," I said. "If I stole all your guitar secrets, first I'd have to get rid of you, then I'd get a red wig so I could replace you."

"Oh, you'd be a killer hot redhead," she said laughing, when her face suddenly turned serious, if not a tad emotional. "Thank you, Tony."

"For what?" I asked.

"For being my friend."

March 5, 2001

It was a cold spring, but I was looking forward to where it might lead. As the university slowly thawed, so did my depression. My knee was healed, and baseball training had just started. I felt good, like I had overcome adversity and now stood on the precipice of something great.

I was content—and I had a group of great friends in my corner who supported me and kept me motivated, through even the toughest times.

The first warm day of spring arrived during the second week of training, and I was already out in front of the pack, turning heads. Even Assistant Coach Mullen pulled me aside to say how impressed he was with my improvement. Things were looking up, and I was feeling untouchable.

Practice ended that day with me throwing out a runner at home plate from center field—a feat that only those with the strongest throwing arms could accomplish. Competition was a whole side of me that had been neglected while I was recovering, and it was beginning to flourish once again. I felt in control of my own destiny—and as a junior, I was ready for my time to shine.

I was on a high, and Coach Mullen slapped my butt as I came off the field—one of the odder baseball norms I never quite understood—but took it as the compliment it was. Everything was coming together, and I felt unstoppable.

As I grabbed my equipment and began jogging back to the locker room, I passed a group of freshmen teammates who were tied up and being "Naired" by upperclassmen. Rick was leading the show, making the kids walk on all fours as the older guys squirted them with hair removal products aimed at their privates while hurling insults. Some even spat at them.

I was appalled, but Rick was the team captain—and there was nothing I could do about it. Ever since that night at Jacinda's party, Rick had left me alone. It was one of the better outcomes of my friendship with her—despite the heartache.

I was lucky the team didn't haze when I was their age. It wasn't until Rick took over as captain that the rituals started, and the stunts were getting crueler by the day.

I showered and grabbed my bags to leave before the rest of the team came in from the field—I wanted to avoid the shit-show and evade getting pushed into becoming a part of the mess. The longer I was around guys like Rick, the more I loathed them, and I had heard rumors of other things—worse things than being "Naired" and spat on.

"Looking back, maybe I should have stuck up for them. Maybe I should have said something to the coaches, but I never did—maybe things would have been different..."

"Why didn't you?" asked Doc.

"Fear," I replied. "I spent so much of my life trying to fit in. To blend. The lesson I hadn't yet learned was that I was never meant to blend. I was meant to be my own person, and I was about to learn that lesson once and for all."

Sid and Marshall were ordering takeout from the China King—one of my favorites—before we hit the bus to spend an evening downtown in Mercy Point along the river walk. Jaycie was invited, but undecided, and I was holding out hope that she'd join us.

The sun was already falling from the sky when I left the locker room. I needed to get home quick, and Jaycie's red cabriolet was parked nearby. As if on cue, I spotted her talking to some teammates from the track team before they broke off to go home.

"Hey, need help?" I offered. She was lugging around her backpack and guitar case, and I couldn't imagine they were easy to carry together.

"Oh, hey," she said. She looked left and right, then smiled. "Sure."

She offered up her guitar case and we began walking to her car.

"Hey Tony," said Jess.

I hardly saw her—my mind was too occupied. "Hey, Jess."

She waved and continued on her way into the locker room.

"Who was that?" asked Jaycie.

"Jess?" I asked. "She's our neighbor at the dorms. She's majoring in Sports Medicine and works in the trainer's office."

"Oh," she said.

"Why?" I asked.

"You should ask her out," said Jaycie with a smile.

"Jess?" I laughed.

"Yeah," she said, nodding like it was obvious.

"I'd be lying if I said that didn't hurt."

"What hurt?" asked Doc.

"Jaycie's suggestion that I ask out Jess."

"Why?"

"The last thing anybody wants to hear from the person they love but can't have is that they should be focusing on someone else," I said. "Of course, I should have. I wish I could have! But there were vast reasons why I never once looked at Jess in that light."

"Which were?" he asked.

"Jess was sweet. She was pretty. She was kind and fun to talk to."

"Sounds like someone you should have paid more attention to," interrupted Doc.

"How could I have ever paid attention to the girl next door when the woman of my dreams was right there?" I said. "Jess and I were just friends. I never even looked at her that way."

"You mean, you looked at her the same way Jacinda looked at you?"

said Doc.

"Yes," I replied. "That's insightful, Doc. Good job. Though, I should mention that Jess was gay."

"Oh."

"I didn't know that till later, but your assessment still holds water," I said. "Still, it would have been nice to have been the dream guy, not the friendly guy next door."

I ignored Jaycie's suggestion with a shrug, then asked, "Coming out tonight?" Jaycie looked away from me briefly, as if to shake off her own struggle with our friendship. "Brad knows a karaoke bar that has every song you can possibly imagine."

"Oh, really?" she said, sounding interested.

"I figured you could rock out to some—Simon and Garfunkel," I said with cocked eyebrow, and she immediately started singing "Celia." "Or maybe Toto?" Without missing a beat, she switched to "Hold the Line." "I'm never going to stump you."

"Nope! Never," she laughed.

"What was that?" asked Doc.

"It was a game we played. I'd name a band and she had to sing one of their songs, but it couldn't be their top hit," I explained.

"That's impressive. Did you ever stump her?"

"Not once."

We were five feet from her car when the locker room door opened behind us. I thought nothing of it. I was having a great time with her as always, and I never wanted it to end.

"So, you're dropping me off, getting changed, then coming with us, right?"

She never heard me.

Jaycie's face transformed to cold stone in a snap, and I didn't see why until it was too late. She looked away as if stifling a tear.

"I can't—"

"Hey! Cocksucker," someone shouted nearby. "Why are you talking to my girlfriend?"

I knew who it was. I didn't even need to turn around.

"Rick," said Jaycie, "it's okay, he was just helping carry stuff to my car."

"I'm sure he was." Rick snatched her guitar case from me.

I held my hands up defensively, asking myself how this went so bad so fast. I was under the impression that Rick was okay with us being friends. He was a muscle-head with a six-pack I couldn't compete against—he couldn't be jealous, could he?

"Trying to score with my girl, punk?" When I didn't respond, he pushed me. "Fucking answer me when I ask you a fucking question."

"We're just friends, man," I said calmly, but that only made Rick angrier.

"You think a girl like her could be interested in a scrubby shit like you? You're lucky if some dumpster trash bitch would wag your toothpick dick."

There were "oohs" and even an "aww snap!" from an audience that had gathered.

"Rick, leave him alone," said Jaycie, but he ignored her. She stepped in between us, attempting to put out the fire, but Rick stared through her like she wasn't even there.

"C'mon, Rick, let's go," said Bill Whatley—he was our left fielder and was rooting for me to take over in center field. I liked the guy, and he seemed anything but willing to participate, but Rick was captain...

I was surrounded. Half the baseball team was there watching, along with some of the girls' track team.

"Fuck that, Bill. This asshole deserves it," Rick replied.

"Deserving or not, that doesn't mean you should kick his ass," Bill shot back. When Rick and the others didn't back down, Bill slid away from view. "I'm not a part of this."

"Do you think you deserved it?" asked Doc. "I've noticed you carry around a lot of guilt. Do you carry guilt over this event?"

"No," I said honestly. "I carry rage."

"I'm going, Rick," said Jaycie. "You can either stay here and measure dicks, or you can come by and pick me up in an hour. We can *go see that movie you wanted to see.*"

The way she said "go see that movie you wanted to see" felt like code for something else. Something that grabbed Rick's attention, if only for a second. Then she got into her car as Rick loaded her guitar case into the back seat. The crowd was starting to break up; I saw my opportunity to leave and took it.

Rick and Jaycie had a two-minute conversation through the car window while I was already walking home. As she drove past down the lane, she didn't look at me, not once. It was like I wasn't even there.

I was shaking involuntarily. I was angry and scared, embarrassed and humiliated, and on top of it, my dream girl was dating the biggest asshole on campus. I felt like I was back in high school, not playing ball at a respected university.

I checked my watch and realized I was going to miss the bus to Mercy Point if I didn't get moving. I jogged down the lane from the locker room parking lot—a winding driveway through a thick, dark patch of forest—as the sun dropped below the horizon.

I was halfway down the driveway to the main road when I heard them laughing.

"Who was laughing?"

"Rick Jansen and his friends," I said.

"What happened?"

"I don't remember much," I said. "Rick came out of the woods and tackled me to the ground. I remember my face hitting the pavement and the taste of my own blood. He punched me more times than I can remember, until one of the coaches drove past on his way home."

"Did anyone catch them? Did they get in trouble?"

"No. They scrambled as soon as they saw headlights."

I was pinned down. Bleeding. The world was spinning away and fading. I saw lights and thought it was the end.

"Stay away from her," Rick growled into my ear. "Or I'll kill you." Then he leaned in extra close and yelled, "I'll kill you, faggot!" He slammed his fist into my ribs one last time and ran into the woods.

I had a bad concussion. Several bruised ribs—one cracked—two black eyes, a broken nose and orbital bone, and a bad gash in my forehead around my left eye that needed thirty stitches. The doctors told me I was lucky I didn't lose a tooth or an eye.

Funny, I didn't feel very lucky.

I was in the hospital for three days.

Marshall, Sid, and Brad had no idea where I was. They spent all night in Mercy Point thinking I ditched them, only to find the message posted from the local cops on our dorm room door early that next morning as they stumbled in.

"What happened to Rick?" asked Doc.

"Nothing," I said. "My dad made the trip to campus immediately. He hired a lawyer, a local guy named Joe Berry, who accompanied us to the police station as we tried to sort the whole thing out. One meeting led to another, until finally a board member accompanied the dean into a meeting with us at the police station. They were well aware of the situation and had been performing an internal investigation since the incident. Rick gave his alibi and claimed that no confrontation outside the locker room ever occurred. Chief White explained there was nothing he could do, even though the look on his face told me the truth."

"Which was?"

"They were lying."

"How did your father react?"

"He was angry. I don't think he ever forgave himself for failing me that day, not that I ever felt he had. I never got the chance to tell him that."

"When did your father pass away?"

"Years later. While I was at Northcreek," I said.

"What happened after that?"

"Mr. Oscuro, as you can imagine, we are deeply distressed about the incident, and will do all in our power to make sure this never happens again," said Dean Nichols with a slight southern drawl.

My father was a good man. He was kind, courteous, reserved, and classy, but even I could sense the rage in his voice when he talked to them that day.

"How can you assure us that it won't happen again?" he asked.

"We have taken the necessary precautions of adding lights along the driveway in and out of the parking lot. We have also added security cameras."

"What about the perpetrator?" asked our lawyer, Mr. Berry. I sat in my chair beside him staring at the floor from behind a pair of sunglasses hiding two black eyes. "Richard Jansen."

The looks on the administration's faces were not what any of us expected.

"There's no proof that Rick Jansen perpetrated the attack," said Dean Nichols.

"No proof?" said my dad. "The proof is all over my son's face. Thirty stitches. Two black eyes. Broken bones and a concussion."

"There were no eyewitnesses. Your son never saw the perpetrator's face," said Chief White.

"It was Rick," I said. "He told me to stay away from his girlfriend. There were others. They were laughing at me while he pinned me face-down and punched me. Then he rolled me over and kept punching. I had blood in my eyes, but I know there were other people there."

"I'm sorry, Anthony," said Dean Nichols. "But Richard claims he was *with* his girlfriend at the time you were attacked. She even submitted a written affidavit."

The news hit me so hard, I began shaking. Why would she do that?

"You believe him? Over me?"

"I have no reason to disbelieve the son of a legacy," said Dean Nichols, "whose family has done so much for this town and university. Richard's captain of the baseball team and a standup young man and—"

"Fuck you," I said. "He's an ape on 'roids."

"Needless to say, I was kicked off the team," I said.

"No charges were ever brought against Rick?"

"None. To make up for my pain and suffering, they offered free tuition, since my scholarship was over."

"And Jacinda? How did she react?"

I took a deep breath and let the memory come back to me. "Rumors spread quickly after it happened. I don't know how much she knew or when she knew it, but I was sure Anne told her everything."

Every student on campus knew some version of what happened—some whispered I was hit by a car. Others claimed I was jumped by drug dealers. The truth had only one version, and only a handful of people besides me knew the truth.

I found Jaycie waiting for me by my front door one evening after class. She stood several feet away and made no attempt to get any closer, like she was afraid of what might happen if she did. Her eyes were nervous, and the corner of her mouth kept involuntarily snagging on a frown. She appraised me, taking in the horrors of my battered face. Then, she averted her eyes and started crying.

I never wanted her to see me like that. I looked like a monster—black and blue and stitched together, and her presence only made my injuries feel worse.

I was angry. I was angry at Rick. I was angry at the university. And I was angry at her.

"Fuck off," I told her.

She turned away, still crying, grabbed her backpack from the floor, and quickly left.

I didn't see her again for months.

"How did the attack and Jacinda's reaction make you feel?" asked Doc.

"Betrayed."

XVIII
dreams

TONY
Somewhere…
Now.

There was heat. Intense suffocating heat, and then for a moment, as I watched Mammon burn and wither away to ash, everything went black.

My eyes opened, staring up into a gray overcast sky. I was lying at the bottom of a hill, and the bare treetops had the beginnings of tiny green blooms. It was cold and wet, and the sound of running water forced me onto my knees.

I was once again in the forest of my dreams, but things were different, like the long winter of the last six years had finally brought forth the early beginnings of spring. I was wearing my brown leather jacket and jeans, just as I had at Marshall's, but I felt different inside. I felt synchronized—calibrated to my surroundings.

Although it was a dream, it felt more real than it ever had before. My pants were wet from the damp soil, and my lungs savored the fresh air. Every step was spongy with twigs snapping below my boots in the fresh soil. The place was so real, so alive, it made me begin to question reality—was this actually a dream?

I leapt over the gully with the babbling creek below and landed on the other side firmly, then trudged up the hill—a task that was once as difficult as scaling a rocky cliff—but was now effortless after my transformation. I was different, not just in the real world, but in this one as well. As I pondered how great I felt, I became aware I was being watched. Hidden eyes observing, gauging my intentions—was I friend or foe?

At the top of the hill, the old warehouse and mill stood in the middle of an overgrown grove. The building hid secrets—I could almost spot them, like beyond the façade was the truth of its existence. The building was old and abandoned, at least three stories high with a sliding barn door. The roof had collapsed in parts, and most of the windows were boarded up from the inside.

I could hear the gentle rumble of the waterfall, and then, on cue, the rain fell, rapping against the metal roof.

The brier within the clearing had grown extra thick, weaving like layers of razor wire, creating a nearly impenetrable barrier between the warehouse and me. The fallen tree was starting to rot with vast mushroom growth sprouting from its sides, and the weeds were as tall as I was. Moving through the grove was possible, but slow, with no apparent trail to mark my path.

The trees creaked and moaned as if speaking to each other. Their messages were sluggish whines, alerting the others to my arrival.

Not only was I being watched, I was being hunted.

I moved forward, pushing into the weeds toward the barn doors, and the clearing came alive. All at once there was movement around me from every direction—movement attempting to mask itself against the falling rain, knitting through the tall grass. From the corners of my eyes, monsters slipped and crawled into position to pounce.

Was this a trap? Was I under attack?

Danger was everywhere—I could smell it as easy as I could taste it. Adrenaline, aggression—like honey and pollen. They were closing in around me, at least a dozen of them, stalking like jungle cats. I had to move, to break their advance or be trapped. Finding a break in their formation, I sprinted for the fallen tree. In three quick strides I was beyond their lines. I leapt onto the fallen trunk, unnaturally gliding through the air like an Olympic long jumper and landed like a gymnast sticking the landing without a hop or clutch.

This place, wherever I was, brought out the best in me. I felt fueled. I felt whole. Like all of me was finally physically coordinating in perfect harmony, bestowing unnatural gifts that I was only beginning to explore.

I ran across the tree trunk toward the warehouse, sprinting for the landing, when something sprang from the tall weeds and bounded directly into my path. It landed like a cat on all fours and hissed a warning.

When she defiantly stood before me, she was no taller than a child, and yet she was a beautiful, fully matured woman of the wood. A nymph. I recognized what she was almost immediately—as if I had known her kind all my life. Along with that knowledge came more extensive information—she was an Alseid, caretaker of glens and groves, and her sisters could only threaten me with superior numbers. She had pale skin, long wild hair, and was mostly nude with eyes of sky blue.

She hissed again and splayed all ten fingers, each with a talon sharp enough to rend meat from bone. Then she leapt and viciously swiped for my throat.

She missed, but not because she wasn't fierce, fast, or accurate.

I ducked and spun away, sensing three more leaping from the weeds—each vying to take a piece of me with them. I dodged by sliding back across the rotting wood and dug my heel in to ready my next move.

Nymphs were protectors, honorable for the most part, but vicious when you crossed them. They were only trying to protect something, and I was an invader. I didn't stop to think of what threat they thought I posed—I only knew that the path to escape the dream was through them. I was playing my part, like riding a rollercoaster named destiny—over the gully, up the hill, across the glen, into the warehouse, up the stairs, across the never-ending hallway, and beyond the demon door—that was how I ended these nightmares.

All thirteen nymphs revealed themselves, and all thirteen looked like variations of the same tiny woman, with eyes as big and bright as the natural world they were sworn to protect. They were colorful like summer flowers, each blossoming with vibrant beauty, starkly contrasted to the dismal gray that permeated our surroundings.

I didn't want to fight them. They were only doing their job.

"I'm not here to hurt you," I said, as the rain intensified. "I only want to go inside." I pointed to the warehouse, hoping they'd understand. The nymph who faced me turned her head apprehensively, following my pointed finger to the barn door, then returned her gaze to me.

She spoke in a language I didn't know, but one I could strangely comprehend. "Leave. This place is not for you," she said in a high, musical voice.

"I've been here before. I need to get inside," I told her.

"Leave. Mistress waits not for you," spoke another nymph with the same voice. She was crouched on the ground below with bright ruby eyes, claws ready.

"Who does she wait for?" I asked, playing along.

"Her love," said another.

"I am her love," I said. My voice sounded firm and confident, despite my uneasiness. Were we speaking of the same "Mistress"? And was I really her love after all that had happened?

"Not her love," said a third, defiantly.

"Different," said a fourth.

The rain was coming down in great big torrents while the winds picked up and blew through the trees, dragging wet leaves and swaying the tall undergrowth with its force. I could feel the energy in the air, the tingle all around me, the smell of atmosphere starting to sizzle. The power was there, begging me to touch it if I wanted to.

I saw no other choice.

"Let me pass," I asked one last time.

"No. Different."

"I'm sorry," I said, giving the nymph with the sky-blue eyes a wink.

It was right there, dangling in the air, waiting for me to take it. I could feel it and recognized its power at my fingertips.

The nymphs were fast, sitting on the edge of a hair trigger and waiting to strike, but all I had to do was reach out and touch the energy—to will it into effect.

They snapped at me the instant I twitched, but I was faster than they were. The moment I touched the spark, the ground trembled and a great flash of white-blue static shot up through me and into the sky. The shockwave sent the nymphs sprawling, dodging away from the deadly bolt, and they took cover.

Thunder roared, echoing off the mountains and provided the opening I needed. I ran for the landing with the barn doors, leapt over a nymph with sapphire eyes, and sprinted up the crumbling concrete steps. I swiped aside the sliding door, and replaced it across the opening, wedging it into place with a piece of rusty metal from the inside.

I expected them to follow. I expected them to tear aside the barn doors and charge inside after me—but they did not. They retreated, as if I had more to worry about inside than in the glen with them.

It was quiet within the warehouse, except for the torrential rain slamming against the metal roofing. The wood and concrete walls were decayed but sturdy, and the abandoned equipment looked to be from a bygone era. There were cranks and pullies with dangling rusty lengths of chain, staging lanes and dusty tables filled with rotted pulpy sheets of paper and plywood. There were giant rollers, large wooden rafters, and broken pallets, as well as a catwalk and sets of metal stairs leading up to a second floor overlooking the expansive room below. I had never taken notice of the broader room prior to that moment—as if it had come alive, a fully realized place, and was no longer just the pre-determined nightmare from my past.

Thunder boomed in the distance, and lightning began to flash through the remaining panes of the antique glass windows. I heard something between the rumbling and waited patiently to hear it again—it sounded like wooden flooring creaking under someone's feet.

Moving through the warehouse seemed easy but knowing where to go was difficult. Sound refracted at strange angles, confusing my ability to track the creaking noise. Every time I felt I was closing in on the source, a crack of thunder chased the sound away to another section of the building. It was like chasing ghosts. The creaking mystery led me into a portion of the building where the floor was weak, and without warning, several of the floorboards crumbled apart and opened up into a yawning black void.

The void hummed like television static—a white noise beyond imagination, where the unconscious and conscious mind met. Without a floor beneath my feet, I fell and was quickly swallowed up by the void.

As I dropped, time slowed—my senses roared into hyper-relativity, and at the last moment, when I felt I was beyond saving, my hand lashed out and caught a length of chain dangling from the edge. However, despite my greatest efforts to save my own life, the chain gave way and fell into the black hole with me.

As I sank into the pit, death impending, my center of gravity shifted and nearly vanished altogether. The chain continued to fall into the pit like an impossibly long snake, one link at a time, but I found it capable of withstanding my own weight, as if anchored. I pulled myself back to the surface more quickly than the chain fell. As the last link tumbled over the edge, I thrusted myself upward and caught hold of a sturdy plank. Then, before that too crumbled away, I shot up through the hole and landed on solid ground.

I wasn't winded. I wasn't even tired, but the experience took my breath away. I gasped for air and said, "That was close." It was silly to think that I had survived all this time, and through the last few nights of insanity, only to fall to my doom in a black hole within my own dream.

When I turned back to investigate the hole, it had vanished. Closed up and healed over like it never existed. I tossed a discarded brick onto the weakened area and watched the wood break and crumble, swallow the brick, then heal over like a milky film on water.

The warehouse didn't want me there. I could sense it. It was trying to stop me from finding its secrets at all costs. When I found the stairs leading up to the second floor, I leapt over the railing and ran up, taking two stairs at a time. After every step, the metal stairs gave way and tumbled to the ground in a crashing equal to the rising thunder outside the warehouse walls.

Upon the landing, I looked out over the room and felt I was still being watched.

The floor continued to creak in the distance, and a door slammed in the opposite direction. Despite my instincts to investigate, I thought better of it the moment I heard her voice.

"Help me," she whispered.

I followed the voice down my usual path, through the door on the landing, around a corner and into the long, never-ending hallway. Windows lined the outer wall every few feet, overlooking the mill and broken water wheel. The far end, however, remained in perfect darkness. After a few steps, the grotesque face of the red devil laughed at me as I strode toward it, waiting for the hall to stretch out of reach. I felt the panic fluttering inside, waiting for the horror to begin.

The demon's mouth opened, and its forked tongue flitted out like a snake, hissing at my approach. However, the hall never extended, but merely waited for me to span its length. The wood creaked loudly, and the storm outside continued to thrash. When I passed the second window, I witnessed a bolt of lightning streak across the sky and watched as the raging river waters tumbled over the edge and rumbled onto the rocks below.

At the end of the hall, I stared into the face of the demon but found no handle to open the door. It smiled and laughed at me, daring me to find my way through—when I caught its flitting tongue and yanked the door open violently before it could bite down on my wrist.

I was over its intimidation. I had accepted the pain beyond that door and wanted to get it over with, to have this confrontation and move on. I wanted to get back to reality. I wanted to get back to the…fire?

I had forgotten all about the real world and what was happening there. Was I dying? Burning alive? Was I already dead?

The room beyond the door revealed itself as my eyes adjusted to the dark. Shapes slowly sharpened and clarified until they came into perfect focus.

The Mistress stood at the center with her back to me, a single shaft of light illuminating her from the shoulders down. Her long red hair hung halfway down her back, and she was wearing an old green dress. Her feet were bare and dirty, and the floor was damp and muddy, like she had just walked inside from the rain.

There was an old couch and beer cans spread around the room, as well as a broken cheval mirror in the corner.

Everything about the dream had changed, and I was embarking on new territory. This was not what was supposed to happen, and I nearly stumbled back in fear.

I was afraid of her. I was afraid of what she might do.

"Who are you?" she asked before I could ask the same.

"What do you mean? It's me. Tony," I said. She refused to turn and look at me, but stood there, stiff and rigid.

"You're different. I can't recognize you," she said as if she didn't even hear me.

"Jaycie, it's me," I said, fighting off my emotions. If she wouldn't look at me, I'd go to her, then force her to look at me. But when I made that first step forward, I couldn't move. I was stuck in place, restrained.

"You're lost. You need to find your way," she said, shaking her head.

"What do you mean?"

"You're missing something."

It was as frustrating as our final conversation. What was I missing? Why wouldn't she look at me?

The lightning and thunder filled the room with quick flashes of light. The storm was right on top of us, and every rumble filled me with renewed dread.

"I don't understand."

"Your heart," she said, like she was trying to jog a part of my memory. "You need to reopen your heart. It is critical you unbury that which binds us. Without it, we will never be able to find each other in the darkness."

"My heart?" I asked.

I didn't understand.

"Find it, before it's lost forever."

December 21, 2013
Philadelphia.

The fire burned unlike any I had ever seen. In a matter of seconds, it went from melting plastic and searing bone to blowing itself out, but not before it had scorched nearly everything in the room to ash.

Mammon and Marshall's remains were still smoldering when I finally came to, caught my breath, and stood up. I was dazed, confused, and had no idea where I was.

"Tony!" yelled Montoya. "Shit, man, we thought you were a goner!"

"I'm here," I said. I was still disoriented, trying to remember what happened.

"Yeah, but you weren't," said Jamaal. "You were long gone."

"What do you mean?" I coughed a bit of ash from my throat.

"You weren't with us. You vacated your body for about thirty seconds," said Henry, inspecting his pocket watch.

"I was?" I asked.

"Yeah, my man, where were you?" asked Montoya.

"I was dreaming," I said, when I heard voices and a far-off siren.

The blast had rocked the entire neighborhood, and there were already people rushing outside to see the damage.

"Dreaming?" questioned Chappy as I knelt down beside Marshall's scorched body. "That was some dream. It looked like you were dead."

"I wish I was," I said.

"We're sorry for your loss," said Chappy, kneeling beside me.

"Marshall wasn't just my friend; he was my best friend. He was my brother." I choked on my tears. Now he was just a ragged mound of ash, and that was my fault. "I should have listened to you. I brought Mammon here. This is my fault." I was wrapped in guilt and grief. I thought I couldn't experience the pain of loss anymore, after all I had lived through, but I was wrong. There was always more to lose.

"Leave, Tony," said Doshin. "Leave now." It was hard to determine if he understood what the sirens meant, or if he thought they were something else. He was a man out of time, but his intuition was spot-on—and the sirens were growing uncomfortably close.

"What's that?" asked Jamaal. He was pointing to a shiny object floating in the middle of Mammon's ashes. I fished it out and held it in my hand. It was still hot and probably would have burned my skin before my transformation. It was a golden coin with imperfect edges—ancient and stamped in the likeness of a Roman soldier.

"Leave. Now," demanded Doshin.

I wanted to grieve. I wanted to mourn. But I wasn't stupid. I knew what was coming and the kind of questions they'd ask if they found me here.

"You need to go," said Jamaal. "I'm sorry, but you have to go now."

Crowds gathered across the street, and people pointed up at Marshall's living room window. I spotted a camera on the front entrance of a dry cleaner on the corner—I could sense its signal the moment I went looking for it—and ruled out both the window and stairs facing the street as escape routes.

"Is there no other way out?" asked Henry.

I took the coin and ran for the bedroom. I agreed with Henry; there had to be more than one way out of Marshall's apartment. The window beside my friend's bed overlooked the neighbor's back patio and was shaded by a tree and an ivy-covered cinderblock wall separating it from the lot on the other side.

There were no other options.

I leapt from the window before anyone could see me and landed in the patio. After climbing the cinderblock wall, I sprinted away toward Center City.

"Where are you going?" asked Jamaal, who leaned against a lamppost as I ran past him. "I mean, what's the plan?" he asked a second later, as I passed him waiting on the other side of the street. They were in my imagination, and they appeared whenever and wherever they pleased.

Must be nice letting me do all the physical work.

"I have to find my heart," I said absentmindedly.

"What?" asked Montoya. "What does that mean, my man?"

"Yeah, Tin Man, what does that mean?" asked Jamaal.

Two times. Two times now someone had mentioned my "heart." It seemed to be the only clue I had to move forward. My echo had said it first, last night, before he burst into flames.

"Retrieve your lost heart. Get it back. Let her be your inspiration, Tony. Never let her go," he had said.

The second reference was from my dream.

"You're missing something," said the Mistress. *"Your heart. You need to reopen your heart. It is critical you unbury that which binds us. Without it, we will never be able to find each other in the darkness."*

"I need to go get something I left behind a long time ago," I explained.

"Is that wise?" asked Chappy.

What was I supposed to say? Yeah, trust me? I know what I'm doing?

I had no fucking clue what I was getting myself into. There were no manuals. There were no instructions. I didn't have a Yoda or Obi-Wan—heck, I didn't even have a T-800 with an Austrian accent, or an Egg-Shen with his six-demon-bag to guide me straight. All I had was the brain trust—who were just figments of my shattered mind.

I was off script. I had lost my best friend. And I was barely holding it all together.

"It's important," I said. "But first, we need a car."

"What kind of car do you need, my man?" asked Montoya with a devilish grin, eying up a sporty Beemer parked next to a fancy rowhome with an even fancier security camera.

"Something inconspicuous."

"Where are we going?" asked Henry.

"Somewhere I used to live."

XIX
evolutions

TONY
Then.

"How did the attack and Jacinda's reaction make you feel?" asked Doc.

"Betrayed."

"How so?" he asked.

It couldn't have been more obvious, but I guess that was the point—for me to overexplain myself in search of clarity.

"I realized where I was on the food chain. I was at the bottom, and Rick was at the top. Jacinda could have any guy she wanted, and she chose the asshole, the alpha male."

"That's quite an archaic way of looking at it."

"I should have known better than to fall for a girl who was taken by a Neanderthal. Seeing her sob over my fragility broke me."

"Do you think she may have felt guilty? That those tears were the manifestations of that guilt?"

"I'm sure that was a large part of it. Guilt or not, she chose him and helped him cover up his actions. I never wanted to feel that weak and

powerless again."

"How did you go about making that change?"

"It started the very next day. I looked at myself in the mirror, and underneath the battered face, I didn't like what I saw. I didn't like how easy it was to break me. I didn't like living in fear. I didn't like feeling weak. I didn't like much about who I was, and it was time I did something about it."

"What did you do?"

"First I healed. I took the pain, the emptiness, and the hurt and I plugged it up with whatever I could to stop the bleeding. Anger. Rage. Fury. The bitter emotions worked best.

"Then, over the summer, I trained like I was still playing ball. I grabbed a punching bag and some gloves, and I hit that bag over and over until my knuckles bled, every night.

"My dad got me a job working for him, manual labor at a construction site moving heavy things, like cement, rocks, and rebar. I felt like I was a castaway—a prisoner on an island with time to pay.

"I earned money, saved quite a bit, but spent some on myself and re-emerged a new man. I went through a metamorphosis that summer."

"I think we've come to the part in your story where most of your trauma lies," said Doc. "I feel like we're finally learning something."

"Thanks, Doc. Glad I could be of assistance," I said sarcastically.

Disappointment and betrayal can alter relationships. Jacinda had sided with a psychopath over me, and that hurt cut so deep, I thought the pain would never go away.

Happier days were behind me, and I was back to where I started—miserable and alone, analyzing and overanalyzing, contemplating my self-worth. Every day when I looked into the mirror and saw the bruises and scars fade, I was filled with anger.

I was at home in New Jersey, sitting in my old bedroom, looking at all the childish things I owned. Comic books, baseball cards, video games—everything seemed so pointless. I didn't like clinging to childish things and immature ideals. Identity was discovered, not made—

and it was so much easier to discover my identity when I stopped to actually listen to myself.

That summer, I discovered who I really was inside.

I learned I was edgier than most. I was two parts punk diluted into equal parts artsy. I had found my style—Doc Martens, Chucks, wallet chains, torn jeans, band tees, thermals, and a vintage brown distressed leather jacket—like something Layne Staley would wear. I grew a goatee, shaved my head down to the skin along the sides, and gelled the rest into a mess—topped off with a pair of black shades.

I grew my music taste and was rarely caught without a Discman—with bands like Stabbing Westward, Filter, VAST, God Lives Underwater, and Nine Inch Nails on heavy replay.

I still loved horror movies and comic books, but I had found a way to let the inside out—and I'd never felt more comfortable in my own skin.

The gash and stitches on my face healed, except for a light scar—like a pale line curling along the left side of my face, from eyebrow to cheekbone. It was a visual reminder of what I never wanted to be again—a victim.

September 1, 2001

It was the second day of the Grace Falls Labor Day Fair. My roommates and I decided to go, but we needed a ride. I expected Anne was going to drive us, like usual, until Marshall explained they had broken up. After my attack, Anne's loyalties were challenged, and according to Marshall, she failed the test.

Marshall loved Anne, and I could only imagine how hard that was for him.

But Marshall was confident that things would be okay.

"Why's that?" I asked.

"Tony, sometimes you have to flip the script. Write a new one."

"A public event like that, weren't you worried that Rick and Jacinda would be there?" asked Doc.

"I was living in a brave new world, with, quite literally, the visible

scars of my past. Part of me wanted to see them. I wanted Rick to see he couldn't break me. And I wanted Jaycie to see that I was a better man than I was before. But all that went out the window the moment I saw her."

We arrived after six, as the sun set and the air cooled, by taking the shuttle bus from campus. I was wearing my Stabbing Westward t-shirt and fatigue button up—dark jeans with a pair of Doc Martens, and a wallet chain at my side—to which Marshall kept asking if I was expecting someone to actually steal the wallet of an unemployed art student.

"I can hear your wallet sigh from over here, T," he said in his latest comedic assault on the new me. "Sounds like starvation."

"Oh!" mocked Sid, "because he's a starving artist?"

"Exactly," said Marshall, giving Sid a pound for the assist.

However, Marshall's playful attempts to bust my balls were his way of admitting my growth. I never felt more powerful, more at home with who I was, than when I felt like my outward appearance matched my inner self.

The same could not be said about Brad...

Bradley, all five-foot-one inches of him, wanted funnel cake, then ice cream, then hot dogs, followed by cotton candy, and then chased it all down with a beer. When we were done chasing after Brad's stomach, we decided to explore the fair from one end to the other.

But when I spotted the Speed Pitch booth ahead, I felt obligated to stop and give it a whirl.

Coach Mullen, the assistant baseball coach, was running the booth that year. He wore his Milton State Red Devils baseball cap with reflective aviator sunglasses and smoked an unlit cigar. I liked Coach Mullen, but never thought the feeling was mutual.

The Speed Pitch leaderboard already had more than twenty names, but only the top three were publicly posted on the chalkboard behind Coach. At the top was Rick Jansen with eighty-five miles per hour. In my opinion, that was underwhelming for a twenty-one-year-old built like a bulldozer.

"Hey Coach," I said as I stepped up, accompanied by my roommates.

"Well, Mr. Oscuro. How ya doing, kid? I almost didn't recognize you. I see your face healed up." Coach Mullen had the social tact of a drill sergeant.

"I don't know," said Marshall, before I could respond. "Do you really call that healed?"

Coach laughed and said, "Chicks love scars, boys. Wear 'em proudly."

Sid laughed—he and I had that in common.

I handed Coach eight bucks and received three tosses each for the four of us. Brad went first, stepping up and looking around for instructions.

"What am I supposed to do?" he asked.

Coach shot me an annoyed glance, then took a deep breath and removed the unlit cigar from his mouth. "Alright. Listen up, buttercup. What you want to do is toss the ball down that way. Get it as close to the target as possible for an accurate read on the radar gun. How does that tickle your fancy?"

"Tickles it goooood," said Brad, as he wound up and tossed all three balls in rapid succession.

"One at a time, numb-nuts," groaned Coach. Only one of Brad's three throws registered, at a pitiful thirty-two miles per hour.

"Thirty-two? This fucking thing's broken," cried Brad.

"Bradley," said Marshall, "I could probably roll my balls faster than you throw 'em."

"I'll roll your balls," groaned Brad.

Marshall went next, tossing a fifty-five, a sixty, and a fifty-four respectively. Then he and Brad exchanged more ball-tossing jokes. Sid threw one that topped sixty-eight, but the rest were below sixty.

When I stepped up, I had all three of them heckling me with every bad and immature "balls" joke one could imagine.

When I threw my first pitch with a cold arm, the readout gave me a measly 65 MPH—to a chorus of jeers from my hecklers. I wound up for my second throw and tossed something a bit more complementary to my skill and talent.

"Seventy-eight!" yelled Coach. "Finally, some competition."

A small crowd gathered behind us, but I was too focused to look back, even when I heard Marshall groan, "Fuuuuuuuuck."

I readjusted my grip a few times before taking a deep breath and readying myself for my final throw. Throwing a ball hard and accurate was about proper mechanics as much as it was the strength of one's arm. If you threw correctly, you could throw much harder and faster than you could if you just wound up and tossed it using arm strength alone. It was instinctual and came as natural to me as riding a bike. I took my step—transferred momentum—whipped my arm around in a perfect arc—then released the ball with a snap of the wrist—and followed through onto my front foot.

The ball hissed as it sliced through the air and slapped the backdrop with a loud *thwap!* The readout blinked three times before it finally displayed.

88 miles per hour.

"Holy shit!" shouted all three heckler roomies.

"A new leader!" yelled Coach with a smirk, shouting as if for someone else's benefit.

"Fuck that!"

From the moment I heard Marshall groan, I could have guessed who was standing behind me. His angry rasp only proved it. His blonde hair was gelled back, and his blue eyes were gleaming with rage. The collar was popped on his expensive golf shirt, and his shorts and sandals were worth more than my entire wardrobe. Rick and I couldn't have been more different. His pompous aura was so thick and irksome that I couldn't stand to look at him without the compulsion to bury my knuckles into his face.

"Oh, look who it is," said Coach. "The second-place contestant. Do you have a problem, son?" If I didn't know any better, Coach was setting us up—and I couldn't tell what side he was on.

"This little faggot threw eighty-eight?" growled Rick, stomping in hot like a rocket reentering the atmosphere.

"You throw around a lot of homophobic slurs," I said with a smirk, "for a guy who takes shots in the ass from dudes in bathroom stalls."

There were audible gasps, and Marshall cackled.

"I'm gonna beat the shit out of you. You tried to get me expelled, faggot!" Rick shoved me. For some reason, he didn't look so big anymore. I was no longer afraid of him, and I was not about to get pushed around either. "You owe me a new shirt," he growled under his breath so only I could hear him. "The cleaners couldn't get your blood stains out."

I shoved Rick back, and it took him by surprise. He nearly tripped over his expensive sandals trying to maintain balance.

"Kick his ass, Rick!" yelled someone from the gathered crowd.

Rick shoved me again. It took all my agility to remain standing. I wasn't there to fight, but I wouldn't allow myself to get pummeled again.

"You and me have problems that need resolving," he said, his hot rancid breath splashing my face. It stank of hot dogs and sauerkraut with a vodka chaser.

"Try it," I said.

"Instead of beating on each other like a couple of cavemen, why don't you have a throw- off," said a girl from the crowd. "Settle it right now. Fastest pitch wins." I let my guard down just enough to see Jaycie leaning against a wooden lamppost as it flickered on in the fading twilight.

All the built-up anger I held toward her evaporated the moment I saw her.

She was radiant, her red hair as vibrant as ever, wearing large, dangling star-shaped earrings—the earrings I gave her. She wore an old vintage cream-colored David Bowie t-shirt beneath an old leather jacket, with a short plaid skirt and Doc Martens similar to my own.

Jaycie wouldn't look at me, not even a glance. Her face was cold and impassive.

She stood out from the rest of the group, like she didn't belong. A few locals had been drawn in by the prospect of a fight, along with Milton State students and athletes—including most of the starting baseball team and a full sorority.

"I think she's right," said Anne from beside Jaycie—the two girls exchanged a quick glance, before Anne added, "A throw-off seems like the most logical way to handle this."

Their suggestion made sense to keep the peace. Rick was on the verge of a roid-rage blowout, and my roommates and I were outnumbered and surrounded—as more and more people flocked to the area like sharks to chum.

"That sounds like a great idea, Ms.," said Coach, who immediately tossed a ball to Rick and me. Rick snatched his out of the air with an angry swipe of his arm. "Three tosses. Fastest pitch wins." As Rick stepped up to throw, Coach added an extra stipulation. "If Rick wins, he gets the record and can do whatever he wants. I won't stop it. I'll only call for help."

Rick looked venomous; his smile spread from ear to ear. For a second, I'd actually thought Coach was on my side.

"C'mon!" yelled Sid. "That's not fair!"

"But," added Coach to Rick, "if Oscuro wins, you walk away with your tail between your legs, without touching him or his friends. Got that?"

"Oh!" nodded Sid. "That's a good deal."

"Good deal? That guy's a Lurch!" growled Brad, referring to the Addams Family butler.

"Probably runs like a Lurch too," said Marshall discreetly, mimicking a Frankenstein-ian walk. "If this goes sideways, meet you back at the dorm."

"Glad I wore my Jordans," groaned Brad.

"Oh yeah," said Sid, admiring his sneakers, "look at those. They even look fast."

"Yeah," said Brad proudly.

"Too bad they're not real," laughed Sid.

"Hey! I paid twenty bucks for these!"

Marshall gave me a semi-confident nod, but I wasn't sure how much more I had left. I hadn't thrown a ball in five months.

"You're dead," said Rick. "This will be over after one throw."

There was a fine line between confidence and arrogance—and Rick trampled over that line on the regular. Coach had given me a way out, but I felt like David facing off against Goliath.

"Were they really such impossible odds?" asked Doc.

"Rick was an all-state ballplayer—star quarterback and pitcher. He had championships under his belt and the swagger to prove it. He never lost a game on the mound. Broke a kid's leg once with a wild pitch—some say he did it on purpose. When he wasn't pitching, he was catching, and held the state record for throwing out base runners attempting to steal."

"Oh."

Rick's first throw hissed like an angry snake and struck the canvas backstop so hard that it bounced off into the next booth.

"Eighty-seven miles per hour," announced Coach.

Rick scoffed and grunted, then backed away, staring me down like we were about to quick draw with a pair of six-shooters. He was putting on a show for the crowd, and they were eating it up.

I stepped forward, then glanced back at Jaycie, catching her before she abruptly retracted her eyes and stared at the dirt. She was emotionless, like she'd rather be somewhere else.

When I lined up and slung my first pitch, something felt off.

"Seventy-four miles per hour," announced Coach.

Some of my former teammates laughed and mocked me. The entire crowd was on Rick's side, and why not? He was the All-American boy with the All-American good looks and the All-American bank account. I was just a punk kid, right? I even caught Brad slinking away, like he was getting a head start on his escape.

Rick's next throw hit 90 MPH, and the mob roared.

My second pitch was a measly 86, and the crowd jeered, anticipating a bloodbath.

Rick was in my head. Everything was going wrong. I felt the situation spiraling out of control, and when Rick tossed his final ball, a 94 MPH laser, I began plotting my own escape.

"Babe, you see that?" said Rick to Jaycie.

"That's great," she said with a smile, "a personal record." That smile quickly dissolved into an icy stare when Rick turned and high-fived his buddies. She didn't appear to be enjoying herself, yet this was her idea—embarrassment and a beating, packaged and delivered by the woman I couldn't stop loving. I'd put her up on the highest pedestal, and even after her betrayal, I still wanted her to notice me.

It felt like my new world was already crumbling. This new identity, the new attitude, the new clothes, everything had changed and yet stayed the same. I was angry at myself and at the world for being so unfair. The situation couldn't have been any worse. I had to throw harder than I had ever been recorded throwing just to avoid having to fight a psycho menace.

"Flip the script," said Marshall, placing a comforting hand on my shoulder. "Write a new one." Amidst the entire scene, my best friend was there, offering the words I needed to hear. Suddenly I let go of everything I was trying so hard not to lose and decided to fight for everything I wanted so badly to win.

I took a deep breath, reset my mind, then took two confident steps toward Jaycie. I boldly stared at the woman of my dreams. I wanted her to see me—to really see me. No bruises. No broken face. The real me—the improved version—and to hell with Rick and what he thought of it.

Jaycie and Anne were discussing something serious when my stare caught Anne's attention. She elbowed Jaycie, and our eyes met the moment she turned. I stared straight into her eyes, and I didn't dare to look away. The last time she saw me I was a broken, bruised mess, but now I was standing taller than I ever had—defiantly proclaiming that I would not be crushed, not now, not ever—not by her, and most definitely not by Rick.

"Nobody," said Coach, "under the age of twenty-two, in the history of this booth, has ever thrown faster than ninety-four miles per hour."

Another round of applause and insults was hurled into the air when a few people in the back started chanting "Rick's an asshole!" It was a girl with pink hair and a group of her friends. They were quickly booed, but it was enough to break the mounting pressure.

"I hope you brought the spicy mustard," growled Rick, "because I'm going to eat you and your friends alive." If that was his attempt at humor, I realized just how awful Jaycie's relationship must have been—he was as humorless as lint.

"No, but I brought the Listerine," I said, seething with sarcasm. "You can have some if you like. Please."

Rick didn't get it, but Coach chuckled.

I stepped toward Coach and instead of flipping me the ball, he said, "If you start running now, you might just make it out alive." I ignored him and aggressively swiped the ball straight from his hand. "Good," he said, "Shut that prick up."

My passion and determination roared when I looked at Rick, and all the pain and fear he instilled in me burst into a fiery furnace inside my chest. The ignited flames soared and made me feel powerful. I felt unstoppable.

"I never understood the flames. They never made sense to me. Were they real? Were they a figment of my imagination? I don't know."

"Was this the first time you experienced this phenomenon?" asked Doc.

"Yes. And many times since. Until Northcreek. They stopped burning after that."

"Do you believe these flames were a manifestation of your emotional state?" he asked.

"I don't know," I said, and the doc jotted down a quick note on his legal pad.

The crowd went quiet, or maybe I had just blocked out all the noise. I could sense everything around me—Marshall, Sid, Jaycie, Rick, the crowd, the air, the dirt, the smell of funnel cake, Brad tying his laces extra tight—but nothing penetrated my concentration. I wound up and hurled the ball with every part of me in complete control. But as I let go—the ball zipping toward the canvas backdrop—a deep regret immediately extinguished the flames. I didn't put all I had into it—it was like I had purposely backed off—like I had given only the minimum effort.

The ball struck the backdrop, and I waited.

The radar gun flashed three times, then displayed my fate. The numbers were like gibberish. My understanding of their meaning was lost until Coach read them out loud.

"Ninety-eight miles per hour!" Coach gushed. It was the most emotion I had ever witnessed from that man. The crowd, which had been screaming the whole time, went silent.

Rick came barreling at me like a man possessed, but Coach leapt over the booth and jumped in between us. "You made a wager, Jansen. Honor it!"

The crowd chanted for us to fight, but Coach made sure that didn't happen. He asked me to leave with a smile. I took my cue, waved for Marshall, Sid and Brad to follow, and we walked out of there with our heads held high—and still intact.

"Was that the end of the rivalry?"

"Far from it. No matter how hard I tried to flip the script and write a new one, the script was always being dictated to me—every confrontation made things worse."

"Why do you think that was?"

"Power. Control. I was a threat, and that made me a target."

"Did you and your roommates leave the fair?"

"No. In fact, the night was far from over."

The moon that night was neatly curled and crescent, but it still shone brightly in the clear night sky. It hung from the heavens like a shiny new ornament, and I couldn't stop looking up at it, as if it had a deeper meaning.

I was meandering through the crowds, trailing Marshall, Brad, and Sid as they decided to take another pass at the food tents. Brad was going on his third tour, but my stomach was tied in too many knots to feel like eating.

I thought about Jaycie, and how much I wanted to talk to her—just to be near her—despite everything that had happened between us. I thought about Rick. I thought about Jaycie and Rick, then wanted to pry a fork up my nose to scramble my brains for mentally picturing the two of them together. Then I thought about the zoning permits for such a huge fair, just to get my mind off the previous thought. I thought about everything until there was nothing left but the endless rumble between my ears.

Marshall noticed my mood souring moments after we left the Speed Pitch booth with my name proudly displayed in the top spot. He took a photo of it before we abruptly left the raging lunatic in the popped-collared polo having an identity-crisis-level meltdown.

I should have been on cloud nine. I should have felt on top of the world. Somewhere in my extra-hopeless romantic mind, I had visions of Jaycie jumping into my arms after I beat Rick. A complete and total fantasy that only ever happened in the movies.

Brad suggested we try some arts and crafts to cheer me up, because I was "artsy and dig that sissy shit."

Marsh suggested I go find that girl with the pink hair and "knock some boots."

Sid thought a beer or two might make me feel better, but truthfully, there was nothing that could have changed my mood—except Jaycie slicing through the crowd, yanking me aside and leading me off toward an unknown destination—which was exactly what happened.

"Hey, what's going on?" I said as she tugged at my wrist to keep pace. She was moving like she was late for an appointment.

"The fair's going to close in less than an hour, and I still have to ride the Ferris wheel," she said with a smile.

"What?" I said, tugging my arm free, and she stopped. "I don't understand."

"You don't want to ride the Ferris Wheel with me?" she asked.

"Yes," I said. "I mean no. Wait. Which one means yes, I want to ride the Ferris wheel with you?"

"Both," she shrugged, then laughed and shook her head.

"But why?" I asked. "What about Dicky Jansen?"

She gave me a discreet laugh but shrugged off her boyfriend's new nickname. "I want to spend the rest of tonight with someone I enjoy being around."

"And that's me?"

"That's only you," she said, then reclaimed my hand and dragged me onward.

The Ferris wheel was by far the largest I had ever seen. It kept growing as we approached from the other side of the fair. Jaycie nodded to the operator, who knew her by name, and she boarded the ride like they were old friends.

As we rotated our third trip around the wheel, the ride slowed and stopped just as we arrived at the very top.

"Yes!" Jaycie shouted. "This is the best part!"

"You like getting stuck?" I asked. She looked at me with danger in her eyes and began to rock the car back and forth. "What are you doing?" I grabbed hold of the guard rail with both hands.

"Oh my! You're scared of heights!" she laughed.

"No! I'm just scared of falling out a rinky-dink car, a hundred feet in the air."

"More like two-hundred-fifty-feet," she said matter-of-factly with a mischievous grin.

"What?" I croaked.

"Relax," she said playfully as the stars twinkled all around us. "It's so beautiful up here." She said it quietly, and I began to take in the view. "My Grammy and I did this every year. We'd ride the Ferris wheel and she'd pay the operator to keep us stuck up here for as long as possible. She used to say *'Tomorrow's not a promise. Gotta earn each one.'"*

"Your Grammy sounds like one heck of a woman."

"She was," she said, smiling. "Thank you."

"You're welcome," I said.

"No, not for the compliment. For forgiving me," she said.

When she started to tear up, I placed my hand onto hers, resting on the safety rail. "Let's not," I said, and she nodded. I wasn't ready to let it all go, but I was happy to have her back in my life, if only for the duration of the ride. "Are you okay?" I asked, after the tears started to multiply.

"Yes? No. Maybe?" she responded. "I really don't know."

"If you need to talk, I've got two ears," I offered.

"Oh, because you're the perfect person to talk to about all this."

"What I'm suggesting," I said, "is that I'd sit here and listen to you.

I'm here for you, no matter what." I meant every word. I was there for Jaycie and her well-being. No tricks. "No strings attached."

She stared into my eyes, glancing from one eye to the other as if searching for honesty and maybe something more.

When her search was over, she finally said, "You are definitely not normal."

"Thanks, I think."

"No, no," she said, and placed her hand on my shoulder. "I didn't mean it that way. I mean," she began to say, then thought for a second before finishing, "most guys when they look at me, in less than two minutes they'll try to look down my shirt. They're like hunters looking for the next kill." She pulled her eyes from mine and began to gaze up at the stars. "But you," she said, turning back to me, "you look me in the eyes. You talk to me like someone who cares. Like someone who wants to know me. Even after all I've done to you, you're still here. Still willing to do whatever it takes to make me smile." Then she quietly added, "You respect me. It's different."

Staring into her eyes was transfixing, and something I would have never attempted months ago when I was dangling around, a friendly fish on her hook. There was power in the eyes. Unspoken words transferred between us with nothing more than a look. When I gazed at Jacinda, I was telling her everything she needed to know about me. She gave a shy smile—like a flinch—before she fully opened up to me.

If I had looked away right then, she may have been able to pass it off as insignificant. Instead, I held, and her smile slowly faded.

I was no longer staring into her eyes, but rather, she was staring back into mine. There was peace around us. The low rumbling of the crowds in the background surrounded us both and stripped away everything else.

I studied her under the moonlight. Her freckles scattered across her cheeks like a constellation of stars. The sweeping curls of her hair, flowing like fiery ocean waves. The suppleness of her lips like pillows. The brightness of her eyes and the small flecks of blue that mixed into the emerald, like an elixir of life. She was perfect, her skin catching the reflected light from the moon, radiating like a star. She was too incredible for this world, like she was made of pure dreams and fairy tales—like she didn't exist.

Then, like all good things, that perfect moment came to an end.

"Sometimes I think there has to be more to life than what I'm feeling. Sometimes I feel so empty," she admitted. "I feel so alone. I feel so ugly inside, that I can't understand why anyone would find me attractive or interesting."

I nodded to let her know I was listening. She hurt and bled and was insecure like anyone else, and that made me even more crazy about her.

"I know I'm only twenty," she continued. "The whole world is ahead of me. I want to graduate college and I want to sing and play guitar. I want to do so much, yet I feel so stuck."

"Why are you stuck?" I asked. Why couldn't she just *unstick* if she was so unhappy?

"I'm scared," she cried, then stifled her tears. She leaned her head onto my shoulder, and I wrapped my arm around her. "Why is it so easy with you?" she asked, and I had no answer, even if she was looking for one. "There's something different about you."

"Good different? Or bad different?" I asked.

"Good. You seem more confident. Stronger."

"It's probably just the shirt. Maybe the cologne."

"Fuck that," she said as she sat up. "It's more than that, and you know it."

"Did you just curse?" Jacinda never cursed, ever—the last time was the day I gave her those earrings. "Jacinda O'Neill just cursed, everybody!" I shouted, and Jacinda laughed.

It was beautiful.

"Tony," she said, giving me her undivided attention. "You're such a beautiful human being. Inside and out."

Jaycie's eyes hung on mine and I sensed something—an intuition maybe? Like the dynamic between us was shifting.

I was never clever with important words. In the moment they always escaped me, and I'd often found myself thinking of better things to say well after the fact.

"When I look at you, sometimes I want to say a lot of things without saying everything," I said, and her forehead furrowed like I spoke in riddles. "I mean, I want to be profound, but not too profound, ya know? Like, I want to be witty but sincere. To make you smile, but not laugh. I mean, laughing is okay, but not ha-ha laugh, because I don't want to be that kind of funny in the moment, right?" I was a dying fish, baking on the desert sand. I was speaking nonsense and quickly withdrew to start over. I took a deep breath. "What I mean to say is, you've touched me in places I've never been touched before."

What the fuck was I saying!?

Her smile bloomed, and she shut her eyes to fight back the urge to giggle. "I haven't touched you, Tony. At least, not like that," she said, and we both laughed.

"Jaycie," I said, pulling myself together, "it's no exaggeration to say I'd take a bullet for you, without thinking. You've brought out the best version of me, and I don't know where I'd be without you. You've kept me grounded, motivated, and you make me feel like I matter. You are irreplaceable. I've had a crush on you since the day we met, but it's no longer a crush."

The look on her face said everything—shock, fear, confusion, overwhelming emotion. I pushed on, realizing I'd always be damned if I do and damned if I don't. At that point, I would rather have no regrets than to leave that night without having bared my soul to her.

Then I said, "I'm always so afraid to be the blunt object that destroys everything in my own pursuit of happiness, which is why I waited till now to say this.

"I would literally do anything for you, Jace.

"You're beautiful. You're cute, even when stressed out or sweaty after track practice. You're always the prettiest girl in any room. You can wear sweats as gracefully as a fancy dress, and I have never once looked on you with anything less than complete adoration. You are undeniably sexy, even when you're not trying to be, and you have this look, when you're trying to be matter-of-fact, that makes me melt every time.

"I may believe wholeheartedly that your beauty is unrivaled, but that's not the reason I care so deeply for you. The truth is, despite those beautiful green eyes, that big beaming smile, the movie-star hair, and the legs of a goddess, you are as beautiful inside as you are on the outside.

"I have never met a more warm, compassionate, sweet, kind, and loving person. I have never met someone who commits so thoroughly to lifting others up. I have never met someone who inspires me more. I have never met a more honest, humble, genuine woman. I adore your awkwardness and find you so fascinating and beautifully quirky. I have never wanted to know someone more, your thoughts and interests—what makes you tick, your soul—and when you bare that soul with your shielded, apprehensive vulnerability, it leaves me want to protect you, as if you were the last pure thing left in this world. I have never met a more competitive, determined, ambitious, and strong woman. I have never met someone who is unequaled and yet my equal, all at the same time—classy, brilliant, smart, and sassy at times. A truly unselfish spirit with a heart of pure fucking gold. Seriously, where did you come from with that heart of yours?

"I see the real you, and there's nobody like you out there.

"For you, if time was all that mattered, I'd wait a lifetime. You're the person that makes everything okay. Caring for you, like I do, is not a mistake. You're the best thing that's ever happened to me. You've stolen my heart."

"Huh?" she said quietly as I finished. Her eyes went wide, and her jaw tightened.

Had I read the moment wrong?

"I like you," I said, committing the biggest backpedal of all time.

"Are you done?" she asked. She sounded slightly annoyed.

"Stick a fork in me," I responded, and a microwave *ding* played in my imagination.

Jaycie took a deep breath, and her eyes freshly glazed over with tears.

"Thank you," she said. There was a long pause of silence, so quiet I could hear conversations from the crowds below and the creaking of the Ferris wheel, as we continued to dangle a few hundred feet up. "Thank you for the kind words. I really appreciate it. Nobody has ever said anything like that to me before."

The spiraling sunken feeling of disappointment settled into my stomach. I was stranded at the very top of a Ferris wheel, with the woman of my dreams, who appeared as confused and polar about me as I was about her just hours ago.

She slid to the far side of the car and began staring off into the sky, away from me. I turned to give her space, and the sky flashed, like a strike of summer lightning with outward ripples—like heat rising from August blacktop, followed by the cawing of nearby crows.

Then she was right beside me, grabbing hold of my shirt and pulling me toward her. Tears streaming down her face.

I was a slingshot rebounding. I was psychologically whiplashed.

"It's not fair," she said. "I'm sorry, please understand."

My arms thought for themselves. They wrapped around and pulled her close, and she hugged me back—apprehensive at first but tightening with every passing moment.

"Don't give up on me," she whispered into my ear. "I don't know how, but you get inside me. You can see me. Who I really am—not what everyone else sees. You see the real me. It's like you've known me forever. Nobody has ever—nobody has ever—" She cried. "What's wrong with me?" She sobbed into my shoulder, gripping my shirt.

"Nothing's wrong with you, Jaycie," I whispered over and over.

Minutes passed, and her sobs slowly died away. Eventually, she cleared her throat.

"I don't want to let go," she said weakly.

"Then don't," I replied.

"Eventually," she coughed, clearing her throat again, "I'll have to."

"I know." Or at least, I thought I knew.

"I'm sorry."

"What for?" I asked. What could she possibly have to apologize for?

"For not being who you need me to be," she explained.

"It was a riddle I couldn't solve. She was saying conflicting things. One moment I saw the real her—who she really was—then the next she wasn't able to be who I needed her to be. All I wanted was her. I guess I

was too distracted to see the clues."

The doc just nodded and listened.

"Don't be sorry." I was confused and didn't know how to respond.

"Thank you for understanding," she said, then pulled away from me, but took my hands in hers and smiled. "What is that?" She was looking at the key around my neck.

"You know what this is," I said, like she was joking. We'd already had that conversation at least twice—once when we first met, then again at her place the night of her party last fall. She looked confused. "It's the key to my heart. And it's yours if you want it."

"Tomorrow's not a promise," she whispered.

Without warning, she leaned forward and kissed me. First kisses were supposed to be mystifying—but there was something extraordinary about the kiss that left me breathless. It wasn't just intimate and sweet and frightening—it carried with it a pain so deep and beautiful that I believed it was the overwhelming joy bursting inside me. It was like fire and ice—love and loss—a dull, rapturous ache that pleasantly scorched my lips and burned blissfully into my chest. It was the most addictive, most overwhelming and satisfying experience of my life—and I desperately wondered if Jaycie experienced it the same.

The kiss wasn't an answer, but I realized that maybe she didn't have the answers. Maybe the future was still a mystery.

Moments later, the Ferris wheel began turning, and we were dropped off at the bottom after another rotation. I walked her to her car as the fair closed, holding her hand the whole way. The long walk across the lot went by in a matter of seconds, and we walked in silence, occasionally staring into each other's eyes.

Once at her car, we stood there, each waiting for the other to solidify what had transpired between us.

"Can I see you? Tomorrow?" I asked.

"Of course," she replied. "I was planning on it."

"Where?" I asked, giving her the option.

"The Grace Falls Diner, near the town square."

"Six o'clock?"

"Perfect."

We kissed one last time, then Jaycie got into to her car, opened the door, and turned the ignition.

"See you then," she said with a smile, then put the car in gear and drove away.

I watched Jaycie's taillights disappear as she drove out of sight and felt like I had taken control of my own destiny.

"Bro," said Brad. He was standing behind me, flanked by Sid and Marshall. They were eating from a single bucket of popcorn, as if enjoying the show. "Big night, huh?"

XX

tragedy

TONY
Then.

"I supposed life really changed after that moment?" asked Doc.

"What do you mean?"

"You and Jacinda kissed. You shared an emotional moment together. I assume that was the start of a relationship between the two of you."

"Doc, some love stories are complicated. This story is byzantine."

"That in itself is a complicated word," he said.

"There has never been a single thing about my life that came easy," I said. "That night after the Labor Day Fair, I couldn't sleep. I couldn't wait for our date the next evening. But I should have known the other shoe was about to drop.

"I don't believe in luck anymore because it doesn't believe in me. Back then, when I was twenty-one, it felt like I was constantly trying to balance my life on a seesaw. One moment of positivity was met with a downpour of misfortune. Before the weekend was out, I'd learn that lesson once again—and not for the last time in my life."

September 2, 2001

I arrived at the Grace Falls Diner around 5:45 in the early evening. The sun was still shining, though plummeting. I was fifteen minutes early but approached the hostess inside the diner and asked if there was anyone there waiting for me. The lady looked like she had never been asked something so peculiar, but all the same she answered no.

I sat down at a booth by the window and waited.

By ten minutes after six, I told myself she would be there anytime soon.

By six-thirty, I had used the Diner's payphone to give her apartment a ring, only the number had been disconnected. Then I called Marshall, asking for Anne's new number, but he didn't have it, and was equally as confused as I was.

When seven-thirty came and went, I decided to leave, after ordering a soda and cheese-fries, picking at only a few bites. My stomach was in knots.

"She stood you up?" asked Doc.
"She did."
"I'm confused."
"Me too."

December 11, 2001

For the next three months, I never saw Jaycie. And despite the fact that Marshall got back together with Anne, I never once asked about her.

Sid, Brad, and I went out as the "Three Bachelor Amigos" while Marshall stayed at home and got fat on Anne's cooking. I met girls. Lots of girls. I used them and they used me, and I spiraled for a while. Then, the second week of December, I met someone who shook up my world.

Brad spotted her first and called dibs.

She was playing video games in Jess's room. Jess, our neighbor, was a hippie bookworm and was as kind as anyone I had ever met. She was quiet, honest, innocent, loved music and poetry, and was never seen without her glasses and squinty smile. Jess never said a bad word about anybody and always managed to see the good in things. She was cool, smart as hell, and let us come over anytime we wanted for just about anything—that day we were looking to borrow an ice tray so Brad could attempt to make Jello shots to impress the bartender from Down the Hatch. That's when we spotted her—a pink-haired emo girl with an unseasonably-short-skirt and mouthing off at the TV like it was arguing back. She was playing her way through a difficult level of old-school Mario Bros, belly down on the floor with her bare feet kicked up in the air.

"Fucking hell! How the fuck did we fucking play this fucking game when we were just little fucking shits? Screw you! Fuck off goomba! Bite me!"

"Dibs," said Brad with a diabolical smile.

"Tori, we have company," said Jess.

"I don't fucking care if you're banging them in the next room, Jess. I'm trying to fucking head stomp my way through fucking goombas to find out if my princess is in another fucking castle."

"I like you," said Brad. "Marry me, sweetheart! Have my Asian babies!"

She turned, looked up at Brad from the floor, and laughed like she was at a comedy show. Then she hopped over, powered off the Nintendo, and scowled at him. "I'd break you, sweetheart." Then she looked at me and said, "But you—wait, I know you."

"Labor Day Fair," I said, noting the pink hair. "You yelled *Rick's an asshole.*"

"Yeah!" she shouted. "But no. We met before then. Same place, different time. You're friends with Amanda Hemmels."

"Oh, right," I replied. "I remember you." I was so distracted that night I almost forgot the rest of Amanda's friends—Maynard Morris and the others.

"Yeah, Jess is my sister," she said with a smile.

"From the same mister," Jess replied. "Literally. Different mother." Despite their dramatic differences, you could tell they were close by the way they spoke to each other.

Tori was pretty, but wild, with a voice that always wavered like she was about to lose it. She followed me back to our place and kicked Marshall out of the bedroom, tossing his notes and textbook into the living room before locking me inside with her. Then she jumped on top of me like an animal—cursing like a sailor bringing her ship to port.

Tori and I hooked up seven more times, once for each day of the week. When she showed up on the eighth day, she proclaimed she had experienced all she needed to experience with me and asked to be friends.

When I talked to Jess and told her what had happened, she laughed, and said, "Poor T! Tori doesn't do relationships. She meets someone here and there and hooks up with them till she's done. Then she takes her time till she meets the next one."

Taking Tori up on the offer, I met up her and her friends at Down the Hatch. Each of them remembered me as the guy who drooled all over Jacinda O'Neill, then bought me a shot to apologize for Tori breaking my heart—which was kind of a running joke amongst them.

"This is my ex-lover, Maynard, but Manda called him Morris," said Tori, patting Maynard on the back. He had gotten tall over the last few years, and his hair was longer than the three girls.

"Name's Robbie Maynard Morris, but everyone just calls me Maynard," he said with a beer in hand. "Or Nard, if you please."

"Please," groaned Tori. "And this is my ex, Trent." She ruffed Trent's moppy hair. He didn't even bother fixing it. Trent always matched his canvas shoes to the color of his clothes. That night he had red Chucks to match his red button-up shirt.

"Drink up, Tony," said Trent. "This is an exclusive club for the un-sober only."

"And this is Cyndi," said Tori, "but we call her Cyn. She's my ex too." Then she winked, and the two girls giggled—but I couldn't tell if they were being serious or not. Cyn was pretty, but even when she smiled, she looked like she was plotting ways to eat your face.

"What about him?" I asked, pointing to Kurt. "Was he an ex-lover too?"

"Ew, dude!" groaned Kurt and Jess together.

"Ugh! What's wrong with you, T!" shouted Tori. "That's my cousin."

"Sounds like quite the group of friends you made there," said Doc, shaking his head.

"They were an interesting bunch. They sounded weird at first, until I got to know them." I was worried the doc thought I had detoured right off topic, so I took a deep breath, then reconnected the story. "The group told me quite a few things, including a disturbing story about Rick."

"What a prick," groaned Tori after we discussed the scene at the Labor Day Fair. "That fucken guy is such a piece of shit, for real."

"He always was, Tor," said Jess.

"Well, not always," added Trent. "I mean, we were all friends once."

"Not since we were fucking five," growled Maynard. "Before his family got re-rich."

"Re-rich?" I asked.

"He was rich. Then he wasn't. Then he was rich again," said Cyn, who smiled at me seductively while playing with her lip ring.

"How does that happen?" I asked.

"His father made some bad choices, and when the paper mill shut down in '81, he was broke," said Maynard.

"Then in the late 80s, after the killings—you know what I'm talking about, right?" asked Jess, and I shook my head. "The Mum Murders?"

I shrugged. It wasn't the first time I had heard the phrase mentioned, but nobody really spoke about it. It was an era in Grace Falls history that many of the townsfolk seemed eager to forget—and I stopped snooping after I found the newspaper stories about Amanda's older brother.

"Back in '86," said Maynard as he sipped on a stout, "a couple of guys went around murdering women with flower names for some weirdo cult."

"Flower names?" I asked. "You mean like Rose? Lilly?"

Once I had said Lilly, the whole table went rigid.

"My mom was murdered by them. Her name was Lillian Martin," said Tori. It was the first time I ever heard her speak calmly.

"I'm so sorry, I didn't know," I apologized.

"I know, it's cool, T," she said, and gave me a quick kiss on the cheek.

"Yeah, so anyway," said Trent, picking up the story. "These lunatics were holed up at the mill. Kidnapped a few women and tried sacrificing them to some insane fucking god at the falls."

"What the fuck?" I spat.

"Yeah," nodded Kurt. "The fuck, indeed."

"This fucking town, man," said Cyn.

"Anyway, both those jerks died," said Jess. "One inside the mill, and the other fell from the falls, but not before they killed a couple high school boys who got mixed up in the whole thing. The mill was eventually investigated. A total death trap, but it was sitting on top of public land. There was a big legal battle and Jacinda's dad left his legal partner, Mr. Berry, to represent Rick's dad—and they won."

"What did they win?" I asked.

"A huge fucken settlement," said Tori. "Then Rick was re-rich."

"Some loophole," said Maynard. "They didn't even have to fix the place up. The two families became close—Joseph O'Neill stayed on as Everett Jansen's personal attorney, and they made boatloads of money together." Then Maynard took a big swig of his beer. "You know the O'Neills used to be my neighbors? On the other side of Amanda's old house." I shook my head. "Yeah, they made so much money they moved to the fancy section of Grace Falls. Elm Way Acres, near the Elm Way Bridge."

"Jacinda went to private school in Mercy Point for years," said Trent.

"Enough of the boring stuff!" yelled Tori as she finished her beer and slammed the empty glass down onto the table. "Kurt, tell him your story."

Kurt was a quiet guy until prompted. I could only imagine what it was like growing up with a cousin whose mouth was as big as Tori's.

"Tony, Rick is about as deplorable a human being as I have ever seen," he said.

"Oh, deplorable," cried Jess. "Great word!"

"When I was nine, Rick and I were on the same Little League baseball team. He wanted to play catcher, but coach wanted him to play second base instead—a more useful position on a little league team. Coach put this kid, Tommy, at catcher. An innocent little guy with a lisp and a bad case of ADD. He was the nicest kid you'd ever met. Never hurt anyone or said anything bad about nobody.

"Anyway," Kurt continued after draining his pint glass, "after practice the whole team would race down the hill to the concession stand to buy a quarter's worth of candy and wait for our parents to pick us up. My shoelaces came undone, and I heard Tommy screaming as I bent over to tie them up. It was the kind of scream you couldn't ignore, like he was in serious trouble. I ran to the top of the hill just as the coaches went running by. They had to tear Rick off poor Tommy. Rick was beating him senseless with a baseball bat. Rick was always a big kid, and at nine, he was already twice Tommy's size. There was blood everywhere. I've never been able to forget it—little Tommy being carted off on a blood-stained stretcher and loaded into the back of an ambulance. It stuck in my mind."

I shook my head, unable to comment.

"But you know the worst part?" Kurt continued. "The cops had to wait for his father to arrive before they could question him—because Rick was a minor, and that's how serious it was. They asked Rick why he did it, and I heard it all, man. I was only a few feet away. I wanted to know like everyone else, and nobody told me to scram. So, Rick, he looked up at the cop and politely said *do what? I didn't do anything. The devil did it.* I still get chills whenever I think about it, man."

Just as Kurt finished speaking, a car engine roared past. It sounded like a Harley.

"Speak of the devil," said Tori, as a red Mustang passed outside the window, speeding down the road.

"That's Rick?" I asked.

"Yeah," said Jess. "Birthday gift when he was fifteen. He drives around like that everywhere. The whole town's afraid to do anything about it. Even Police Chief White."

"Why?" I asked.

"Because Rick's father owns everything," said Cyn.

"This isn't Roadhouse," I laughed. "People aren't above the law."

"Tell that to your face, T," said Tori. She asked me about my scar one day as we were lying in bed, and I told her the whole story.

"Unbelievable," I said, shaking my head. "Does he hang out around town often?"

"Not really," said Trent.

"I see him occasionally down at the mall," said Maynard. "I work at the record store."

"The Music Shoppe?" I asked, and he nodded.

Then Cyn said, "I've only been home for a year, but I see him cruise by the salon all the time on his way out of town."

"Where were you?" I asked. "Before you came home."

"Philly. I dropped out," she said. "My roommate was this gothy bitch named Deedra. Drove me nuts."

"Where was Rick going, Cyn?" asked Jess.

"Probably some new fucking party site," said Tori, putting in her two cents before she swallowed a gulp of beer.

"What party site?" I asked.

"Grace Falls tradition for the blessed and popular," groaned Jess.

"In high school," growled Tori, "the fucken popular kids always found a secret fucken spot to party around town. Rick was the fucken king of Grace Falls party sites. Probably found a new fucking site somewhere outside of town for him and his fucking douchey college pals."

"How do you know about this?" I asked. It wasn't meant to be an accusation, but it landed like one.

"Damn," said Kurt, laughing. "Tell him, Tor."

"Because I used to date that fucking psycho. Happy now?" she growled, then drowned her memories out in her beer.

"You? And Rick?" I was baffled. "That's like a gorilla dating a giraffe."

"Who you callin' a fucking giraffe, T?" shouted Tori, as everyone laughed.

"I'm just saying, you're extreme opposites," I laughed, defending my metaphor. "Besides, I didn't think you dated?"

"Why do you think that is?" added Cyn. "Rick broke her."

"What can I say? I went searching for myself. Discovered he was a lunk and I was a fucking punk." She said it like she was glossing over an epic story. Then she downed the rest of her beer while flashing *the sign of the horns.*

"Scary shit, man," said Kurt.

"Yeah," added Jess. "What about you, Tony? Got any skeletons in your closet?"

"Nah," said Tori, answering for me, "he's just in love with the lying psycho."

"What do you mean?" I asked.

"You'll find out, eventually," she said.

"No, seriously?" I asked, as the waitress returned with a full round of beers. "What?"

"Damn, T, getting pushy," groaned Tori. "Fine." Then she smiled devilishly and gave me a flirty wink. "Jacinda's a witch."

"A witch?" I laughed. "Firstly, I'm not in love with her. She doesn't want anything to do with me. Second, she—was—one of the nicest people I know."

"Not true, she's been plenty fucked up to you," said Tori. "Also, not what I mean."

Cyn started laughing. "We mean she's an actual witch."

"Trent and I want to go on record as disagreeing with that theory," said Maynard, almost choking on his beer.

"I third that movement," said Jess.

"Same," added Kurt.

"Well, Cyn and I would know," said Tori. "We're fucking witches too."

Jess rolled her eyes. Trent nearly drowned himself in beer, then went looking for a napkin as he tried to stop his coughing fit.

"Why do you think she's a witch?" I asked, unable to stop myself from laughing.

"Shut your pie-hole, T!" shouted Tori. "We're not joking."

"Answer the question," I said, trying to straighten my face.

"We can prove it," said Tori. "Hang out with us tomorrow, and we'll show you."

"Can't, I have a final tomorrow."

"Okay, the day after," suggested Tori.

"Can't, I'm going home for Christmas."

"Ah, the festival of Saturnalia," said Maynard as he fiddled with his lighter.

"Okay, fucking hell! New Year's Eve then! Maynard's having a party. Come out and we'll show you."

"Am I invited?" I asked. Maynard offered me a thumbs up as he chugged, and I said, "Okay."

"Okay, we'll settle this then," said Tori. "You're going to be so glad you met me, T."

The rest of the evening was some of the best fun I've ever had. We piled into Maynard's black van—a late 70's Chevy model that was customized on the inside with small sofas welded into the frame, and an airbrushed grim reaper on the left side—the right side was composed of three different black panels where Tori had spray painted the words *"Under Consideration"* in red—and drove across town.

"Under consideration?" I asked. Trent and Kurt laughed from the back sofa while Tori and Jess sandwiched me in the middle seat. Cyn was up front with her legs propped onto the dash.

"Yeah, got any considerations?" Maynard asked, gesturing to a tip jar that was glued to the front console next to the emergency brake.

I dropped change into the jar and said, "What about the Garden of Eden?" Cyn glared at me over the front seat as Tori looked like someone had asked her to lick a frog. "Yeah, like naked Eve being tempted by a demon snake to bite from an apple. While angels circled the sky above with spears aimed at them." I was acting it out and saw Maynard's eyes flashing up to a mirror he'd installed so he could see the other passengers while he drove.

For a moment I thought I lost them.

"Fuck! That's fucking cool!" yelled Tori as she wrapped her arm around me.

"I like it!" said Trent.

"Yeah, not bad," said Maynard, stroking an imaginary goatee on his face. "I'll take it under—"

"Consideration!" everyone in the van yelled, like a game they had played before.

"Damn, T!" Tori groaned.

"What?" I asked as Jess started laughing.

"I didn't know you were so fucking creative," she said.

"Tony's a design major," said Jess as she rolled her eyes.

"Fuck, T!" shouted Tori, like the news had illuminated a whole new world to her. "We should bang some more and have some double-T babies!"

"No," groaned Trent and Maynard, while Kurt shook his head silently from the back seat.

"Bad idea," said Jess.

"What!? Why?" growled Tori.

"Not for you," said Maynard, "for Tony."

"Nard!" whined Tori.

"What!?" he responded as he turned onto Cemetery Drive.

"You're such an asshole," she said, laughing.

"Where are we going?" I asked.

"Grace Falls' best kept secret," said Trent.

Maynard pulled onto a small, paved driveway that wound through the cemetery. The driveway twisted around a hill at the back and up a steep incline toward an overgrown lot beyond a wrought-iron fence. Eventually, we pulled up to an old house and funeral parlor that once belonged to the Hallows family. It had been abandoned for more than a decade, and was as big as a hotel, with a turret that overlooked the cemetery.

Maynard parked the van next to an old shed, and we climbed out into the brisk December air. It was cold but not windy, which made it easier to stay warm as I wrapped myself up in my leather jacket, scarf, and gloves.

"Don't get too close to the house," warned Kurt.

"Why?" I asked, but nobody offered an answer. The house looked brittle and ready to collapse, yet strong and sturdy like it would outlive us all.

We were high in the foothills that surrounded Grace Falls, staring off a steep cliff that dove into the rushing waters of the river below. A few miles upstream were the waterfalls by the fairgrounds, and way off in the distance we could see Mercy Point and beyond. It was snowing, shrouding the town under a hazy gloom.

"Keep the headlights on," said Trent to Maynard, who was still sitting in his van. "CDs, please?" Cyn handed him a fat CD wallet and gave me a conspiratorial smile.

"Mkateewa River," said Tori, standing next to me. She was sounding out the word, like she was practicing. "It means *black* in Shawnee."

"Black river," I said. "Doesn't look so black to me."

"Black and white doesn't exist, T," she said. "Everything is shades of fucking gray."

"Why can't we get too close to the house?" I asked her.

"T, have you ever really paid attention to this town?" she said as Jess wrapped her arms around her sister and held her tight for warmth. "Strange shit happens here."

"Growing up," said Jess, "rumors and stories were rampant."

"What kind of rumors?" I asked. "What kind of stories?"

"Dude, why's it not working?" groaned Trent from the rear of the van.

"Bang on it," suggested Maynard.

"Ghost stories," said Jess, answering my question.

"Yeah, remember Nikki Twist?" said Cyn, jumping into the conversation.

"What about Tommy Lee?" added Kurt, "Not the drummer, obviously."

"Veronica Green went missing," said Trent. "And that kid, Sean-something."

"Did Amanda ever tell you about her brother?" asked Maynard. "She swears she saw him one night, when we were kids. Years after he jumped off Goner's Cross."

"This town is fucked, Tony. Bad things happen here."

"If bad things happen here, why do you stay?" I asked.

"Where are we going to go?" laughed Jess.

Then Tori winked at me and said something that in the moment seemed really strange. "Hey, how many of you fuckers are left-handed?"

"What does that have to do with anything?" I started to ask, when each and every one of them raised their hands, again, with the same conspiratorial smile—like they knew things I didn't. "All of you? That's—"

"Impossible?" asked Jess, finishing my sentence.

"No," I replied, "improbable. Only ten percent of the population is left-handed, including me." Tori smiled and placed a hand on my shoulder.

"Then you're one of us. The fucking sinistra," she said.

"It means *left*, but it's also the origin for the word *sinister*," said Jess—always a bookworm. "Tony, this town is weird. You'll find more lefties our age than you'll find anywhere else in the country."

"But why?" I asked. "What does it mean?"

"Who knows! Besides," said Tori, "we are the Children of the Mkateewa. We're fucking cursed."

Suddenly the quiet night burst into music as a gentle snow fell from the sky. Tori and Cyn shouted as Maynard took Jess's hand and began to dance as only Maynard could—which was to say, a lot of shimmying and gyrating that only a lanky guy like him could get away with.

"Who is this?" I asked, referring to the music. It was something I hadn't heard before.

"Sisters of Mercy!" shouted Tori. "Let us fucking educate you, T! You're gonna love it!" Then she grabbed me and forced me to dance with her.

We had fun being goofballs together, and as the night progressed, I felt like maybe Jaycie was right. Maybe tomorrow wasn't a promise, and maybe the answers were right in front of me.

"T, if you're going to hang with us, you need to start swearing like a fucking sailor," said Tori. "Fucking hell."

"Did you believe that?" asked Doc.

"That I needed to curse more? No fucking way," I said, chuckling.

"No, about the cursed children and all the strange stuff."

"Oh, you know, I hadn't really thought about it," I lied. I thought about it a lot, but that was irrelevant, wasn't it?

December 31, 2001

After spending the Christmas holiday with my dad, I took the bus back to Grace Falls for New Year's. Looking back, I wish I had stayed to spend some more time with him, but I was young. When we're young, we don't think about that kind of stuff—we don't think about how im-permanent everything is.

Tomorrow's not a promise.

That's what Jaycie always said, and I wish I had listened.

We arrived at Maynard's house on Cross Road sometime after 10 PM on New Year's Eve, and the driveway was already full of cars. Mar-shall was spending a romantic night with Anne, and Sid had disappeared, leaving Brad to come with me.

"How do you know these townies?" asked Brad.

"Dude, be nice. They didn't have to invite you too."

"What did I say?" He shrugged. "I like townies. They're creepy. They're weird. And oh yeah, they're usually racist."

When the door opened and Maynard answered wearing a satin robe and his hair in a ponytail, Brad gasped in horror.

"Buffalo Bill," screeched Brad under his breath.

"Gentlemen," greeted Maynard in a sing-song voice.

"Nard!" screamed Tori from the next room. "Let them in already!"

"Come in," he repeated with the same voice.

"This is Brad," I said as I passed through the door.

"Are you a townie?" asked Brad.

The night drifted along pleasantly to music, conversation, and an enthusiastic ball drop countdown that was highlighted by Cyn drunken-ly making out with Trent in a corner. Jess looked on, mortified, as she sipped on a cup of Jack by the TV.

There were tons of people there, most I didn't know, and some I only vaguely recognized, but overall, it was a good time—until Tori stood up and pronounced it was time to "prove this bitch wrong" while pointing at me.

"Yeah! My favorite game!" yelled Brad, despite not having any clue what it was about.

A group of us moved into the study, where Maynard's dad had a robust collection of Civil War memorabilia, including old revolvers and muskets, most of which were just collecting dust. At the center of the room was a table, where Tori and Cyn had placed a shoebox covered in black construction paper with the words "Witch Evidence" painted across it in red fingernail polish.

"Cool room, bro," said Brad as we entered.

"Nard's dad collects Civil War shit," said Tori.

"This isn't even half of it," said Maynard. "The rest is in the garage. My mom refuses to let him keep it all in the house."

"Why's that?" asked Cyn.

"She's afraid some of it's still live—old gunpowder and all. He'll blow up the house or some shit."

"Where are the 'rents?" asked Trent, plopping down onto an old leather sofa against the wall and absentmindedly thumbing through a cigar catalog.

"Barbados. Bahamas. Who knows," he said. "They go every year for Saturnalia."

"What?" asked Brad.

"Christmas," explained Jess. "He's talking about Christmas. It was a pagan holiday before Christianity co-opted it into one of their own."

"Co-opted? They stole it," said Maynard. "The white man steals everything."

"Yeah!" shouted Brad, "but dude, you're white."

"I'm seventy-five percent Shawnee," said Maynard defensively.

"Oh, rad. So, what's this all about?" asked Brad, pointing to the box on the table. He was excited to get to the part where he could call me a bitch.

"They invited me here tonight to prove Jacinda's a witch," I said.

"What!?" Brad shouted.

"We have proof," said Cyn as she swatted away the cigar catalog and plopped onto Trent's lap.

"Get to it then. What's your proof this time?" groaned Jess.

"You guys have discussed this before?" I asked.

"Numerous times," said Jess. "Look, I'm not Jaycie's biggest fan, but she's not a witch."

"I'm a witch," said Cyn, "And I know when I see a witch."

"Really?" said Jess, eyeing Cyn up. "You perform spells and have wild bacchanal orgies in the woods?"

"What the fuck has gotten into you?" spat Cyn.

"Nothing," said Jess, as she left the room.

"What's her problem?" Cyn asked Tori.

"I don't know," she said. It was the first time I had ever heard empathy in her voice.

"Let's get this over with," said Maynard. "We're missing the party."

Cyn jumped from Trent's lap and walked over to Tori, who lifted the lid from the box, allowing Cyn to grab a single page from an elementary school yearbook.

"First piece of evidence," said Cyn. "Third picture from the left."

It was an old black and white yearbook page from the 80s with terrible print quality. Third from the left, in Mrs. Snyder's 2nd Grade class, was a little blonde girl with a big toothless smile. She was wearing a flowery dress with lacy sleeves.

"Where'd you get this?" asked Maynard.

"I tore it out of Kurt's yearbook," said Tori.

"Hey!" said Kurt, speaking for the first time in hours. I forgot he was even there.

"Look at the name," said Tori as she pointed it out.

"Jane O'Neill," I read aloud. "Yeah, so?"

"Has Jacinda ever spoken about a sister?" asked Cyn.

"She doesn't have a sister," said Maynard. "Amanda and I would know. She lived three houses down." Then he counted it out for everyone, "My house, Amanda's old house, the Berrys', and the O'Neills'—before they moved."

"Maybe there was another O'Neill family in town?" I suggested.

"We thought you'd fucking say that," said Tori, who removed a manila folder from the box and slapped it down on the table. "Check it out."

The tab read *Jane O'Neill*, and the very first page after opening it was a handwritten photocopy of basic information, like emergency contacts. Beneath Jane's name was a space for her parents' names—Joseph and Saoirse O'Neill.

"Sa-oir-see? That's not even a real name," said Brad.

"It's Irish," said Cyn. "Pronounced Seer-sha."

"That can't be," said Maynard. "Those are Jacinda's parents' names."

"How does this prove she's a witch?" I asked.

"You heard Nard," said Cyn. "He was her neighbor. Kurt was her classmate." She pointed to a goofy toothless guy in the middle of the page. It was Kurt.

"I don't remember her," Kurt said. "I don't even know if I would. It was second grade."

"So, what are you trying to say?" I asked.

Tori reached into the box and pulled out one last item. It was a print-out from a microfiche machine at the local library. It was a newspaper article with a distorted black and white photo of a busted-up tractor trailer and a small car. There was a little girl crying in the photo, standing next to a familiar woman I couldn't place.

"Head-on collision," said Brad, reading the headline. "Little girl dead."

Reading the first few lines of the story, it mentioned a VW Bug's transmission failing, and a tractor trailer swerving to avoid it, then crashing headfirst into an incoming car on Route 13 toward Mercy Point. It mentioned Jane O'Neill dying in the crash. The article was dated October 13th, 1986.

"I'm trying to say," said Tori, "that Jaycie fucking O'Neill made her sister disappear. Maybe she killed her. Maybe she didn't, but one thing's certain. Jaycie made everyone forget Jane ever happened."

"I really didn't have the stomach to be near Tori and Cyn after all that. Jess asked for a ride, so we loaded into Brad's new car and left. I drove because Brad couldn't handle more than a few ounces of liquor."

"How did their presentation make you feel?"

"Disappointed."

"Did you ever talk to them about it?"

"I never had the chance."

We pulled out of Maynard's driveway onto Cross Road and headed back toward Grace Falls. Jess was up front with me, while Brad laid across the back seat.

"What's wrong, Jess?" I asked.

"Yeah, what's up, girl?" said drunken Brad.

"She doesn't know," said Jess.

"Who?" I asked.

"Cyn," she said. I peeled my eyes away from the road and saw the way Jess was looking at me. The combination of her words and her expression carried new context.

"Oh," I replied. "I didn't know."

"No," she replied. "Nobody does. And she doesn't like plain, bookish girls, anyway."

"I like you, Jess," said Brad, attempting to make her feel better, but he didn't know what Jess meant. He didn't see the expression that outed her secret.

I placed my hand on hers to comfort her. "I know how you feel," I said.

"You're a good friend, Tony."

We were only a few miles up the road when I spotted headlights in the rearview mirror. In the time it took me to glance down at the road, then back to the mirror, the car zipped by, passing me uphill. Jess said, "Careful," and despite being sober, we almost didn't make it.

I took my foot off the accelerator to give the car plenty of space. When we crested the hill, the other car shot back into our lane—and suddenly we stared down the headlights of an incoming car swerving to avoid a collision.

I yanked at the steering wheel and sent us spinning out on the slippery road toward the guardrail. There was a huge drop at the forest edge that plummeted a few hundred feet into the river. Our car came to a complete stop against the bent guardrail, teetering on the edge, as other cars raced by and of sight—a whole line of them flying down the road.

Jess popped out of the passenger seat as Brad threw up. She was crying, but I was somewhere else.

"What do you mean, somewhere else?"

"I can't explain it," I replied.

"Do your best."

"I had the worst feeling in my chest. Like someone had just walked over my grave. In the headlights of the oncoming car, I saw something."

"What did you see?"

"I thought I saw a woman screaming in pain, calling out for help. But I also saw something else. Blood on my hands. Pain. Angels circling the skies."

"Do you believe it was a hallucination?"

"Hell, yes." Then I said, "But why? How?"

The Doc jotted down a few notes, and I continued.

After the nerves settled, we got back on the road. I had never driven more cautiously than I did for the remainder of that trip. We had only been back at the dorms for an hour when there was a knock on our door. Brad was out cold, and Sid and Marshall were still away, leaving me to drag myself out of bed to answer it.

"Tori's dead," cried Jess, and she fell to her knees.

XXI

contracts

MALUS
December 21, 2013
Now.

What was evil?

Evil, by definition, was profound immorality. Wickedness. Depravity.

Few beings that ever existed believed themselves to be evil. Evil was a construct, a label to identify those whose morality had deviated from societal norms.

An individual does not begin evil. Each of us is the hero of our own journey. Some of us are pushed further—pushed into doing things that others dare not.

Can a truly evil individual identify the wickedness within them?

I only saw myself as the hero until I came face to face with my reflection and saw how far I had fallen. Sometimes, it was hard to find the righteous path beneath the feet of the morally blurred traveler.

Sometimes, the end justifies the means.

When the spark was marked, his essence lit up across time like candles burning in the darkness. It was an extermination—my Thirteen scoured the timeline, ridding the world of the spark pests—and yet, something felt wrong. As if I had missed an important detail.

When a contract was voided, I was notified immediately. A sharp pain seeped from my ring and burned out the name of the contract tattooed to my skin.

Summanus was dead.

The dark thunder-god, with his ever-faithful witch, marked the spark so that his shattered spirit could be cleansed from the Earth across all time. Mammon, god of greed, along with the rest of my Thirteen, journeyed out into the timestream—a gift given to us after consuming the flesh of the titan, Chronos—searching for marks and destroying them.

Then, a second name burned from my skin.

Mammon, also dead.

I'd made a grave miscalculation, and I was in need of retribution. I began to reexamine my confrontation with the spark—*the devil is in the details*, so they say.

"I failed her," the spark had said when he confronted me within Votan's tomb. My rage over Frigg's duplicity had blinded me to the most obvious answer. The spark knew about me. The spark was hunting me. He knew where I'd be, and he knew my past sins.

Who was The Raptor? And who was the woman he had failed?

It was time for me to learn more about the spark and what he was capable of.

Walking amongst humans was always a strange sensation. I felt like a tiger walking amongst a herd of deer. Yet as considerably different as I was to them, my beginnings were very similar.

It did not take long to find the right building. A morgue was a place of death, so it was only a matter of letting the dead show the way. They pointed their fingers toward my destination, doing their master's bidding without consternation. Once I became aware of them, it surprised me how many of the modern dead had not left the world of the living, clinging to their familiar surroundings for eternity.

I slipped inside the hospital through the back entrance, where supplies were loaded into the building through large bay doors. Then I walked into a main corridor and down the brightly lit hallways without anyone daring to stop me. Few offered an unsure glance, wondering if I had the credentials roam the halls freely, but nobody challenged me. I made them anxious. Looking upon me left even the bravest man feeling dread—maybe it was my eyes? The two different irises often made people apprehensive, as if they were unnatural. Funny, my eyes were one of the only natural things about me.

Even if one dared, could they stop me?

I had no qualms about being careless, not now. What did I have to fear? Nothing on this planet could thwart me, and there would be no interference from the other side—Heaven or Hell. Earth was neutral. Its fate was to be decided by those who existed here only. All Fallen gave up their wings and halos to become denizens of Earth, like breaking the celestial shackles for freedom. This realm was where the Fallen could take their own destiny.

The dead revealed the stairs to the basement level where the morgue was located. Down a long empty hallway abandoned by patients, nurses, and doctors. It was as if the hall led to nowhere, to nothing. It was just me and the ghosts as they continued to point the way.

The door was locked with a modern digital touchpad—technology was useless compared to the old ways. Leaving a hex bag or scrawling an ancient knot in pig's blood upon the door was more effective. Nobody could enter but the one who locked it. However, lock a door with electronics, and you were only barring other humans—and some of them were crafty enough to break even the most sophisticated pieces of technology.

I ripped the handle from the door and walked through without breaking a sweat. At the bottom of the stairs was a small open area with a lazy old security guard watching television and eating pastries. He barely saw me coming.

"Hi there, can I get you to sign in?" he asked.

With a wave of my wrist, the dead were upon him. His eyes erupted from their sockets and his heart exploded. Sometimes it was easy to forget their bodies were a bit more fragile than ours. He fell backwards into his chair, a lifeless mound of flesh, as I pushed on. His ghost stood by, helplessly watching and confused.

Quick violent death often left human souls bewildered—wandering aimlessly in a loop of perplexing thought—like a vinyl record skipping. Too perturbed to understand their predicament and too stubborn to let go.

The morgue itself was a temperature-controlled room, inside an insulated area that was entered through a latched door. I opened it and walked inside, my breath exiting in plumes of white vapor while I studied the room.

In front of me, lining the opposite wall, was a grid of freezers holding the remains of men, women, and at least one fallen angel.

It was in the fourth row from the left and third from the top. I opened the stainless-steel door, latched airtight, and slid the long tray out as far as it would go. Then I unzipped the black body bag containing Mammon's remains. As it opened, the greedy god's putrid stench filled my nostrils. His charred remains were mostly ash, and his skull laid in several pieces, making it hard to identify.

Still, the barbed teeth were plainly non-human and would alarm the professional who would inspect the body sometime within the next few hours.

It was not my concern. I did not care to hide the realities of the world away from the ignorant. In fact, I was actually amused that this discovery might shake the pillars of their own existence. I zippered up the black bag and shoved the shelf back into the freezer, then closed the door.

Mammon's remains were not the reason I was there.

I asked the ghosts if there was another, one similar to Mammon, here within the room. The dead did not reply, so I reached out with my power, groped through the darkness, and sensed each of the dead bodies that laid within the coffin-sized freezers. One by one they spoke to me, telling me their secrets, until I came upon one who rambled in circles. I quickly opened his freezer door and unzipped the bag holding his remains. They were charred right down to the bone. Assuredly, it was the kind of heat and burn symptomatic of hellfire, but this man had no Grace. He was no angel, Fallen or otherwise.

"How did you die, Marshall Pryor?" I demanded.

"I was with my best friend," he said, then hung there, unsure of what had transpired. Then he repeated himself. "I was with my best friend." Confusion. Befuddlement. An archetypical case of violent end by unnatural means.

"What came next?" I prompted.

"...pain..." he whimpered.

I examined his bones and found many of them broken, splintered and ripped apart. He did not die from hellfire; he was merely disintegrated—burned to ash after death.

"Who was your friend?" I asked calmly.

"Tony Oscuro," he said.

"How do you know him?"

"We went to college together."

"What happened to Tony?" I asked and fed additional power into the aether. Sometimes a small nudge was all it took to get the departed back on track.

"I don't know," he said, just as I sensed a new presence behind me.

"I know," she said, eager to answer.

"Who are you?" I asked the ghost.

"Anne Whittaker," she said. I took note of the mixed ash in Marshall's body bag. There was just enough of Anne to bring her here. Whatever happened to the rest of her, it was destroyed.

"Anne, what happened to Tony?"

"Gone. He ran after the explosion."

"He killed Mammon?"

"He's cursed. He brings bad luck on everything he touches," she said. Her spirit was angry, and in death she became spiteful and wicked. "Tony killed the monster who killed me. Tony brought death to Marshall's door. He killed us. He murdered Jacinda. He should burn for what he has done."

"Jacinda?" I asked. "Jacinda O'Neill?"

She nodded.

My past sins were coming back to haunt me.

TONY

"And sometimes, when it's a foreign car, the starter sticks and you have to know when to separate the wires," said Montoya, thoroughly explaining how to hotwire a car.

"Why are you still talking about this?" asked Jamaal. "We rented a car like civilized people."

"I know," said Montoya with a shy smile. "I just thought it woulda been far out to steal one and split. I always wanted to do that, you know."

Leaving Philadelphia, I took 76 West to 476 West, then through the tolls to the Northeast Extension of the PA Turnpike toward Scranton. A long drive lay ahead, and I was already feeling weary.

"What exactly are we after, Tony?" asked Chappy from the back seat.

There wasn't enough room for all the personalities to sit comfortably in one car, so they took turns fading in and out. At first it was distracting, but after a while I got used to all the yammering.

However, I ignored Chappy. I didn't want to explain the whole thing. The story was too long and too personal, too painful to even begin. And Marshall—

—everything happened so fast, I never even properly mourned Marshall. Every few miles the emotion would bubble to the surface and overflow—like a child blowing milk bubbles through a straw. I'd no sooner excise the thoughts from my mind, digging them out by whatever means necessary, when they'd creep back in stronger than before. Without an outlet, just miles and miles of asphalt ahead, I slammed my fist into the steering wheel. I was so hopelessly alone and felt so endlessly guilty.

Marshall was gone. I'd pushed him away for years, and the one moment I let him in, to share my confusion and inner darkness, it got him killed. I killed him. It was me.

But we were on a mission. Things were out there hunting me, and the faster I moved, the less chance they'd have to catch up.

"Guilt is a terrible thing," said Chappy. "It has a way of holding onto us, even as we try to let it go."

"What would you know of guilt?" I said. "Today I got my best friend killed. And that wasn't even the worst thing that's happened in my life."

"We all have had terrible experiences, sir," said Henry. "To compare them is folly. Every man, woman, and child perceive reality through different lenses. You feel awful, and nobody is attempting to take the guilt away from you. We are, however, concerned about the toll it may take on your judgment."

"My judgment is fine," I said. I had been balancing my inner turmoil with reality for years. I was a pro, and it was frustrating to have some-one question it—especially a handful of voices inside my head.

"Is it though?" asked Jamaal. "You're drifting into the other lane."

A burgundy SUV laid on the horn as it flew by, swerving around me as I drifted halfway between lanes. I yanked the wheel back into my own lane and took a deep breath—I was frazzled, not just from the horn noise blaring through my heightened hearing, but the near impact gave me a startle.

Maybe I was too distracted.

"How embarrassing," said Chappy. "I misunderstood the rules of roads. I thought we were supposed to drive over the lines, not between them."

"In the future, we don't even drive," said Jamaal. "Driverless autos. And all this land?" He pointed out the window to the trees, the moun-tains in the distance, the cars, the people, everything. "It's gone. One big giant mega-city from Boston to D.C."

"The world has changed," said Henry.

"Hell, it's been only fifty years since my time," said Montoya, "and everything looks different. I can't imagine my kids growing up in all this."

"You have kids?" I asked.

"Yeah, my man," he sadly replied. "Gabriela was two. Junior was four. I finally had the money to buy a ring for Maria. Two weeks, man. Just two weeks and I was going to be a free man—debt and service paid to my country in full."

"I'm sorry," I said. I understood him all too well. "What about you, Henry?"

"I left behind my wife, Martha. Two adult children, and my life's work."

"What kind of work were you doing?" asked Montoya.

"I was studying dementia praecox," said Henry. "However, I was specifically focusing on the splintering of the mind. The development of alternate identities."

"Dissociative personality disorder," said Jamaal. "That's kind of funny, isn't it? Multiple personalities."

"How so, my man?" asked Montoya.

Jamaal stared at him with his jaw wide open, and it made me chuckle. "There are six of us in this car," he said. "But, only one actual person. We are all in that jawn's head." He pointed at me. I was "that jawn."

"Is that what jawn means?" he asked, and Jamaal and I shrugged. It really was an undefinable word.

"This circumstance—splintering personalities," asked Chappy, "it happens to other people? Frequently?"

"I would not say frequently," said Henry. "It is rare. I believe I was suffering through the earliest stages. I was having vivid dreams and speaking languages I never learned."

"In other words," I said, "you were prematurely experiencing our current situation."

"Likely so," he said with a nod.

"There are more things in Heaven and Earth, Horatio, than there are dreamt of in your philosophy," said Chappy.

"Shakespeare," said Jamaal.

"That was Shakespeare?" asked Montoya, to which Chappy nodded. "What does it mean?"

"It means," I said, "that the world is a strange place."

"Much has changed," said Doshin. "I imagine time eases change. One form, one thought, one evolution at a time."

"Did you have a family, Master Doshin?" asked Jamaal.

"No," he said sadly. "Samurai were arranged to marry. My love married another. My students became my family. They were my greatest triumph."

"My flock," said Chappy, "I worry what became of them." Then Chappy sighed in deep thought. "Tony, I couldn't help but notice your best friend was a man of color. I must ask, is the world a better place?" He was looking to me and Jamaal—those in the furthest future from his own time.

"I'd like to believe it's better now than it was," I said. "But there is distance yet to go."

"In the future, we have other things to fear than each other," said Jamaal cryptically.

"Fear and love do not go together," said Doshin.

"I like that, my man," said Montoya. "Is that an ancient Japanese proverb or something?"

"No," said Doshin with a shy smile. "Saw it on sign a short time ago."

When Jamaal started laughing—a full throated jovial snicker with a snort every five laughs—the whole car erupted into laughter with him. Talking with them—knowing them—was helping. We all suffered. We all bled. It was a lesson I needed to learn.

We were five hours in—a few miles from Mercy Point—twenty-five minutes from Grace Falls, when my pocket started buzzing. It was a long drive made bearable by, of all things, the voices inside my head.

"What's that?" asked Henry.

"A cell phone," I said, as I shifted around in the seat to retrieve the phone from my pants pocket. I was confused—who would be calling me?

"Waitaminute, my man," said Montoya, "you have a phone that goes everywhere you do?"

"That's nothing," scoffed Jamaal. "We have implants in the future. You can call anyone with just a thought." He pointed to his head to show that the implant was placed behind the ear into the base of the skull and neck.

"Is all technology so intrusive?" asked Chappy, who then added, "and loud?" once I pulled the phone free.

It took a moment to recognize the image and the name that appeared on screen. I hadn't seen her face in so long that I almost didn't recognize her—even after some light social media stalking a few years ago.

"You look like you've seen a ghost," said Montoya. "Who's phoning you?"

I swiped to answer the call, placed it to my ear, and said, "Hello?"

"T?"

MALUS
Five minutes ago…

Her apartment faced the south side of the building, away from the road and prying eyes. I walked up the building's facade and snuck over to her window, then watched as she changed clothes. She had pale perfect skin without blemish—smooth and supple and curved in all the right places. She was a carnal delight, like honey and floral pheromones. I watched until she was dressed—there was no point in taking her before—I enjoyed unwrapping presents.

After she was done and checked the mirror, perfecting her ponytail, she slipped into the next room while I let myself in. I entered without a sound, like a stalking predator. Once inside, I slid my hand across a table and found a long piece of her pale blonde hair stuck to my fingertip. I slurped it up into my mouth and tasted her, and the sparkles of flavor shook me with anticipation.

I was going to make the spark wish he had never been born.

"You are a monster," spat a voice only I could hear.

Her apartment was small, just a bed with a nearby couch and television, and an adjoined kitchen. There was no place to hide, so I stood beside the bed and waited for the right moment.

She had no idea I was there inside the room when she returned. She did not even notice me standing by the window as she walked past and fiddled with her purse before shutting off the light. I could have hidden within the Veil, but where was the fun in that?

She turned her back to me and began to write something down on a sheet of paper when I moved across the room and stood directly behind her, sniffing her hair. I did it so lightly, she barely sensed my presence just inches away. Only the tiniest of blonde hairs along the back of her neck seemed to prickle. It was just enough to get her attention.

She stiffened like a board. Her pathetically weak senses finally registered my proximity. I allowed my breath to tickle her skin just as soft and gentle as a spring breeze. I could hear the blood pumping frantically through her body, and the hissing release of adrenaline being added as she secreted the rotten smell of fear.

She turned and swiped at her back. I anticipated her movements and stealthily slid behind her, out of sight. When she had determined it was all in her mind, I softly exhaled across her bare neck, eliciting an angry spin—and still, she saw nothing. I remained just beyond her sight, tickling her skin and planting seeds of doubt and paranoia. She sighed and pondered her situation—was she sensing something that wasn't actually there? Then I allowed my body to lightly brush against hers, and she trembled and quaked with revulsion. She swung her arms around and feverishly swiped at her unknown assailant—

—but this time, I let her hand brush against my face. The shock derailed her as she screamed and ran for the door, but it did not budge no matter how hard she tried. My hand held it shut above her head. When she realized there was something obstructing the door, she curled around and saw me for the first time. She flattened her back against the wall.

"Hello, my dear," I said. I felt the need to charm her. She was one of his favorites. An adored friend, and I admired her strength. After all, it was the strongest ones that were the most fun to break.

She kicked me between the legs and ran to the far corner, then began rummaging through a desk drawer. I almost laughed at her assault but decided to keep our encounter serious. I did not want her to get the wrong idea.

I was there to kill her.

"I need you to do a favor for me," I said pleasantly and stalked toward her, imagining her begging me to let her go—when she spun and shoved a letter opener into my chest, then ran once again for the door.

In in blink, I was blocking her path. If she did not understand what I was, my speed was beginning to inform her.

She gasped as I removed the metal object from my chest, then handed it back to her in a sign of good faith. "I'm sorry, love, but I'm afraid your attempt to harm me was rather ignorant. All I'm asking is for you—"

She lunged forward and shoved her weapon up through my throat and into my skull, just missing my right eye from the inside.

I was being too easy on her.

As she backed away, I carefully slid the metal object from my skull and threw it into a corner. If she had taken an eye, I'd be halfway to the pit.

Eyes were like corks—they kept our Grace from escaping and grounded us here on Earth. Without them, we'd be sent home and thrown into the Pit. An eternity of damnation serving a Prince of Hell amongst countless circles of suffering. Earth was freedom, so long as we played by the rules.

I was angry, and if not for my intent to make the spark suffer, I would have ripped her to pieces right then. She did not run, there was nowhere to go, and her last attack was all the fight she had left. I could see in her eyes—the coldness of submission.

Had she known what I was about to do, she would have kept fighting.

"As I was saying, I'm asking you for a favor," I said through feigned politeness. It took her several moments to comprehend over the involuntary chattering of her teeth. Her crystal blue eyes teared, but she did not cry. Her silky blonde hair began to stick to her face and neck where cold perspiration moistened her skin.

"Wh...at do you need?" she asked. Her throat was so choked and sore that she had difficulty speaking.

"I need you to make a telephone call for me," I said. Technology these days had advanced so much, it was hard to keep up. I had witnessed automobiles and planes, moon landings and computers, atom bombs and guns, but the usefulness of the computer age was lost on me. I didn't have the need for the kind of information stored on magnetic devices in temperature-controlled rooms thousands of miles away. When I needed information, I could get it from the source, wherever and whenever that might be.

"Who?" she asked, shaking ferociously.

"Ah, the bane of my existence, my dear Amanda. But you know him simply as Tony," I said.

Tony was such a silly name for a spark. Antonius, Anthony, those were names of kings—but he was so much less than a king.

"But I haven't talked with Tony in years?" she said while removing a small silver rectangle from her bag.

"Do you presume me to give a silly fuck?" I said. She winced at my words, and tears trickled down her cheeks when she squeezed her eyes shut.

"Okay," she whined. She slid her fingers around in a geometric pattern, and the screen on her phone lit up. She quickly opened a second screen, then pressed a single button and moved the phone to her ear. I imagined that to call someone she had not spoken to in years would have taken more effort, yet she was not lying to me. I could sense it. Her connection to Tony was woven into the very fabric of her existence. She held him close, despite years and distance.

I could hear the signal connecting, the disturbance in the air from the phone as it technologically sent and received voices from great distances.

"When he answers, I will help you communicate my message," I said as I heard the phone ring through the earpiece. "But first, I need you in the proper frame of mind."

When I hurt her, she screamed appropriately.

TONY
Now.

My whole body started shaking. I slammed on the brakes and pulled over, coming to an abrupt stop that sent several cars swerving out of the way. I know the others were only part of my imagination, but I hopped out of the car to be away from them and said, "Amanda?" When she didn't answer, I asked, "Are you okay?"

I'd made an ill-advised phone call to her last night, but something told me this went beyond my indiscretions.

"No," she said. "No, I'm not okay. Someone's here with me and I think he's going to kill me." She spoke through heavy, erratic gasps, like she was in equal amounts of pain and fear.

"Who's with you?" I asked.

I looked at the car, and thought about driving to her, but I didn't know where she lived.

Even after all the time that had passed, Amanda was still a keystone in the foundation of my life. Even though we didn't speak, my heart wasn't built to let her go. I still cared for her and needed her in a safe and happy place. I never blamed her for being absent from my life. I hated myself so much that I was willing to accept that I wasn't worth the effort.

But hearing her voice in distress, I was brought back to that night in high school, with Paul Lucas's gun to my head. The night she decided to walk out of my life.

"A white-haired man. He knows your name, T. He told me to call you," she said as cars whipped by on the highway. Was it Summanus? Was he still alive?

"Tell him," said a voice on the phone next to her, "how you feel about him." There was a noise like cloth ripping and a deep thumping sound like something shifting or popping, a bone or joint, followed by a terrible shriek.

"Amanda!" I yelled.

There were sounds in this world that evoked certain indescribable negative emotions, none of them more profoundly heart-wrenching and destructive as listening to a loved one stricken with pain from an attacker and being unable to do anything about it.

Experiencing that once was more than anyone should endure.

I'd experienced it twice.

"Tony..." she wailed, followed by a series of painful whimpers. "Tony, I-I-I," she stuttered, the emotion overwhelming her—and me. I sank down onto the ground, listening to her suffer through what I knew was going to be goodbye.

There was no way for me to stop it. The area code prefix on her phone number was 971—an Oregon number, on the other side of the country. I had no other choice than to listen and accept it.

"Tell him," demanded the voice. She yelped, followed by an immediate change in concentration—as if she was given dire reason to be precise.

My fingernails dug and scraped at the asphalt like it was soft linoleum.

"Tony," she whimpered, "I'm sorry I abandoned you. I know you needed me, and I wasn't there."

"It's okay, Amanda," I said. If these were the last words she was ever going to speak to me, I didn't need an explanation or an apology. I didn't want her to ever think I held any anger or ill will. I missed her, but I never hated her.

"It was the worst decision I ever made," she said. "Please forgive me, please?" She was crying so hard, the pain in her voice was relentless.

"Amanda," I said, choking on my own words. "I forgive you."

"I love you, T," she said.

"I love you too," I told her. The phone made a bizarre series of cracking sounds and then went silent. "Hello?" I called into the phone, hoping to stop the inevitable. My mind raced for answers. Maybe I could reason with him? I could trade myself for her! I would gladly do that if he would stop hurting her!

There was nothing but silence, yet the line was still connected. Would I have to sit here and listen to her being snuffed out? How do you hang up on a friend's last moments?

"You're fucking things up for me, Tony," a cold voice growled into the other end of the line. There was a solid high-pitched ring inside my head that grew louder and louder, matching my anger. It felt as though I was going to blow a gasket, like flames were going to burst through my ears. I felt the fire inside, burning high and hot, hoping for the opportunity to hurt him back. I wanted to rip him apart, to make him bleed and snap his bones. My fury was a monster, ready and willing to hack him to pieces.

"I thought you were dead."

"I'm shocked you would confuse me with a pawn."

"If you're not Summanus, then who are you?"

"How quickly you forget me. We only just met."

I glanced at Henry, who was standing nearby with a concerned look, and wracked my brain for a connection. We only just met? There were only a few strange people I'd managed to bump into recently.

I quickly constructed a mental list:

- Summanus, but he was dead.
- The nightmares in the masks?—but they were dead too, weren't they?
- The invisible voice? It said, "Be seeing you, Tony Oscuro," before it disappeared.
- Anubis? Did he survive the explosion of green fire?
- Mammon—but he was ash, I saw it with my own eyes.
- My Echo? Couldn't be. He was me, and he wasn't white-haired.

Had this asshole confused me for someone else?

"Who are you?" I asked.

"Who are you?" he replied to my question. "Tony Oscuro? The Raptor? We all have many names."

The Raptor? What in the Jurassic Park was he on about?

"What do you want?" I asked after a momentary pause. My voice was stern and smooth like an interrogator.

"Suffering."

My skin tingled, and I was beginning to shake. I felt nuclear, the way my mind and body were raging out of control. My composure was gone, and I began to shout and cry openly. I couldn't restrain the anger any longer—my chemical walls were gone—they kept me even—and now I was a rollercoaster of extremes.

"Leave her alone!" I screamed into the receiver. I wanted to grind this man into a bloody gooey mess. I wanted him to pay for every single tiny scratch on Amanda's body. I was vengeance, pure hot vindication.

"I cannot. Once I got going, I couldn't stop," he laughed. It was a creepy laugh, the kind reserved only for the criminally insane.

"Let her go!"

"I told you, I can't."

"Don't you dare kill her."

"It's far too late for that."

"I'll kill you," I whispered.

"Tony, I will track down and kill every human being you have ever loved because that is what I do. You pained me, now I will pain you. Would you like to guess which of us is better at this game? Perhaps your old friends in Philadelphia would like me to pay them a visit? Thaddeus and Christopher? John and Meghann? Perhaps Robbie Morris or sweet Cyndi? Jessica maybe? Bradley?"

I was speechless and stunned. I couldn't feel a thing as my body went numb. My mind couldn't grasp it. All those names and faces from my past, all of them targets because of me. I felt disconnected, like none of this was actually happening. Those people, all of them were almost strangers to me—people who had left me far behind and hadn't looked back. My heart felt cold and dead, and my thoughts were frozen in a loop like a broken record skipping over and over again across their names.

"What? Nothing to say?" he asked.

"What do you want from me?" The tears had dried, and a calm resolve had replaced them. I could only be pushed and threatened so far before the clarity of hate settled in.

"I already told you. Suffering."

"Come after me. Leave them alone," I said.

"No."

"Don't be a coward! Come after me! Come after me!" I yelled. I could almost hear him smiling over the phone, enjoying it.

"Amanda and I say goodbye, Tony," he said, and the call ended.

How many times can a man lose the people in his life before the heart breaks permanently? How many times can a heart break before it dies? Everything and everyone I touched, I broke. This was my fault, just like before. It was all, and always was, my fault.

THE BARTERING OF HEKATE

1991 A.D.

Step by step, Malus strode further into the forest, as quiet as shadow. He passed an abandoned house a mile behind, food still warm on the kitchen table, lights left on and a fire smoldering beneath a stone hearth. There were four bedrooms and five beds, but not a trace of those who lived there. Her mark was left at the foot of the front door—a sprig of hemlock, in full bloom. It was his first clue that she was near, miles down a narrow gravel road deep into the Icelandic countryside.

She had disappeared long ago, only recently resurfacing in modern times at the brink of civilization. She was known by many, each claiming her as their own, but in truth, she did not belong to this world. She was queen to another.

A warm light caught Malus's attention, drawing him through the thickest, wildest portions of the forest, with twisted trees at the base of a craggy ravine. A great bonfire roared and snapped, sending tongues of red and yellow flames high into the air as hissing high-pitched voices caught his sensitive ears. From afar, he retrieved a hag stone from his pocket and peered through the hole, spotting exactly what he expected to find—creatures, large and small, dancing gleefully around the fire. Some were twisted and scrawny, others pale and beautiful—sprites and fairies and goblins alike.

Unseelie, the darkest, most deranged of Fae.

He replaced the hag stone within his pocket and approached the fire assertively. He could not see the creatures, but he could smell them and feel the motion vibrating on the air—when suddenly it stopped.

They knew he was there.

Malus stepped up to the fire and peered into the flames. Three bodies. Parents and an adult son. Fae enjoyed the young and only the young.

"What do you want, stranger?" hissed a voice. It sounded as if it came from everywhere all at once and echoed off the ravine wall.

"I came to offer you an opportunity," said Malus. His offer was immediately met by cackles and giggles. The Fae considered him a joke—a courageously stupid creature who was in over his head.

"Poor, poor man. There is nothing you could offer me, except to fuel my fire."

"I'm not here for fairy games," warned Malus.

"Funny, I do not play games, sir," said the voice.

There was motion on the air—vibrations. The Fae, out of phase with Malus's reality, were surrounding him. He quietly inhaled a lung full of smoke, then blew it through the hole of the hag stone, revealing the Fae as if removing the curtain that concealed them. Creatures large and small, some vicious, some beautiful, but all perverse came at him in a snarling, angry rush.

At once Malus called the spirits of the burning dead upon their bonfire and threw their recently departed anger at them, all while generating a flaming sword from the ether. In two quick motions, the dead had torn apart goblin, troll, and faerie—while Malus chopped down a banshee and embedded his sword into the skull of an angry erlking.

"Stop!" shouted the voice, cold and angry like an avalanche.

"Will you hear my proposal?" asked Malus.

From the shadow came a woman in black wearing a mask of pure white. It appeared like a barn owl, with two wide vacant eyes and a nubby hooked beak. At her sides were two children, a boy and a girl, with eyes rolled back into their heads. They were mystified, enchanted, and moved as stiffly as the undead. Her black hair drifted on an unknown current, and her long black ballroom dress was embroidered with a demented pattern like children screaming.

"What do you offer, Pale Wanderer?" she said.

"Hekate, Unseelie Queen, in return for your assistance, I will gift you anything you desire," said Malus.

"You cannot provide what I want," said Hekate, humorlessly. Her remaining Fae giggled at the thought. "Nobody can."

"Tell me what it is. Name it," said Malus. "And I will provide."

"The land of Fae has been stolen from me. My crystal key has been shattered. Airne, goddess and Queen of the Seelie Court, has locked me out of my home. I want her head. I want her dead. Bloodshed, blood red, and behead-ed," she said. "Her court must fall. Mischief and mayhem shall reign no more. Long live the court of darkness, the court of catastrophe."

"So be it," said Malus. "Sign my contract, help me achieve my goals, and it shall be yours." Malus extinguished his sword and approached the Unseelie Queen with arms open.

"No," said Hekate. "Bargains are for fools. Treaties are for humans. Contracts are for demons. Pacts are for Seelie. But Unseelie—we agree to nothing without stipulations."

"What additional price do you require?" asked Malus, hesitantly.

"A down payment," she said. "Help me destroy the Seelie Court first, and I will sign your contract. Upon the terms being met, I require one thing."

"Name it," said Malus.

"Children. For every three born in this realm, I require one."

"So be it," said Malus.

XXII
the set up

TONY
Then.

"I didn't know Tori for very long, but I grieved just the same. Jess asked me to go to the funeral, and Tori's friends accepted me as one of theirs. It was a tough few weeks. Jess eventually dropped out and moved away. I think Grace Falls had finally become too painful for her. Nobody knew where she went, except Kurt, and he wasn't telling."

"That is a really awful experience," said Doc.

"Yeah, it was. Life has a way of bringing back these greatest hits, over and over." I thought for a moment, before I said, "The trouble is, you think you have time. Buddha said that. I found it in a fortune cookie once, and I think it adequately sums up everything about my life."

"Did you ever learn how Tori died?" he asked.

A lot of things happened on New Year's Day, just after midnight. Things I only managed to piece together over the years. When we stormed out of Maynard's house that night, Tori felt bad. She felt bad about how things went down, and she felt bad about Jess. She hopped into her car and sped out after us. She didn't even get out of Maynard's driveway when a red Mustang with no headlights crashed into her. The impact sliced the whole front half of Tori's car right off, and sent it tumbling until it came to a complete stop more than a hundred feet away. The cops said the Mustang was going over a hundred miles per hour when it impacted Tori's car. She died instantly.

The driver, however, lived, with hardly a scratch on him.

Rick Jansen was put in handcuffs and taken into custody that night, with nothing more than a bum knee to show for it. Maynard, who was there, said Rick was screaming "She did this! She did it!" into the night as they loaded him into the back seat of a police cruiser.

The speeders that nearly ran us off the road were students, racing away from the scene—probably from a party somewhere further up on Cross Road.

Something happened at that party. Something that spooked them all, including Rick. Maybe they were underage or trespassing, doing drugs or other illegal activity—afraid of getting caught, or maybe they just didn't want to sink with the ship. Whatever it was, they abandoned that party in a hurry.

However, it wasn't until Marshall came home two weeks later and told me the rest of the news that a chain of events began to unfold in my mind. Jacinda had broken up with Rick in a blowout fight on New Year's Eve—and the rest of those events were just dominos falling in their wake.

February 14, 2002

Sadness was like an avalanche when you let it take over. I buried myself in schoolwork, trying to keep my mind busy so I'd stop thinking about all the bad things that kept happening. I was beginning to think that Tori was right about Grace Falls—bad things happened there. It was like there was negative energy surrounding us and pulling us all down with it.

Marshall was always the most empathic of us. The guy knew when to give you space and when to step in. After giving me just enough slack for just the right amount of time, he showed up from class on Valentine's Day and walked right over to me at my desk, put his hand down, and swept the entire thing clean.

I could have murdered him.

I wanted to, but the guy looked at me and said, "Enough!" Then he walked out into the living room and screamed it three more times before he came back and tossed me a bar of soap.

"What the fucken hell is this?" I said. Tori would've been proud.

"Soap. Go use it. We leave in an hour," he said.

"For what?"

"Anne and I are taking you out. We decided to open up our hearts and our romantic evening to a third, and you're the lucky winner," he said.

"No, I've got stuff to do."

"A devil's three-way?" shouted Brad from the living room.

"Yes, Bradley," said Marshall. "Tony turned us down. You're up!"

"Really?" he said, as he came bustling into the room.

"Fuck no!"

"Aw man," groaned Brad. "You're no fun."

Then Marshall turned to me and said, "Bullshit, you're already two weeks ahead in all your classes. I've been paying attention, T. You've got the time. You're one of these guys that internalizes everything. You place guilt onto yourself when you don't deserve it. You lock yourself off from the world hoping all your problems will go away, but here's the thing you haven't learned yet."

"What's that?" I asked, being a smartass.

"Nothing ever changes if you don't try to fix it," he said. Then he paused to let that sink in before he continued. "I don't want you to be a forty-year-old with no friends and no life because you couldn't figure out how to get yourself on track when you had the chance. You have a hero complex. A deep need to save someone, and you don't even see it. You need to save yourself."

"Everyone always thinks they have time until it runs out. You always

think that just because it's not working today, that maybe it'll work to-morrow. Maybe I'll find love tomorrow. Maybe I'll get my career going tomorrow. Maybe I'll write that book tomorrow. Everyone always thinks that. Tomorrow's not a promise. The trouble is you think you have time.

"Losing Tori should have taught me something."

"Sometimes," said Doc, "we have to learn lessons over and over again before they sink in. Sometimes they never sink in. Look at how many people every year sign up for gym memberships, claiming this is the year they lose weight. By March, most of those memberships have hardly been used. And by the end of spring, nearly all are abandoned."

"I wish I could say I'm not that kind of person, but I think I am," I admitted. "I think I'm the type that only lives for today when it's present—when I'm motivated to do so."

"Were you motivated after Marshall's speech?"

"Hell no. I was annoyed."

I took a shower and got dressed with ten minutes to spare. Anne showed up shortly after and immediately gave me a big hug, telling me she was sorry for my loss.

Anne was always the sweetest.

We loaded into Anne's car, and she drove us to Mercy Point. There was an upscale bar along the River Walk. It had a reclaimed wooden floor with a tiled bar, and tables and chairs made from wood and old industrial piping. It was the kind of place you took someone on a first date—classy, but still a bar.

Marshall bought us a round of beers and added a shot of something that burned the whole way down—because "T needs to relax." We had ordered a plate of nachos and a few more beers when the lights dimmed and someone walked out on stage behind me.

When a practice chord was strummed, I knew why Marshall insisted I sit in that chair, with my back to the stage—and their cheesy "we got you" grins became obvious.

"Happy Valentine's Day, everybody," said Jaycie into the microphone. "I'm Jacinda O'Neill. I hope you enjoy."

She immediately launched into her set. At first, I didn't even turn around. I didn't want to see her, and I didn't know what Marshall and Anne were playing at. That ship had sailed between us, and I needed someone who wanted to be with me—not someone who stood me up.

"Aren't you going to turn around and watch the show?" asked Marshall. "Or are you going to pout there like a little bitch?"

I reached out for a nacho and grabbed the one chip everyone was eyeing up and eating around. It was the one chip with the most toppings that looked tastier than any other chip—every order of nachos has one. I grabbed it, and with that nacho came half the remaining toppings. I set it down onto my plate and saw Marshall glaring at me.

"What?" I said. "That's considered one nacho." I proceeded to stuff the whole thing into my face, as if on principle to show how much I didn't want to be there. Once I had swallowed it, I guzzled down my beer, then looked at them both and said, "How romantic."

"You're not even going to look at her, are you?" asked Anne.

"Look at who?" I said childishly.

In all the years I've known Marshall, I never saw him actually get mad. I'm talking, neck-vein throbbing mad. He stood up, walked around the table, grabbed my stool, and forcibly tried to turn me. As I fought him, the chair made the worst screeching noise you could ever imagine. So loud, everyone in the restaurant glared at us, and Jaycie, mid-song, said, "Gee, I hope you fellas are enjoying the show."

She was looking right at us, playing, with a gentle smirk that showed she was as shocked to see me as I was to see her.

"This was a setup for you both?"
"Yup."

Incorporated into her set were original songs sandwiched between love song covers I had never heard Jaycie sing before. One of her originals sounded like a plea to me—*sorry, I'm not who you thought I was.*

I tried to ignore her music, but as stony as I tried to be inside, seeing and hearing her stirred up things I didn't want to feel. Eventually her set ended, Jaycie placed her guitar on its stand and Anne got up to speak with her roommate—to clear the air and soften the unwelcomed surprise.

She was talking to Jaycie for at least twenty minutes from the hall that led to the restrooms. I didn't have the best angle, but Marshall did, and I could tell by his face that things weren't going so well.

"Happy now?" I said. "Neither of us want to see each other."

"If I get you another plate of nachos, do you promise to stuff your face again? If your mouth is eating, at least it's not being a total dick," he said.

Anne came back to the table, and for a moment I thought I was off the hook.

"Hey Marshall," said Jaycie happily, and then she turned to me and said, "Hey."

"Hey kid, great set tonight," said Marshall, filling the silence. "Were those some original Jaycie O's I heard sprinkled into the mix?"

"Yeah," she said bashfully, her nervous smile twitching.

"Jaycie O's," I grumbled. "Sounds like a cereal."

She laughed, maybe politely, and said, "It does sound like a cereal. With strawberry- flavored marshmallows?"

"Well, it has to be," I said. "I mean, the whole box is red. You can't have a bite of Jaycie O's without tasting strawberry."

"What are the O's?" she asked, "Just sugary hoops? Or do we give the kids something healthy? —"

"—like a whole grain?" we both said simultaneously.

Marshall and Anne sat there in complete befuddlement, until Marshall said, as un-humorously as possible, "And you two fuckers don't think you're made for each other."

The rest of the night was perfect.

Jaycie and I fell back into a groove, like we'd never left it, despite the six months since the last time we spoke. We laughed, we cackled, and we challenged each other like we always did. We brought out the best in each other.

At the end of the night, I helped Jaycie pack up her microphone and amplifier and realized Marshall and Anne had ditched us. Jaycie offered me a ride, because that's what our matchmakers had planned, and we loaded up into Jaycie's red cabriolet and headed back to Grace Falls.

It was a good car ride—we laughed, and we carried on, and when she pulled up in front of my dorm and put the car in park, it felt like we both didn't want the night to end. We were both very aware that our journey together was at an impasse—that I could either say good night and get out of the car, or I could make a bold move—of which there were varieties. She could sense I was jumping over a few dozen mental hurdles, and I could tell she was doing the same—overanalyzing and feeling through every possibility.

"Go out with me," I blurted, but not until I had thought through everything I was going to say. "On a date." I waited and watched for her reaction, but when none came, I continued. "No pressure, it can be just like it was tonight. Something low-key. Talking. Laughing. Nothing has to happen."

"Okay," she agreed. Then she reached over and grabbed at my neck, pulling the chain free of my shirt, with the brass key dangling from the end of it. "Just making sure it was still there."

"Always."

Then we made plans to meet at the town square by the fountain.

February 15, 2002

We met at the town square in the late afternoon and walked with no destination in mind. Everything started light and fun, but as time went on, we ventured into deep waters.

Without prompting, Jaycie told me information about herself I knew nothing about.

"Tony," she said as we walked by the Grace Falls Diner. "I'm sorry I stood you up that night. I was there," she said, pointing to a nearby tree across the street, "watching you."

"You were?" I said, surprised.

"Yeah, I panicked. I was dealing with a lot, and I had no way of meeting you and explaining myself that didn't come off worse than if I had not shown up at all."

"What do you mean?" I asked as we stopped at the corner. Jaycie was bundled up in a green peacoat, looking gorgeous as ever in her white knit cap with the pom-pom on top.

"I run from my problems. I always have. The night we first met back in high school, something happened," she said.

"What happened?" I asked.

"It's not really important," she said, avoiding it, "but one thing led to another, and when I tried to discuss my problems, my parents and I got into a horrible fight. When I struggled, their first answer was to throw money at the issue and send me away to private school. That night, I left. I told my parents I needed to get as far away from Grace Falls as I could. My mother said some things I know she wished she could take back. I got in my car, and I drove. I thought about calling them, but I never did. Not for a very long time."

She grabbed my hand and held it, then we started walking again and she continued. "I dreamt about you that first night on the road, sleeping at a rest stop in my car. It was random. Some guy I met only once, and I had this vivid dream. We were walking through a forest together, then a horn went off and I was startled awake before some trucker drove through my car because I was blocking the truck lane.

"I drove to Lincoln, Chicago, Boise, Reno, and San Diego. I kept going. I just couldn't stop," she explained. "I couldn't shake all the bad things from my thoughts. I replayed them over and over again in my head. No matter where I went, or what I did, I couldn't escape my demons. I was too afraid to. I needed to live a little, because if I didn't heal from old wounds, I'd never be whole enough to return. I was so broken, disgusted with myself, and angry. Before I knew it, almost five months went by and I was working as a waitress at a hotel casino bar in Vegas. I woke up on Christmas Day and realized I hadn't done anything with myself. I hadn't even taken the opportunity to pursue my dreams. I got depressed, really, really depressed. I had gotten so far away from my one goal that it was too hard to get back on track. I wanted to die, I wanted to find a way out.

"Anyway, eventually I pulled it together. I got my GED, then signed up for classes. I made some friends, and I kept writing and playing.

Then, I moved home. It took a while to get transferred to Milton State, but I kept playing, and got a few gigs around town, Mercy Point, even one in Philly. Then I packed up my things and moved in with Anne," she said, taking one last breathy sigh. "And here I am."

"I didn't know you had gone through all that."

"It's not something I like talking about."

"Speaking of not talking about things, I didn't know you had a sister," I said.

"What?" she asked. Her eyebrows and forehead creased.

"You had a sister, didn't you? Jane? She passed away a long time ago?"

"I never had a sister," she said. "Why do you think that? Did Amanda tell you that?"

"No," I said. "Sorry. It's a long story."

"Do you think she was telling the truth?" asked Doc.

"Of course," I said. "She had no reason to lie to me. Tori and the others were wrong."

"So, where are we going?" she asked. "Or are we just going to walk every inch of town? Not that I mind. I think I could probably walk and talk with you till we ran out of sidewalk." She was rambling like me when I got nervous.

"Jaycie?" I said, staring into her eyes.

"Yes?"

"Would it be okay if I kissed you right now?"

"If you didn't, I think it might hurt my feelings."

"In that case, I suppose it's best to do it right away," I said, leaning in slow. I was scared out of my mind, but I wanted it more than anything. It was like having a first kiss all over again.

"Yeah, yeah, you should," she whispered just before our lips touched. It was like a magnetic attraction, our lips traveling the last few centimeters as if drawn by natural forces. An explosion went through me, like fire and electricity, like I had just done something that only I was meant to do. It was destiny.

Kissing her, loving her, was the only thing in my life from that moment on. My passion poured out of me and into her, but now it was reciprocated. I could feel her passion rivaling mine, like our souls were connecting, completing one another.

It was beautiful and intense, but it was painful as well. It was as if kissing someone after missing them for a lifetime. Beyond the emotion was a beautiful pain that felt as if my heart was about to explode. Like barbed wire being dragged through my veins.

Nobody ever kissed and experienced this, what we felt, the both of us, something beyond us. It wasn't normal, and it took all my strength to pull away. As soon as our lips parted I felt lost and needed to reconnect, like a junkie needing another fix to sustain myself. My lungs ached and my head throbbed to the beat of my hammering heart.

For a moment I thought it was just me, that only I experienced the kiss that shook the very pillars of existence. But when I looked into Jaycie's eyes and saw the tears welling up, I realized she felt it too. She felt all of it, like I did, and we were both forever changed because of it.

"I'm confused," asked Doc. "What you experienced sounds supernatural."

"Yes," I explained. "I feel like it was."

"How do you explain that?"

"I don't. Not really," I said. "But I have a thought."

"Which is?"

"That soulmates exist, and that we had found each other."

XXIII
stalker

TONY
Then.

"You believe in soulmates?" asked Doc, skeptical. "You don't strike me as a believer."

"There are few things I believe in," I said. "I believe that there are strange forces at play. I don't necessarily believe in an almighty entity, but I believe there are things—phenomena—that cannot be simply explained."

"And soulmates?"

"I believe that Jacinda O'Neill was the other half of my soul. Maybe not in the literal sense. But there was a connection that went deeper than flesh or chemical reactions in the brain."

The doc nodded. "Continue."

February 15, 2002

We were standing on a corner along the edge of the town square near the Pin Falls bowling alley when we started making out, and it was getting late.

We had been kissing for seconds—maybe minutes—fifteen or more at most, the way reality sped up when I was with her—when I felt something. A presence? As our lips parted, I sensed someone standing nearby—like they were breathing down my neck.

CAWWWW!

A crow squawked overhead, pulling my attention upward. It stared at me and squawked again, then a few of his friends joined in. There were six of them, lined up along the power cables spanning two telephone poles.

"That's weird," I said.

"What is?" she asked.

"The crows," I said, remembering the night we first met. "They really don't like us kissing."

"What do you mean?" she asked.

Over our time together, I'd resigned from being critical over the unimportant things. Jaycie never had a great memory, but that was okay—even if she didn't remember the night we first met, and our almost-kiss ruined by crows.

"Never mind," I said, but couldn't shake the feeling like we were being watched. "What do you want to eat?"

"Ever try sushi?" she asked.

"No, never," I said. "Never thought I would either."

"You're going to love it," she said. "I promise."

Back then, even when things felt like they were going in the right direction, there was always something to bring us back down. We had a great night—our first together. When we arrived back at Jaycie's place, knowing Anne would be out with Marshall, we burst through the door grappling at each other. She had my shirt over my head when I tripped over something on the floor and tumbled.

I landed in a crash, but not because I ruined anything. It was dark, but from where I landed, I could tell there was something all over the floor.

She gasped after she flipped on the lights and said, "Oh my god."

Jaycie and Anne's apartment was torn apart. Sofa ripped, dishes smashed, furniture broken—and placed onto the floor, staged like a dead body, was Jaycie's guitar—the acoustic guitar her Grammy had given her, broken and smashed apart.

Jaycie cried like she had lost her grandmother all over again.

There was a message left behind—Jaycie and Anne used alphabet magnets on the refrigerator to leave each other notes and reminders, including what groceries to buy. All the magnets had been removed from the fridge, with the exception of four letters—M-I-N-E.

Anne arrived with Marshall just after the police.

When they asked Jaycie who might have had the motive to break in, she immediately named Rick Jansen.

"Wait, Rick was arrested, wasn't he? Vehicular manslaughter?" asked Doc.

"I told you, doc. Rick was untouchable."

"How is that possible? He committed a crime. A serious one."

"Do the rich ever pay for their sins? Rick was arrested and charged with second-degree murder. His blood alcohol level was nearly twice the legal limit, and he was stoned on a combination of MDMA and methamphetamines. They also found high levels of testosterone from steroid abuse. And yet, when the time came, Rick's father paid an enormous amount of money to get him out on bail and hired his go-to lawyer—Joseph O'Neill, who kept tying up the court and delaying the trial.

"Jaycie and her father had quite the conversation on the phone. I hadn't met the man, but from what I could hear on her end of the conversation, he was a stubborn prick, ordering his daughter to retract Rick's name from the police report.

"On top of all that, knowing Rick was walking free reopened all the scars of Tori's death. Tori's mom, Lillian Martin, was murdered when she was just six. The Martin family never had their day in court, and something told me they never would."

Despite the darkness, I was happy. We were happy. It's human nature that when you get everything you've ever desired, you want more.

For some reason, I didn't want any more. Being with Jaycie, every moment was special, and every day was exciting. I couldn't want anything else. I knew that just being with her made it all great.

We spent hours on end talking, connecting.

Some days we met between classes, grabbing lunch together or taking walks around campus. Other days we'd meet up after class to study or relax. We even double dated with Marshall and Anne a few times. Then, once a week we'd all go out with Brad and Sid to hit up a bar or party or find some local event around Mercy Point—like Karaoke Fest, and the time Marshall wanted to run a 10K—we ended up rescuing him after the second mile for a beer and burgers.

When Jaycie slept over, I often found myself lying awake after she fell asleep in my arms to study her, memorizing everything. She had four prominent pale freckles on her cheeks just below her eyes—three on her left side, one on the right, like a constellation. I committed every perfect feature to memory.

Some mornings I'd find her lying awake beside me, memorizing me as I did her. I'd pretend to be asleep just to listen to her soft breathing as she studied me.

I couldn't get over how beautiful she was in the morning, like bed head and morning breath were a disease from which she was immune.

Or maybe I didn't notice her imperfections because I was so in love with her.

On lazy evenings, I would lay on Jaycie's bed and perfect my Photoshop and Illustrator skills while she sang to me and played guitar. Every moment listening to her sing was special, and I often found myself staring at her with droopy hypnotic eyes while she played.

During our long talks, we began to open up about past loves. I told her all there was to know about the string of women who came and went, but I left Tori out of it. There was no reason for me to hide anything, but the hurt of losing her was still too recent.

The doc took quick note of that.

Jaycie had a hard time opening up at first, telling me only bits and pieces. We were together for two full months before she could even say Rick's name to me.

Then, one Saturday afternoon, Jaycie finally told me all about Rick.

April 23, 2002

"You have to understand," she said, looking up from her salad to impress her point upon me further, "I wasn't the same person I am now. I was a kid. We met in the fifth grade, over summer break. My parents sent me to an all-girls school in Mercy Point when I was eight. Rick was one of the few guys I knew, so of course I had a crush on him," she said, then crunched into another bite of lettuce. We were sitting in a booth at the diner, enjoying an unseasonably warm April. "I remember going to a party with my neighbor Whitney, and I chased him around the whole night, right after I started at Grace Falls High. My first few days there were right before holiday break. Everyone already had friends, and I was strolling in with clothes I had gotten the day before in an emergency back-to-school shopping spree. I never had to worry about those things before—I always had a uniform for school. I very rarely wore anything other than t-shirts and lounge pants when I was home."

"You really didn't have anything to wear? No jeans or dresses?" I asked in between munching on a French fry.

"Can I have one?" she asked, losing interest in her salad.

"Of course. Eat as many as you like," I told her and angled my plate for her reach.

"Thanks." She smiled and continued to rub her bare foot against my leg. "No, unless you count like church clothes and uppity things like that. If I had worn that stuff, I would have been exiled immediately to the losers table."

"You mean to say we could've sat at the same table?" I joked.

"Babe, you're no loser. Stop that. That's not what I meant," she said, then grabbed another fry and continued. "I showed up that first Friday in this yellow funky dress, and I totally thought I was rocking it. Until I—oh, is there any more ketchup?"

"Yeah, I got it. Go on." I opened the ketchup bottle and dabbed some onto my plate of rapidly thinning fries.

"Until I overhear these girls making fun of me. Calling me Raggedy Anne, because of my dress and red hair. I cried my eyes out that night, and I nearly told my parents I made a mistake and wanted to go back to private school. I cried in my room all weekend. I just wanted to fit in. Then suddenly those whispers stopped. The girls stopped making fun of the way I looked when the guys took notice of me—and new whispers began. The kind that a girl never wants to hear."

"Huh?" I asked, but then she shot me a look and I figured it out on my own.

"I loved the attention, but not that kind of attention. I only knew two boys around my own age. Rick and your buddy Robbie Morris."

"Who?" I asked. The name only vaguely rang a bell.

"Robbie Maynard Morris?" she said.

"Oh! Yeah, Maynard," I laughed.

"He was my neighbor before we moved. I'd see him every now and then around the school, though I wouldn't recognize him now even if I saw him. We used to play together sometimes when we were young, but I think he was scared of me or something. I'm sorry, I'm boring you, aren't I?"

"No. I like listening to you talk. I want to know everything about you, so I think you need to stop eating my fries and concentrate on talking," I joked while noticing my fries were down to the last three or four. She feigned being insulted, and I caved. "Fine, you can have the rest."

"Ha!" she cried out in victory. "So, the guys were noticing me, and there was no guy more popular than Rick Jansen. All the girls talked about him." Then she paused, her tone loaded with sarcasm. "I'm sure you love hearing this."

"It's okay, I got the girl," I replied proudly. She smiled brightly and continued.

"Rick was the alpha's alpha. He was good looking, rich, and captain of all the sports teams. All the girls swooned when he was around, and they'd stab each other in the back to get his attention. He was dating this girl named Tori, and I wanted so badly for him to notice me." She took a deep sigh and thought for a second, then shook her head. "The things girls do to get noticed…"

She remembered something that bothered her but pushed it away and moved on. While she shook off the memory, I took a healthy gulp of my soda to avoid looking guilty over omitting Tori from our talks.

"I ran away from home before anything actually happened. Rick played the field, and he made every girl feel special. When I moved back to town, we ran into each other and he asked me out.

"Sometimes," she continued, "I wonder how things may have been different, if you and I had run into each other first." There was pain and distress in her voice as she examined their relationship, so I reached across the table and took her hand in mine. "All the things I could have avoided if I had just—"

"But we all can do that," I explained, cutting in before she got upset. "We're all the products of our own experiences. You're in a better situation now, and you ganked all my fries," I finished, joking to make her smile.

"I still can't believe I didn't leave him. Especially after what he did to you. There were times when he could be so Jekyll and Hyde, like there was something wrong with him. I made so many bad decisions. I did so many things I'm not proud of. There were so many things—" Her eyes glazed over in thought.

"Were there ever any good moments?" I asked, half in jest.

"Of course, it wasn't all bad. There were moments of kindness. But it got confusing, and I realized I was in too deep. I didn't like who I was with him," she said, trailing off. "Eventually, I got back to basics. I played guitar. Wrote in my notebooks and drew. Rick never cared about those things. It was always about him, football and baseball, and where was the next party."

"You know, I wish I could've said or done something, anything to make you leave him," I said. She could hear the pain in my voice. "If I had just found the right arrangement of words…"

"It wouldn't have mattered," she explained. "If it had, you'd never have the best version of me. I was too hurt. I wasn't myself. I needed to get away on my own. Things happened the way they did for a reason. But, if we didn't get to know each other like we did, I would've never known how wonderful you are. You're everything I could have wished for." She paused as a few crows landed outside the window to peck at some bread left behind on the ground. "Tony, there were things that happened—strange things that I don't know if I could ever speak of. Things that don't make any sense. Things I'm afraid of, like a nightmare—"

"Is everything okay here?" our waitress asked, checking in with us. She was an older lady who wore too much makeup and perfume.

"Yeah, can I get another order of fries for the fry-thief?" I said. "And another bottle of ketchup please? This one's almost empty."

"Of course." The waitress smiled and walked away.

Jaycie gripped my hand tightly with growing affection. I tried to press her about the nightmare things, but she smiled and told me they were unimportant.

"Ever have a bad feeling, but you pass it off as nothing, because maybe you're just being paranoid?" I asked Doc.

"Certainly," he replied. "I think there is some truth to the way our minds and bodies are in tune with the world around us. Accumulating stimuli that register on a subconscious level, raising internal alarms."

"My life is marked with hundreds of them. Every major event in my life has been preceded by some kind of positive or negative feeling. The day I met Jaycie? I felt it. That evening Rick jumped me? I felt it before I ever started walking away. The night Tori died? There was a mosh-pit in my gut."

"What do you think that means, Tony?" he asked.

"Probably nothing," I admitted, despite the paranoia.

"Or maybe it is something?" suggested Doc.

May 3, 2002

"What do you mean?" she asked. The look on her face was devastating. She was peering back and forth between Marshall and me as if waiting for us to explain that she had heard incorrectly. She looked shocked, confused, and definitely hurt.

"I thought I told you," I said, "I don't really talk about it."

"So, it's true?" Jaycie asked, and Brad looked like he was about to cry.

We were halfway through a game of Jenga, a game of balance and skill, of all things, to celebrate the end of senior year, when a small faux pas turned into a full-blown problem. Marshall and Anne were petrified by Jaycie's response—Marshall had been drinking his beer for a full minute straight without putting it down.

"I'm sorry," I said. "I thought I told you."

"You dated Tori Martin, and she died," she said, like she was putting together clues, "on New Year's Eve?"

"Yes," I said, as I glanced over at Sid. The blood had drained away, leaving him paler than usual. He looked mortified.

"Rick," she choked, "hit her in his Mustang?"

"Yes," I said.

"Shit," she spat. I couldn't tell if she was angry at the cruelty of life, at Rick, at me, or at herself. She looked embarrassed and angry, then said, "I have to go."

She grabbed her purse and cell phone, then bolted out the door with me in hot pursuit. I caught up to her just outside the door and said, "Please don't go."

"Why didn't you tell me?" she asked.

"I thought you knew," I explained, and I couldn't shake the feeling that there was something more going on. "She was my friend. We only dated for a week. I don't like reliving that kind of thing."

Jaycie nodded, then said, "You're right, I wish I had found out some other way. Not like this. Everyone in the room knew but me."

"I knew I had omitted things. I wasn't proud of it. I omitted it as much for me as I did it to protect her," I said.

"Lies by omission are complicated," said Doc. "The people we love want to know everything, even if it means being hurt."

"Yeah, but what if I omitted things because I didn't want to hurt myself?"
"Are you speaking about your mother?" he asked.
"No." The question blindsided me. I shook it off.
"Did you ever tell Jacinda about her?"
No. I didn't. And I'd never have the chance to do it now.

"Are you that mad at me?" I asked as she turned to open the door to the stairs that led down and out of the dorm. She sighed, and I followed that up with, "Are you breaking up with me?"

Jaycie spun around at once and kissed me. "No," she said, "I'm not breaking up with you. But I need to be alone tonight. I have another final tomorrow anyway."

I nodded, despite the fact I didn't feel good about it. Something felt off.

"I'll text you when I'm home," she said.

"Okay," I swallowed. "I love you, Jaycie." We had just recently started saying that to each other, and we both agreed it was right.

"I love you too, Tony," she said with a weak smile, followed by another kiss. "Always."

"It would seem Jacinda felt your omission was a betrayal of trust,"
said Doc. "She was willing to forgive you and move on. Did you ever
tell her about your mother? Or are you refusing to answer?"

"I told you, one ghost is all I'm willing to discuss today," I replied. I
thought for a moment, then continued. "I knew she felt betrayed. I never
wanted to do that to her. Everyone in the room knew what I had gone
through, except her—the one person I was closest to. I always felt like
I was never good enough for Jaycie, even when I had her. I was always
making mistakes and chasing after her." Then I took both hands, pulled
them into fists, and rubbed both eyes. "But that wasn't the worst thing
that happened that night."

And the doc jotted down more notes.

Jaycie left our room at 9:31 that night. On average, it took about twenty minutes for her to cross campus and walk down the street to her apartment building. It was an easy walk down a well-lit path through campus, with lamps every thirty feet and plenty of people enjoying a warm spring night.

At 9:52 PM, I sent her a quick text to check in.

"Hey, just making sure you got home okay," I wrote.

By 9:55, I was having a small panic attack, asking myself if I had really screwed up—if she was hurt—or worse. By 10:01, after I'd counted each and every second over that eight-minute span, my phone rang. I picked up on the first ring and brought it to my ear so fast the line had yet to fully connect.

"Help me," she cried. She was hysterical and her breathing was erratic. Jaycie was the kind of gal who could take care of herself. She was smart, strong, healthy, and capable, and to hear her voice so chaotic and distressed sent me into a frenzy.

I bolted from my room and leapt over the couch, all while yelling, "I'll be right there!" into the cell phone. Brad was watching TV on the couch, and his big bowl of popcorn flew into the air. "Where are you?"

"I'm outside my apartment," she whimpered.

"I'm coming." I ran for the stairs.

A million thoughts went through my head as I ran to her. A million thoughts that meant nothing if I couldn't be there to protect her. I never ran faster than I did that day, cutting through campus and running through the dark, barreling through hedges, in the name of love.

"Please don't get off the phone! Please stay on the phone!" she yelled as I ran.

"I won't leave you alone," I promised.

The flames in my chest rose. I was burning up, hot and sweaty, and I never once felt tired or winded. I ran like a bat out of fucking hell.

I cut across the campus gardens, over the covered bridge, and came out the other side in clear view of her apartment building, where I saw her slumped on the ground under shrubs. She was lying against the side of the building in a dark corner where the light couldn't reach her. I raced over and slid along the ground, trying to get to her as fast as I could. She flinched at me before she noticed who it was, putting her hands up in front of her face to protect herself.

"It's me!" I yelled as she defensively slapped me away. "It's me!" I yelled again and grabbed hold of her wrists to restrain her. Her phone was on the ground next to her, still connected to mine. "Are you hurt?" She didn't appear to hear me. "Jaycie, are you hurt?" She was covered in blood.

As I frantically looked for a gaping wound, I suddenly noticed the chunky spray across the brick façade and followed the pattern toward a lifeless heap in the bushes.

I turned back to her, but she looked at me like she didn't even know me, then said, "There were so many crows." Her eyes darted around the sky, like she was tracking them flying in the dark.

"Jace, babe, you're scaring me," I said. I had no idea what had happened, but everything about it chilled me to the bone. Then she grabbed hold of me and sobbed uncontrollably.

"I love you," she cried, and I thought she was going to fracture into a thousand pieces.

I heard heavy footfalls as someone came running up behind us. It was Sid, and he already had his cell phone out, dialing 9-1-1. He kept his distance.

"She's okay," I said to him, who nodded just as the operator picked up. While he was relaying information, my attention returned to the body.

"I'm going to let you go now," I said to her. "I have to check on the body." I didn't want to, but what if he—she—it?—was still alive?

Her pupils were like nickels. She was in shock, so I gently lifted and slid her aside so I could access the bushes beside her.

"Don't," she said, but I continued. The body was dressed in black from head to toe, and as I grabbed hold of the shirt around its massive neck and pulled it up for a closer look, there was a giant piece of his skull missing.

I was staring into the lifeless eyes of Rick Jansen.

After a few minutes a crowd had gathered around us, one that included a nice lady who was a nurse. She stayed with Jaycie and me until the ambulance and police arrived. The nurse and I moved Jaycie away from the bushes and away from the body.

Brad, Marshall, and Anne had followed me out the door, and they eventually found us after seeing the flashing lights. Overall, Jaycie wasn't seriously hurt, but she was bruised around her neck and ribs, and her shirt was torn with scratches down her side. Sid was walking around, pacing back and forth angrily, while the others kept their distance.

When the police finally got the chance to ask Jaycie questions, I was sitting beside her in the ambulance, holding her hand.

"I left Tony's apartment around 9:30," she said. "We had a fight." She glanced at me as if to say she was sorry. "I walk home all the time from his place without any problem. I take the path through campus with all the lights, and I usually see a lot of people. I got about halfway home when I saw someone. They said something *strange* to me."

"What did he say?" asked the policeman, his pen resting on his notepad awaiting her details. Jaycie was wrapped in a blanket, her feet dangling off the back of the ambulance, and she was shivering despite the warm night.

"I don't know," she said. "Found you? We found you?"

"We?" said the policeman. "Was there more than one attacker?"

"I don't know."

"Did they say anything else?"

"You'll always be mine. The sooner you realize that, the better." She repeated it as if she were a thousand miles away.

"Did you call for help?"

"No. I just ran. I ran to my apartment." She gestured toward the building. "I couldn't get my key out fast enough and he tackled me to the ground."

"Did you scream? Did anybody inside the building hear you?"

"I guess not." She shrugged. "He put his hands around my neck and mouth."

"How did you get away?" the officer asked.

"I don't know. I closed my eyes and tried to scream and when I opened them, he was dead."

I thought about what she had said, and the whole thing didn't add up to me. It normally took her twenty minutes to get home, and if she ran in fear for a portion of that time—a former track star—then why did it take half an hour to get home? I didn't think she had a reason to lie. I tried not to think about it. She needed me.

"Did you know the perpetrator?" the cop asked.

"Yes," she said after taking a deep breath. "His name was Rick Jansen." She said it while looking me straight in the eyes. I'd never seen such fear in her before. It rattled me. It was a horrible and helpless feeling. I wanted to take it away from her, to cure it like medicine.

"Do you have any idea why he attacked you, then took his own life?" he asked.

"Maybe," she said, her eyes still staring into mine, as if she was worried about what she was about to say. "He's an ex-boyfriend."

"Why would he want to assault you? For what reason?"

"I don't know. Revenge?"

"I don't understand," said Doc.

"Yeah," I chuckled. "Get in line."

"Do you know what happened?"

"I only know what Jaycie told me, which was similar to what she had told the cops that night. She was walking home, she saw someone, she ran. He caught up to her as she attempted to unlock the door, there was a tussle, she closed her eyes, and when she opened them, he was dead."

"Was there a gun? A gunshot?"

"She claims she never heard the shot, but I thought that maybe in the moment, it didn't register," I explained. "There was a gun though, yes. He was holding onto it. But it was empty."

"It wasn't loaded?"

"There was evidence that it had been fired recently, but there were no casings nearby. No bullet in his brain or in the building facade. And the serial number looked like it had been melted off."

"Was it suicide, or was it murder?"

"Are you suggesting that Jaycie—?"

"Absolutely not," said Doc. "Was there someone else?"

"Doubtful," I said with a heavy sigh. "The police found a letter on the passenger seat of his Mustang, parked a few blocks away."

"What did it say?"

"Jibberish."

"What do you mean?"

I angrily stared at the doc for a moment. The letter itself was an excuse for all the wicked shitty things Rick had done in his life, and I hated that something like it existed in the world. "The letter said that he was still in love with Jaycie. That he needed to take her to stay alive. That without her, he was a dead man. That he would take her or die trying. That the voices had gotten so loud that he couldn't hear anything else. They told him that killing her was the only way."

"He was a disturbed individual. Likely suffering from a psychotic episode," said Doc.

"Ya think?"

"You still feel angry? Even though you know he was suffering?"

"Of course, I do! That piece of shit was evil. It's hard to put it behind me when all I ever loved is gone."

"I'm not judging you. I think you have every right to feel the way you do."

"Jaycie said the same thing."

Marshall and I stayed at Jaycie and Anne's place that night. Jaycie was having a hard time sleeping and kept startling herself awake. I, on the other hand, was too enraged to sleep. I kept her tight in my arms as I thought about all the things that had transpired that night.

"I'm sorry," she whispered to me sometime after three in the morning. I was spooning her, and I didn't even know she was awake.

"What for?" I asked.

"I brought all my problems with me," she said. "And now you have them too."

"What problems?" I asked, but she didn't answer. "I feel like I can't protect you."

"You do an excellent job protecting me," she replied. "Like all the times I forget something, you're there to remember. Or when I set my glass too close to the edge of a table, and you move it, so I don't spill. Or when you kick broken glass away from my path when we walk together. Or when you make sure that I'm happy, and the way you go out of your way to love me and cherish me. Those are great things, and I need them more than I need your fists."

"What are all those things worth if I can't protect you from living in fear?" I asked. I could feel her pulse quicken.

"I have no doubt you'll be able to protect me if the situation presents itself. I understand how much you hated him, and you have every possible reason to, but it's over now. Let it go. I can't lose you, okay?" Her voice was so emotional and pained that I learned right then and there that she was right. It was hard to let go of my anger, but for her, I had to find a way.

"I'm sorry I didn't tell you about Tori," I said.

"That's okay," she said dreamily, then fell fast asleep a minute later.

"That night, I had the strangest dream."

XXIV
no fair fights

Tony
December 22, 2013
Now.

"Do you think he heard us?" said a voice.

"Fuck if I know," said a second voice. "Look at his face."

"Uh huh," said the first, "and what the hell is that?"

"Did he claw at the pavement?" Then an exasperated, "Shit."

"Call it in," said the first. Footsteps and shuffling. "Sir? Sir, can you hear me?" Then a pause. "Damnit. Why does this always happen to me?"

The heart is finite. It beats for roughly eighty or so years, on average, then gives out due to age, disease, or a combination of both. The heart, as the symbolic epicenter of emotion and spirit, is far less durable. Lose a parent or loved one, it will crack. Lose all the people I lost over the years—including the people who walked out—and if there was anything left but dust after that, it would be a miracle.

My miracle was coming to a close.

Amanda was killed in a phone call—a fucking phone call. I listened and couldn't do a damn thing about it. I was a helpless bystander. Caught between being there for her in her last moments and sinking into my own despair for failing her when she needed me most, I was impotent to change the outcome. When the line went dead, so did I. Sinking into a catatonic state was like submerging into a warm bath. I sank into the farthest reaches of my mind, retreating into a distant corner where I didn't have to feel or think or dream. I can't say who or what I was when I was there—was I even anything at all?—but I wasn't planning to come out for anyone or anything.

I heard my brain-trust calling me—

"Tony! Tony, my man!"

"Sir, we cannot do this without you."

"We understand your loss, Tony, but for the sake of us all, we need you."

—but it didn't matter. Why would I want to live in a world without the people I loved?

I was so far gone, so far into the nothing, that I didn't realize when the thoughts—the memories—were surrounding me until they were all that I could hear, feel, and see.

"*Retrieve your lost heart. Get it back. Let her be your inspiration, Tony. Never let her go.*" The words of my echo.

"*You're lost. You need to find your way,*" said the Mistress.

What if I didn't want to be found? What if I wanted to slip away? Life was so hard and sinking into the nothing was so…easy…

"*Tony, sometimes you have to flip the script. Write a new one,*" said Marshall, once upon a time.

"*I don't want to let go,*" said Jaycie, whispering into my ear.

"*Then don't,*" I heard myself reply.

"*Eventually,*" she coughed, clearing her throat, "*I'll have to.*"

"*I know.*" Or at least, back then I thought I knew.

"*I'm sorry.*"

"*What for?*" I asked. What could she possibly have to apologize for?

"*For not being who you need me to be,*" she explained—prophetic words from the woman I loved.

"Tomorrow's not a promise, T. Gotta earn each one."

"I brought all my problems with me," she said. *"And now you have them too."*

"I don't need a white knight—but you need to be one," said Amanda, and she was right. All those years ago, and she was right about me.

"Friends protect friends. There's a better future coming. I know it," said the Alchemist from behind his mask, just before he died. I couldn't help but wonder, did I know him in another life?

"Who are you?" asked the man—my enemy—over the phone. *"Tony Oscuro? The Raptor? We all have many names."*

"Tomorrow's not a promise, T. Gotta earn each one."

Marshall screamed, *"You've spent a lot of time cutting off from all the friends you once had. I'm the only one stubborn enough not to give up on you. I know you went through hell, stuff I wouldn't wish upon my own worst enemy. I don't know if you're actually stupid enough to be suicidal, but it's shit or get off the pot time. Just do it and get it over with!"*

Marshall. You were like the wind at my back, pushing me to be better…

"Black and white doesn't exist, T," said Tori. *"Everything's just shades of fucking gray."*

"I know that not everyone comes into your life for long periods of time, sometimes we only get a moment, but I wish I had someone like Tony in mine," Jaycie wrote inside her journal.

We had a moment, and it's gone now.

"Tomorrow's not a promise, T. Gotta earn each one."

"And you two fuckers don't think you're made for each other," growled Marshall.

"Always."

"Jaycie?" I said, staring into her eyes.

"Yes?"

"Would it be okay if I kissed you right now?"

"If you didn't, I think it might hurt my feelings."

How could I possibly go on? How could I do this without you?

"Tomorrow's not a promise, T. Gotta earn each one."

Hadn't I earned it? Hadn't I earned one fucking day of happiness?

I'd been kicking, and scratching, and goddamn clawing my way out of this! Every time I fight my way up to the top, someone kicks me all the way back down! Life shouldn't be a game of Chutes & Ladders. Life shouldn't be this hard!

"Tomorrow's not a promise, T. Gotta earn each one."

"…this is the only wish I need to come true," I told her. *"Jaycie, you're everything to me. You're my last thought before I fall asleep and my first thought when I wake up in the morning. I can't live without you. I would rather die. I just need to know that you're mine forever."*

"I'm yours," she said, and grabbed me tight. *"Forever. We'll grow old together and hold each other's hands as we die."*

How do I move on?

"I thought you were the moon."

"Tomorrow's not a promise, T. Gotta earn each one."

It was raining. Dark overcast skies and I was soaked. I could feel the cold water encroaching into places that should be warm and insulated. How long I had been there in the rain was a mystery to me, but it had been sunny when my phone call ended.

The blue lights of a police cruiser were flashing, and a state trooper hovered over me, but I did not move. My eyes were already open, and I was staring down at my cell phone, sitting on the shoulder of the road with my back against the rental car's bumper. A truck flew by on Highway 13, kicking up wet gusts of drizzly vapor as it soared past.

"…aaaannnnndddd the lights are on," said Montoya with the perfect game show host delivery, kneeling down in front of me with a toothy grin. "You gave us a scare, my man."

"Tony," prompted Jamaal to my left. He was like a pavilion the way he lumbered over me in his quadruple XL t-shirt, and yet he provided no cover from the rain—an opaque but incorporeal entity projected from my splintered mind. "Listen, don't move. There are two troopers. One beside you and the other in the cruiser running the rental plates."

"If we had stolen a car like some had suggested," said Chappy, shooting Montoya a glare, "we may be in an even more difficult position."

"All I'm saying is, it would have been fun," he replied with a shrug. Beneath the army fatigues was a wild man driven into service for a higher purpose.

Henry was studying me—were there physical symptoms of a psychotic break? Like a rash? Chicken pox? Psycho-pox?

"Wait till the right moment," said Doshin. "Be patient." The man already had an escape plan, and something about the way observed the world made me trust him with my life.

Despite their lively banter, I was still coming to terms with being back. The last twenty-four hours felt like I was moving from one intense obstacle to another—and after the horrors I'd seen, confronting two state-troopers was like facing off against a pesky little league team.

"The guy's gone," shouted the trooper beside me after he did a full three-hundred-sixty-degree inspection of me and the car. He wouldn't find anything—no personal effects, no information, no identity—and I was still sitting on my wallet. If they had the opportunity to run my name through their system, they'd have more than enough information to grow suspicious.

"What's that?" the second trooper asked, sticking his head out of the open cruiser door. He was punching information into the dashboard computer and could hardly hear his partner over the rain and traffic noise.

"He's gone," repeated the trooper. Then to himself, "I'm gonna catch the fucking flu because of this motherfucker? Shiiiit."

To serve and protect—sorry for the inconvenience.

Wings were flapping nearby. The sound of feathers somewhere above me to my left along the noise barrier—a large wall beyond the highway shoulder to prevent the constant traffic rumbling through the nearby neighborhoods.

CAWWWW!

Crows. Always fucking crows. They were always there, weren't they? I couldn't go anywhere near Grace Falls without them following me, and now it was like they were here to welcome me back. The welcome wagon—or harbinger of evil?

The temperature was hanging above freezing—but the moment the crows arrived, it began to plummet. A layer of ice was developing so quick along the blacktop I could hear the atoms constricting.

It wasn't natural.

"You sense it too?" asked Chappy—we were on the same page. "Something is not right."

"What is it?" asked Montoya. "More of them? The Thirteen?"

Nobody answered. Nobody knew. The glassy surface of the frozen blacktop shimmered, like dark shapes were moving on the other side of the reflective surface.

"That's it," growled the trooper. He was frustrated, cold, and wet. "I'm getting back in the car." He said it like he needed to justify his actions to me—but that was the moment I was waiting for.

He left my flank and started walking back to the driver's side of the cruiser, about fifty feet behind the rental. By the time he had paced halfway to his cruiser, I had the rental car started and shifted into drive.

"What the—" said the trooper.

"Hey! Hey! Stop!" shouted the second trooper.

As I slammed my foot onto the gas, the car lurched forward—we'd rented a 2011 Honda Accord, which just so happened to be the most boring car in America—and the effect was a less than stellar zero-to-40MPH in ten seconds. It wasn't what I imagined—and I admit, I had watched too many movies in my day—but I was hoping for a little more tire-squeal-peel-out than the groaning chug the car crawled through. Still, by the time the trooper got behind the wheel and started up the cruiser, I was already doing sixty and weaving through traffic.

"What am I doing?" I grumbled rhetorically. Back to ruminating over the self-destructive patterns I suffered through when I was backed into corners. Was I being stupid? Reckless? Where exactly was I going to go? Where was I was going to hide?

"Tony, my man," said Montoya. He sat in the passenger seat like Bo Duke with a big cheesy grin. "You're my hero."

"Fuck," I groaned as I peeked into the rearview mirror. The cruiser was shaving off ten feet from my lead every five seconds.

"What did you expect?" said Jamaal. "This ain't no muscle car. It's a fuel-injected economy-class four-cylinder gasoline chugger. They outlawed these jawns in the 2040s."

"What's the plan, sir?" asked Henry. He was still studying me like I should be behind the glass of an observation cell.

"The plan?" I replied. "The plan was don't get arrested."

"A noble plan," added Chappy, "but how does our current situation prevent that from happening? It appears your car is slower than theirs."

"Great observation," I sassed. "Why don't you get out and push?"

"I do not believe that will help," said Doshin, looking at his fellow figments like he was missing some logical leap.

"I think he was being facetious," said Chappy, wearing a sour frown.

In the rearview I could see the flashing lights through the misty haze. Cars were pulling over as the cruiser pursued me, and it was getting harder to see through the rain. However, that wasn't what concerned me most as my lead was cut in half. The cops weren't the only ones following me. A swirling cyclone of crows swarmed behind us, attempting to keep up with my escape. It looked like a tornado if not for the flapping wings—but the surrealist terror of that sight became the blossoming panic in my gut.

"Now that's something you don't see every day," said Montoya, his statement an underwhelming observation of the danger.

"That can't be good," added Jamaal. "And the physics are impossible."

"How so?" asked Chappy.

"You could take a thousand birds, and they still wouldn't have the ability to create something like that. The force necessary to create a tornado is," he explained, then paused, "something found only in nature."

Through the rearview mirror I tracked the cyclone's path as it wound uncontrollably like a top, spinning wide and sweeping left and right through the misty rain. The windshield wipers were on their fastest setting, but even they couldn't keep up with the water spray emanating from cars and trucks cruising over the wet, half-frozen roads. One by one, the cars behind us pulled over—some spun out as they attempted to dodge the sweeping cyclone, while the cruiser maintained pursuit, effortlessly closing the gap between us.

I was running out of time.

I remembered a story my dad used to tell, about when he and my mom were first dating. They were driving through a storm and the rain was coming down so thick and heavy that they couldn't see ten feet in front of the truck. My mother was worried, but Dad was attempting to calm her down by telling her stories about the farm he grew up on—he said she was always mystified by his childhood, fascinated with the simple life at peace with the land. He was driving along at twenty miles per hour, mid-story about some hijinks with his brothers, when my mom yelled, "Stop!" as if she could sense what he couldn't.

He slammed on the brakes just in time. The downpour had washed out the road, and dad was about to drive right into it. He always ended the story saying that he "ran out of road and survived to tell the tale."

That phrase loomed in the back of my mind as we sped past another mile-marker.

Either the troopers were going to arrest or shoot me, or the crows were going to shred and peck me to death. The rental, try as it might, was never going to out-pace a V8 or a supernatural tornado of birds and rain—and I was running out of road.

Grace Falls was only 15 minutes away.

"What is happening with the glass?" asked Henry. He removed his bifocals to clean them, as if the problem was with his own perception.

The windshield was fogging over despite the defroster running. It started at the edges and was spreading toward the center, like an icy manifestation. I flipped the defrosters on high, but that did nothing to prevent the spread. Then I cranked the heat and fiddled with the gauge when Jamaal said, "Tony, look."

On the frosty window was a message, like someone had written it with their finger to display its secret when the glass fogged over.

As if on theatrical cue, the moment the message fully absorbed into the gray matter of my brain, a gnarled hand clawed into the hood of the car. Something was crawling out from beneath, up over the front bumper. The creature, moving in sudden jolts, quickly pulled the top half of its body onto the hood. It wore a white mask over its face, like a barn owl, with its yellow eyes watching me from beyond the foggy window.

"Hekate," I said aloud. She had killed her fair share of the voices inside my head, and their fear of her became my own. Her arms, neck, and head were wrapped like a mummy in lace, clinging to her body as a protective covering. Where it dangled from her limbs was like a black shroud, drifting out of phase with the violent wind and friction outside the car. It was a swarming shadow, fluttering from her form in vaporous tendrils.

"Jamaal," I said urgently, "you're a living encyclopedia, right?"

"I remember everything, and I had a lot of time on my hands," he explained. "When you suffer through the phobia of everything there's not much else—"

"No offense, no time," I said, cutting him off. "What do you know about Hekate?"

"Greek goddess, associated with crossroads, secret passages, witchcraft, herbology, ghosts, necromancy, and sorcery."

"Anything else?" I asked, urging him to spit it out before she climbed her way into the car with us.

"I don't know!" he shouted. "It's mythology! Who knows what parts are real and what's just a stupid story." After I swerved to avoid a car that had pulled over—the rental's tires slipping on the freezing road until regaining traction—he added, "Also, some say she's the dark queen of the Fae."

"The what?"

She was crawling closer, and I could almost see her smiling beneath the mask, as if excited to hear us discussing her legend.

"The Fae," repeated Jamaal. "As in fairies and goblins."

"You're telling me she's David fucking Bowie?"

"Who is David Bowie?" asked Chappy.

"*Labyrinth*," said Jamaal. "Imagine if Jareth had a dark, twisted, evil as fuck sister—that's Hekate."

I glared him down as the icy roads started to affect the car's traction. A million angry thoughts snapped through my head like a mouthful of Pop Rocks.

"Of course she is."

The goddess crawled right up to the windshield and stared into my eyes, blocking my view of the road, and putting me on a collision course for any vehicle in my path. What she didn't take into account was that we had the same intentions.

We were traveling through a section of highway with twenty-foot sound barriers on either side of the dual three-lane road. There was no exit ramp or space to pull off to the side of the highway. We were funneled into a narrow space with only one option available.

When I rammed into the side of the pickup, I was aiming to have it slice through the passenger side, clipping Hekate and sparing my destiny a few additional moments. What I didn't expect was for the collision to be so violent, slicing the car in half long-ways and smearing the goddess across the broken windshield like a bug—then tossing her away into the chaos.

The next several seconds were a blur of glass and plastic, metal and burning fumes blasting into my face and through the air around me. The car spun six times before it was hit by the cruiser, then spun another three on the ice, finally resting in the opposite lanes across a twenty-foot-wide grassy median, facing the wrong direction.

Once we had stopped moving, it took the longest fifteen seconds in history to gather my equilibrium and brush the loose glass from my face. The pandemonium on the highway lasted another ten seconds as a vast array of vehicles piled up into a twisted pile of wreckage spanning almost a quarter-mile.

"Everybody okay?" I asked.

"My man," said Montoya, "we're not actually here, remember?"

Chappy looked at them and asked, "Did he hit his head again?"

"I believe he's fine," said Henry, quickly inspecting my injuries as I unbuckled myself and shouldered the door open on the third try. I thought my hand and arm were broken, but as I crawled out of the wreckage, everything seemed to be properly functioning without pain.

"Actually," I said with a shrug, "I feel pretty good."

Blood was trickling down my face, and as I checked myself in the cracked driver's side mirror, I watched my skin pry loose embedded pieces of glass, then miraculously stitch back together. I had to trace my hand over the wounds just to be sure they were gone—with the exception of the scar on my face, the one I received second-hand from my Echo, everything had healed.

"What the heck—" I said to myself, then excitedly stood up to show my brain-trust. "Did you guys see that?" It was a moment of elation that went against good sense and thrust me right into literal crosshairs.

Something hissed through the air past my shoulder, immediately followed by a popping sound in the distance.

"Get down!" yelled Montoya, and I dropped to my knees below the steaming hunk of fiberglass and metal that was once the rental car.

"That was a warning shot!" yelled one of the troopers. I could hear him shuffling around a few hundred feet away. "Accident on Highway Thirteen. I need backup. Trooper down," he said into his radio. I could hear the whole thing as if I was standing right beside him. "We need ambulances. Fire and Rescue. Over."

Peeking over the wreckage, I could see the trooper—holding his ground behind the open driver's side door as his partner suffered through a series of injuries from the impact. I could smell the iron—his blood—and hear his rapid breathing and pulse. He was in pain, but it didn't seem life-threatening—at least, not if he got proper, timely care.

The cruiser's entire front half was accordioned, and the flashing lights flickered on and off, but there was no sign of the cyclone—like it had abandoned its pursuit and blew itself out once I had been stopped.

"Come out with your hands up," shouted the trooper.

Did I want to test his accuracy? Where was I going to go? Traffic was stopped in both directions and there was nowhere to run.

The misty rain was still falling and freezing, and we were at an impasse.

Then there was a scream in the distance, from somewhere further down the road, behind the cruiser. A mass of cars lined up with their flashers on, each a random yellow blink of light in the mist. However, it wasn't until the explosion that everything went from horrible to nightmare.

A flash of fire burned through the mist, its black smoke darkening the already gloomy skies, and there were shadows moving—people abandoning their cars and running for cover.

Out of the mist came tall dark shapes. They walked like men, but their heads were covered in something tall and pointy. There were five of them from what I could see, and they were dragging something heavy and metal behind them—scraping across the blacktop as they moved.

"What the fucking hell is that?" asked Montoya.

The trooper looked over his shoulder and saw them looming in the mist. A car door opened, and someone made a run for it. In a blink, a giant hook attached to the end of chain, thick enough to tow a bulldozer, caught the man through the mid-section. The creature then swung the chain aside—shearing the top half of the car in a screech of ripping metal and glass, whipping the man clean off the hook and into the distance. Another creature caught the poor soul one-handed, then ripped the man apart over its head, drenching the creature in blood.

"Lord, have mercy," said Chappy, as he gave himself a sign of the cross.

"No," said Jamaal. "Lord has nothing to do with this."

The monsters each wore some kind of meaty red hood—like flesh tented over their heads. Their skin was lean ripples of muscle, as gray as the overcast skies, and they wore only pants, made of patchwork cloth and leather.

"What are they?" I asked.

"Red Caps," said Henry. "I think they're Red Caps." He was British, perhaps even part Scottish, and if anyone grew up learning about the Fae-Folk, it was him.

"A what?" asked Montoya, while Doshin studied the creatures. I imagined he was already searching for weaknesses.

"Red Caps," said Henry. "Malevolent Fae that use the blood of their victims to stain their hats red. If their hats dry out, they die."

"What kind of backwards shit is that?" growled Montoya.

And he was right. This new world, where the things of nightmares, mythology, and fairy tales were coming true, was backwards shit. Why were they suddenly coming out of the woodwork? After centuries of being nothing but campfire tales and textbook studies on ancient man's ability to explain the world around them, why were they suddenly here? For me? Why? Why was I so important?

"A fairy tale," I replied. The deck was stacked against me. My echo had bailed me out against Summanus. I got lucky against Mammon. I'd narrowly avoided Hekate, for the moment. How long was I going to last? I was a simple man from a simple backwoods Jersey town. I wasn't anything special. I was wholly unremarkable, and after spending a large portion of my life trying to prove I was something more, the last six years had confirmed the world was right about me—and I'd been wrong all along.

"Freeze! Stop where you are!" yelled the trooper—but, you guessed it, the monsters didn't freeze. There was a good possibility they didn't even understand the trooper's demands. When he fired on them—three pops followed by a fourth, followed by additional orders to freeze—they did not slow, they didn't even appear to care about the lead slugs propelled in their direction. They didn't flinch or twitch. They didn't feel it at all.

They were like tanks, forming an impassable barrier.

Then scraping.

Metal on pavement.

The sound was coming from the opposite direction.

"Oh, you're kidding me," said Montoya as he ran a frustrated hand through his black hair and down his face. The dour mood didn't suit his usual upbeat, curious personality.

Six more Red Caps approached from the north, dragging battle axes the size of street signs. They were only looming figures in the mist, but I was stuck with nowhere to go.

"What is it they want?" asked Chappy.

"They're here for me," I said to myself. "The man on the phone, he wants me to suffer."

"But why?" asked Jamaal.

It was a mystery. What had I done to piss off some creature I had never met? What had I done to upset him so much that he'd send these creatures after me? I always had a gift for pissing off bullies, but this was something else.

Self-destructive thoughts flew through my head. How could I sit back and watch innocent people die for me? Why wasn't there anyone to help? Where were the forces of fucking good in all of this? Or was it all up to me?

Was it really all up to me?

"This isn't a fair fight," said Montoya.

I looked at him with a conciliatory smile. "There are no fair fights."

TONY
Then.

"That night, I had the strangest dream," I said. "I don't ever recall remembering my dreams before that night. They were the typical weirdness you forget the moment after waking. But this one dream was the first that felt different. This one scared the shit out of me."

"You've been having dreams like this since before Northcreek?" asked Doc.

"Yes. I didn't have them as frequently. But nothing made me feel like they were meaningful. Not like the ones I came here to discuss with you."

"Tell me about this dream."

I dreamt of Jaycie and of a place I had never been. It was dusk, and the sun was falling through the sky like a comet with a trail of light. We were in a wide golden field surrounded by mountains, a cool late summer breeze blowing across tall amber shoots of mixed brown grasses. Her hair stuck out amongst the gold, like flames burning a path through the field as she pranced over to me wearing a long green dress with yellow flowers, which she held in her hands about her waist to keep it from dragging across the ground. She was barefoot and laughing like she was having the time of her life.

"Where have you been?" I asked, and she giggled playfully at my concern.

She moved closer to me and parted her lips as if preparing to kiss me. Our lips had almost touched when she stopped and whispered into my ear, "Find me."

Then she pulled away and ran, on her tiptoes and giggling, still clutching her dress so it didn't snag. Her hair flowed wildly behind her, large flowing waves of it dancing over and between the tall stalks of gold, drifting further and further away from where I stood.

I chased after her, yet she continued to pull away from me, swiftly escaping onto a small path cut into the forest at the field's edge. I continued to chase her playfully, her giggles echoing back to me as I entered the forest after her.

Within the forest were shadows of twisted shapes, loose dirt covered with twigs, and crumbling brown leaves. Not even the light penetrated the thick canopy above. After a moment I spotted her crimson hair, dancing up the side of a steep incline, on the opposite side of a gully filled with rushing water.

I saw no reason to rush. It was all just a game, after all—a simple game of tag. I followed her over the stream and up the hill, but when I reached the top, she was nowhere to be found. I was standing at the edge of a clearing with a couple of old buildings at the center.

One of the buildings had a barn door, with crumbling cinderblock and rotted wooden planks, the soft rumble of falling water nearby. The last glimmer of sunlight was dissipating, and the cold embrace of the evening chilled my body. The darkness dimmed my spirits, and the game was no longer fun.

"Find me," she giggled.

I ran, racing toward the barn doors and leapt up the concrete steps, taking them two at a time. When I grabbed hold of the door handle and attempted to pull it aside, the door would not budge.

Jaycie kept giggling on the other side, calling me to follow as she ran deeper into the mysterious building. Fearing I might never hear her sweet laugh again, I yanked at the handle and bashed at the door until suddenly, unexpectedly, a roller gave way and broke free from the track. The door swung aside, and I rushed through the threshold into an immense room filled with old machinery and rusted metal. It was dark and fuzzy, like my eyes couldn't focus, but I spotted her—a red blur running across a platform on a second level.

I took the stairs up to the second floor, moving quickly without upsetting the intense quiet. At the top I turned left, following her path, and down a long hall toward a closed door. The door seemed to breathe as I approached, swelling and seething with pressure.

When I opened the door, I found the room empty.

It was just a room—four walls with no windows. Only a broken cheval mirror was sitting in a corner, but I could feel the demons there. Shadows of every sad moment, of every painful memory became part of the room, part of the still air. They'd awoken and drifted into reality when I disturbed their peace and gave them an audience by opening the door.

But the memories… they weren't mine.

I witnessed every humiliation, every shame, and every heart break. I saw every worry, and every nightmare that crept into her mind while she slept. I saw things I couldn't understand and things I knew. I saw myself, a reflection, an image of me through the eyes of someone else, and I was stunned to find the man there was so much different than the man I thought I was. So much better than I could ever be.

I saw the world that could be, the world without me, and the cold loneliness, the emptiness, and the misery and despair my absence brought her. I saw timelines that never were and felt loss that never was. I felt the fear of abandonment in her heart, having touched her one and only love and lost his warmth forever.

I experienced it all in an abstract explosion of things I could never understand—and in the midst of it all, the door slammed shut, and I was alone in the darkness.

As I searched through the gloom, I became frantic and deeply upset, unable to see my own hand in front of my face. I didn't want to play this game any longer, and I began to lose control, thrashing around in the darkness until I found myself lost in the great black void. It was at the peak of my frustration, when I thought I was going to die alone in the void without her, crumbling in the blackest pitch of darkness, that I saw her.

She was lit like an angel by a mysterious light that shone for only her, bouncing off her perfect skin and glowing like a beacon in the darkest pits. She walked towards me from far away, a glimmering star at first, from far beyond the walls of the room I was locked within. She stepped silently and gracefully towards me, floating through the void, the nothingness that surrounded us in every direction. I only realized I was on my knees when she arrived and looked down on me with a sympathetic smile.

"I thought I lost you," I said.

"You did lose me, silly, but you will always find me," she said playfully.

"Where did you go?" I asked, and she shook her head, refusing to answer, her hair tossing from side to side. "Can you show me?"

"If I show you, you won't like what you see," she said thoughtfully, and her smile dissolved into a pout.

"I need to see," I said, pleadingly, "so I can find you again if you ever go missing."

"Silly, I can't get lost," she said, holding her hand out to me. I took it, and she looked a little disappointed by my decision. She began to lead me away into the black beyond.

"Where are we going?" I asked. "Why won't I like what I see?"

"Nobody likes to see the Truth," she said with a polite smile.

"We're going to see the truth?" I asked. I was confused.

"Yes. I don't like to go there, but one day we won't have a choice," she said somberly and frowned. I did not understand her and decided to wait before I allowed myself to ask any more questions.

She stopped then, suddenly, let go of my hand and faced me.

"We're here," she said. We were standing in the middle of the blackness, which spread out all around us into infinity.

"We're at the truth?" I asked her hesitantly. She had begun to walk around me, circling, but kept her eyes focused on me.

"Yes," she said, nodding her head like a child.

"There's nothing but black?"

"The Truth, for you, begins and ends in black," she said. "The rest, between, will be revealed."

"Is there nothing else? Is my truth only black?"

"Silly," she said and smiled again. She was highly amused by my ignorance. "When you're ready to see, you will see it."

"When will I be ready? How long will I have to wait?" I asked. She cocked her head to one side and looked at me with thoughtful eyes.

"That's up to you," she said. Seeing my face twist in confusion, she approached me. "Soon enough," she decided. "I'll take you back now." She took my hand again and began to lead me away.

We weren't very far when I said, "This kind of reminds me of an old song," as the tune rose all around us—a gentle piano lifting from nothing into something. "Tears for Fears. *The dreams in which I'm—,*" I sang lightly to her. She stopped still and kissed me, a sweet fleeting kiss, almost congratulatory.

"Perhaps you see more than you think," she said with sad eyes.

I awoke just as the sun crept through my window. Something was nibbling at my neck. "Are you hungry?" I croaked, my voice rusty and sore from the long night.

"Mmm hmmm, for you," Jaycie said, her voice clear and soft. She kissed my neck and wrapped her legs around mine, pulling herself closer.

"I would kiss you, but I have a horrible case of morning breath," I said, the rust still thick in my voice.

"Shut up and kiss me anyway," she demanded, and I obliged.

"I love you," I said suddenly.

"I love you too, baby. What's wrong?"

She was behaving strangely, as if her ex-boyfriend and stalker hadn't attacked her the night before, then blew his own fucking head off right in front of her.

"Nothing. I just had a bad dream," I told her, shaking it off.

"Aw, about what?" she asked.

"You were trying to show me something, but I didn't understand," I said, trying to sum it up without the details.

"I think it's just the stress," she said. "I want to take you somewhere. Right after graduation."

"Where?" I asked.

"It's a surprise," she said. "But first, I'm going to wipe that bad dream right out of your mind." A sly smile spread across her lips, then she rolled on top of me and made all the bad dreams go away, as promised.

"I was surprised by how quickly she let things go. The night before, she was sexually assaulted. Her ex-boyfriend blew his own brains out. That morning, she was cheery and pleasant, like nothing ever happened," I explained.

"Tony," said the doc with a concerned voice. "I'm beginning to suspect that Jacinda was suffering very deeply about a great many things. As you have detailed this story to me, I fear you may have unnecessarily attributed her suffering and her choices to yourself, in the form of unforgivable guilt."

"I think you're entirely right," I said. "She was hurting. I thought I could fix it. I thought I could make it all better, but I was so very fucking wrong."

May 31, 2002

A few weeks later, Jaycie forced me into her tiny red car, and we drove a few hundred miles to the Jersey shore for my birthday. Sid, Brad and his new girlfriend, Marshall and Anne—all of them followed us down in Anne's car. I had gone to Wildwood as a child with my family, and Jaycie wanted to take me back for a day. We spent the day walking the beach and grabbing a bite to eat along the boardwalk. After checking into our hotel, we went back to the boardwalk to take in all the sights and sounds.

Eventually we split off into groups, and Jaycie and I came across a mini-golf course. She argued that it was called "putt-putt" not "mini-golf," which prompted an impassioned debate that left us with only one alternative: to play for the right to call it whatever we wanted, and the loser had to comply. After the first five holes, that bet turned into general bragging rights and more—to the winner, went all the spoils. Things got dirty, but all in good fun. Jaycie even tried flashing me when nobody was looking.

"She looked so beautiful that night," I said, remembering the green barrette she had in her hair and the way she glowed under the stars. I started crying in front of the doc again.

"Go on when you're ready," he said.

The words "who's going to hold my hand when I die" kept rebounding around my brain like they were trying to maim me for life.

Heading into the final hole, I was only up by a single stroke when Jaycie sank a hole-in-one, forcing me to impossibly match her for the win—two strokes to tie, or, god forbid, three or more for the loss. Her celebration on the hole-in-one was something to behold—it included a cartwheel and a whole lot of trash talk, bordering on obscene.

"Put that in your mouth and suck it!" she said, laughing the whole time. The couple behind us were several holes back, but I was pretty sure they could hear our banter and decided to ignore our obnoxiousness.

"Depends on what it is," I quipped back, then whispered seductively into her ear, "I might enjoy it."

"Oh, you wish," she laughed.

"Amendment!" I shouted.

"Amendment?" she said, looking incredulous. "It's your last putt-putt, putt. You can't change the winner's spoils this late in the game!"

"Can't I though?" I said with an eyebrow raised. "I think you might enjoy this new stipulation."

"Okay, what is it?" she asked, as she stepped closer to me to adjust my t-shirt, even though it didn't need adjusting. Her gamesmanship was otherworldly. She knew touching me was a distraction.

"Whoever wins gets to have one fantasy fulfilled by the other person."

The look on Jaycie's face was like an explosion of hilarity and joy. She hardly had to think about it before she said, "Deal!" Then she added, "You're going to look so cute painting my toenails."

"That's your fantasy?" I laughed.

"Tomorrow's not a promise, T," she said with a serious smile. "I definitely need to see that before I die. It's on my bucket list."

When I placed my ball onto the green and began to line up my shot, I felt her club hooking at my shorts.

"Don't mind me," she giggled.

"You're going to rue the day if I win," I said.

"Oh yeah?" she said, cocky, and I quickly took my shot before she could do anything else to distract me—which was something of a stroke of genius, if I might be allowed to pun.

The ball rolled down the green, up and around a tilted wall, then back down the other side, miraculously splitting two obstacles and progressing between a plastic pirate's legs before rolling to the edge of the cup. It paused there, hanging by a thread, until suddenly falling into the hole.

The look on Jaycie's face was full of shock and awe.

I had never seen someone so completely spun, and it was glorious.

"And that's what I call snatching a win from the jaws of defeat," I bragged.

"No!" she groaned. "I want my wish!"

"I beat you fair and square, O'Neill," I said.

Jaycie tossed her club into the air and pretended to walk away in disgust when she came walking back humbly. "I can't believe you beat me at putt-putt!"

"What is it?" I asked with my head cocked to the side.

"Mini-golf! You beat me at mini-golf!" she laughed.

"Haha!" I laughed along with her.

"Fine, you win. What's your stupid wish?" she asked as she paced over to me. She looked embarrassed and moderately afraid of the fantasy I was stirring up inside my head.

At first, I was smirking—I was really trying to lay it on thick. Jaycie was a gifted athlete, and she was super-competitive. She often beat me at things, so there was a real level of accomplishment when I came out ahead, especially so miraculously.

It felt like destiny, so I decided to write my own.

"Tomorrow's not a promise," I repeated back to her, my face stone. I dropped the golf club and took both her hands in mine, then dropped to one knee before she had the chance to react. "Jaycie, would you marry me?"

We had only been together three and a half months, but I knew what I wanted. It didn't feel like an immature decision. It felt right, despite anything anyone "more mature" might say.

Her face morphed from shame to confusion to shock, all in less than a few heartbeats. Her eyes widened, and her skin went paler than the Irish features she was born with.

"What?" she gasped, like her breath had been stolen from her lungs.

"My one wish is to spend the rest of my life with you. I don't have a ring or anything," I said, feeling a little embarrassed to be asking her to marry me without any of the classic traditions that would make it official. "I didn't even mean to say it until just now, but I know this is where my heart is. This is my fantasy. This is what I really want, more than anything."

"I was going to make you to do a naked cartwheel in the hotel room," she said with a weak voice. She was so shocked, she almost looked sick.

"Sorry, I didn't mean to drop something like this on you." I stood back up.

Then she placed a hand on either side of my head and kissed me as hard and passionately as she ever had. The pain of the kiss was deep, and exhilarating, and had all the passion a kiss like that could bear.

"Yes, you fool!" she cried out. Her voice was frantic and happy, like the answer was boiling away inside her. Happy tears fell from her eyes. "Don't you ever think of apologizing for this." She scolded me with a sudden streak of anger. "I love you so much! And yes, I want to spend all my life with you."

"I don't have a ring," I said again.

"We have time," she said with tears, treating the idea like a promise.

"You didn't have to make a wish for this, you know!" She was so happy she was moved into a mess of emotions and frazzled nerves, and she couldn't stop smiling and crying.

"I know, but this is the only wish I *need* to come true," I told her. "Jaycie, you're everything to me. You're my last thought before I fall asleep and my first thought when I wake up in the morning. I can't live without you. I would rather die. I just need to know that you're mine forever."

"I'm yours," she said, and grabbed me tight. "Forever. We'll grow old together and hold each other's hands as we die."

Her heart pounded away in her chest, and I could feel it even though we stood inches apart. Then I reached into my shirt and pulled out the key, my good luck charm, then slipped it over my head.

"I don't have a ring," I said, and she looked terrified for a moment. "But I do have the key to my heart. It's always been yours. And now I'm giving it to you."

I took the chain and put it over Jaycie's head. When I lowered it around her neck, Jaycie flipped her hair up and over the chain, accepting my gift, then she gripped it tightly in her shaking hand. Her whole body shook, and I held her close to steady her quakes.

"I wish I had something to give you," she whispered to me.

"You've given me everything," I said. "I can't take any more from you."

"We need to go," she said impatiently, looking at me with needy eyes.

"Why?" I asked, confused.

"Because what I am about to do to you, I can't do out here in public," she said. "I can't bear another second without having all of you to myself."

"It wasn't official, of course. We both knew that," I said. "It was too soon, and we were too young, but we also knew we were betrothed to each other. After that night, we talked of marriage every now and then, pretending what it would be like in five years—living in a house and coming home to each other every day. It was so real imagining these life events with her.

"I never told anybody about what happened that night, and neither did she. It was our special secret, and I cherished that memory more than any other."

"When you think about this memory now, does it make you happy or sad?"

"It makes me feel," I started to say, but changed my mind as I began to feel my mental walls crumble to dust, "sad." I could feel the panic rising inside me, knowing what came next. "Even back then, everything felt like it was on borrowed time, and still, I kept thinking I had all the time in the world. Deep down, I knew this kind of happiness wasn't meant for me."

"How long was it after this event?" asked Doc. "When it happened?"

"Years. We had five years of happiness. We graduated college together. Signed the paperwork to lease our first apartment in Mercy Point and furnished it with as many second-hand pieces of junk as we could afford. We laughed. We cried. We loved. We hosted game nights and parties. We struggled. When her mother died, I was there to hold her hand and keep her going. When her father stopped speaking to her, I was there to pick her chin up and put a smile on her face."

"Why did her father stop speaking to her?"

"There was a long history there. Something about an accident and her parents' distaste for me. They didn't approve," I explained.

"What accident? Tori's accident? Why didn't they approve?"

"She never told me. I never pushed for answers there. It was old pain. The kind I didn't want to uncover if it meant upsetting her. As for why her parents didn't approve, I couldn't say. They had money. I think they expected her to be with a guy who also had money, like Rick, but we were as content as ever to build our lives together from the ground up. Brick by brick."

"Did you ever have the feeling that Jacinda was suffering?"

"Never. There were moments from our time together that didn't add up. I once came home to her standing in the middle of the living room, shaking. I thought nothing of it, and when I wrapped my arms around her, she screamed. It was a bloodcurdling terror kind of scream. She claimed I startled her, but it never really sat right with me.

"There were other things. Like her reasons for leaving Grace Falls—or her reasons for staying with Rick. I always felt there was more to the

story, but I never once thought that I wouldn't have the time to find out.

"As the years passed, we grew up, and my love for her only deepened. She was my lover, my best friend, my confidante, and at times, my moral compass. My reason to get out of bed in the morning was to be as successful as I could so that she could work on her music. She was so close to her dream! She was selling out small venues around the city and was always being asked to collaborate with other musicians. She even had interest from some small-time producers..." I paused to remember. "She was making her dreams come true. I was so proud of her." And as I finished, I realized I was crying again. I sobbed openly for a few seconds before managing my tears.

"Tell me about that day," asked Doc.

I immediately understood what day he was referring to.

XXVI

truth

TONY
December 31, 2007
Then.

The ride over to the store seemed to last for hours. I had so much going on inside my head, and my plan was perfect. All I needed was to pick it up and hand over the final payment. It was more than I had spent on anything—a worthy investment for that kind of symbol.

When the store clerk handed me the felt-covered box, I felt excitement and panic all at the same time. The clerk must've recognized my expression immediately, because she placed her hand on my arm and said, "It'll be fine. She's going to say yes."

I took a quick peek inside by lifting the lid and letting it snap open on its hinge. It sparkled like a disco ball—a white-gold setting with twelve small gleaming stones surrounding one large, beautiful, crystal clear diamond. I imagined what it might look like on her hand—to show the world that she was mine—and a big smile conquered my face from ear to ear.

"Thank you," I said to the clerk, and I left at once.

Jaycie and Anne were out shopping for something special to wear for later, which gave me plenty of time to finish up everything else I had planned. Jaycie was no ordinary girl, and I would never consider an ordinary proposal for her. There was orchestration that needed to be confirmed, the final touches put on all the moving parts. I wanted her to feel as loved and as special as she was to me. I wanted to give her bragging rights to every woman who ever asked the question, "So, how did he propose?" I wanted her to have that smile every time she looked down at that diamond and remembered.

Though, even the best-laid plans of mice and men often go awry…

When I stepped out of the cab and onto the curb in front of our apartment building in Mercy Point, I noticed a red Mustang parked across the street. None of our neighbors owned one. It was the kind of coincidence that made me feel uneasy, like I was traveling the wrong path, despite my confidences otherwise.

My mind was swimming in anticipation—mentally listing out all I needed to accomplish as I started texting Marshall to make sure he was following through on his end. When I arrived upstairs on the third floor, the front door to our apartment was open. Jaycie's favorite lamp was smashed onto the floor in the middle of our living room.

"Tony!" yelled Anne, running toward me. "Thank god!"

"What's wrong? Where's Jaycie?"

"I don't know what's happening." She pointed toward the bathroom door. "I was just about to text you. She grabbed something out of the broken lamp and locked herself in the bathroom."

"She did this?" I said, pointing toward the shards of lamp on the floor. I felt like I was being pranked—Anne was in full-blown hysteria and I was abruptly disrupted from planning the biggest night of my life thus far.

Anne nodded and said, "Tony, I don't know what's going on. She started hyperventilating and had a full-blown panic attack at the mall. We took a cab back and she did that as soon as we got inside the door."

Nothing Anne said sounded like my girlfriend and soon-to-be fiancée. Even on Jaycie's bad days, she was pleasant to be around. She could shake off a disappointing day as easy as anyone I had ever met.

She always inspired me to do the same.

"Did anything happen after the show last night?" asked Anne.

"No," I said as I approached the bathroom door, "Why?"

"She was rambling about it on the way home," said Anne. "She kept saying *show's over*."

When I got to the door, I placed my ear beside it to see if I could hear anything. She was moving around, but not doing anything that would cause immediate alarm.

"Hey, babe," I said. "What's going on?"

The movement stopped, but she didn't answer at first. I could hear her sniffling, like she was crying behind the door. "I'm so sorry," she sobbed.

"What are you sorry for?" I asked.

"It's all over," she said.

"What is?" I asked. "Jace, you're scaring me. Why don't you come out and talk to me?"

"I can't," she cried. "They're going to get me."

I looked over at Anne, who was starting to cry. She was looking at the felt box in my hand like it was the saddest thing she had ever seen.

"Who's going to get you?" I asked.

"They've been after me for a long time."

She sounded delirious, and that's when something Anne said struck me.

"You said she took something? From the broken lamp?" I asked Anne. "Did you see what it was?" Anne shook her head, but she began to cry even harder. "Call 9-1-1. Right now." Anne nodded and pulled her cell phone out of her pocket and stepped out into the hallway. "I need to see you, Jace," I said through the door. "Can I come in?"

"I don't want you to see me like this," she said.

"Like what, love?" I responded. When she didn't reply, I started to feel a different kind of panic set in. "Jaycie, what are you doing in there?"

"I'm sorry," she said. "I love you, but I'm sorry."

Some people snap under duress. They fold up and lose the ability to think and react. You find out a lot about yourself when an emergency strikes, especially when the life of a loved one was involved. I knew I had to get into the bathroom, and I knew I was on borrowed time.

"Jaycie, unlock the door for me," I said.

"I can't. They'll get me."

"Please, I need you to open the door. I can protect you," I said.

"No, you can't. Your spark isn't bright enough."

"Hon, I don't know what that means," I said as I began to contemplate a way in.

"It'll all be over soon," she said, and every part of my being went into desperation.

I tested the door handle, twisting it back and forth. I didn't care if it made me look desperate, because I was.

"Anne!" I shouted, and she stepped into the doorway. One of our neighbors walked by and peered inside, then went about his way. "Are they coming?"

"They're dispatching now," she said through a series of trembles.

"They need to hurry!" I said.

I slammed my fist into the door out of frustration, then heard a siren go off in the distance. One of the best things about living in a suburb was the proximity to emergency services. Once the call went out, an EMT could get to your front door in under five minutes.

I was twisting the door handle back and forth and thinking about how I was going to pick the lock, or kick the door down, when the torque in my hand seemed to power through the locking mechanism and snapped it right off.

I pushed and yanked at the door. Each time, the bolt slid further out of the cylinder until the door finally swung open. On the other side, sitting in the bathtub with her legs over the edge, was Jaycie huddled into an upright fetal position. She looked at me through swollen dazed eyes, and almost smiled.

There were hypodermic needles in the sink and a lighter, along with a bunch of other things I had no time to investigate. She didn't fight me as I lifted her out of the tub, she only went limp and rested her head against my chest.

"You always find a way to amaze me," she said, and I carried her into the hall and to the elevator. By the time we got down to street level, the ambulance was pulling up, and Anne ran out ahead to wave them down.

"Are you her husband?" asked the EMT.

Before I could answer, Jaycie said weakly, "My fiancé."

"What did she take?" they asked.

"I don't know," I responded. "I saw needles."

They helped me get her into the ambulance and placed her onto the stretcher, where one EMT hopped into the back with us while the other got the ambulance moving.

"You need to keep her awake," said the EMT. "We can only do so much for her until we get to the ER."

I nodded but didn't know what to say. As I looked down at her lying there, slowly dying, I was at a loss for words—until I saw the key. She always wore it. She never took it off. I removed the felt box from my pocket and looked at it for a brief moment before opening it.

"You know, I had plans for today," I said, and her eyelids opened a fraction of an inch. Her green eyes stared up into mine and the fear seemed to drain away. She didn't speak. She seemed too weak to do anything but watch and listen. "I was planning something big and spectacular, and at midnight, I was going to give this to you." I lifted the ring box so she could see it. "A long time ago you accepted that key as a symbol. I made a promise that I was going to get you a ring. I know you didn't need one, but I had to. I wanted to see that ring on your finger. I wanted the whole world to see it. I wanted to catch you staring and smiling at it." I took it out of the box and held it between my thumb and forefinger. Her eyes bounced back and forth between me and the ring, and when I saw tears forming, I knew she was fighting for me. "This isn't how I planned it, but I chose to give you this ring today, and dammit, it is going onto that pretty little ring finger of yours."

I took her left hand and slid the ring onto her finger. It fit really well, considering I didn't know her size—I merely guessed. Her eyes were wide open, and she started to speak, but her voice was too frail. When I leaned in, she said, "Yes, always," and then she squeezed my hand.

I stayed with Jaycie as they unloaded her from the ambulance and rolled her on the stretcher into the ER, then forced a concoction down her throat, in case she'd swallowed something poisonous. They hooked her up to several machines, tested her every which way, and got her settled into the ICU before the sun went down. When she was stable and asleep, I ventured out into the guest area and found Anne and Marshall waiting there. I nearly fell to pieces when they gave me a hug. I cried it out right there just as Jaycie's father came through the door.

It took only a matter of minutes before he was accusing me of being the reason his daughter was there. He said I was the one who got her the drugs, that I probably shot the heroin straight into her veins. Marshall and Anne stood up for me, but her father pushed past us and went right to his daughter's room.

I sat down on a chair and stared at the floor. It felt like the world was spinning. People were getting dressed up in their fanciest clothes and going out to ring in the new year, and I was sitting on a cheap plastic chair in the waiting room of the ICU because the love of my life overdosed. I kept asking myself, what had I missed? I thought I knew everything there was to know about Jaycie—good and bad.

Before too long I was being questioned by a police officer, who seemed intent on questioning me about my past with illegal drug use and other nefarious activities while Mr. O'Neill watched with a smirk. When it was over, I left the hospital and went home—not because I wanted to, but because the officer suggested it could be considered harassment if I stayed. Mr. O'Neill was quite a lawyer and was going to throw the book at me when this was all over.

"On what grounds?" asked Doc. "You had every right to be there."

"Mr. O'Neill was crafty. He made up some story about me being arrested and how I pushed his daughter into a life of drugs and alcohol. That I had brainwashed her and was holding her against her will."

"I saw your report," said Doc. "You were arrested ten months prior to the events of New Year's Eve in 2007."

"Unrelated," I replied. I didn't have to explain anything to him. I'd

suffered enough over those circumstances. "Mr. O'Neill did his best to fabricate a story that was so very far from the truth. I never did drugs. I never owned, or sold, or bought them. I never witnessed Jaycie ever using, buying, or consuming them either. However, he was her father, and after Marshall and Anne promised to keep me posted on any news, I relented and went home to try to get perspective."

It was strange being in our apartment without Jaycie, and as I sat on our couch staring at the fragments of her favorite lamp on the floor, knowing now what it contained, made me wonder what else might have been hidden in plain sight.

I searched the room, high and low. I checked between the mattress and the box spring and went through her makeup drawer. I flipped over the couch and checked each cushion thoroughly. I inspected the food cabinets, looked under the sink—I even checked the television and her collection of lip balm—but found nothing. When it was over, I laid on the bed staring at her guitars, and the collection of notebooks she kept with lyrics and personal thoughts.

"Hidden in plain sight," I said aloud, and popped up to investigate.

Taking a flashlight, I lit the interior of her acoustic guitar and found something taped to the inside. The only way to get to whatever was stashed inside was to unstring the guitar. I thought about how angry she'd be if she knew I was going through her stuff—but I needed answers.

The stash was a small roll of plastic with what appeared to be a handful of various colored pills and a heroin kit, with a powdered substance inside a small vial, along with a small note in Jaycie's handwriting.

"USE ONLY IF YOU'RE SURE THERE IS NO OTHER WAY," it said in all caps.

"That note frightened and confused me more than any other Jacinda mystery," I said.

"Did this realization make you love her any less?" asked Doc.

"No," I said, almost angrily. "Nothing could have made me love her any less. At the time I was just thankful I had found it. I didn't know

what it meant, but I wasn't as concerned with that as I was saving her from whatever had pushed her down that path. I was frustrated that I didn't know. I told her everything about me. She knew absolutely every-thing—even my darkness. Why didn't she tell me everything?"

"Everybody has their demons, Tony," he said. "We make the mistake in believing that we know all there is to know about the ones we love. Just because she kept certain things hidden from you doesn't mean she loved you any less."

"That's the thing though, Doc," I said. "She really did have demons."

After flushing the drugs down the toilet—I didn't care if that was the right or wrong thing to do, I just wanted that shit out of our apart-ment—I went back into our bedroom and grabbed a few of her most recent journals. I flipped through the pages well into the early hours of the new year and found absolutely nothing that led me to believe any-thing was wrong. Her most recent song was about the lost relationship with her grandmother. I felt like I was committing a serious sin—I had never looked at her journals without permission. They were her private thoughts, her art, and I did not want to intrude on her privacy—but now there was a reason. I had a warrant for suspicion.

Jaycie managed to fill one to two notebooks a year, and every page was stuffed with doodles, drawings, and poetry. There were too many pages to count about me—and I learned almost nothing, except that even her most private thoughts were more complimentary to me than I de-served. After hours of searching, spanning only notebooks from the last few years, I took a break and checked my phone for the first time in hours.

I had three messages—two from Marshall and one from Anne, as well as a handful of texts from Sid asking me to text him back—he was away in Philadelphia for work and must've heard what had happened.

Loading the text app, I walked back into our bedroom, stared at the pile of journals on the floor, and felt the sick sensation of having to put them back in order. I ran my hand through my hair and pulled, wonder-ing where the hell everything went so wrong? How did we get here?

The screen flashed as it opened Marshall's latest message first. It was in all caps with so many exclamation points that it was hard to decipher on first glance.

"!!!!!!!!WHERE ARE YOU?!!!!!!!!!!!JAYCIE MISSING!!!!!DO YOU HAVE HER?!!!"

Whether it was the jolt of distress or the trembles that polluted my motor functions, I ended up slipping on her journals as I pressed play on the most recent voicemail. Slamming into the dresser, I dropped the phone as it played back the message.

Anne shouted, "Tony! Please call us back!" but her message wasn't the most upsetting discovery. Something that had been tucked inside one of the notebooks slid out as I slipped—something that stood out, like the dope kit hiding in the hollow of Jaycie's acoustic guitar.

I took the notebook, set it down on the dresser beneath the lamp, and opened it. Inside was a handful of torn pages that had been folded and stuffed away within a notebook from 1998, just days after the entry about the night we first met, at the Labor Day Fair in 1997. She'd shown that notebook to me years ago in her bedroom, before we were even dating. The dates on the pages spanned several years—the earliest in December of 1996.

The drawings were terrifying.

The first drawing had a white-haired man with a pair of sinister eyes—one gray, the other brown—watching from a window with the words "who is watching me?" scrawled across the page. The next of a little girl in pigtails and a bloody dress. Scribbled so terrifyingly hard that the colored pencil ripped right through the paper was the phrase, "Not Jane."

There were many others. Dark faceless soldiers dragging a little red-headed girl through the forest, and another with a red sports car surrounded by fire, and a body strewn into the tall grasses at the side of the road.

Along with the drawings were several pages of notes to herself, with names, places, details, and questions—some were scribbled, others retraced for prominence. At the center of the last page was a drawing of my key, the one she'd been wearing for years, with a note that said, "the key to whose heart?" traced over and over in black ink.

My heart sunk further with every page, as I came to one very awful realization—

—Jaycie was a time bomb.

She had a real mental illness, and I had only just found out.

We had been together for almost six years, and I never once had any clue to the level of trauma she was dealing with. I was devastated. I was sad and confused about everything I thought I knew. But most of all, I was so terribly scared for the woman I loved.

Through the wad of drawings there was one thing that stuck out the most. It appeared over and over on multiple pages with the same wording. It was a door with a smiling devil, and the words "death knocks here" written several times beside every instance.

The devil on the door looked like a twisted version of the Milton State University mascot, with a forked serpentine tongue spiraling from of its mouth. I quickly snapped a photo of the door drawing and sent it to Sid, Brad, Trent, Cyn, Maynard, and Jess, even Amanda—asking if they recognized it, then immediately pocketed the papers, grabbed my coat, and ran.

XXVII

voicemail

Tony
December 22, 2013
Now.

The trouble is, you think you have time.

Buddha said that, or so I think he did. It could have been Lou, the old man from the Gas & Go in Grace Falls. The guy kept the town's dentists in business, selling candy and sodas to kids, and eventually decided to sweeten their minds by giving them each a quote when they brought their haul up to the register.

Mine, one evening on a sugar run, was "The trouble is, you think you have time."

Regardless, that phrase has haunted me…

…amongst other haunting phrases.

With everyone I've ever known, I thought I had more time—time to spend, time to make amends, time to enjoy.

But that's the trouble. The things I put off ended up being the things I missed out in the end.

I was a walking regret.

When the series of sirens in the distance became a gathering of flashing blue lights and cruisers coming to a screeching halt—four local cops and two state troopers rushed in to bring peace to the chaos. They didn't know what they were walking into. The literal fog of war that surrounded the accident hid the horrors within. As brazen as it was to attack innocents, the terrors did so under concealment.

"This isn't a fair fight," said Montoya. Bring every cop in the tri-state area into this fight and it still wouldn't be enough.

I looked at him with a conciliatory smile. "There are no fair fights."

"Maybe not for them," said Chappy. "But with you? Maybe some innocent lives will be spared."

"You're suggesting I go in there and fight those things?" I asked, while Doshin sized me up like one of his students.

"I'm suggesting you do what's right," said Chappy. "You were put on this Earth for a reason. Maybe you're here for this very moment."

"Destiny is bullshit," I said. There was nobody that was going to tell me that all this was supposed to happen. And the suggestion made me feel used—like a cosmic slut, tortured and left to rot so I could end up losing my mind on a highway, on my way to the site of the worst day of my life, all so I could be here, today, to stop a bunch of psycho 'roided up fairies from killing people? It was a joke.

Two of the officers were herding people away from the stalking Red Caps while the rest were trying to evacuate the officer trapped in the ac-cordioned cruiser. They were wedging the door open with a stray piece of metal and they were running out of time.

I watched them together unload four clips of bullets into the Red Caps, but nothing stopped their advance—like a troupe of Jason Voor-hees intent on coming to murder-town.

The brain-trust was arguing, but I wasn't listening.

I was trapped. It was over. Tomorrow's not a promise—did I do enough to earn the next?

"Let's go," said Montoya. "While everyone's distracted."

"I second that," said Jamaal.

"What about the innocent lives?" asked Chappy.

"What about them?" replied Jamaal. "They've got two legs. They can run just like us."

"We're leaving them to die?" asked Henry. "You would have run all the way to Amanda if you knew where she was, just to get slaughtered by the mysterious man on your pocket telephone." Then he looked at the others before he turned back to me. "You knew her. You loved her. Do you not have empathy for them? They love. They are alive, and many of them will die if we do nothing."

Would the Red Caps slaughter everyone to get to me? Had I hidden myself away for so long that I'd become a callous asshole intent on saving my own skin?

I looked at Master Doshin. Our eyes met and I could sense he was waiting for me to ask. "What would you do?"

Doshin nodded as I gave him the opportunity to speak, uninterrupted. He was the quietest of my brain-trust, but his voice was their equal.

"Fighting them all, head on, is foolish. Even the greatest warrior would not survive," he said, then looked out into the mist. At the current rate, we had fifteen minutes with the slow pace of the monsters, like a methodic noose tightening at every angle of escape. "When a net is at its widest, butterfly gets caught. When a net is at its most narrow," he said, using his hands to display the angles a butterfly could escape from when the enemy was drawn close, "easier to fly away."

"You're saying we should draw them in," I said, repeating the lesson back to him, "away from the innocents, then slip away?"

He nodded.

"Oh, that's a great plan," said Jamaal with enough sarcasm to roll even Doshin's eyes. "You guys, that's brilliant. They've got giant axes and fucking hooks on big-ass chains!"

Montoya was quiet as he eyed everything up.

"What other options do we have?" asked Henry, trying to play peacemaker.

"Stay alive," said Doshin, "like cat and mouse."

"There's like a dozen Toms to my Jerry," I said as I counted them.

This wasn't like playing NERF wars in the dorms with Brad, Sid, and Marshall covering my back.

"My man," said Montoya with a twinkle in his eye that spelled trouble. "I've got the start of a plan. It's waaaayyyy out, but it's still a plan." Then he shook his head. "Actually, I've only got the end of the plan, but that's beside the point."

"I'll take it," I said. It was better than nothing.

The icy roads had created a chain reaction when I slammed the rental car into the truck. A quarter-mile of highway on both the north and south bound lanes turned into a maze of cars and trucks, most of which were caught in fender benders and small crashes. However, there were a few instances of severe collisions that left broken glass, crushed metal, and leaking fluids along the road. The scene, what could be observed of it through the mist, was like the setting of a post-apocalyptic movie, including a few car fires—both of those from accidents, and Red Cap-created.

A Mercy Point taxi had flipped onto its side, and a mini-van full of holiday gifts had spilled out onto the road. There was even a jackknifed semi-truck that had slid off the highway and was stuck in the frozen mud of the grassy median.

It was a labyrinth of places to hide, and a small gathering of those who had fled for safety had found shelter cowering from a position beneath the jackknifed truck. Amongst them was a small family—mom, dad, and a little girl—the beer-bellied trucker in a John Deere hat, a man in an expensive suit, and a teen power-chewing on a stick of fruity gum I could smell from a few hundred feet away. At the front of the truck, keeping watch, was one of the many policemen who arrived on the scene only to find themselves in the middle of a bad horror video game.

The Red Caps stopped and searched nearly every vehicle, peering through the windows and ripping doors off hinges for a better look inside. Some people were trapped within their cars—those that couldn't flee, who cowered from the creatures that lurked in the mist, praying the monsters would pass them over like some biblical plague.

A group of the dispatched policemen moved through the abandoned cars, attempting to escape the closing gap between them and the monsters stalking through the mist. Every time they attempted to move from their position, a hook and chain lashed out, cutting off any opportunity for escape.

There was a cop with his gun pulled, picking up the rear as the group retreated through the labyrinth. One of the Red Caps rounded a corner and cut off his escape, pinning him between two cars as the others slipped away. While the Red Cap pried apart the two cars, the cop scurried away and found refuge inside the cab of a semi. He ducked into the space behind the driver's seat, leaving the door open as he found it.

He was in his late forties, with a grayed mustache that stood out against his dark brown skin. I could tell he was having a hard time slowing his heavy gasps as the Red Cap stalked by.

He had just sighed and closed his eyes after the creature passed beyond his view, when I whispered, "Hey." As the word left my mouth I grimaced, half expecting the man to jump right out of his skin. I was standing in the open door, having climbed up to look inside.

"Kid," he said as he peeked over the back of driver's seat—just two big eyes in the darkness. "I don't know what's going on, but you need to get out of here."

"There's more of them," I said calmly. The misty drizzle made for the perfect cover, masking our hushed tones against the gentle taps of freezing rain.

"Where?" he asked.

"Moving in, southbound," I said, gesturing with a head nod. Behind me was a woman about my age, with her young daughter wrapped around her—head buried in her mother's winter coat. There were three others besides them—all rescued from their cars when I swung by and promised to get them out before the Red Caps terrorized them, or worse.

"How many?"

"Ten. Twelve. Maybe more." Then I said something he must have found ridiculous, because his heart rate slowed, and his irises refocused. "I'm going to lure them away. You take these guys, gather everyone you can, and go the opposite direction while they're distracted."

"Who are you? Bruce Willis?"

"It's a good day to Die Hard," I replied with a smirk.

"Are you stupid?" he guffawed, "or just crazy?"

I shrugged, then leaned out the semi door to check the mist. I could smell the Red Caps coming—like musk and exotic patchouli, and I wondered if the others could smell it too. It was foul, like garbage on a summer's day, and made my stomach sour.

"Uhhhhh," I combo-ed a sigh and groan after hearing the C-word, "six of one, a few dozen of the other."

"I think you said that wrong," he replied.

"No," I said, shaking my head. "I didn't." Then I grabbed him by the collar and began pulling him out of the truck before he hunkered down and refused to come out of his hole. "C'mon, let's go."

"Kid," he shouted with a hushed tone, "You can't yank me around like that."

"Why?" I said as we both hopped down onto the pavement.

"Because I'm a police officer," he said.

"Apologies, but I have a high distrust of police."

"Why's that?" he asked suspiciously, like we were still in the real world and not this nightmare universe. Like it mattered if I told him I was a klepto or serial killer.

"I just don't." The coast was clear, but for how long? "Besides, I'm the one who's going to get you out of here."

I crept to the front of the truck and peered around the hood.

"Is that so?" he said.

"He got us out," said the woman as she gently bounced to keep her daughter calm. "Those things killed the man in the next car. He got me out before they got to us."

An elderly couple beside her and a man in an ugly holiday sweater carrying a bottle of wine in a death grip, nodded along with her. They were all I could find—the rest were either dead or had managed to escape.

I looked back at the officer with a smirk and said, "Don't look so shocked. Where are you from?" I could hear his heartbeat rising and needed to keep him calm until we could find our way out.

"I transferred ten years ago. Saw too much in Philly," he said quietly. "My aunt's the medical examiner for the Grace Falls police department." We were so close to Grace Falls, their local cops were among the first to respond. "A fresh start in a new place."

"Yeah," I said. "Funny, I went the other way for my fresh start." Then I said to myself, "The trouble is, you think you have time."

"Ain't that the truth," he replied. After a quiet moment, he whispered, "Can you see them? Are they gone?"

I was about to shake my head—when the air around the officer flared a vibrant red, followed by the immediate squeal of his radio—like I could see the incoming transmission.

"Pryor? Where are you?"

There's an expression my father used to say. "That's how they get ya."

He said it when discussing the ins and outs of taxes, or when he found something overpriced at the grocery store. That same phrase was used to express his dissatisfaction with all the added sugar in my morning cereal, as if to say that was how addiction started. He used that phrase so often, mostly in jest, that it would pop into my head at odd times, always in his voice.

"That's how they get ya," I heard him say in response to the ill-timed transmission, as a Red Cap stalked out of the mist from behind the nearest sedan. It didn't see us, but it knew where we were. There were too many Red Caps lurking, like waves—as one passed, another was sure to follow through. There was no way we were going to out-maneuver them and their destruction.

"Hide them," said Doshin.

"My man," said Montoya, "put them into the trailer."

I moved without warning and waved for them to follow me while Officer Pryor turned off his radio. At the back of the semi, I unlatched the trailer door and opened it just wide enough for the ugly sweater guy to crawl inside and help the others in after him.

"Get them into the trailer," I whispered.

"What are you going to do?" asked Pryor as the woman and her daughter climbed in.

"Lure them away. They're here for me."

"For you?" he asked.

How ridiculous did that sound? These creatures were here for me? Of course, Officer Pryor would find that silly—who wouldn't?

When my stomach and shoulders tightened—a warning my body was attempting to tell my brain despite the two not speaking the same language—like Morse code connected to the internet—I spun away from the others to keep them hidden. None of that mattered, though, because in the split second I realized something was wrong, a gigantic hand palmed my head and slammed it into the side of the trailer—putting a head-sized hole into it—and tossed me aside a hundred feet.

Between the skull rattle and the toss, there was a moment of dizzying weightlessness where gravity and propulsion disappeared, then reappeared when I hit the wet grass of the median and bounced away with clumps of dirt.

"Get up!" shouted Montoya, channeling his inner drill sergeant the moment my body came to a complete stop. "Push aside that pain and keep moving."

The pain, the dizziness, the fear and confusion—these things dulled impulses. I was always an overthinker—analyzing, reanalyzing, over-analyzing every sentence, movement, and thought—but when I ignored them, when I escaped into the mindset of reaction, when I let them melt away, like tracking down a fly ball right off the bat—I could feel the resurgence of the flames. Flickering. Waiting to be called upon.

Three shots went off before I got to one knee—my cop friend took several steps back from the Red Cap that towered over him—all eight feet of terror beneath a pointy red hood—and watched as it lifted the rusty old chain and swung. The hook hissed around in a large arc, aiming to cleave Officer Pryor in two as the Red Cap released.

I was a hundred feet away, if not more. The time it took for the beast to lift and whip the chain down at Officer Pryor was between two and three seconds. The officer closed his eyes and trembled, waiting for death as the hook made impact.

"Get back," I said, shaking his eyes open with my free hand.

The look on his face asked everything I didn't want to answer. Yes, I caught it. No, I don't know how I got all the way over there that quickly. And yes, it hurt like fucking hell.

The hook went into my palm and snagged around the wrist. There was a decent amount of blood, but instinct had fully taken over. When the Red Cap yanked, I gripped onto the chain and used the beast's strength to propel me into the air—then I wound up and unloaded with my left fist. I socked its hooded jaw with a superman punch, something straight out of comic books—a soaring airborne punch that was equally dramatic as it was devastating. I expected the creature to stagger and fall—the amount of strength I put into that punch could have broken an elephant's jaw—but the thing took the punch as if I had plucked it on the chin, like flicking a paper-football. In fact, the punch should have hurt me just as much as it did the Red Cap—a broken hand, or at least a few bloody knuckles—but I felt nothing. It was like punching a sack of dirty laundry.

Before I had the chance to follow up with another attack, it took me by the throat like a WWE choke slam. It pinned me over its head against the side of the semi-trailer next to the logo of a laughing clown and began to squeeze.

The brain-trust shouted instructions as I gasped for air—

"Hit him!"

"Fight back!"

—But it was all just noise.

The pressure in my head felt like a swollen zit about to pop. I wrapped the chain around my ruined hand and hit the thing over and over where the nose should have been. Every impact was like hitting a soggy cardboard box and did absolutely nothing to stop the Red Cap from squeezing. My lights were dimming, the flames were burning low, and I had only moments.

"Hey ugly!" shouted Officer Pryor, wielding a broken car door like a shield just before he rammed into the Red Cap like a linebacker hitting a tackle sled. It didn't drop me so much as it loosened its grip enough for me to pull away—then I fell to the ground, gasping for air.

My friend had the Red Cap pinned against the trailer, but he was losing his leverage. It thrashed like a wild animal—pushing, kicking, snarling, and swiping to free itself.

"Little help here!" said the officer.

I had just gotten a lungful of air back into my chest when I slammed my own shoulder into the door, driving it back into the trailer.

"Thanks for the assist," I said through gritted teeth.

"We can't hold it forever," Pryor replied while fighting off its free hand as it swiped for a grip of his nostrils.

"Tony," said Doshin into my ear, "the wrist."

His vague instruction lacked instruction. It was as if someone had said, "look up!" without any details as to what they were intending me to find. But when I looked at the hand grappling with the officer's collar, there was something that stood out—literally.

Was it a piece of hair? Was it string?

Before the thought had finished sprouting, we were tossed aside—the Red Cap found its leverage and slung us down into the frosty grass. It snarled, then emitted another sound, like something was stuck in the back of its throat—a call. It was calling to the others, and it had me snared by the hand.

When it yanked at the chain, I slid across the frozen ground like I had fallen from water skis. When I was within five feet, I took a leap of faith.

Dangling from its left wrist was something that had sprung loose—or maybe it was a flaw in its design? All I knew was that Doshin wanted me to see it, and I felt compelled to find out what it was.

Leaping, I grabbed hold of it and pulled—

—it was like pulling a shirt from the dryer and finding a dangling thread, where the more I pulled the more threading came loose. This was similar, but with different results. Instead of a long piece of thread, it was like pulling a rip-cord.

The Red Cap body—all three-hundred pounds of lean hooded muscle—collapsed next to me like a sack of laundry. Springing from the pile a moment later came a small, ugly gray creature with a red cap that disappeared beneath the semi-truck, scurrying away like a scared cat running for cover.

"Did that just happen?" asked Montoya, "or did I imagine the whole thing?"

"Wow," said Jamaal excitedly. "They're just little people riding inside big people clothes."

"Remarkable," added Chappy, "and truly terrifying."

"Is this the level of subterfuge we should expect?" asked Henry.

"Holy hell," said Officer Pryor. "What was that?" He hadn't fully come to terms with the giant hooded creature carrying a murder-hook, let alone the last few seconds. The shock in his eyes was evident, his irises as wide as when I first found him.

"A creature from another place," I responded. Why bother the poor man with the details he could never understand?

I pulled the hook from my hand and grimaced, then tossed it onto the pile of giant clothes. It was like a big onesie—even the skin was stitched and sewn, despite it feeling nothing like cloth.

"Hekate," said Doshin, kneeling beside me to investigate the pile. "Fae witchcraft."

I never believed in witchcraft—especially when the love of my life had been accused of it—but that didn't matter now. What was in front of me was a murder machine that could be slipped on and off like a robe. If that wasn't witchcraft, what was?

"We need to get you to an ambulance," said Officer Pryor.

"I'll be fine," I replied. "Get inside the trailer with the others."

"Where are you going?" he asked.

"Out there." I gestured into the empty expanse. "Stay hidden. When they converge on me, take the others and make a run for it. Get them out of the mist."

"You're going to fight them?" he asked. "Alone? With one hand?"

"Officer Pryor," I said, "they're here for me, and they'll kill anything that gets in their way."

"Why do you think they're after you?"

"Because I've dealt with their kind before," I replied. "They want me dead."

"Kid, you're in shock and injured—"

"Who's injured?" I said, showing him my hand. There wasn't a blemish on it. Not only could I sense things beyond what a normal human could—smell, taste, sound—and perform some insane athletic feats, but I was able to heal fucking fast—so fast that it was surprising even me.

"Who *are* you?"

"Just some guy," I replied. "I need to go." I left before he could argue with me anymore—plus, he seemed pretty freaked out about my hand.

Officer Pryor retreated to the trailer and disappeared inside as I danced out into the open. The rain was easing and the mist was thickening, cutting visibility in half. Every few moments I could hear movement—but there was nobody in our vicinity. There were no scents or heartbeats, no whispers or shoes on pavement—just the exotic patchouli stink from the approaching Red Caps.

I was all alone with the monsters as they appeared. Shadows in the mist tightening their circle around me. Tightening the noose.

They stopped their approach when they got within ninety feet of me and waited. Doshin's butterfly proverb had sounded pretty good, but as I faced down a dozen giants with vicious weapons, I began to question my ability to break through their lines—and they were still too far away for me to make my move.

Each of the Red Caps were dragging something behind them, and as I realized what they were doing, they tossed them one-by-one into a pile near me. Dead bodies. A dozen of them. Men, women, children—all dead. The sight of it made me angry—I'd saved six people, and they'd murdered twice that amount just to gather them here?

Then I heard laughing. Not like people, or children, but creepy high-pitched laughs like something out of a Grimm Brother's adaptation. There were things all around me—things I couldn't see, but I could feel them moving—rushing past my feet as they gathered near the dead.

A sound, like crunching, started within the pile of the dead. From it, crawling free into this world, was their queen in her white owl mask— wrapped in lace that dangled from her lean body like creepy fringe clothing gone wrong.

"I saw you like a candle burning in the darkness, and I decided you would be mine," said the goddess.

"Yet you had to kill all those people just to get to me?" I asked angrily.

"You are not just a spark as they claim," she said, ignoring me, stepping down from the piled bodies, "but you are not one of *them*." She stopped when she was within five feet. "Come with me. Unseelies would benefit from our union."

I had a problem. I had a very expressive face. Amanda used to tell me I had a disease, that I could never hide my emotions like most people. When someone said something off-color, I had very little ability to hide my true opinion. When someone said something repulsive, Amanda claimed I looked like I had been "forced to watch the Double Dragon movie on loop for twenty-four hours straight."

"No thanks," I said, and I could feel my face contorting into Double Dragon-movie- levels of disgust.

Montoya and Jamaal started laughing.

"I hope we live through this," snickered Jamaal, "because that's some funny shit."

"I only offer once," said Hekate. "Your fate has been sealed."

My throat suddenly went sharp, and I began a hacking cough to clear the obstruction. It felt like I was going to suffocate. When it finally dislodged, I spat out a bloody wad of pins. I was bent over with tears streaming down my eyes—the pain was excruciating. I had never felt anything like it, and as Hekate stepped forward, her Red Cap guard moved in.

"I can make your last moments miserable, or I can end it all at once," she said. Then I was struck again with the same affliction—painful sharpness in my throat and chest. My arms and legs trembled, and with the trembling came additional pain. I gagged on the blood rushing down the back of my throat, locked in a cycle of torment.

She grabbed me by the hair and lifted me to my feet—her yellow eyes staring into mine as she brushed aside my leather jacket and tried to bury her claws into my chest. She stank of fish and stagnant ocean, and the ivory owl mask over her face did nothing to prevent the rancid odor of her breath.

The Red Caps gathered, each with their axes and hooks raised, ready to chop should I take an advantage, while I heard the tittering of something small crawling around me—small creatures—pixies?—scurrying out of the surrounding shadows.

Then, it came to me. A name. I don't know how, or why it hadn't come sooner, but as I stared into her eyes, gagging on the pins and needles in my throat and lungs, I was struck with the intense need to speak it out loud.

"Entropia," I choked, and the effect was immediate. The pixies fell into shadow, cast out of this realm, and the Red Caps dropped like discarded clothes. The needles in my throat and chest eased and fell away—and Hekate recoiled at her true name as we grappled, her claws digging into my chest.

From afar, I spotted Officer Pryor leading the rescue group away from danger as I reached out and slapped the mask from Hekate's face.

Beneath the white owl mask was a thing of pure nightmare—the goddess had no skin, no eyelids, no lips, no nose. She was just the muscle beneath—a slimy disfigured creature of pure ugliness.

I ran as the goddess wailed and dashed after her mask, my repulsion as great as my instinct to survive. I darted through the wreckage, aiming for my destination, when I heard something crash over my shoulder with bits of glass and metal spraying into the air.

A goddess—a different goddess in a black feathered cloak, her pale bare legs stalking toward me from the tops of wrecked vehicles—then, from the sky came a flock of red-eyed crows, squawking as they soared after me like a weaving current.

There was an abandoned car in the right lane all by itself—door open, keys in the ignition—Montoya had spotted it when he surveyed the area. It was his idea of an escape plan, ready to go. The occupants of the car went missing after the Red Caps stalked out of the mist, leaving it on its own with a straight, but narrow shot through the wreckage and into the open road beyond.

I dove in, slammed the door shut as a handful of crows smacked against the window, turned the key, and hit the gas. The car, a modern hatchback Kia Soul, had even less power than the rental, but it was small and light and could fly once it got out on the open road.

A few hundred feet from the wreckage, the misty rain subsided—it was obvious that the evil goddesses had brought the foul weather with them, like a storm cloud following Charlie Brown—all I needed was the yellow zig-zagged t-shirt to complete the metaphor as I sped out of the mist and into the cold overcast December skies.

My brain-trust were a mixture of polarized reactions, and I could feel each of their emotions within our shared mental space—

Montoya said, "My man, that was so close!" like we had narrowly escaped a game of dodgeball with a win. Henry was gasping, like he had been holding his breath the entire duration. Chappy removed a handkerchief from his pocket and began padding his damp imaginary brow. Jamaal held his head in both hands and was still giggling over my harsh denial of Hekate's indecent proposal. While Doshin, as sharp under fire as ever, was peering out the back window.

This was a joyride to them—a roller coaster—and I didn't know how I felt about that. It was my life on the line. They were just along for the ride, right?

The sound of a whistle, like an old-fashioned locomotive pulling into a station, started howling with increased intensity. I thought it was the stress at first—

—I wasn't expecting to get away easy. Nothing in life was ever so uncomplicated. I was expecting the other shoe to drop at any moment…

…when a New Balance bounced off my hood, followed by a whole SUV slamming into the road directly in my path—I swerved and kept the gas pedal floored, narrowly avoiding it as I spotted the traffic back-up in the other lanes, southbound. The passengers were evacuating their cars and rushing from of the road—and I didn't need to look back to know exactly why.

We were being followed by the cyclone of red-eyed crows as it spun and swung like an uncontrollable top. In the rearview, I spotted something inside the tornado as it swung right and tore trees right from the ground—a shrouded figure within the twisting rain and wind—the Morrigan, forcing her will into the spinning storm.

Inbound, driving on the frozen median, were two ambulances and a fire truck. Both slammed on their brakes and abandoned the vehicles just as I soared past. The cyclone picked them up and tossed them aside like they were Matchbox cars. The car was at eighty miles per hour and climbing, but it wasn't pulling away from the cyclone.

Maybe I could survive a handful of black magic Fae warriors. I could get lucky and speak the name of a goddess and slap away her mask. I could burst into flames and burn a god till he was nothing but ash, and I could survive a harrowing night while being hunted by creatures through the streets of Philly—but was I really going to survive this?

My emotions, without the chemical walls, were like a pendulum. I swung from normal into the lowest lows with such frequency that I couldn't live a normal life without the pills. When I was at my lowest, my most desperate, I always thought of her.

I don't know why I did it. I'd thought about doing it several times over the years, but it seemed like this was going to be the end. My cell phone was in my pocket. I grabbed it, swiped through the geometric lock pattern with one hand and loaded up my favorites. The first slot was Marshall, followed by Work, Brad, Sid, and Amanda—the latter three I'd collectively called a grand total of twice since Northcreek—including the ill-conceived call to Amanda last night.

The last favorite at the bottom, the one without a picture or name attached, I would not dare to call—and there were moments when I wondered why I still kept the number.

I tapped the unnamed contact, put the phone on speaker, and placed it into the cup holder on the dash. A trill of dread crawled up and down my spine—I was truly afraid of calling it. More afraid than I was at facing off against evil goddesses and monsters.

It didn't ring. It went straight to voicemail as I expected it would.

"Heyo! You've got me. Leave a message after the beep," she said, and her voice gave me shivers. After the beep, I took a deep breath and started speaking.

"Hey Jace, it's me. I promised you I'd never call, but I kept your number if there was ever a situation when I needed to hear your voice one last time." The front half of the ambulance hit a tree along the side of the road. "I need you to know that I tried. I tried to make a life without you.

"You told me once I was relentless," I said, my heart spilling out its guts on cruise control. "A fighter. You said I'm at my best when I have something to fight for. You wanted me to stop fighting for you. You wanted me to fight for myself. You needed me to have a reason to live that wasn't just you. You needed me to find something more. But I don't know if I have that in me without you.

"I had fire with you," I cried. "We had bottled lightning. Without it, I'm chasing a dream.

"I miss you," I said. "I wish you were here, holding my hand at the end, like you always said you would. I still love you, with all my heart." Then the phone beeped, and a digital voice prompted me.

"Press 1 to re-record or hang up to send."

As I pressed the button to end the call, the exit sign for Grace Falls came into view.

TONY
Then
January 1, 2008

"What happened next?" prompted Doc.

I was looking up at the tiled ceiling. I needed a new focal point to help bring my story to a close. I needed new perspective to get started, because even the most powerful chemicals suppressing my erratic emotions were failing as I attempted to move on—reliving these events secondhand blunted the assault by only a fraction.

"There's a feeling I get when things are completely out of my control. It's a feeling that goes beyond helplessness. It feels like falling, even when I'm standing on solid ground. My heart races. My throat tightens. My fingers and wrists tingle, and my knees feel weak. It's a horrible feeling, but on the inside—if a panic attack was a stomach-full of butterflies, mine was a twister of hornets.

"I haven't been well since that day. I get panic attacks from time to time, and I didn't start getting them until…

"Imagine trying to solve a mystery, when the person you love is in perilous danger, all while in the throes of the worst panic attack of your life?"

"Sounds awful," said Doc.

"Yeah. It is." I took a deep sigh, then said for the last time, "As I said before, this isn't a love story."

I met Marshall at the hospital parking lot at 5:45 AM. I was driving Jaycie's car and managed to arrive in less than ten minutes. My mind was a chaotic jumble of half-formed theories, emotions, and a tremble in my hands that I couldn't suppress. I was barely holding it together, and for whatever reason I half-expected to find it was all a big joke— that Jaycie was safely inside, resting in her hospital room and on the road to recovery, because reality didn't seem real. This wasn't my girlfriend. This wasn't who she was, and I didn't know what to do.

"Where have you been?" growled Marshall as I stepped out of the car.

"Have you ever seen this before?" I asked, holding up the drawing of the door with the devil face.

"Haven't a clue," he replied angrily. "What is this? We've been calling you for an hour! What does this have to do with anything?" He grabbed the drawing from my hand and shook it a few times before I snatched it back from him. It was important. I could feel it.

Marshall was sick with worry, and I was showing him surrealist art. I was lucky he didn't slap me past silly and right back to serious.

"I don't know," I replied. "How long has she been gone?"

"An hour," he said. "Why didn't you pick up the phone?" He asked like he was accusing me of purposely avoiding his call.

"I had the ringer turned off," I said absentmindedly. "How'd she get out without anyone seeing her?"

"I don't know, man," he said as we approached the sliding door entry to the hospital. "Where do you think she's going?"

"I wish I knew. Not the apartment. She would've shown up while I was there."

I got a text from Sid before Marshall and I entered the waiting room. All it said was "Stay away, Tony. There are no happy endings."

I didn't have much time to contemplate the message. Sid was always vague and weird, and he'd been oddly patronizing since he left for Philly a few years ago. But it wasn't the off-beat nature of his message that prevented me from trying to interpret it—it was Mr. O'Neill accompanied by two policemen stalking my way that forced me to shove my phone back into my pocket.

"Mr. Oscuro, do you have a moment, sir?" asked one of the two cops. His hand was hovering behind him, and I'd seen more than enough cop shows to know that's where they kept their handcuffs.

"We need to find her," I said, appealing to Mr. O'Neill. "Arresting me isn't going to help."

"Where is my daughter?!" he demanded. "Tell us where she is!"

There was an event—something had transpired ten months prior, something that made him think I was a danger to Jaycie. I wasn't, but that didn't seem to matter to him.

Anne peeked out from behind them and looked confused, like she didn't know what to believe. Who knows what lies Mr. O'Neill was peddling, but Anne knew me, didn't she? She knew I wouldn't do anything to harm Jaycie, right?

"Mr. O'Neill is looking for his daughter," said the second policeman in the most cop way possible—cold, presumptive, and full of anticipation. "Let's take a ride and see if we can find her. Just keep your hands where we can see them."

The other cop fanned out to my left and Marshall turned to me, as if to say he had nothing to do with this. All of it happened within moments. I felt overwhelmed. Mr. O'Neill was accusing me of taking Jaycie, hiding her, and we were losing valuable time. When the officer on my left got within five feet—my mind attempted to circumvent the incapacitating fear that froze me in place with the need to run or lose everything— my phone buzzed in my pocket and set me free.

I took off like a thoroughbred at the Preakness Stakes.

Marshall and I always had this telepathic ability to anticipate each other. Sometimes it was just a natural understanding of the flow of banter—other times, it was like the beatdown we gave to a couple of mouthy freshmen in a pickup game of basketball. Marshall was stocky, but the guy could dribble like Jason Kidd.

When my pocket buzzed, Marshall stepped out to block the policeman just as I made my break, like a world-class left tackle protecting his quarterback's blind spot. I spun and ran toward the sliding glass doors as the whole world slowed.

The flames were back, and every possible scenario played out in my head. I knew, no matter what, I'd have to face the law. Some people would say innocents don't run. I ran because I didn't trust the cops to listen to the truth—if anyone was going to find Jaycie, it was me.

I could see myself in the glass door's reflection, and everything happened behind me in slow motion. The cop reached for his gun as Mr. O'Neill screamed for them to stop me. I watched Anne's jaw drop as Marshall was slammed to the ground. And a nurse running into the room to stop them from doing something regrettable.

The doors were on a motion sensor and weren't opening fast enough. I didn't have time to wait for them to widen. I didn't even have the time to think of a better plan. On instinct, I spun sideways, slung myself through the cracked doors, and sprinted around the corner, just as the cop pulled his gun free of its holster.

I ran back to Jaycie's car and sped out of there without looking back. I didn't see any flashing lights in my rearview or hear any sirens, but that didn't mean I was going to go for a casual spin. Mercy Point was a terrible place to hide, and as I weaved my way through side streets, waiting for inspiration to strike, my phone buzzed a second time.

I flipped my phone open to two new messages. I expected one of them to be from Marshall or Anne, filling me in on the immediate aftermath of my escape—but I was wrong.

The first message was from Amanda, asking "who's this?" All those years of hoping for a reunion with her were put on hold—but the second message was from Jess, asking me to call her back.

Jess picked up on the fifth ring and screamed "T!" into the phone.

"Hey, listen, I'm in a lot of trouble," I said.

"Oh, I'm sure," she replied sarcastically. "How ya been? And why are you sending me creepy sketches of the old party house?"

"What?" I asked.

"The devil door. That's in the old Jansen Mill, where they used to throw all the parties up by the falls on Cross Road. Tori told me about once. It's like a frat house or something."

"Jess," I said, "Thank you. I'll call you back."

But I never did.

Jaycie's little red car wasn't the most inconspicuous vehicle, but it sure could fly down a highway. I arrived in Grace Falls just after 6:25 AM on New Year's Day. It was still dark, and the temperature was a frigid twenty-three degrees. There was still two feet of snow on the ground from the last storm, and wide patches of ice along Cross Road, which had only a modest plowing and a sprinkling of salt that failed to keep the ice at bay.

Jaycie's little red car didn't appreciate the ice.

The car slid off the road and crashed into a tree. The airbags never deployed, and my face found the steering wheel. I didn't feel the pain in my forehead or the cracked ribs in my side—everything felt numb. The adrenaline fueled my urgency to keep moving. My mind was solely focused on finding her despite all odds. I jogged for a mile and a half through the snow until I came upon an ice-covered sign that mentioned the historical mill site, as well as a sign for the state park and sightseeing destinations up the road.

It was my first time back in years, and most of my friends were long gone. I'd heard only Maynard was still in the area. I had no more ties to Grace Falls, but there was something about that town that kept sucking me in. All I wanted was to put it far behind me, so long as Jaycie was by my side. And here I was, following her into the town that brought us together and nearly tore us apart.

The snowy path down the unpaved road toward the Mill was a tough hike. I was wearing a pair of converse Chucks that had already soaked through and gave me little to no traction on the icy parts—but I knew I was in the right place—mine were not the only fresh footprints through the snow.

The old warehouse loomed off in the distance beside the low rumble of the falls. The mill wheel was stuck in the ice, but the water beneath the frozen surface still flowed downstream and over the rocky shelf. The white noise drowned out everything else—it was just the sound of the falls and me when I grabbed hold of the heavy barn door and slid it open.

The interior was trashed. Someone had swept the floor, but never circled back to pick up the piles of Solo cups, cans, and beer bottles that were left behind. It looked like the place had caught on fire. There were small scorch marks here and there, but nothing that threatened the integrity of the building. Tori had died five years ago to the day—when Rick and his pals hastily abandoned their party.

Were they fleeing a fire?

The mill was shrouded in evil. I could feel it the moment I stepped through those doors. There were ghosts here. A series of yellowed newspaper clippings were thumbtacked to the wall, some more notorious than others, detailing the mill and the town's awful history.

The Mum Killer Strikes Again, read one of the headlines in big bold type.

A symbol spray-painted in black was on the wall beside them—an ominous black circle with lines coming out of the top, bottom, and sides.

I caught a glimpse of wet footprints—bare feet—on the floor leading off into the dark. My cell phone buzzed again in my pocket.

Anne texted me a long list of swears, followed by a few accusations, letting me know that Marshall had been arrested for helping me.

A second text was from Sid, once again imploring me to leave it alone.

"Don't go to the mill, Tony!" it said.

I followed the wet prints up a flight of stairs that led to a long hallway lined with windows overlooking the river as it led to the falls. Every footfall was followed by the wailing creak of old wood. There was no sense in trying to be sneaky, so I called out to her.

"Jaycie," I said. "I know you're here. Can we please talk?"

The door at the end of the hallway was shrouded in shadow, but as I got closer I saw the devil face hiding beneath the gloom. It was an old mascot costume nailed to the door, from a previous era of Milton State sports. Out of context it was hideous. In current context, it was absolutely horrific.

When I opened the devil door, the room beyond was a frat-palace, with old couches, dart boards, empty kegs, bottles and cans, and beer pong tables. There were decorations hanging from the ceiling, proclaiming "Happy New Year 2002." The room smelled like old puke. There was a stack of moldy pizza boxes in a corner beside a sink, and a cheval mirror by an old stereo. In the mirror's reflection, I could see Jaycie sitting on the floor against the far wall—and there was something heavy in her hand.

"Hey," I said.

She looked at me like she had just gone through hell. Her eye make-up was smeared, and her hair was a mess, but she was definitely sober.

"Hey," she said. She was wearing her jeans from yesterday, as well as the hospital gown for a shirt, but her feet were bare and looked painfully cold.

"Can we talk?" I asked politely.

"Yeah, we can talk," she said, but when I motioned toward her, she showed me the gun. "Stay there."

"Okay," I said and stopped right where I was standing. However, I couldn't hide the involuntary shiver from seeing the gun in her tiny hand. It was a paradox of beauty and the grotesque—love and death. It looked wrong. It was the scariest thing I had ever seen. "Let's start small. How'd you get here?" I asked. It felt like I was talking to a stranger.

"You wouldn't believe me if I told you." Then she looked at me strangely and said, "How'd you get here?"

"I drove your car," I said, but I didn't mention I'd crashed it a mile up the road.

"You should have watched the ice," she said. My face betrayed my confusion, and she said, "You're busted up pretty good, babe. It's pretty obvious."

"Yeah. Sorry," I said.

"Don't be. I won't need it."

Those words stung. "Why are we here?"

"Existentially?" she joked with a straight face, but then adjusted once she saw the seriousness on mine. "I know why I'm here. Why are you? Trying to get laid one last time?"

"Are you trying to push me away?" I asked. If I wasn't so scared, I would have been fucking pissed. What was she trying to say? What was she attempting to do? "You know that won't work on me." She choked on my words. "I was the one who never gave up on you, remember? I loved you so much that I would have suffered a lifetime as your friend just to be near you. So do not try and push me away. Not now, not ever." She began to cry, and I felt a slight tremor in the floorboards.

"Do you remember what you said to me that day? At the Labor Day Fair?" she asked. I nodded. "*I see the real you*, you said."

"I still do."

"There's so much, Tony," she cried. "So much I haven't told you. You couldn't have possibly seen the real me because I've never shown it to you."

"That's bullshit," I said harshly, then dared to take two steps closer. "I know all about you, Jaycie. You're the only person in this world who makes sense to me. I know that you like lilies and hate smelly feet." She almost laughed at that. "I know that your favorite song is 'Wish You Were Here' by Pink Floyd because it makes you think of your Grammy. I know you love the sound of distant thunderstorms in the summer but hate the rain. You love French fries, but you'll never order them for yourself. And you absolutely can't stand mayo because—"

"Stop," she said. She was bawling her eyes out. "I don't want to die before I've actually lived." Then she sobbed. "I don't want to go."

"Then don't go," I pleaded, and took another step toward her. "Stay with me, please."

She saw my advance and put the gun to her head, then said, "Get back."

I was terrified. I felt like I was walking in quicksand—like the more I tried, the faster I sank. Seeing that gun to her head was like every bad nightmare come true. I felt like I was going to puke, but I held it together because I had to. I had no other choice. Failing her was the only thing I couldn't allow.

"Who is this?" I asked, removing the drawing of the white-haired man with two different eyes from my pocket. She grimaced and began to cry differently. She wasn't hurt or angry, she was scared when she saw it. "Did he sell you the drugs?" I don't know why I thought he was a dealer. It seemed the most rational—as if any of this made any real sense.

"No," she said shaking her head. Tears were rolling down her face as quick as the falls outside. "I saw him here, last time. You don't understand."

"Help me understand," I pled.

"He wants me, Tony. But he can't have me. He will hurt you too, and I can't have that. I can't let him get you too. I'll show him I'm no fish on a hook." Then she looked away to the window on the far side of the room overlooking the grove outside. "He sees me right now. Take a good look, asshole! Before I take it all away!"

"Who is he?"

"No!" she scolded me. "Don't you dare go looking for him! I'm doing this for us, Tony. Don't you see? This is for us. What he'll do? And he won't stop. Not ever."

She was waving the gun around as she talked, and it made me nervous. "Where'd you get the gun?" I asked. "Can you please put it down?"

"It's Rick's," she said, "He kept it under the floorboards over there." She gestured. "In case a deal went bad or something." Then she looked real serious. "He got to Rick. That piece of shit was just a puppet." She was beginning to look angry when she started to cry again. "I think he took your friend Tori. He took her, and it was my fault!"

"That was an accident, Jace," I said. The situation was spiraling. She was becoming frantic and speaking nonsense, and I shoved my hand into my pocket so she couldn't see it trembling. I couldn't let her see what this was doing to me.

"Listen to me very carefully, Tony," she said. "There are no accidents. No coincidences. They are everywhere. The crows know."

"Jaycie, you're scaring me so much," I said, and finally broke down and started to cry.

"I'm sorry," she wept, then grabbed the key from around her neck with her left fist and held it up in front of her wet eyes. She looked at it—her ring and the key, the two symbols of our love in her left hand, together. "I've been looking at it all night. It makes me smile, just as you said it would. This world wasn't meant for us, but I would have been the happiest woman on the planet to be your wife. I would've held your hand, till our very last breaths, forever." Then her face went cold, almost graven. "He's here, Tony." She was looking at the far wall. When I turned to look over my shoulder, I saw nothing there through the tears in my eyes.

"I don't see him," I said.

"It's okay, love," she said. "It's my turn to protect you." Then she placed the gun to her head once again, and said, "Tomorrow's not a promise." There was a pause, when her eyes on me filled with love and loss, and the battle inside her waged. Then the emotion on her face left all at once, and I was too slow—too stunned—too unconvincing to do anything to stop it. "I thought you were the moon."

When the gun went off, it was like the world was on pause and then moved suddenly in fast forward. I don't remember running to her. I don't remember cradling her in my arms or sobbing my fucking head off. I don't remember any of it quite that way. I remember watching myself from afar, like I was having an out of body experience. The only thing I remember was sobbing "Who's going to hold my hand when I die?" over and over as the sun came up, breaching the horizon with a ray of golden light. My hand was wrapped around hers, holding the key and her ring.

"I was arrested later that morning," I said. "The cops found me sobbing hysterically with her body in my lap, my hands and shirt covered in her blood. They said they could hear me from the road and followed it to the mill.

"The next several days were a blur. I was released on bail into Marshall and Sid's custody. I went to her funeral—it was a closed casket—but the O'Neill family asked me to leave. Marshall made sure they buried her with the ring. The key I kept for myself. It was the only thing of hers I had left, and it got me through the trial."

"The trial?" asked Doc.

"Jaycie's dad was a lawyer, and a really good one. He blamed me for everything, and he made sure they threw the book at me. None of it stuck. His former partner, Mr. Berry, made sure of that. I was acquitted on all charges, but the trial destroyed my life. I was in debt, I lost all my friends—many of which couldn't decide if I was innocent or not—and my dad was suffering from two broken hearts—the loss of his wife from years ago, and the shame of his son.

"At some point in time, I had a complete breakdown. I went catatonic. My mind shut down, and I was admitted to Northcreek, where I spent the next four years of my life. In the fourth and final year of my stay there, my dad passed away.

"It took a very long time for my mind to come back together. When it did, they made sure to pump me full of so many different anti-depressants that I couldn't even feel the needle when they ran the blood tests. I had to pass several psych evaluations, and in the end, they finally allowed me to enter the real world.

"The day I was released, Marshall was supposed to pick me up, but I ditched him and took a bus."

"Where did you go?"

April 13, 2011

I took a public bus to Grace Falls. By the time I arrived in town, the freezing rain had turned to large flakes of snow. I had a jacket, one that was provided to me as a gift since they couldn't release me into society only to have me freeze to death. I wrapped my arms around myself, attempting to keep warm, and walked through town on my way to one very specific place that had been on my mind for years.

I was wet and freezing, and the sky was almost black when I reached the wrought-iron gate to the Grace Falls Cemetery. It didn't matter if you were rich or poor, if you lived in the town of Grace Falls, that's where you were laid to rest when your time was up. Although the more affluent families were easy to find, since they were the ones with larger monuments, there was no separation between the headstones. Some markers dated back over a hundred years, while others were newly placed.

It was a vast necropolis built on ten acres of land, but I wasn't deterred. Although it was faded, I had a memory of where to go, and I planned to search all night until I found what I was looking for. A name caught my eye after I had walked up and down three dozen rows. My feet were frozen solid, and I couldn't stop my teeth from chattering, but I knew I had to stop.

The epitaph read *Richard Thomas Jansen, 1980 to 2002, Beloved son, friend, and star athlete. Well done, thou good and faithful servant. Matthew 25:21*

I took a moment to pay my respect. Over the course of time, I may not have forgiven him for what he had done or the type of person he was, but I believed that everyone deserved peace in death. I hoped Rick finally found that peace.

Moving row by row, shuffling through the snow and carrying the backpack that held all my belongings—those that weren't locked away in a storage facility—was more exhausting that I could have imagined in the frozen temperatures. I was down to the last corner of the cemetery and was losing hope quickly. I was worried that I had walked right past her, or that maybe I was in the wrong place all together—my memories from those days were like a blurry photograph.

I don't know what I would have done if I couldn't find her.

In the far corner, the last place left to search, in front of an old willow tree and under the cover of its branches, I found her.

She had a beautiful rose-colored headstone that stood almost three feet high. It was made of the finest marble and chiseled into its smooth broad face was the inscription, *Jacinda Moira O'Neill, 1980 – 2007, Beloved Daughter, We will hold dear our memories of her, her smile, the sound of her laughter...forever.*

I wiped the tears from my eyes, then knelt and brushed away the snow that had gathered on her precious stone. Even through the chemicals, it felt like hell. All the pain and the torment, the suffering and the loss, came back to me all at once. I cried for a long time, sitting beside her in the snow.

I kissed her name—the cold stone nearly bonded with my lips. Then, after I had gathered up all my courage, I did what I came there to do.

I reached into my pocket and pulled out what always belonged to her.

"I gave this to you the night I asked you to marry me. It was all I had to give, because you had already taken everything else—my mind, my body, my heart, my soul, they were all yours, and always will be. You accepted my proposal—what woman in this world, except an amazing one, would accept a marriage proposal from a guy who had no ring? Instead, I gave you a silly brass key I wore for good luck—a gift from my mother—with the promise to give you a real ring one day." I laughed, then thought of her smile.

"You were the better part of me. I can't stop loving you." I fought back the tears to say what I needed to say. "Forgive me. I wasn't strong enough to protect you, or convincing enough to make you stay. I was never good enough for you. You were a force of nature, and I was just a leaf caught up in your storm."

I then fell onto my knees in the snow and dug through the ice and frozen earth with my bare hands. I dug into the dirt and I didn't stop until I had a hole that was almost a half-foot deep. After that, my hands were too bloody, too mangled to dig any further into the frozen ground.

"This is yours." I placed the key into the hole, then covered it back up neatly, taking extra care to make it look nice for her. "It's the key to my heart. The door is now locked. Nobody else will open it ever again."

I got to my feet while the snow was still falling gently around me and looked up to the night sky. I could see the stars beginning to peek through the snow clouds, shining brightly, like tiny little beacons of light, blinking above. I had memorized the constellation of her freckles and swore I could see them there amongst the stars.

"God, please, protect her. I never had much need for prayer in my life. I don't even know how much I believe in you, or anything these days. But please, protect her. She's a rare jewel. Keep her safe, for me."

Then I looked down again at her grave one last time. "Goodbye, Jaycie. I love you, always," I said and walked away.

"In the years since, I feel like I've been living a half-life. I've never been able to get over that kind of loss. How do you learn to move on from that? If I had known that time was running out for us, I would have done something, anything to change the trajectory of our lives. To lead it as far away from the mill and Grace Falls as I could. If I had only recognized the pain in her eyes—maybe things could have been different.

"I warned you," I said, "This wasn't a love story."

"But things weren't different," said Doc. "Things turned out exactly as they did. There isn't anything you can do to change that. You have to learn to accept reality and move on. No more holding onto the past. Tony, it's time to let go."

betrayal

TONY
December 22, 2013

I watched *The Wizard of Oz* for the very first time with my mother when I was four. It was one of the only memories I still had of her. After watching, we would pretend to be tornadoes, spinning around in circles, magically whisking each other away to wonderful new lands beyond.

"Do all tornadoes go to Oz?" I asked her.

"No, hon," she said. "Most of them go to a better place."

"Better than Oz?"

"Yes," she said with a distant smile. "A much better place."

She died a year later.

In second grade science, my teacher asked us to name different kinds of weather. Suzie Hughes shared with the class the story about how her family survived a tornado when she lived in Oklahoma. Suzie recalled being scared and hiding in the old cast iron bathtub as the storm passed them by. When I raised my hand and asked why they were so scared, because "my mommy told me" they were magical portals to a better place—Billy Woodward made sure to call me an "idiot with a stupid dead mommy" in front of the whole class. He got himself two detentions for it, but the damage was done.

I remember crying so hard, my dad allowed me to stay home sick the next day.

You can't contain memories. You can shove them aside, build up mental walls and create all kinds of coping mechanisms—but they always manage to surface, even at the worst possible times.

The Kia hatchback was starting to drift—the spinning winds had finally closed the gap and now began to affect the car's traction. It was only a matter of moments until the tornado would reach me, with the Grace Falls exit lingering a mile away. Still, I was struck with memories from when I first arrived for college—my dad and I loaded up onto his pickup, the tall pine trees on either side of the road like centurions, guarding the town from intruders—the two of us, talking baseball and sports instead of the gaping holes inside us—the void my mother left behind.

But now I was an intruder, and I was dragging evil along with me.

Animals scurried out of the forest, some dashing across the road, while a bloom of birds kicked up into the air like pollen in spring—but when those birds fanned out and began flying toward the car, I was convinced we'd reached the end of the road.

"Crows!" I shouted. "They're everywhere!"

"It was a heck of a ride, my man," said Montoya.

"Against impossible odds," added Chappy.

"Wait," said Henry, as he scrutinized the flock.

"They're different," said Jamaal. "They don't have red eyes."

"Red eyes?" I asked.

"You can see their eyes?" questioned Montoya.

"What's the difference?" I asked.

"I can't see their eyes," whined Montoya.

"Morrigan's crows have red eyes," said Jamaal, like he was solving a mystery.

"What does it mean?" asked Doshin.

I shook my head—the red-eyed crow-cyclone was on our tail while the other crows were flying straight at us. They didn't deviate; they didn't even appear to care that death was imminent.

"Shiiiiiit!" yelled Montoya, as the crows swooped down—dozens of them—gliding toward and around the car, riding the air flow as it broke around the hood. The sound was like a trumpet—a thousand squawking birds all crying at once. It was deafening, followed by a high-pitched tone that slowly faded beneath the sound of the car's engine.

"Are we still alive?" asked Jamaal.

"We're dead, dummy," said Montoya with a wink.

"It's gone," I said, looking into the rearview mirrors for signs of the cyclone, but there was nothing but a scattering of black birds and dust, pine needles and loose branches.

"Tony," said Chappy, "ease off the acceleration. Calm yourself."

I was a nuclear man, soaring down Highway 13. The vinyl-wrapped steering wheel in the car had melted—the flames inside me were like solar flares erupting from the surface of the sun. Would I have ignited like before?

With the threat fading away into my rearview mirror, I took the exit to Grace Falls, from the ramp onto Cross Road, and pulled off in front of the town's welcome sign.

Everything came rushing back to me—the memories, the horrors, the stress. I couldn't breathe as a panic attack was beginning to take over.

"Breathe," said Henry. "Listen to my voice. Concentrate on what I am saying. Breathe." His instructions were helping, but my collision course with a breakdown was still on track. "Focus on the sign ahead. Read the words on the sign. Repeat them to yourself. Keep reading. Repeat. Read. Repeat."

"Welcome to Grace Falls, Pennsylvania. Where Water Falls and Dreams Soar! Est. 1886." Someone had spray-painted the sign to alter the message, replacing it with "Where Angels Fall and Demons Soar!"

My heart rate slowed, and I was beginning to control my emotions.

The altered sign reminded me of Maynard Morris and the way he saw the world through a different lens—any other day, I would have chuckled at the thought. After I was done with the business at hand, I needed to find him, if nothing more than to make sure he was okay. The man on the phone had threatened everyone I ever knew, and that included Maynard.

And that was when I remembered the phone call.

The dwindling panic attack was replaced with rage, and I exited the car for fresh air. I stomped around the driver's side, took two deep breaths, and expelled them in a cloud of white vapor. The rage, however, kept coming—I was a buoy in its storm. When I put my hands on my knees, it was all I could do to keep my anger from exploding—literally.

The threat against my friends was something I couldn't shake. These things, these monsters, went after innocent people—people who had nothing to do with me. Life was a joke to them. They were immortal, and we were cattle.

I wanted to protect my friends. I wanted to protect them all, everyone, but I was just one man. I didn't even know where most of my friends lived—and I scolded myself for having let the friendships slip over the years. It was my fault as much as it was theirs. Of those I knew, some were hours away back in Philadelphia, and the rest were scattered to the wind. When my future self, my echo, said there were decisions that needed to be made, tough decisions ahead, I never imagined this might be one of them.

"You have to keep moving forward," said Chappy, daring to speak. "Going back would be certain death."

"You mean like the death sentence I inadvertently signed for everyone I ever cared for?" I snapped. "I'm supposed to be okay with that?"

"What could you even do about it?" asked Jamaal. "You said yourself you don't know where they live. You don't even have their cell phone numbers."

"You'd have to be everywhere all at once," added Montoya. "You'd have to be…God?"

"We admit that you, as us all, are sacrificing everything for an unreal predicament," said Chappy. "We are all taking a leap of faith into the bizarre, the otherworldly, in *reality,* and in you."

It felt like I was running away from my problems once again, but this time I was running toward answers—prompts from my Echo and the Mistress inside my crazy dream. Was a silly hunch worth more than the lives of my friends?

"The sooner you learn that you cannot control everything, the better off you'll be," said Henry.

"I know I can't control everything!" I roared. "I can't even control anything! If I could, I wouldn't have lost everything I ever loved! Do you really believe I need to learn that lesson? I lost it all! I can't get any of them back! And now I have to let go of those that were still here?"

"Maybe it was a bluff?" said Montoya.

Maybe it was. The man on the other end of the phone took Amanda's life. Would he really follow through on hunting down everyone else?

"C'mon," I said, as if they had to physically load into the car with me.

"Where are we going?" asked Jamaal.

"To do what we came here to do," I said.

The weather kept people off the streets. It was cold and damp, and the light rain was mixed with snowflakes. From the smell and taste of the air, I knew the precipitation would end soon, but the temperatures were on the verge of plummeting again. Despite the cold, I didn't feel the need to turn on the car's heat. Maybe this was a byproduct of the flames? Or maybe I was concentrating too hard to feel much of anything?

The town looked almost the same, with a few new businesses and a technology park. I even spotted a new playground before I turned onto Cemetery Drive and drove through the tall wrought-iron gate. A red brick wall kept the consecrated ground private from the main road. It was covered in ivy and weeds and looked uninviting in winter.

I parked the car in the empty visitor's lot and got out into the frozen night, then began my trek through the necropolis. I couldn't help but remember the last time I was there, and all the circumstances that led to that moment. My suffering didn't end that day at the Jansen Mill. It had only just started. Every day since was suffering.

I lost all my friends, except Marshall—and now he was gone.

I was arrested. I was tried. I was exonerated only to lose my mind.

I spent four years inside a mental institution at Northcreek.

I spent the last two years sifting through the damage.

And now I was back in the one place I swore was too painful to ever visit again.

The Grace Falls Cemetery—fuck me.

Though it was night, I could see the Hallows House on the hill behind the overgrown trees and shrubs—its tower peeking over them.

There was no way to tell how many were laid to rest inside the brick walls of the Grace Falls Cemetery, but headstones covered the entire landscape as far as the eye could see. If all the dead stood up at once, there wouldn't be much elbow room to go around. It was a historic town, and many of the grave markers dated back to the Civil War. The prime burial spots, where the tallest markers were placed—everything from ten-foot spires to above ground crypts—were located near trees with benches donated to the cemetery from estates of the beloved departed.

I began to read the names of the dead as I passed. So many people, all of them loved. They all had ambition. They all had passion. They all had lives.

My life was wasted. Fool's gold. A fantasy that never culminated. There would be no happily-ever-after for me. How could there be?

As Sid once said, *"The sooner you come to the conclusion that there are no happy endings, the better off you'll be."*

Whatever happened to that guy? Such a bright ray of sunshine, but he was right.

Whatever happened to me from this point forward, I would be at peace. I would play my part and be done with it—so long as I went down swinging. Beyond that, what else was there for me? I was alone.

All I ever wanted was to be happy, to be with *her* and to live out my days. I didn't belong here, and without *her* I would never be happy.

I placed my hand upon Tori Martin's headstone as I passed. Thoughts of her and the rest of the gang that night, as we partied by the Hallows House overlooking the Mkateewa River, flashed through my mind. *"We are the Children of the Mkateewa. We're cursed,"* Tori once said. How fucking right was she? This town was cursed.

Mom, Amanda, Tori, Jaycie—why did all the women in my life leave me?

"Guilt won't do us any good, Tony. It is best to leave it in the past," said Henry. They were all there, walking with me, like an entourage of pain and suffering. Montoya, Jamaal, Doshin, Chappy, and Henry—my brain-trust, following me down this path into darkness.

I knew Henry was right, but my past was never behind me. It was always staring me right in the face, like a haunted reflection, anticipating every move. Every time I tried to move on, it rose from the dead like Michael Myers and hunted me down. There was no escape.

Had my time in Grace Falls cursed me too?

My journey took me through a labyrinth of headstones and sepulchers. Some of the vaults were as large as a small house, with enough room for a full family. There were statues of cherubs and other large stone monuments, even an ominous hooded reaper with a long menacing scythe. As I stared down the statue of death, I couldn't help but think that this journey through the cemetery was going to get worse before it was over.

The scent of rain vanished, and the air dried out as temperatures continued to fall below freezing. It was getting so cold, I felt the steam rising from my arms and shoulders.

When I spotted the willow tree a short distance away, a lump formed in my throat. It was as heavy as cinderblock and as sharp as broken glass. I stifled an initial sob, and the horrific memories of what I had suffered hit me like an anvil dropped on a cartoon coyote. My body conspired against me, telling me to run, but I refused to listen. I had a job to do.

Her headstone looked as perfect as ever. Rosy marble with the inscription, *Jacinda Moira O'Neill, Beloved Daughter. We will hold dear our memories of her, her smile, the sound of her laughter...forever.*

I heard a memory of her laugh, and the emotions overtook me. I was thrown out of her funeral and visiting her one last time after being released from Northcreek was supposed to be a final goodbye. Being back, looking at the marker that represented her life in this world, knowing she was six feet below, was a special kind of terror.

I was already losing control—the flames were roaring.

The ozone around me sizzled, and steam thickened into wispy tendrils hanging on the still air. The pain was growing beyond my threshold, and I stifled it with clenched fists and gnashed teeth.

Over time, there was one awful image my mind grappled onto—a traumatizing snapshot I could never shake—Jaycie's cold eyes with the gun firmly pressed to her temple. It stuck in my mind's eye like a pesky fly swarming an overfilled dumpster. When the image faded, driven out of my mind with willpower and grit, I unclenched my entire body.

"Breathe," said Henry.

"You're here for a reason," said Chappy. "Focus on the task at hand."

"Focus," added Doshin.

Seeing her name chiseled onto the tombstone made all the nightmares real. I rarely used Jaycie's name—a simple defense mechanism I developed to heal my mind. Her name had magic in it, a lyrical connection to the very core of me, and hearing, or reading, or speaking it was to rip open the scab of her memory.

Henry and the others disappeared. I didn't need them for this.

I knelt in front of the headstone and pushed my hands into the frozen dirt. A clump of grass broke free, and I tossed it aside for another handful. The most difficult task wasn't digging with my bare hands but keeping my mind stitched together. For every concentrated effort forward, a blast of the surreal burst from my subconscious.

In the middle of grabbing fistfuls of dirt, Jaycie's decayed hand burst forth from frozen soil and snatched me by the wrist, her fingers dug into my skin and drew gushes of blood. I jumped back, jittering, and tugged my arm free, until I realized it was all in my head—my subconscious playing horrible tricks.

After a deep breath, I went back to work brushing soil away from a rock and uncovered what appeared to be one of Jaycie's green eyes staring back at me. I kept on, identifying the delusion, and ripped away another portion of the frozen ground.

Every inch I dug aggravated my psyche like I was ripping the skin from my face, cracking open my skull and stirring my brains about with a blender. I witnessed thick drips of blood leaking from her headstone, oozing from the chiseled serifs of her name—and heard the sound of her laughter from the shadows of the willow tree.

The heat from my body forced a fog to congeal from the frosty air, as thick as clouds. It surrounded me in a cold embrace, like the world beyond did not exist. It was just me, and her, and death.

I furiously scratched and clawed at the ground as my desperate heart jackhammered. With every inch I dug, the more anxious I became.

I hoped it was still there.

Did I bury it this deep?

Had someone come by and taken it?

Had it fallen into my enemy's hands?

MALUS

Pleasure was limitless once you moved beyond morality—endless enjoyment as infinite as the heavens beyond and the space between stars.

Inflicting pain was as addictive as lust.

Tragic was the life of Amanda Hemmels. She lost her brother when she was young, only to have her own life cut short. It was a pity she had to die.

I savored the experience as I travelled the ancient halls of my home. Pain.

This world was nothing but pain. Pain and torment, followed by pain and torment. A cycle from the beginning of creation until ultimate destruction. Yet, which fate was preferred? Withering away on this rock, living out my immortal days amongst the sheep? Or the endless flaming pit for all eternity? Was there a lesser of two evils when both presented such absolute anguish?

I was not like the others. I could never be what they were, gods tricking men into loyalty and adulation—believing their false gods would guide them to a better existence.

I could never take pleasure in seeing men and women bowing before me, paying homage or sacrificing themselves for the sake of my goodwill. I could never find a place in this world like so many others of my kind had found. What I needed, what I wanted, I could never find here, and could never achieve anywhere else. My goals were unique, and I kept them to myself.

My identity and my purpose were mine and mine alone to know. My success and survival hinged upon secrecy.

I wasn't always like this.

I was once in love.

"You were always a monster," she said to me.

Tragedy can sour even the purest of heart.

It was easy persuading the others to follow. Maybe all Fallen suffered from the same flaw, but they were all too eager to sign my contract once the bait was dangled in front of their greedy eyes. There was not a single member amongst my Thirteen who did not have intentions of swooping in at the last moment and taking from me that which I had designed. Fallen, like us, did not survive this long without having certain qualities—most notably a disposition to deceit.

We were untrustworthy by nature. Trust was only earnest when there was a need for collaboration. Once that need was gone, every one of us would be on our own, fending for themselves and their own intentions. I did not have any delusions otherwise.

For now, our goals were still aligned.

I sent my Thirteen into the world to cleanse it of the spark. Whether or not he was a threat, albeit the many shards of him scattered throughout time, I did not care. I wanted him gone. Wiped from existence so that I could proceed unfettered.

Summanus was dead. Mammon followed him into the Unbecoming.

While the others scattered to clean up scraps, I was having fun torturing the spark. And if one of my Thirteen happened to clear the pawn, this Tony Oscuro, from the board, I'd be all the better for it.

"Lord," cried a voice in the darkness.

"What is it, goddess?" I asked. Hekate stepped free of the shadows and threw herself to my feet.

"Lord, your power sacked the Seelie Court on my behalf," she said, nearly weeping. "Your half of our contract was paid in the blood of my enemies—but I have failed you."

"Explain," I said, as I contemplated the growing dread her groveling inspired within me.

"My power against him is gone," she cried from beneath her mask, her hands caressing my boots—begging for mercy. "He knew my name. He spoke it aloud and my magic can no longer harm him."

"Who?" I asked.

"The spark," she explained.

When I kicked the goddess, I cared not for mercy. Her mask cracked, exposing a peek of her ruined face. She was another failure against an insignificant threat, and as I stormed away, she shouted after me.

"I looked into his eyes and witnessed a ghost of old!"

Distrust.

One is never served so well as by oneself. The dramatist Charles-Guillaume Étienne once wrote those words, and they inspired my thoughts once more. I have often pondered the fallacy of collaboration. There was more might in many, but more accuracy in few. Failure kept me vigilant. Failure was a reminder—hubris was the great destroyer. However, too much failure could not and cannot be tolerated.

It was that vigilance that forced my distrust to operate on high alert. It was that alert that flared in my chest when I arrived inside the house. As soon as I stepped foot onto old wooden floor, I knew something was wrong. I'd left Lilly asleep, forcefully driven into the deepest recesses of her mind by a simple spell—

—but there was something in the air. Not a smell or a taste, but a vibration. An unusual disturbance.

I was standing at the bottom of the stairs attempting to decipher the meaning of the vibrations when a sense of dread traveled down my back.

I had made a terrible mistake.

"Nemesis!" I yelled, but the warrior goddess did not answer my call. Her contract was not responding to my command, yet it was not voided. It was still intact. The rights were still mine to control.

I leapt up the stairs as a presence behind me kept pace—a threatening presence—albeit the devil I knew.

"What has you so spooked?" asked Loki as we tracked through the hallway. "Where were you, if not here the whole time?"

"I had an errand," I said under my breath, while concentrating on the shadows ahead.

"I see," he chuckled. "While you were out erranding, you left our prize behind? How vast is your arrogance to leave her here? All alone?"

"I left our prize guarded by my most faithful servant."

Never verbally spar with a Trickster. They twist every word spoken into a maze of wordplay and deceit. Loki may have been the best of them. He quibbled with every phrase, doubling and tripling entendre at will.

"Faithful? Servant? To whom? To you or to the girl?" he said as we came upon her room, and every agonizing suspicion revealed itself. "When is a door not a door." It was not a riddle, but a statement.

The door was left ajar.

Every impeding spell, every bolting incantation, every ancient locking symbol—broken.

She was gone. Lilly had escaped.

"The pet's off the leash," he squawked, as if our predicament was only a minor obstacle. He seemed to enjoy my setbacks, but what he failed to understand was that Lilly could be anywhere—

—and anywhen.

What, other than my humiliation, would Loki have to gain by my failure?

She was laughing at me, as if I was a fool. "Shut up," I said.

"Fuck off," replied Loki, but I was not speaking to him. I was speaking to a ghost.

As I contemplated what transpired, reconstructing Lilly's escape with the aura of clues left within the room, Loki spun and smashed his hammer through the wall—not out of anger or disgust, but defense. There was a flash of metal followed by a thud when Loki's severed hand hit the ground, then another flash, and his body slammed through the wall like he had been hit by the payload of a catapult.

Something was in the room—was it Lilly?

No.

It was much worse.

Another flash of metal, and I raised my flaming sword just in time to parry the attack. This attack followed another, and another, until I jumped back and away from danger.

"The Helm of Darkness has many names," I said. "The Cap of Invisibility. The Helm of Hades, another. I stole it from the God of the Underworld's own head when I killed him. Do not assume I cannot repeat the same feat while it rests on your head, Nemesis."

Another flash, followed by repeated strikes—one of them cleaving an ear. It grew back the next instant. This was foolishness, a wasted effort. Her spirit was mine, signed and sealed, and I could free her from contract…*and life.*

"Contract terminated," I growled, and waited for the pop—only nothing happened. There were few things that could arouse my most venomous rage—losing control over my favorite weapon was one of them. "How did you do it? How'd you break our contract?" I kept my distance, unsure what she was after. "What do you want? To recondition the terms? To replace me? What do you want!?"

Then she whispered, "To send you into the pit," directly into my ear.

The metal flashed before my eyes—attempting to pluck them from my skull. I spun away, and by the time I brought my sword around, aiming for her invisible crown, I heard four hard taps across the ground, like someone had spilled their coin purse.

Distracted, my sword glanced across the Helm, striking it from atop her head as she kicked out her foot, and sent me sprawling backward into the mirror—shattering the glass.

The Four Keys of Eden were as unalike to one other as any of my Thirteen. The Key of Aries I plucked from the mouth of Votan was shaped like a tooth, with ridges cut into its twisting roots. The Key of Libra, made of jade, was flat with two wyrms attached at the tail, snaking around the bow and down the stem. The Key of Cancer, like the golden ankh of Pharaohs. And the Key of Capricorn, a simple piece of brass—a loop with a single bit along its stem.

They were the culmination of one full year of plotting and planning—

—and I watched them bounce and settle onto the wooden floor—the four keys, cut from my neck when she swiped for my eyes and missed—or perhaps, she did not miss at all.

"Why?"

"The girl touched me, and she burned away the evil that clouded my heart and mind," said Nemesis.

Her gray eyes flashed as she wiped the war paint from her face—no, not war paint, blood dripping from her lips. Either I had struck a solid blow, or she had swallowed a mouthful of flesh.

No, not just any flesh. Chronos.

"Your contract was with Nemesis. Goddess of Retribution, I am no longer."

With a thought, I summoned my Thirteen. They would arrive at any moment.

"Your halo is broken. You cannot go home, Carina," I said, and the scent of her fear filled the room like someone had struck a match. "I know your true name. We will hunt you down."

"You'll never find me where I am going," she said.

Loki flung himself into the room—a half-regenerated hand growing from the stump— and dove for the keys—

—Morrigan arrived in a pack of crows, followed by Anubis waving his khopesh.

We had her surrounded—but she was faster.

Carina snatched the Key of Capricorn and Loki's severed hand, then disappeared into time before anyone could stop her.

A second later, a psychic blast of enraged ectoplasm smacked into Loki and Anubis and sent them spinning into the far wall—my attack, like their arrival, was too late.

As I picked myself up from the floor and the mirrored glass fell, I was struck by the sudden realization that the mirror never had any glass. It was a glassless frame that sat in the corner. Lilly was awake, and so was the Dyad. She'd voided one of my contracts and created a powerful agent from a loyal servant.

"I'll fucken rip out her fucking ovaries and stuff them down her fucking throat!" roared Loki. He was seeping blood from the attacks—both from Nemesis and the dead. "Why'd she take my fucking hand!?"

"What was on that hand, Trickster?" I asked as I gathered the remaining keys. I knew what he took—and under the circumstance, it made sense for Carina to steal it back. "Where were you?" I scowled at them all. They arrived moments too late.

"I do not remember," whispered Morrigan, as I unleashed the dead upon her.

Failure simply cannot be accepted.

They had no idea *who* we were dealing with…

Nine days.

Three-hundred-fifty-six days had passed without problem—then everything began to fall apart in the last nine. The last nine before everything was mine.

"You will fail," she said, "like you failed me." Only I could hear her.

I silenced her with my ring and slammed my fist into Loki's face. While the Trickster spent the next few minutes regenerating a shattered, mutilated skull, I mused over two important details. The first: Lilly was still mine. I had control over her, though not the control I once had when she was under my spell. However, no matter where she went, I would eventually find her.

The second, and the most important, was that no matter how gifted she was, she did not know her limitations, or lack thereof. She was a blank slate. A tortured mind. A frail human body sheathing something extraordinary.

And maybe, I thought, her escape might become my advantage.

rebirth

TONY
December 22, 2013
Now.

This was a bad idea.

My life was brimming with them. I once replaced Brad and Marshall's Coronas with vegetable oil. Our entire dormitory floor suffered through that misfire—the stink emanating from the shared restrooms were enough to call an immediate truce.

That was a bad idea.

This was something more akin to grave misjudgment—with double entendre noted.

I dug through the dirt in front of Jaycie's grave while the fog rolled in, and I was losing my mind one handful at a time.

I remembered the first days after. I remembered breaking apart, when each and every thought was consumed by the idea that I could have done something different. It's not like you could take a college course in preventing tragedy or receive do-overs for life-altering events.

Maybe I could have said this. Maybe I could have done that.

That kind of guilt drove me mad.

When I was admitted to Northcreek, it wasn't because I admitted myself. I was admitted because I had a very public breakdown and was legally forced to go.

Screaming at the top of your lungs in the streets of Mercy Point, seeing your dead fiancée everywhere you go, was the first step toward being committed.

The second step was violence.

I struck a police officer who attempted to get me off the street. The problem was that I didn't know he was a cop. I saw a dead man that day. I saw Rick Jansen threatening to drag me down to hell and fought for my life.

Hallucinations, however absurd, are the scariest experiences ever. Imagine dreaming while you're awake, and there's no way to tell they're not real. There's no waking up. There's no pinching your arm to miraculously discover everything was all in your broken head.

Back then, I'd see Jaycie and her smile on my left, then turn to see her jamming a gun to her temple on my right. It was a complete and total meltdown, and I was beginning to experience it all over again.

"You killed me, Tony," she said from somewhere in the fog. She was angry and bloodthirsty. A wraith ready to strike me down. "I wanted you to go, but you kept pushing. You should have just let me go."

"I couldn't let you die," I sobbed. I was speaking to my delusions. I was falling into that abyss, and after all that had happened over the last few days, one could argue I was already there.

There was a thump, then another. A heartbeat, rhythmically pumping from the earth—her heartbeat from below.

"Rick was a better man. I should have stayed with him," she said from somewhere behind me within the thick swampy haze. "He could have saved me from my demons." My mind knew exactly which buttons to push. Each word stung more and more as I frantically dug. "And Mason? He was a gorgeous man. And rich!"

The hole in the ground had widened two whole feet—if I could only find it, I'd leave and never come back. She'd never be tortured by my presence ever again.

"You're nothing. A never was," she said from somewhere in the mist. "Pathetic."

"Why would I ever choose to be with a loser like you?"

"You could have stopped me from killing myself, but you were too weak."

"You're so weak," she laughed, responding to her other voice.

"It's all your fault you couldn't save me."

My hands continued to rake the dirt but found nothing. The illusions were worsening, and my body quaked as my nervous system fried under the pressure. I was losing it. I could hear the pounding of her heartbeat getting louder—or maybe the heartbeat was my own? I couldn't tell which through the throbbing behind my eyes.

"Leave me alone!" she cried into my ear.

"Why don't you just leave me alone!" she shouted into the other.

"I'd still be alive if it wasn't for you!" she screamed from a distance.

The wind blew, stinging my eyes as it froze my tears. My urgency to stop the voices led me to uncover a rock the size of my hand. Once unearthed, I discovered a long strand of metal.

There it was, hidden beneath the rock, clean and gleaming as if the dirt had never touched it. The shiny brass key with its sterling silver chain coiling beneath it, as bright and pristine as the very first time I wore it.

"Leave it be!"

"That key has nothing to do with me!"

"Go away! I don't want you here."

"What a fucking waste you turned out to be."

"Why did I ever love a pathetic piece of shit like you?"

The voices were getting louder, and I could sense movement nearby. I could even smell her scent. Strawberries and lavender. The fragrance slithered up my nose and threatened to drive me completely mad. I was on my knees trembling, I was sick, I was crying and scared. I was falling apart—her words, her voice—my worst fears—terrorized me to the brink of a terrible decision. I became very aware of the pocketknife stashed in my jeans—a way out?

As I wept, broken and alone, I wrapped my hand around the key, and everything went silent. Complete silence, like drifting in the void of space.

"You found me," she said one last time, several beats after everything had gone still. Her voice was sweet. Innocent. With the love and passion my tortured mind had lost and forgotten. It was as if the pain had forced the memory of her voice to hollow, and what I heard was everything the memory had lost. On my knees, my jeans soaked through and muddied. With my eyes shut, I cradled the key in my hands and took a long moment of silence to come to grips with the end of the nightmare.

A twig snapped behind me.

I could hear shallow breathing.

Was this another hallucination? It didn't feel like I was in danger—not like before, while being hunted by faeries and evil gods. What I felt was something closer to dread, but that wasn't quite right either. Perhaps it was anticipation—preparation that reality was about to slap me down once more.

When I turned toward the snapping twig, I discovered my mind had gone to a whole new level of insanity. *Supra-insanity?* Were there levels of un-sane I had yet to hit?

"Tony?" she asked. There was fear in her voice, and my heart broke like it did every time I heard her panic.

I stood and faced a silhouette looming in the dense fog. It was a woman, barefoot, wearing a raggedy old green sundress with embroidered yellow flowers. She had long flowing red hair and two sparkling green eyes. She took another step toward me, and the fog sifted away from her path as she roamed. She was shivering, but her eyes were fixated on me—gazing like she had found lost memories after struggling through the haze of dementia.

"You look different," she said, with a quick smirk flitting at the corners of her mouth, the way she used to when she was nervous. I didn't exactly look innocent standing in the middle of a graveyard with dirty clothes and hands and a giant scar across my face. I looked like a grave robber, or worse.

"Jace," I said, expecting another horrifying delusion to take her away.

Her eyes darted to the hole at the base of the rosy headstone, and after a few ticks she finally read the name chiseled onto its face.

"What's going on?" she asked and wobbled. I took a single step towards her, and noticed the constellation of freckles on her face, as perfect as ever.

It was really her…

Jacinda O'Neill was alive, and she was standing right in front of me.

To be continued in
The Second Book of Cataclysm:
THE OMEGA

a letter from the author

Hello Friends!

Thank you for reading **THE RAPTOR!**

This book and it's three sequels have been stuck in my head for the last twenty-six years. Though the story has changed over the years, the spirit of the story has always remained the same. I hope you'll continue this journey with me through the next three parts: **The Omega**, **The Pale Demon**, and **Cataclysm**.

In the meantime, please go to your favorite book site and leave a review. Reviews, especially written reviews, are the lifeblood of every author. A book's success is dependent on reviews and referrals from readers just like you.

If you enjoyed The Raptor, please go and review—tell your friends, your family, your neighbors, and anyone who's willing to listen.

Thank you for starting this journey with me.
G.A. Finocchiaro

G.A. Finocchiaro lives in the suburbs of Philadelphia, where *"Bad Things Happen"* and furry orange, ice hockey mascots wreak havoc on anyone who belittles the city and its spirit. In the time of Covid, G.A. has spent most of his free moments dreaming and writing.

Check out his website: http://www.gafino.com
Follow him on Twitter: @G_A_Fino
Follow him on Facebook: https://www.facebook.com/GAFinocc
Sign up for his Newsletter: http://www.gafino.com/Newsletter/

449

THE RAPTOR